THE RUMOR GAME

ALSO BY THOMAS MULLEN

The Last Town on Earth
The Many Deaths of the Firefly Brothers
The Revisionists
Blind Spots

THE ATLANTA CYCLE

Darktown
Lightning Men
Midnight Atlanta

THE
RUMOR
GAME

A Novel

THOMAS MULLEN

MINOTAUR BOOKS
NEW YORK

First published in the United States by Minotaur Books, an imprint of
St. Martin's Publishing Group

THE RUMOR GAME. Copyright © 2024 by Thomas Mullen. All rights reserved.
Printed in the United States of America. For information,
address St. Martin's Publishing Group, 120 Broadway, New York, NY 10271.

www.minotaurbooks.com

Library of Congress Cataloging-in-Publication Data

Names: Mullen, Thomas, author.
Title: The rumor game / Thomas Mullen.
Description: First edition. | New York : Minotaur Books, 2024.
Identifiers: LCCN 2023036532 | ISBN 9781250842770 (hardcover) |
    ISBN 9781250842787 (ebook)
Subjects: LCGFT: Thrillers (Fiction). | Novels.
Classification: LCC PS3613.U447 R86 2024 | DDC 813/.6—dc23/eng/20230815
LC record available at https://lccn.loc.gov/2023036532

Our books may be purchased in bulk for promotional, educational, or business use.
Please contact your local bookseller or the Macmillan Corporate and
Premium Sales Department at 1-800-221-7945, extension 5442, or by email at
MacmillanSpecialMarkets@macmillan.com.

First Edition: 2024

10 9 8 7 6 5 4 3 2 1

In memory of my grandparents:
Anne and Ernest Comeau
Mildred and Francis Mullen

THE RUMOR GAME

Chapter One

LOOSE LIPS

The June sun felt hot and malevolent on Anne's skin, but she knew the long walk would be worth it, as she'd learned it was always best to look a liar in the eyes.

She'd taken the stuffy train to Harvard Square, then walked through the university campus, not as sleepy in summer as she would have expected, young men in short sleeves and crisp linen pants hurrying to this classroom building or that. A few of them whistled at her as she passed, the eggheads no better than construction workers, but she ignored them.

North of the oasis of Harvard came the rest of Cambridge: the blue-collar neighborhoods, the three-deckers and cramped blocks. Fewer trees, less shade to hide in.

Still a mile away from Inman Square, she seemed to be headed straight into the late-afternoon sun's angry gaze. She felt the sweat at her back after just a few blocks. Halfway there, she was almost regretting the decision not to splurge for a cab. The reporter characters in the movies never seemed troubled by their low pay, she'd noticed. No one in *His Girl Friday* had damp armpits and sore feet.

The address in question was halfway down a dead-end street off Mass Ave, light blue and in need of a paint job. The steps to the door creaked as she ascended.

How had she found herself here? It had taken two days to chase this particular rumor down, but the gist was:

The barkeep in Scollay Square said he'd heard it from a lawyer.

The lawyer had caught wind of it from the secretaries.

The secretaries all blamed Doris, the new one.

Doris told Anne she'd heard it from a friend of hers, Marty.

Marty? He lived in Central Square. He'd heard it from his buddy Joe, who'd heard it from his pal Mikey, who'd heard it from Hank. Good guy, Hank. Okay, actually, maybe not so good. Kind of an oddball, if you know what I mean.

Anne didn't—could you explain?

Mikey explained. Anne asked follow-up questions. Personal histories emerged. Then she understood, and she asked where this oddball Hank lived.

After her subway trip and a long walk, Anne finally knocked on Hank's door. She clasped her notebook to her chest with both hands, adopting her look of professional friendliness.

There were many different kinds of mistruths, she had learned through years of writing and reporting.

Some mistruths were born of ignorance, almost innocent in their lack of understanding about the world. Some were initially harmless, more mistakes than outright lies, until they were repeated often enough to convince a critical mass of people, in which case they became dangerous.

Then there were the deliberate mistruths that all but dripped with venom, sharpened like fangs ready to sink into gullible flesh.

Some lies were well-camouflaged, particularly hard to ferret out, while others were so obvious that only a fool would willingly reach out and touch it.

The good news for her was that each kind of falsehood felt equally rewarding to chase down and disprove. She loved her job.

The door opened and a thin young man gazed at her suspiciously. "Can I help you?"

She offered her most disarming smile. Anne was not vain, but she knew she was good at appearing harmless and winning people over, a skill that came in rather handy for a reporter.

"Good evening. I'm sorry to drop by so late. I'm not interrupting dinner, am I?"

"No, not yet."

"Are you Hank Doyle?"

"One of 'em. 'Less you mean my old man." Thin, sandy hair fell across his forehead. An archipelago of acne traced his right jawline. He might have been nineteen or twenty. "You selling war bonds? I think we bought enough already."

"No, actually, I work for the *Star*. I was hoping I could ask you a few quick questions."

He hadn't been expecting that. His thick brows scrunched up a bit.

"What, for a ladies' interest column or something? You gonna take my picture?" He grinned. "Writing about all the eligible bachelors left behind?"

How quickly suspicion is replaced with bravado. She'd seen this before.

"Not exactly. I'm looking into some rumors we've heard about Fort Gillem, in Georgia. Do you have any friends there?"

A two-second pause. "Yeah, a few, actually. I'd be there too if they hadn't . . ."

"Hadn't what?"

He looked away. "Ah, it's just . . . They gave me this bum news about my heart."

"Oh, I'm sorry to hear that." She put an overly dramatic hand to her own heart. "I hope everything's all right."

"Yeah, I'm perfectly fine. Strong as a bull. That's what I'm saying. Yet they go and say I have a 'murmur.' Whatever that is. You believe they won't let a fellow serve on account of a murmur?"

She'd heard her share of complaints like this from men ruled 4-F due to one health ailment or another. It was a sore subject for most, as if their very manhood was being questioned. It was best not to overdo it with the sympathy, otherwise they'd feel pitied and take offense.

"I'm sure you're still doing your part. You work at the Gillette plant, right?"

"Yeah. How'd you know that?"

"Your friend Mike Hurley told me."

"You know Mikey?" He still couldn't decide how suspicious to be about this strange young woman on his doorstep, she could tell.

"Just met him today, actually." She'd only spoken to Mikey on the phone, but some of the things he'd said had led her to conclude that her talk with Hank should be in person. Despite that long, hot walk.

"Hank!" An older woman hollered from inside. "Who's at the door?"

He turned his head and shouted back, "Just a saleslady, Ma!"

The lie intrigued Anne. It implied that he might know why Anne was here. And that he wanted to hide it.

"Tell her we don't need nothing!" Ma yelled.

Anne retook the conversational reins. "The thing I wanted to ask you about was this rumor we've been hearing about Fort Gillem." She tried to slow her normally rapid-fire voice. "It's rather a sensitive topic, so I apologize if it makes you uncomfortable, but I really do need to ask."

He put his hands in his pockets. "Okay. What is it?"

"Well, it's about the WAAC. And, you know, some of the things going on with the ladies down there."

She left it at that. It was always best to let people fill in the conversational blanks themselves.

Yet Hank seemed in no rush to fill in anything. He silently assessed her.

She saw the understanding behind his eyes: he knew what she was talking about. He just needed the right invitation to admit it.

She asked, "Do you know any women serving in the WAAC?"

He scratched at his neck and looked away. "Yeah, sure. A few."

Thousands of women had joined the Women's Auxiliary Army Corps, added after Pearl Harbor to fill noncombat roles. Though some found work near their homes, most had to relocate, exercising a degree of female independence not appreciated by everyone.

Anne played dumb: "It's great that so many young women are doing their part to serve, don't you think?"

"I suppose."

"I thought about enlisting myself, but I decided I could do more good here." She tapped her notebook. "Who is it you know in the WAAC?"

"Well, just this one girl, actually. Grew up across the street. She went down to Fort Gillem a few months ago." He scratched at his neck again. "You don't need to know about her for your story, though, do ya? I wouldn't want her name in print or anything."

"That's so good of you to want to protect her. No, I don't need to print her name. Have you heard anything from her since she got down there?"

"Yeah. Got a letter from her."

"Oh, that's nice." She'd had a hunch from the start, but now this made even more sense. "Do you write to her, too?"

A shrug. "Yeah."

"That's good of you. So many men don't know how to express themselves in writing. It's always nice to get a letter from a sweetheart."

"Well, she's not my . . . I mean . . ."

"Just a friend, then."

"Yeah." The dejection plain.

"I won't tell anyone her name, but . . . could you tell me?"

He considered for a moment. "Cindy. Cindy Byrne. Her folks are in 12B there," and he motioned across the street.

"So is Cindy the one who told you about . . ." And here Anne pretended to have trouble with it, even looked down at her notebook as if she were too embarrassed. When he didn't volunteer the answer, she finally looked up and said, "About the doctor?"

He exhaled. The itch at the back of his neck really seemed to be troubling him.

"Yeah, look. About that . . ."

Another pause. Being a reporter, Anne had learned, meant being comfortable with long pauses. Awkward silences. *Don't fill them,* she had been taught. *Wait for the other person to offer something.* Being an inveterate conversationalist herself, this had been one of the journalistic skills she was having the most trouble perfecting.

She told herself to wait, wait.

"Hank." The hell with it—waiting was for the lazy. "I told you I wouldn't use Cindy's name in my story. And I won't use yours either. *If* you cooperate."

Short pause to let it sting.

"Because here's what I think: I think you got angry at Cindy for something. For what, I don't know, and I don't need to know. What-ever happened between you"—or whatever *didn't happen* between you, is what Anne figured—"isn't any of my business. But it *is* my business, and it's my readers' business, to know the truth about what's happening with our military and our soldiers."

She was staring into his eyes now, trying to look empathetic but firm, and he hadn't broken her stare. He looked like just another schoolboy getting the talking-to he knew he deserved from the teacher he most hated to disappoint.

The long, hot walk had been worth it.

"I think that you were angry at Cindy, and so you said something about her to your friends. Something that wasn't kind and wasn't true."

He finally broke the stare and looked away, out to the street. The street where he and Cindy used to play together, no doubt, where he must have developed his crush, his unrequited love for a girl who went off to have exciting adventures without him.

He shook his head, and she saw that his eyes were watering.

Anne continued, "You said something unfair about her, and word got around, and it's really amazing how quickly word gets around these days, especially about that sort of thing, and you really didn't mean for it to get out of hand like that, but it did, and that's why I'm here. And I don't think you *really* feel that way about her, do you?"

"I . . ." His voice tiny. A long exhalation to check the tears. "I shouldn'ta said that."

His mother's voice again: "Hank! Dinner's ready! Where's your sister?"

"In a minute, Ma!" With the yell, his face flushed red. All the sadness and guilt in his eyes a moment ago turned into a fresh anger. That mo-ment of vulnerability gone, hidden once again behind false toughness.

"Okay?" His voice more forceful now. "It was wrong of me. But what's the big deal?"

"So, just to be clear, and for the record: Cindy *didn't* write to you that she got pregnant from one of the soldiers down at Fort Gillem, and she *didn't* say that her girlfriends down there got pregnant too, and she *didn't* tell you that they all got abortions from a staff doctor at the base?"

He stared at her for an extra few seconds. "No. She didn't."

"But you said that to some friends."

He folded his arms. "Yeah. I made it up."

"She rejected you," Anne said, her veneer of reportorial disinterest now fading, "and because she dared to do that, you decided to call her a whore and make up stories about not only her but about all the patriotic young women in the WAAC supposedly getting abortions."

"I said I was sorry, okay?" Not that Anne remembered—no, actually, he hadn't apologized. "Can you leave now, lady?"

She nodded to him and said good evening. She was down the steps and had taken a few triumphant strides toward Mass Ave when he called out, "Hey!"

She turned and he asked, "What was your name, again?"

"Anne Lemire. You'll see the byline in the *Star* on Thursday."

Chapter Two

ESSENTIAL WAR WORK

Agent Devon Mulvey woke in a strange bedroom with a headache, dry mouth, and missing pants.

He waded through the bedroom slowly, as it was the only speed he could muster at the moment. Hungover, he ached in strange places, like he'd been physically assaulted. He *had* been—she'd been a damned jaguar in the sack. And in the hallway. And on the stairs.

The stairs, that's right—she'd taken off his pants in the stairway. It had been funny at the time. He seemed to remember laughing as he'd left the slacks behind. Proud of himself for not tripping as he did so, indeed gracefully leaping from one step to the next. She'd lost her blouse a few steps later, if memory served.

She lived in a fourth-floor walk-up, the trolley rumbling along Commonwealth just outside. He'd had the presence of mind to hang on to his wallet and keys, slipping them into his jacket pocket as he'd stepped out of the pant legs, which had been doubly awkward as he'd still been wearing his loafers.

He spotted his jacket on the floor, nylon stockings coiled upon it like shed snakeskin.

She started snoring again. That must have been what had woken him. He found a clock in the kitchenette: six forty-five! Far too early after a night like that.

If memory served (which it often didn't when drowned in alcohol), they'd had four rounds at the bar. Not a cheap date, but she'd seemed pent up, like everyone else, from the shortages and the rationing, the blackouts and dimouts. Apparently his invitation had been exactly what she'd needed.

From the moment he'd made eye contact with her, at the front desk of Gray and Grayson, Attorneys-at-Law, he'd had an inkling. He had a sixth sense about these matters. He was there to interview one of her bosses as part of a background check for a local businessman who was set to be appointed to a government-industry oversight committee, just another boring errand of the sort Devon was doing entirely too much of lately.

Gray and Grayson was a friendly firm; he had a number of contacts there who provided information about suspicious activity, subversive rumblings overheard at local law schools, odd requests from clients (attorney-client privilege, like most things, was not to be held too sacred during wartime). He had never seen this particular secretary before, so he'd made a point of asking her a few questions about herself before she ushered him to the right office. Her eyes had said all that her lips weren't allowed to, at least not in public.

After the background check, which he'd deliberately dragged out just a tad so that it ended precisely at five, he'd lingered in the lobby once more and asked the secretary if he could walk her to the subway. She'd accepted, and also accepted his next invitation, for a quick drink, which turned into four.

The irony was that he had been planning to take that night off. Stay home, read. But he'd changed his mind the moment he saw her, as if a secret signal had been exchanged between them, clear as any radio broadcast. Some chemical released into the air, and they were helpless to resist, both of them realizing that, if they had to live with air raid drills and ration cards, if they had to pull dark blinds down on every night to protect against potential long-range bombers, then they would grant themselves a release when the opportunity arose. They damn well deserved it, didn't they?

But back to his pants. Had he really left them in the building's stair-way? Jesus, that was extreme, even for him.

The lady of the hour was still snoring. Christine, or Kristin or Chris-tina. Devon was generally good with names, particularly women's names, but all those variations on "Chris" threw him. Some odd Catholic blind spot of his. He'd already put on his shirt and shorts, so now he slipped into his suit jacket, letting her nylons silently cascade to the floor. Lucky nylons they were, to embrace such legs every day.

At the bar last night, they'd toasted to America and victory, of course. He could have proposed that they toast to our boys in uniform, if he'd been an idiot, but he'd already seen her ring. He'd learned that the setup really was this easy: you approached, you implied the offer. If the lady was in any way offended, she would make that plain, immediately. In which case Devon would apologize, say that he hadn't seen her ring, and, depending on her tone, perhaps he'd depart with some line to the effect of how lucky her husband was.

That particular response had actually worked, twice.

Downtown locations were the best. Or chance encounters on main thoroughfares like Boylston or Commonwealth. Trying it in a neighborhood spot was risky, especially the staunchly ethnic enclaves—and was there any other kind in Boston? In such areas, everyone knew everyone, the women were watched, cultural mores were sacrosanct, and even a brief exchange between a married lady (especially a soldier's wife) and a strange man was dangerous for both.

But back to last night.

Let's say it had been "Christina."

Devon and Christina had touched glasses, he sipping whiskey and she a sweet vermouth on the rocks.

"I don't usually drink on a weeknight," she'd claimed.

He pretended he could empathize. "It's good to cut loose now and again."

"It is." She smiled. A bit off-center to the right, but she had full lips. Lips that knew how to do things, or would be eager students.

"My name's Devon, by the way."

"Christina." (Or something similar.) She'd given him her hand, he'd kissed it, and she had not objected. The ring on her finger was thin and probably wasn't even gold.

The hand-kiss had been a bit much. Maybe everything about this was phony and false, but she'd found it impossible not to grin and blush.

Because how false or phony was it, really? Maybe they were pretending, but some things you need to pretend at first, as practice for making them real. Everyone was worried about their husbands and sons and fathers and cousins, worried about how long this might go on, worried about what was happening to the world. How much worse things might get. Positive as the newspapers tried to be, every page contained bad news.

Britain was being bombed into nothingness. France didn't seem to exist. The vast Pacific contained untold dangers. The only countries doing well were those run by lunatic strongmen.

"So, an FBI agent." She couldn't conceal her excitement. "What do you do when you aren't interviewing attorneys like my boss?"

"Mostly war work these days, preventing industrial sabotage."

Each time she sipped, her lips were undressed of more of their lipstick. He could watch this girl drink for hours. He didn't think he'd have to.

"What does that mean exactly? Tightening screws?"

"In a manner of speaking. There were all sorts of shenanigans in the last war, German sympathizers trying to blow up factories and whatnot. It's my job to keep that from happening."

He glanced at the bar's mirror, its reflection of the tavern behind him. A few blocks off Scollay Square, it attracted all kinds. Devon spied a few State Street bankers toasting their newly ascendant portfolios, City Hall staffers flirting with secretaries over gin and tonics, shipbuilders from the Harbor buying beers for sweaty friends.

"You mean like those Germans on the submarine in Long Island?"

"Exactly like them."

It had been one of the Bureau's great accomplishments: a year ago, in June of '42, agents had arrested a ring of German spies who had been secreted by U-boat to Long Island. The story had been covered extensively in the papers and newsreels.

"Does that mean you won't have to ship off to the front?"

"It does. What I do for the Bureau is considered essential war work, so, when it came time to enlist, it was made clear to me that my services were more direly needed here."

Which was mostly true. At least she didn't question him any further. The main thing was not giving a pretty lady the impression that he was 4-F, that he was missing a foot or had VD.

"You ever have that feeling," he'd asked as they'd neared the end of the first round, "that you're in a moment you'll remember later? That things have aligned a certain way, and you need to play it right and take advantage, because it's going to be a memory one way or the other?"

"I do."

"When you know you're living in something, right now, that you'll always look back on. There's this pressure to make sure you do the right thing with the time. That you don't waste the moment."

"My thoughts exactly."

He motioned to her empty glass and asked if she would have the same thing or something different.

She smiled. "I think I'd like something different tonight."

With his jacket on, he looked at himself in her mirror. Enough light emanated through the curtains for him to give himself a cursory finger-comb. He didn't look so terrible. He needed a shave, but a scruffy face would not be so unusual on the morning streetcar.

A man without pants, however, would be noticed.

He quietly inspected the dresser, starting with the bottom drawer. *Voilà*, pants. He and Christina had been a good fit for each other height-wise, Devon a good three inches taller, so hopefully her matrimonial pairing was similarly apt. Figuring the pants on top might be the husband's favorites, he dug deeper into the drawer and removed the bottom pair. Dark blue, not quite the right shade but hopefully close enough not to look too absurd with his jacket.

He tried them on. Her husband was a big one. Did he have a belt? They might work with a belt.

Devon checked the other drawers, then the closet. Perfect: a newish black leather belt. Not actually new, of course, but it had been new a few months ago and had been hanging unused in the closet these many months, waiting for the owner's waist to return. Devon felt bad taking such a good belt; Christina would have to find a way to explain the absence. Hopefully the husband was not as much of a clotheshorse as Devon was. Few men were.

He wandered back into the kitchenette and inspected himself. The pants didn't sit right on him, but they weren't so outlandish as to be eye-catching on the streetcar. A tad long, but not so bad.

It wasn't that he deliberately sought out married women. They were pretty much *all* married, so what choice did he have? Every halfway attractive girl had been proposed to by a nervous man about to be shipped off to war. Some of these men had been legitimately lovelorn, sure, and many were the ironclad pacts between ocean-separated husband and wife. But add to that the uncountable marriages of convenience and haste, of panic and pity. Women who felt that they were doing their patriotic duty to wed that boy who had the nice enough smile and was probably a good fellow, women who sort of, kind of enjoyed so-and-so's presence and could only hope he wouldn't be too transformed by the horrors of war. Women who'd been pressured into mistakes instantly regretted, who'd allowed a young man's fear and desperate lust to ruin their own chance at the good life, a happy marriage to someone they actually loved. All for what they considered their "duty," to give a nervous young virgin his roll in the hay and a tiny portrait to entomb in his wallet.

The truly committed wives would rebuff Devon's advances, which was fine with him. He wasn't out to break hearts or tear asunder those marriages that actually stood a chance of continuing once the GIs returned and the spouses tried to remember what they'd liked about each other back before the war.

The many other wives, as far as he was concerned, were fair game.

He was doing a patriotic duty like any other, wasn't he? Spreading joy, relieving tension, keeping spirits high. Lord knows, he hadn't walked away from any unsatisfied faces.

In the bathroom he found the husband's toiletries behind the mirror, untouched, as if he'd only left for the Army the night before. How thoughtful of her to leave his things like this. Devon opened the can of pomade, glancing at the pasty whiteness, where the husband's fingerprints were still embossed. He found himself thinking of the dust and ash of Pompeii, those domestic moments forever frozen in time.

He dipped his fingers, found a comb, fixed his hair.

He gave the bedroom a final check, grabbed his briefcase. His hat? There it was, under the bed. It would need some blocking, but it was okay. He brushed lint from the bill.

His gun? No, he was smarter than that; he'd left it locked in the office. He hoped.

She lay on her side, the sheet low but her arms gracefully draped across her breasts as if she were hoping to pass muster with a censor. She had certainly passed muster with Devon, not that he remembered as much as he wished he did. That was the problem with drinking and loving, yet he kept making that mistake.

He quietly stepped out of the apartment. There were only three other units on this floor, the other doors down a short landing. His pants were not in view. He walked to the bottom of the stairs, just in case she'd de-panted him on an earlier floor than he'd thought, but they weren't there either. His head was pounding—movement hurt, as did thinking. He was initially inclined to walk away, to write the pants off as yet another patri-otic sacrifice to the good war.

But this was his favorite suit.

Walking down had been difficult, but walking up was a goddamned nightmare. It hadn't seemed such a steep staircase last night; the build-ing apparently had grown taller. Booze bestows a certain weightless-ness, yet in the mornings we grow so heavy.

He needed to cut back on the drinking, he knew. That he'd actually let a woman undress him in a semipublic stairway should be a wake-up call.

Back on the top landing, he took a breath and tried to think. He heard someone open the building's front door and begin to ascend the steps.

The footsteps seemed to be pounding, but maybe that was just the blood in his head. The steps continued until he saw a woman walk-ing toward him. Late thirties, graying hair, even grayer housedress. She didn't look the sort who'd spent the night out on the town.

"Morning," he said to her. They made eye contact as she passed him, and her eyes were not friendly.

Christina had been rather on the loud side last night.

The neighbor lady was sliding a key into her apartment's door when Devon mustered the energy to say, "Excuse me, ma'am?"

She turned to face him—key still in the door, waiting impatiently to be turned—but acknowledged him with nothing more than that.

"I'm a friend of Mrs. Dawson's next door." He'd checked the mail slot downstairs to remind himself of "Christina's" surname. "I was, ah, I was wondering if by chance you came across anything on the stairs on your way out this morning."

She watched him with disappointed eyes, like a schoolteacher. Like a nun. A nun who allowed herself to get angrier than Jesus would have condoned.

"Anything in particular?"

"An article of clothing."

She gazed for a weighted moment at his appropriated pants. Then back at his face.

So that's how she wanted to play it.

"I haven't seen any hats or anything. No watches either, if that's what you mean."

He was holding his hat and he put his other hand in his pocket, adopting his leveling-with-you gaze, or what of it he could muster at that hour.

"How about a pair of slacks?"

She raised her eyebrows. But that was all. She seemed to be waiting for a good line, but what she came up with didn't sound all that good.

"I know her husband. He's fighting overseas."

"Yes, I'm an old college chum of his, from out of town," he lied. "She and I were commiserating and I, well, seemed to spill something all over my suit, and she offered to help clean it up, so—"

"At least she still *has* a husband." Eyes gone harder. "That makes her luckier than some. Much luckier."

His mental arithmetic, like so much else, had been wrong. The pants were not worth this.

"You should be ashamed. Men like you make me sick."

He let the war widow vent. Knew there was nothing he could say.

"Your slacks are downstairs. In the trash. Where you should be."

He wasn't sure if she meant he should be downstairs, leaving, or if he too should be in the trash can. Either way, she was probably right.

He was about to say he was sorry for her loss when she slammed the door.

Chapter Three

THE RUMOR CLINIC

W ho woulda thought a depressed nineteen-year-old could cause so much trouble?"

"Depressed nineteen-year-olds have been causing trouble for centuries."

Larry Barnett, Anne's chain-smoking editor, grinned at her riposte. Thin and manic, he looked to be in his mid-forties, old enough not to have been drafted.

"True, but the way you describe the little wimp, doesn't seem like the type who'd be behind all this."

"He seems *exactly* the type." Anne laughed at her editor's naïveté. "I do think he was rather amazed by all the attention his mouth had gotten him, yes. But everyone has a mouth, Larry. Doesn't matter how *wimpy* they look."

Loose lips didn't just sink ships, they also angered parents and scared teenagers who needed to enlist. They confused, terrified, alarmed. They made us worry we were weaker than we feared, vulnerable in a newly dangerous world.

Larry stood and Anne sat at her desk, in the far, windowless corner of the *Boston Star*'s smoky bullpen. She'd been reviewing her notes and was ready to start typing a draft when Larry had stopped by, asking for the scoop.

She'd filled him in. Even before she'd questioned the sullen Hank yesterday, Anne had called the Army base at Fort Gillem in Georgia. After being funneled through several operators, she found herself speaking to a gruff, Southern press liaison who, after some awkward half-steps that betrayed his lack of comfort even addressing this topic with a female, assured Anne "on my mama's grave" that precisely zero members of the WAAC had been sent home pregnant.

And no, the fort did not employ an abortionist.

So Anne had already known the truth before she found her way to Hank. But printing the truth was only part of her job. Her main task was to disprove falsehoods, and the best way to do that was to trace them to their very source and reveal that source to the public in all his shamefulness.

And yes, despite the stereotype of gossiping women, it was usually a *he*.

Anne wrote for the Rumor Clinic, the weekly *Star* column she'd managed to create for herself after weeks of persistent calls and a few connections. The idea behind the Rumor Clinic was to identify and disprove the many harmful rumors floating around town, some of them spread by deliberate Axis propaganda to weaken resolve and others just random bits of hearsay mixed with fear, ignorance, and bigotry.

She'd been on this beat two months and had disproven several rumors already:

No, the permed heads of women who worked at munitions factories were not exploding. Factory work was perfectly safe for all Rosie Riveters.

No, a rash of stomach illnesses in Quincy was not the result of Nazi submarines poisoning lobsters off the coast of Maine. Please continue to support your local lobstermen.

No, a traveling Negro League baseball team with a Chinese manager had not altered its travel schedule so that it only played in cities near Army bases, and it was not relaying troop information to the Japanese. The team supported the Allies and simply traveled a lot. Also their "Chinese" manager was actually Puerto Rican. Common mistake.

No, none of the Army camps had been hit by a wave of suicides; basic training was not making our young men "camp-crazy."

No, hordes of Indians who lived outside Fort Devens in western Mass were not raping female war workers. The small tomahawks that had been found at the fort were mislaid toys, property of white children who had visited their fathers the previous weekend. Anne herself had returned the toys to two charming, towheaded tykes who were blissfully unaware of how their lost treasures had caused mass hysteria.

(Larry had initially wanted the column to be *called* Mass Hysteria—he loved awful puns—but she'd managed to talk him out of that.)

Anne chased lies down to their dirty origins, like playing a game of telephone in reverse, on the scale of an entire city. By getting to the original source, she could point her finger and demonstrate beyond doubt that the story wasn't true but was merely the brainchild of this one crank, who almost uniformly expressed a combination of anger, embarrassment, and shame at having Anne reveal their role in the rumor.

Her new piece would refute the nasty rumor that WAAC women had loose morals and were corrupting our young soldiers at Army bases. Parents who were worried about their daughters' newfound desire to work outside the home, and for the Army no less, could at least stop worrying about their daughters' chastity.

"You know," Larry said, paging through the rival *Globe*, "it'd be interesting if one of your rumors was *true* for a change."

"They're not exactly *my* rumors."

"Larry was rooting for the exploding-heads one," said Cheryl, from her desk beside Anne's. The only other lady reporter Anne had seen here so far, Cheryl was usually relegated to reporting on the parties of socialites and on matters regarding the welfare of children, but lately her portfolio had expanded, given how many male reporters had been lost to the draft. Anne guessed Cheryl was about thirty, meaning six years older than Anne.

"Can't deny that would have been an interesting story," Larry said.

Larry had been clear from the beginning that he thought the whole Rumor Clinic idea was silly, a frippery for this gal reporter to occupy herself with. The first day they'd worked together, he'd even told her, "You chase down the false rumors, and if one ever turns out to be true, and an honest-to-God news story, bring it to me and I'll write it up."

Hadn't happened yet. Anne wasn't exactly rooting for that outcome anyway.

This was her first job at a paper, but she'd already been a writer for years. Shortly after graduating, she'd helped start an anti-Fascist group, the Boston Center for Democracy, dedicated to alerting Americans to the growing dangers of Nazism. Anne had written several muckraking stories about anti-Semitic and Hitlerite groups in New England. The BCD had been funded by donations; she'd been its sole paid employee, writing its newsletter and warning against isolationism's false security.

Once Japan bombed Pearl Harbor and America finally declared war, though, the BCD's very purpose seemed to have been fulfilled, so people had stopped donating. The BCD all but ceased to exist. Suddenly in need of work, Anne managed to sell a few freelance pieces here and there, then took on a part-time copyediting job at a Cambridge publisher before managing to convince Larry's boss to hire her for the Rumor Clinic.

"So what's next, Lemire?" Larry asked. Like most people, he mispronounced it as "Le-MIRE" instead of "Le-MEER." The name had likely been "Lemiere" originally, but a generation or two of illiterate French Canadians had led to several spellings and an overall disagreement about everything except the pronunciation, which non-Canucks usually got wrong anyway.

"Once I actually write this one, you mean?" She started typing, hoping that would spur him to leave.

"I expect my reporters to be covering several stories at once, sweetheart. You know that."

"I pitched you several other ideas, and—"

"I'd remember them if they were any good."

She stopped typing and reached for one of her notebooks. Her position was only partly funded by the *Star*; the rest came courtesy of the federal government's Committee on Public Safety, which technically made her an employee of the Division of Propaganda Research. But Larry called the shots.

She flipped through her new story ideas. A few had come from random calls to the paper, but most were things she'd picked up from her "morale wardens," people whose regular jobs made them well-positioned to overhear the word on the street: bartenders, waitresses, shop owners, salesmen, socialite bridge players. For most, being a morale warden was a painless way to be a part of the war effort, almost like being a professional gossip: they were rewarded not for spreading salacious nonsense but for passing it on to Anne so she could disprove it.

"How about this," she said, pointing. "I've heard from five different people now that Jews are getting extra ration stamps. *Clearly* it's bunk, so I could—"

"Ix-nay on the hebes." Larry made a face. "Your last few have all been about Jews and Indians and the blacks. Don't think I'm not starting to notice an agenda there, missy. You're here to disprove war rumors, not write about the travails of the dark and swarthy."

They're so often related, she wanted to say. But as usual she forced herself to ignore his casual biases lest she get pulled into another argument she knew she'd lose.

"I like this one," he said, pointing to a line in her notes, "the idea that sailors in Hawaii are turning green from chemicals after Pearl Harbor. That's swell! Should be a fun one."

"Exploding heads and green-skinned sailors," Cheryl said, cigarette bouncing in her lips as she typed. "You should work for the pulps, Larry."

"Don't tempt me."

Anne sighed. "If I cover the Hawaii story, will you throw in a plane ticket to Oahu?"

"Ha! You want Hawaii, join the WAAC. Although I heard a rumor they're all getting knocked up." He winked. "You want to keep writing here? Pick up the phone and earn your keep."

Chapter Four

THE BODY

H̲ave yourself a fun evening?" asked Lou Loomis, Devon's strait-laced WASP partner.

Lou was driving them to the North End. Thin, pale, pockmarked from childhood smallpox, and perpetually nervous when questioning attractive women, Lou was a few years older than Devon but tended to act much, much older, in Devon's opinion.

"I did; thanks for asking."

Lou had no doubt noticed that Devon was wearing the same jacket as yesterday and with pants that didn't match. He and Lou had been partners for only six months, and Devon feared he was constantly disappointing the man.

It was bad enough that Devon had been branded an outsider the moment he'd joined the Bureau, in '40. Barely a year out of law school, he'd been only the second Irish Catholic ever to work at the Boston field office (that other fellow had since transferred to New York). Director Hoover preferred men of a certain background, and Papists had long been considered as suspect as Jews and anarchists. Had Devon been born ten years earlier, he never would have been hired, but over the last few years the Director had met just enough intelligent, influential, God-fearing Catholics to realize that such people tended to share his traditionalism and his hatred of communism, materialism, wanton sexuality, and anything else that threatened the status quo. Thus opened the Bureau doors, slightly, to Irishers like Devon Patrick Mulvey (despite Devon's inability to follow certain scriptural passages, like not coveting thy neighbors' wives).

Most of the other agents, Devon had learned, didn't trust him any farther than they could throw a King James Bible at him, figuring he'd soon reveal himself to be just another Irish badge who drank too much, roughed up innocents, and lived off bribes. Lou had never said as much to Devon, but still Devon felt wary around him.

"So," Lou asked, "who was she?"

He didn't have the heart to tell his possibly virginal partner that he wasn't even sure of her name. "Just someone who probably woke up in a great mood."

"You don't even wake up with them?"

"Well, I had a job to get to."

"Ha, that's funny. It's your wittiness that must win their hearts."

Lou wove slowly through the narrow roads in the North End, the city's densely settled Italian district. Used to be, Italian flags were common here, but they'd all been replaced by the stars and stripes, as the immigrants were defensively quick to demonstrate their new allegiance. Lou parked in front of a butcher's shop, ham hanging in the window.

"Look out, the federals are here!" a cop called out as Devon and Lou approached the gaggle of uniforms assembled at the mouth of an alley.

"Put the flasks away, gentlemen!" teased another. "It's Hoover's boys."

An older cop walked up to Devon a little more closely than was polite. "How many ration stamps you sell to buy that nice suit?"

Devon had been taught that the Fourth Commandment to honor thy mother and father should be extended to all elders, so he tried to play nice. Which in this case meant smiling as he said, "Well, I was going to take kickbacks from all the dope dealers and pimps, but they said you already took their money."

The old cop laughed, but his eyes betrayed little warmth as he stepped aside.

Whenever Devon was in the company of Boston's finest, he braced for this. He endured the occasional comment about how he was "a hoper," someone who goes to sleep Irish and hopes to wake up Yankee. He heard their sneers about how he was an upwardly mobile "lace curtain" Irish or "two-toilet" Irish. And yes, his parents' home in Milton did indeed have lace curtains and two toilets, so he mostly bit his tongue and took the ribbing.

Such a weird phrase, he always reflected: "two-toilet" Irish. A sign of respectability, in theory, but also a reminder that they're never far from shit.

Yankee Lou, he'd noticed, the cops basically just ignored.

Ten feet into the alley, Homicide Detective Jimmy Moore stood beside a police photographer who looked no older than a high schooler; maybe he was, given the manpower shortages. As the agents stepped closer, Devon saw the body, and his breath caught. Feet pointing toward them, pale white face turned toward the near wall. The shirt he had been wearing looked dirty, light gray, but most of his chest was soaked black with blood. The man had been tall, bent legs and arms spread wide across the alley, like a marionette God had lost interest in and released, the strings vanishing.

"Gentlemen, welcome to my alley," Moore said. "Please wipe your feet."

Snap, snap went the camera.

"So, what do we have?" Devon asked.

"People keep killing each other. It's almost like it's part of the human condition."

"No one reads the Bible anymore."

The banter was probably habit for Moore, but Devon had to work at it. He had relatively little experience with murders, having been on the industrial sabotage beat for most of his time with the Bureau. But he knew he couldn't show that here.

Snap, snap.

He and Moore had known each other since grade school, drifting apart years ago when Devon's family moved on from Dorchester. Because of their shared history, Moore was one of the few cops who didn't consider college-educated, FBI-employed Devon a blue-nosed Yankee traitor—or at least, he didn't openly say so.

"This gentleman got himself stabbed last night. Likely bled out in seconds."

Blood had pooled beneath the body. It had mostly dried, but given the morning's humidity some of it still looked shiny.

"Robbery?" Lou asked. "You find his wallet?"

"No wallet, so indeed, I was first thinking robbery as the motive. We did find his Northeast Munitions time card on the ground, though, along with this."

Devon pulled on a pair of gloves as Moore, also gloved, handed him what looked like a crumpled paper napkin. He opened it up and yes, that's what it was, a white cocktail napkin, on which someone had drawn a swastika in black ink. He passed it to Lou.

"This was in his pocket or on the ground?" Lou asked.

"Pants pocket. The one his wallet shoulda been in."

Devon carefully stepped around the dead man's legs and nearer to the alley wall, leaning against it a bit so he could crouch down and get a closer look at the man's face. Dark hair with a few flecks of gray. Small mustache. On the skinny side. Otherwise unremarkable.

"You think the killer left the swastika as some calling card?" Devon asked.

"It's a theory," Moore replied. "Question is, was our man here a Nazi spy, and someone found out and killed him, left the napkin to explain himself? In which case, you had a spy working at that factory. Or maybe the *killer* was a Nazi, left the note as a brag. In which case, why did he kill this particular gentleman?"

Police officers were supposed to notify the Bureau about any crimes that may have been committed by Nazi sympathizers or any other Fascist group. In the year and a half since Pearl Harbor, the Bureau had cracked down on the German American Bund, the Silver Shirts, and a dozen other ultraright organizations, arresting members for treason or violating the Smith Act when they couldn't get them for more easily definable crimes like money laundering, assault, or murder.

Even before Pearl Harbor, agents had been keeping an eye on a number of groups whose praise of Hitler and opposition to the Lend-Lease Act veered a bit too close to Nazi propaganda. Here in Boston, the FBI had arrested several people for being unregistered German agents, yet the country still had more than its share of crackpots, some of them evading detection by lying low and others on the FBI radar but stubbornly immune from prosecution for political reasons that Devon didn't entirely understand.

"Looks like he tried to fight them off," Devon said, pointing at the man's bloody knuckles as he stood up and stepped back.

"Yeah, I saw that too. Maybe it started with fists, graduated to knives, only he didn't have one." Moore shrugged. "Mortician says time of death was somewhere between ten and two. Best he could do before he opens him up. We're about ready to move the body, but I thought you'd want a look first."

"Who called it in?" Lou asked.

"Kid who works for the restaurant next door. Came by to empty the morning trash at eight, saw the body."

The dumpster was only a few feet away. "No one was emptying the trash at night?" Devon asked. "You'd think someone would have noticed it then."

"Not much light in here at night. We'll find out when the other places took out their trash if that helps us narrow the time of death, but it's possible someone coulda stepped out here and just not seen him."

Devon thought for a moment, then looked at Lou. "I've seen enough. You?"

Lou nodded. "You can move him."

Two uniforms were given the honor of lifting the body and zipping it into a body bag. As they lifted the corpse, Devon saw on the alley floor, beneath where the body had been lying, a piece of red plaid cloth. He leaned over and picked it up, thinking it was a handkerchief, but it turned out to be the wrong shape. And frayed.

"That a shirt collar?" Lou asked.

"It is. Could be he grabbed a handful of the killer's shirt."

It was only the topmost section and had been torn at the seam, so Devon saw no tag or tailor's mark. Didn't smell any cologne. He handed it to Moore, who slid it into a small evidence bag.

"We'll see if we can get any prints from the collar or the napkin," Moore said, yawning.

Devon could tell that this represented about as much investigating into this particular crime as Moore was likely to perform. Murders were down in the city—funny what happens when you send nearly all of your young men away to the military—yet cops and detectives still acted overwhelmed by their backlogs. Devon suspected that the best and brightest cops had joined Military Intelligence or other war agencies, or become Army grunts themselves, leaving BPD with its dimmest bulbs.

Of course, civilians could say the same thing about FBI agents. And they had said it, to his face, more than once. *Why aren't you in the military, tough guy? What are you hiding from, you 4-F bastard?*

Devon took another look at the dead man's munitions-factory time card. "And we'll find out who the poor son of a bitch was."

Chapter Five

MORALE WARDEN #1

So many sailors and soldiers on the street. Many of them whistling at Anne, or just making eyes. Salvation Army reps on the corner, hawking war bonds. Flags everywhere.

She was walking over to one of her favorite diners for an early lunch, two blocks north of Faneuil Hall. Shiplighter's made the best fish and chips in town, but more important, it was a good spot for gossip.

Since she regularly checked in with her network of morale wardens, she spent far too much time at diners and bars, which meant she often spent money she couldn't afford. (Larry had laughed at her suggestion she be reimbursed for expenses—"Order water," he'd said.) She feared she was one of the few people in this time of rationing and sacrifice who might be *gaining* weight.

"I thought this place had air-conditioning," she said as she slid onto one of the stools at the sticky counter, which Lydia was wiping down. It was just before the lunch rush.

"You think it's bad on *that* side of the counter? Try being this close to the kitchen. The old man was complaining about the electric bill—said it's our patriotic duty to sweat."

"It's my patriotic duty to drink more coffee. But given the heat I'll settle for a Coke."

"Sure, and the usual, right?"

"Of course."

Lydia relayed her order to the cook, then turned and smiled. "We're going dancing tomorrow, right?"

Anne had forgotten. "Is that tomorrow?"

"Yes, last I checked Friday still came after Thursday. Unless Uncle Sam's changed that too?"

"Oh, sweetie, I'd love to, but I forgot I have a union meeting."

"No, no, no. I'm not letting you get away with that. Can't be all work and no play, Annie. Between your job and that union stuff, there's nothing left of you. We need to get out there and have fun. Remember *fun*? You do realize it's still legal in this country?"

"Getting pawed at by some drunken sailor isn't my idea of fun."

"They won't *paw at* you—there are chaperones everywhere, and they're too scared of getting thrown in the brig. Usually. Plus there's no alcohol at the dances. Well, officially—okay, they usually sneak it in. My point is, you've been working day and night. You need to kick back now and then."

"It just doesn't feel like the time to be kicking back."

Lydia volunteered at the American Red Cross in her spare time. Her girlfriends had encouraged her to come to the USO dances near the Navy Yard, which she'd done twice now. Anne had yet to join her.

"When's the union meeting?" Lydia asked.

"Seven."

"No problem—the dance starts at eight. Go to the first hour of the meeting, then meet me at the USO and we can be fashionably late."

Lydia clearly didn't realize how union meetings could go on and on. "I'll either be overdressed for a union meeting or underdressed for a dance."

"They're sailors, Annie! You could wear a smock and they'd be thrilled to dance with you, you know that." Lydia leaned on the counter. "Sweetie, don't be a prude. It's been so hard to meet fellas lately."

Anne didn't care for the "prude" remark. She'd had her share of beaus, thank you, but none of them were the sort she'd taken seriously. One had even proposed, when she was still at Radcliffe ("If we get married, you can quit this college business!"). She had declined, though her mother called her misguided. And now, with so much vital work to be done, this just didn't strike Anne as the time to be on the prowl for a man, which was Lydia's animating drive lately.

Not that Anne could blame her. Lydia had been engaged two years ago, to another neighbor of theirs. Shortly after his proposal, Jimmy got polio. He was in and out of hospitals for over a year, and had finally seemed on the mend when he suddenly worsened and died. Lydia had only recently emerged from the dark cloud that had descended on her. Taking this job had been a big step, as was her Red Cross volunteering.

"The sailors who come to the dances aren't a bad lot," Lydia pressed. "And besides, you owe me."

Anne laughed. "How's that?"

"Who kept you company when you had to go knock on strangers' doors in the worst part of Roxbury to ask about some Negro baseball team? Who spent her day off trekking through Chinatown with you so you could ask about spy cameras in Mandarin restaurants?"

"Well, that was *fun*."

"Oh, it was a barrel of laughs."

Anne was surprised Lydia hadn't found those missions exciting. What wasn't to love about going new places and learning secret things, especially when there was some risk involved? She felt hurt to realize Lydia had considered it a chore.

"All right, I'll come to the dance."

"Wonderful!" Lydia reached out and squeezed Anne's hands. "You won't regret it."

Lydia was called away to wait on another diner, so Anne ate her sandwich and flipped through that day's *Globe* as well as the *Herald* and *Star*. When Lydia was free again, Anne asked if she'd heard anything interesting lately.

"Some suits from City Hall said something about U-boats near P-town. Think that could be real?"

"God, I hope not." Tourist season had been all but canceled at the Cape anyway, due to the enforced blackouts and concerns about naval invasions, but an actual U-boat sighting would ratchet the terror up a few notches—if it was true. "Anything else?"

"Someone was here the other day, government type—bad suit and bad hair. He was telling a buddy the Germans have been sinking so many of our boats, and so quickly, that it's almost like there are Nazi spies in the government or at the docks, feeding them the info."

"I've heard the same thing." Anne put down her Coke bottle, her stomach tight. One of her brothers, Joe, was a midshipman in the Atlantic. Every day it felt like a new headline mentioned the sinking of another American ship. Despite the ocean's vastness, it seemed to be awash in U-boats. Even before GIs started seeing combat in North Africa last winter, hundreds of Americans had already died in what was being called "the Battle of the Atlantic," a very one-sided battle indeed. "But my government sources tell me the spy angle's hogwash."

It was hard to decide which was more alarming: that the Nazis somehow knew our boats' routes in advance, or that their submarines were lethal enough to sink so many without being tipped off.

"I heard a couple sailors talking about Italian gangsters hanging out by the Navy Yard. Didn't catch all of it, but they seemed excited."

Anne wrote *gangsters at Navy Yard?* in her notebook.

"Businessmen keep whining that taxes are going to go up to pay for the war," Lydia added. "Funny how it's always the ones in the nicest suits who complain the most." Then she reached into her pocket and removed a folded piece of paper. With a sheepish look, she added, "And I thought you'd want to see this. When I bought some shoes yesterday, the lady slipped it into the bag."

Anne had only finished half her lunch, but when she unfolded the paper, she lost her appetite.

Chapter Six

THE HOME FRONT

That night after dinner, Anne was playing Auction 45 with her mother and her mother's cousin Elias at the small table in the kitchenette of their second-floor Ashmont apartment. This was the rare evening when all three adults were home. Elias worked at the docks and Anne's mother was a seamstress, so between the staggered shifts every factory had adopted for the duration of the war, and Anne's own unpredictable hours, one or another of them tended to be out at this hour. At least that made the tiny apartment feel slightly less cramped.

"I'm getting lousy cards," her mother complained. She spoke with a French-Canadian accent, one she tried hard to suppress. Anne's parents had moved to Boston from Nova Scotia when they married in their late teens, and were such firm believers in the melting pot that they hadn't even taught their children French, though Anne and her brothers had picked up a few choice phrases.

"You always say that," Anne said.

"It's always true."

Anne won the hand, then they heard a key at the door.

"Don't give him a hard time," her mother warned Anne.

The door opened and in walked her brother Sammy, seventeen. His right eye was completely swollen shut and purple, and he had a red bruise on the left side of his face, which bore a large red scratch.

Anne's mother had called her that afternoon to tell her about the fight, so she'd expected him to look bad, but still she couldn't help gasping. "Jesus, Sammy."

"It's worse'n it looks."

"Well, good, because it looks awful."

"C'mon, no more sympathy, please." He dropped his satchel on a chair in the living room and poured himself a glass of water. "Mom already made a big deal out of it. I don't want to go through it all over again."

He'd been jumped on the way home from his summer job the night before. Anne and her mother had been asleep when he'd come home, Elias away at work. Then this morning, Anne had left for the *Star* before Sammy had gotten up, so she hadn't known till her mother's call a few hours ago.

"Can I get you some ice?" she offered.

"I iced it all last night and this morning. I'm fine."

Anne looked accusingly at her mother. "Why did he go to work today?"

"It's what men do," Elias said in his thick French accent. He'd only been in America for a few years.

"And women, thank you very much," Anne's mother said.

"He's not a man, he's seventeen," Anne said.

"There are seventeen-year-olds in the Army," Sammy said. "They lie about their age, but, you know, I could always—"

Anne motioned to his face. "Oh, that fight was so much fun that you want to get in another one? With guns and bombs this time?"

"Don't even joke about enlisting," Anne's mother said. "One son in uniform is enough for me right now."

"It's only five months away, Ma," Sammy muttered quietly.

"And I plan on enjoying all five months with your pleasant conversation until then."

Elias meanwhile dealt out the next hand, though neither woman reached for her cards.

"I still think he should have stayed home and not gone right back there," Anne said.

"I like earning money," Sammy replied. "Mr. Henry kept me in the back stockroom all day so I wouldn't scare away any customers."

"You do look like hell."

"I wish I could say, *You should see the other guys*. But, yeah, they still look fine, I bet."

"How many were there?"

"Aw, Jesus, I said I didn't want to go over all this." He walked into the living room, trying to flee the conversation, but that wasn't terribly effective since it was only a few feet away and there was no wall between the rooms.

"Watch your mouth," their mother snapped.

"I like getting my facts directly from the source," Anne told Sammy. "It's what reporters do."

"You are not gonna *report* on this, Anne!" he shouted.

Elias held up a hand. He was only a few years older than Anne, and many years younger than her mother, but still he liked to think of himself as the man of the house, which he technically was in that he was the oldest male, but Anne never wanted him to think his voice carried extra sway. He often took Sammy's side in arguments, masculinity apparently making them natural allies.

"I'm taking him to the gym again this weekend. We been working on how to box, but we'll work some more."

"I don't think that's such a great—"

"We started some lessons after the first time but then we got outta the habit," Elias continued. This was the second time Sammy had been beaten up. "We'll keep working on it, overtime."

"Knowing how to throw a punch can't be much help when it's four against one." Anne raised her voice to Sammy: "Was it four of them again?"

"No comment." Sammy dug a comic out of his satchel and started reading, or staring at the pictures or whatever it was boys did with comics.

A few weeks ago, he had been beaten up coming home from Hebrew school, where he went for an hour after school. At first he'd told his family it was just a high school brawl, nothing serious, brushing off their concerns about his busted lip and black eye.

Later he'd admitted to Anne that it had been worse than that. He and two friends had been chased by older teens—too old to be in school—wielding pipes and brass knuckles. Sammy didn't want their mother to know, and Anne had agreed to keep that aspect of it secret, if only to appease him.

This was how she first learned of the attacks that had become common in certain Dorchester neighborhoods. Groups of young Irishmen—and sometimes not-so-young Irishmen—chasing Jews down, cornering them in alleys, beating them senseless. First Anne had heard only whispers and echoes, but as she'd asked more questions, she realized Sammy's story wasn't unique. Worse, some stories had it that cops refused to help the victims and even joined in on the side of the attackers.

Yet no newspapers were writing about the attacks. Larry had rolled his eyes when Anne suggested they cover it. *You honestly think we should run a story about Irish kids beating up Jews?* he'd laughed. *How do you think that'd go over in this town? Hey, we could also run an exposé on how Irish men drink too much! Then maybe a piece about how Irish mothers are terrible cooks? Sweetheart, who do you think buys our newspaper?*

Larry had ended his riff with a closing statement that "kids being brats is not news," nor was the fact that Irishmen were clannish.

"It's your turn," Elias told Anne, motioning to her cards.

She sighed and picked up her hand, already less interested in the game and plotting her next move at work.

Later, her mother was asleep in their shared bedroom and Elias had left to work the night shift. Anne walked over to Sammy's room, which was really a closet in which they'd crammed a bed. When he'd been younger he'd shared a room with his brother and Elias, but a year ago he insisted he'd prefer his own space, tiny though it was.

He was sitting up in bed, reading *Captain America.* The sight of the comic and his very adult injuries made for such an odd juxtaposition, she realized. He was taller than her now, thin but filling out.

"So, where and when did it happen?"

He lowered the comic and sighed. "Blue Hill Ave and Floyd. I don't know, ten o'clock, I guess?"

"What were you doing out that late?"

"I have a right to be out when I want, Anne. And Mr. Henry needed me at the store."

"I'm not talking about *rights,* I'm talking about common sense. You know this has been happening yet you're coming home that late at night? C'mon, Sammy."

"So it's my fault, huh?" He sat up straighter. "That's easy, coming from you."

How had the world come to this? She was seven years older than Sammy. She felt protective of him, of course, but also some degree of guilt. The first time he'd been jumped, he'd told her, the four who had cornered him asked if he was a Jew. He hadn't said *None of your business* or even *Fuck you*. He'd looked them in the eye and said *Yes*. She wondered if she had the courage to do the same if it came to it.

Anne had been a teenager when they'd learned they were Jewish; the much younger Sammy had known for nearly his whole life. So strange to have this dividing line between siblings.

"You're allowed to go spy on those meetings," he said, "but I'm not allowed to go to *work*?"

Sometimes she wished she'd never told him about the anti-Fascist research she'd done. She softened her voice and said, "You working is fine. But I thought you said you weren't going to work there after dark."

"Somebody was sick and asked me to take their shift, so I did. It's not like I can be turning down money."

"You can turn down money if this is what it takes to get paid."

He looked away again. She wondered if he was lying. Their neighborhood here in Ashmont was safe, as far as she knew. Most families were Jewish or Eastern European immigrants or both, having arrived over the last fifty years and established a strong community. The northern sections of Dorchester, though, where a few Jewish neighborhoods were surrounded by Irish ones, were where the worst of the violence was happening.

The shop where he worked part-time sat at the outer rim of what Anne considered the danger zone. His mother had only let him take the job if he promised to walk straight home and not work late.

"Just be careful, Sammy. And if your job has you walking through the wrong parts of town, quit."

She knew he was trying to act tough, yet he wore the same sulking expression he'd worn as a kid whenever he didn't get his way.

"We need the money. And I'm taking a different route home."

She couldn't understand his stubbornness. Some vexing male trait. Then again, she was stubborn too, probably more so.

She said good night and was stepping away when he said, "Anne, you're not . . . you're not really gonna write about this, are you?"

She watched him for a moment. "No comment."

Alone at the kitchen table, Anne took out the pamphlet Lydia had secretly handed her that morning.

ARE YOU BEING EXPLOITED BY JEWS? Below that headline's lead story was one about "the truth behind the war," little-known "facts" about Pearl Harbor, warnings about the dangers of Zionism, the occasional Bible passage, and instructions on how to raise healthy, virile, Christian children. Lydia had been given it, she'd explained, by the lady who sold her some shoes that day.

Anne had seen more than her share of these lately. She folded the pamphlet in half and slipped it back into her purse.

"Goddamn it," she said to herself, quietly. The walls were thin.

Larry didn't want her to disprove awful rumors about Jews? The hell with him. She'd start her reporting on these pamphlets tomorrow. Then she'd hand Larry the story, and if the *Star* wouldn't print it, she'd find other ways to get the truth out there.

Chapter Seven

ON GRAYNESS

No place did gray like Boston. It may have seemed a time of black and white, of easily definable enemies, of right and wrong, of stars and stripes and swastikas, but Boston had the full palette of grays. Winter was especially gray, but some years spring rivaled it, and even in summer the sun took plenty of days off. Last month had been one of those Mays that felt more like March, with a long pall of clouds that simply would not move, merely changing tones throughout the day. The sun hiding back there somewhere, Devon charting its movement by how light gray or dark gray the skies appeared.

Charcoal, graphite, slate.

Devon owned many suits and hats, most of them gray. He often found himself in meetings with a dozen other men and everyone's suit was gray.

Herringbone, wool, winter sunset.

He'd recently strolled through an Impressionism exhibit at the MFA (an excellent place to meet women), and the thought occurred to him that if Monet and his merry band of painters had congregated in Boston rather than France, museums would be full of canvases displaying the many shades of gray seen by Trinity Episcopal in Copley Square (asphalt, concrete, dowager's hair), or the various gray tones of a farm in Concord (roadside snow, worn tires, despair), or the darker grays of the Harbor shipyards (exhaust, smoke, suffocation).

Morning and evening newspapers were equally gray, his two-cream coffee was gray, and his mother's overcooked Sunday Irish dinners had been, without fail, boiled dead gray. Colors were unseemly, blacks and whites too obvious. This city reveled in gray, goddamn excelled at it.

The murdered Northeast Munitions employee, Devon had learned after calling his contact at the factory and reading the punch-card number, was Abraham Wolff. Age thirty-two, nationality German, hair and eyes brown. No disciplinary information in his file, nothing of note since he'd started working there eleven months ago.

Wolff had spent his last days in a tiny one-room apartment so mildewed that it smelled to Devon like a basement even in that third-floor walk-up. It sat in the northwestern edge of Dorchester, one of the more run-down blocks off Blue Hill Ave, where most of the city's newly immigrated Eastern Europeans and Jews were hemmed in, surrounded by the Irish on every side but one, which was where the blacks lived.

That afternoon, Devon and Lou stood in the narrow hallway of the apartment building and knocked on the thin door to number 324. They could hear a conversation in what Devon recognized as German, and after a moment of silence, the door was pulled open the two inches that the chain lock allowed.

"Yes?" Dark eyes and dark hair, a gray smock. Unmistakable fear at the sight of two unfamiliar men in suits.

"Mrs. Wolff?" Lou wisely let Devon lead when visiting women. "Elena?"

She nodded.

He told her he was Agent Mulvey with the FBI and he was barely halfway through the next part of his spiel when he could see from her eyes that she didn't understand a word of it. She finally raised a hand and disappeared, leaving the door open so they could hear her barking instructions in a foreign tongue. Then another woman appeared, blondish and heavier, and Devon repeated himself.

"Okay, yes," the new woman said, quickly shutting the door to undo the latch and opening it again to let the agents in. "Elena not understand English much. I help."

There followed a brief and awkward dance in which Mrs. Wolff, the first woman at the door, fussed in the miniature kitchenette and insisted on providing something for the agents despite their insistence that they were not hungry or thirsty.

They sat at a small table. Out of propriety, Devon took a bite of bread that he hoped was black on purpose and that had no discernible taste, and he considered whether he should wash it down with the (gray) tea in his mug. The apartment was very small, a bed (gray sheets) along one wall just beneath the one tiny window that you couldn't throw yourself out of even if you tried, the stove and sink (gray) on the opposite wall, a large chest and tiny bureau. The walls (gray) were bare, the chair hard against Devon's back.

He told the widow he was sorry for her loss and she nodded blankly. He hadn't been involved in many murder cases so this still felt like new territory to him. She appeared stunned and shrunken, or perhaps intimidated and afraid, maybe all of the above. Devon was relieved to see no evidence of children in the apartment, no bright eyes newly dimmed.

He asked the translator for her name, address, and relationship and was told "Lucja Majewski," second door on the left, friend.

Yesterday afternoon Elena had gone to a police station to report her husband missing, and one precinct had called another until they connected him to the body in the alley.

"We know she's already spoken to the police," Devon said to Lucja, "but we're a different organization, and we might be able to help in ways they can't."

He looked into Mrs. Wolff's large eyes; she in turn watched him as she listened to Lucja translate. Despite some wrinkles around her eyes and a few strands of gray in her hair, her eyes seemed youthful, like a kid made up as a woman for a school play.

Lou sneezed, likely the first of many. He was allergic to mold, mildew, and the underclass. Devon braced himself for a long day of listening to his partner complain about the way "these people" took care of themselves.

Elena Wolff explained that, on the day of his death, her husband worked the ten-to-eight shift, then he and some buddies had gone to a tavern. This she had only pieced together after the fact, as they owned no telephone, so there was no way for him to call her and say he'd be late. Between sneezes, Lou asked for the drinking companions' names and addresses, which Elena provided, admitting that some of the addresses ("the big blue building around the corner") were approximate.

One of the friends' name was familiar: Jaromir Zajac. A member of the New Patriots League, a Communist labor organization the Bureau was monitoring. Devon filed that away for now.

"Did the friends tell you anything about any arguments they might have had that night? Between themselves, or with someone else?"

She shook her head, *No.*

"He was found in the North End," Devon noted. "Did he have any friends there? A bar he patronized regularly?"

Another headshake.

"I'm a little surprised he would have chosen that neighborhood to go out in."

She had no explanation. The North End was only a fifteen-minute walk, or a ferry ride, from his job at Northeast Munitions, so maybe Devon was overthinking. He asked if Abraham had any Italian friends and she shrugged, said maybe some men from work, but she didn't know.

"How long had he worked there?"

"One year, almost. Started last August."

Lou mumbled to Devon, "Pretty good job for a guy just off the boat." The politics of who should get defense work were raw. The war economy finally seemed to be humming, but the government kept changing its mind about what needed to be built; this resulted in "priorities unemployment," when an entire factory would be laid off with no notice due to some sudden change in military needs. Men were working again, but no one felt secure. Depression-era fear still ran deep.

Devon was struck by the widow's lack of outrage, the way she was not asking him any questions at all, didn't seem to crave from him the slightest sign of hope that he would avenge her husband's death. As if she was so used to grappling with atrocities that she'd already used up all her rage about life's unfairness a long time ago.

He asked her, "In one of your husband's pockets was a piece of paper with a swastika on it. Any idea how that might have gotten there?"

After hearing the translation, she looked at the table for a while. Then she spoke and Lucja translated, "Lived in France for some time but hated the Nazis. Got out just in time."

"Was your husband Jewish?"

As Lucja translated, Elena nodded and pointed to herself. They both were. This ruled out the possibility that he was secretly a Nazi and had been killed for that reason.

"Did your husband ever say anything to you about feeling in danger? That anyone might have wanted to do him harm?"

For the first time, Lucja and Elena had an exchange without Lucja's offering any English scraps to the befuddled agents. Finally Devon interrupted with, "What is she saying?"

"She says No."

"That sounded more complicated than No."

"She says No. Everything fine here."

Lou exhaled loudly, and Devon glanced at him. He couldn't tell if his partner was insulted by the obvious lie or simply annoyed by this entire situation. Since things were already getting touchy, Devon charged ahead with, "Was your husband a member of the Communist Party?"

"No. He is capitalist. He do work, get paid. Capitalist." Lucja smiled as she translated this. Devon, too, smiled to acknowledge the beneficence of American capitalist democracy.

"Did he talk politics with Mr. Zajac, that friend you mentioned?"

Headshake. Blank stare. *Maybe people in shock are better at lying*, Devon mused, *their faces already stripped of every emotion but one*. If she knew that her husband's friend Zajac was a red, she wasn't showing it.

He aimed his next question at the translator. "How would you describe their relationship?"

"What?"

"Did they get along? Did he run around on her?"

She looked confused, then outraged, his question clearly out of bounds. "*No*. Happy marriage."

He had no reason to think Elena had conspired to have her husband knifed in an alley, but he'd needed to ask.

"Ask her if there was anything going on between them we should know."

The translator looked aggrieved by this request. She exhaled, then said something in German to Elena. Her tone of voice made clear that she wasn't asking the question so much as commenting on it: *This idiot here wonders if maybe you killed him yourself.*

Elena shook her head and mumbled something. Lucja translated it, maybe, to "No. Happy marriage."

Devon asked, "Could we see your papers, Mrs. Wolff?"

He'd asked as politely as he could, but he might as well have brandished his gun: Elena's eyes grew wider than before as she heard the translation. She leapt to her feet so hurriedly that some of the tea in the agents' mugs splashed out.

She walked over to the chest and threw open its latches. Then she piled a great number of documents on the table before the agents. On top was the green card, as well as the transit papers from when the couple had entered the country. There were also several letters in German and French—maybe this couple had been well-connected once, and had asked important pals to pen recommendations. Beneath those were more records in German, one of which looked like a wedding invitation; a postcard with a photograph of the Empire State Building (the back was blank—perhaps it was a souvenir they'd bought en route); foreign newspaper clippings; and a few old photographs of what might have been their childhood families. She was giving them her entire life, evidence of her and her husband's dogged journey across the cursed continent of Europe and now her uncertain existence in this not entirely welcoming new land.

Elena offered and Lucja translated that the couple had fled Germany for France in 1937, living in Paris for two years before fleeing that country too, only months before Hitler invaded, arriving in the States in June of '39 and winning asylum. Her husband had been a linguist, fluent in several languages and teaching at secondary schools. They were "hardworking, good people, no care for politics."

He and Lou took more notes, then stood and thanked the ladies for their time. They refrained from making any empty promises about catching the person who had done this.

Outside, Devon and Lou tried to remember where they'd parked. Wasn't that hard—just stand at the corner and look for the only car made in the last decade.

"He was some kind of intellectual," Devon rehashed. "And Jewish. Maybe he was more politically minded than she claims, which is how they got out. Maybe he imported some trouble with him, then years later he's walking down Hanover Street and bumps into some fellow from the old country who'd hated him for belonging to the wrong group, and out come the knives."

"Maybe." Lou shrugged. "Or it was just a robbery. Or he got jumped for being a Jew."

"Heaven forfend."

"What?"

"It means 'forbid.'"

"I know what it means. What I meant was, what do you *mean*?"

Devon rested one of his hands on the car roof. "I guess what I'm trying to gauge is exactly how little it concerns you, Louis Cabot Loomis, that a fellow might have gotten killed for being a Jew."

"I think it's lousy. I'm simply saying it doesn't have anything to do with what the Bureau should be spending resources on."

The murder would interest the Bureau only if it had been some attempt to interfere with the vital war work of Northeast Munitions, or if it could possibly reveal some sinister Fascist (or Communist, or Japanese, or German splinter group or God knows what) plot against the country. The fact that Wolff's buddy Zajac was red could be intriguing, but if they didn't turn anything else up, the case would become irrelevant to them. The Bureau had a clearly defined jurisdiction, and it was careful to avoid the city's ethnic and political fault lines. Director Hoover did not want his men getting involved in the many blood feuds between Irish, Yankee, Jew, Italian, Negro, Canuck, Syrian, Cape Verdean, and other ethnicities that made this town so treacherous (if entertaining) to work in, unless those feuds directly affected the nation's security.

Of course, in a time of war, some of those judgment calls became harder to make.

"And how much do *you* care, Devon Patrick Mulvey? Or are you only interested because she's pretty? Jesus, can't you ever turn that off?"

"Yes, I can turn it off. But the victim was in the wrong neighborhood, he's got radical friends, and there's something the wife's not telling us. Come on, why was a Jew out drinking in the North End?"

His partner gave an empty laugh. "I know. He deserved it, right?"

Devon didn't share the sentiment, but his point remained: a Jewish immigrant wouldn't normally be carousing in the city's most Italian neighborhood, where even a fellow Catholic like Devon didn't feel entirely welcome. "Don't you think that's a little odd?" he pressed.

Lou only shrugged. He seemed to be ignoring the existence of certain obvious boundaries in their fair city. Maybe it was a Yankee thing to do that.

"There could be something here," Devon insisted. "Or would you rather we spend the next few weeks doing more background checks on federal hires? This could be something *interesting* for a change."

The truth was, despite the stories and Hollywood reels, the job lacked excitement. But that never seemed to bother Lou, who seemed more suited to being an accountant.

Lou leaned closer, his arm atop the car. "Devon, let me give you some free advice. You need to stop feeling insecure about not enlisting. And you need to not invent adventures here to make up for it." With that, Lou got in the car.

Devon followed him inside, annoyed at his partner for psychoanalyzing him. Defensive that maybe he'd gotten it right.

He finally mustered a riposte: "And you need to stop clenching up and going cold every time an investigation brings us someplace that doesn't have white linen tablecloths. I know you don't like lowering yourself into neighborhoods like this—not far from where I grew up, by the way—but we can't always get our information from the Harvard Club."

Lou just shook his head and smirked, not taking the bait. Devon turned on the engine, realizing he'd already lost the argument.

Chapter Eight

OUT REPORTING

That same afternoon, Anne made calls regarding the story about the green-skinned sailors. She didn't make much progress until late, when Hawaii was finally awake.

She reached the Honolulu branch of the Navy Information Office and got their official take, then made some more very long-distance calls to Hawaii hospitals, following that up by interviewing two Boston-based sailors who had been in Pearl Harbor on that fateful day and could at least say they didn't know anyone who had turned green and that they themselves were fine, thanks for asking.

As much as she liked her job, she also felt it exposed how impossible it was to truly prevent false stories from spreading. Even as she did her workmanlike reporting, the rumor spread like a cloud of poison gas, impossible to contain. She published her stories and reimposed factual order on the universe, yes, but even if thousands of people read her pieces, thousands more didn't, and those uninformed masses would all continue to open their mouths, and the poison would keep spreading.

She needed to do more.

She found herself looking again at the notes she'd taken during her lunch break. She'd walked to the same shoe store where Lydia told her she'd been given the anti-Semitic pamphlet. Anne had bought some hose, and, just as Lydia had described, the kind old lady at the register had slipped a pamphlet into her bag with the receipt. Anne had glanced at it on the street corner: *THE TRUTH ABOUT JEWS AND THE WAR!*—two short "articles" full of slander, hatred, and gross overuse of exclamation points. Anne had heard that some downtown shops had been passing these out to customers, but this was the first time she'd been given one.

She'd walked back into the store and lied to the old lady, claiming that her father owned a deli in Mattapan and they'd love to get some of those pamphlets to pass out; where could she get some?

The woman had been happy to help, telling her she'd gotten them from Pete Flaherty and showing Anne his business card (PRINTMAKER: MAPS, STATIONERY, NEWSLETTERS), with Flaherty's name and phone number.

Combining the roles of journalist, activist, anti-propagandist, and street detective all at once could get a tad complicated. But Anne felt surrounded by injustice and desperately needed to *do* something about it.

The card had listed Flaherty's office number but not its location. She checked the phone book, but it didn't turn up any such business. Under "Residential," she found several listings for "Peter Flaherty," this being Boston. One number matched the one on the card, the address somewhere in Watertown.

The way Anne typically wrote her Rumor Clinic stories, the ending came when she identified the source of the rumor. Usually it was a tall tale or a piece of wicked innuendo someone (like that brat Hank Doyle) had invented out of boredom or spite; rarely had it been actual propaganda planted by anti-American provocateurs. Exposing the secret publishers of this filth, then, would be a step beyond what the Rumor Clinic had done before. Larry had shot down her story idea about anti-Semitic rumors and ration stamps, so he might well refuse to run this one too and accuse Anne of pursuing her "agenda." But, good God, this green-skinned-sailor piece was ridiculous. It was time to do some real work.

While Cheryl was out on a smoke break and no one was close enough to overhear, Anne dialed Flaherty's number.

"Hello?"

"Is this Mr. Pete Flaherty, printmaker?" She gave her voice a harder accent, one socioeconomic class below her own, replacing her Rs with mere rumors of Rs. Her parents had raised her to talk quite differently, but any local could fake it.

"Sure is. Who's asking?"

"My name's Cindy Byrne. I was hoping I could buy some of those pamphlets."

"What pamphlets?"

"The ones about the Jews. Why, do you have other kinds?"

Silence for a beat. "Usually, people come through folks I know."

"I was buying some shoes downtown and the woman at the register gave me your card. McIllery's Shoes."

"Oh yeah, sure." With that, his suspicions seemed to melt away. "How many you need?"

"Gosh, I don't know. I'm a seamstress in Central Square. I thought I could pass them to my customers, and I get maybe"—she thought fast—"twenty customers a day? I'm terrible with math; how many would I need for a couple of weeks?"

He gave her a recommended amount and named a price.

"That's cheaper than I expected," she said.

"It's for a good cause. I'm not looking to profit from this, you know? I just need enough to cover my expenses."

"I can drive to your office to pick them up." She hoped it didn't sound like a strange offer, but she wanted to figure out where he was printing them. *Maybe* from his house, but that was unlikely, given how much space even the smallest printing press would require. "What time should I drop by?"

"Ah, I'd rather drop them off by your shop."

She'd been afraid of this—she didn't want this man to know where she lived, or worked. "Well, the thing is, I'm not the only one in my shop. There's a couple of other gals, and, honestly . . . Well, they don't see eye to eye with me on this, if you know what I mean."

"Are they Jews?"

"Oh, God no! But they just don't see things the way we do. So I was hoping I could get my hands on these discreetly, and only pass them on to customers when the other gals aren't around. Maybe we could meet somewhere else?"

They chose a diner near Central Square, the next day at noon. She told him she'd be the lady in the yellow dress, thanked him, and hung up, hoping this wasn't a terrible idea.

Chapter Nine

CONFESSIONAL IN REVERSE

"Bless me, Father, for I have sinned."

"How long has it been since your last confession?"

"One week, Father."

Devon in his dark confessional, the priest in his. Separated by the concealing screen. Alone with his thoughts. Not unlike a jail cell, he'd thought many times.

"What would you like to confess?"

Devon had never been a big fan of this whole song and dance. Who was? The ritual flagellation always struck him as a bit much. Then again, sinning was fun, so if this was a necessary part of the package, he'd do his duty.

"Fornication. That's pretty much it. But . . . rather a lot of it."

"Well. I do think that's a more serious issue than your tone suggests."

"I understand, Father. That's why I'm here."

"The power to create new life is a sacred one, my son. That is why we are to withhold ourselves until we've received the sacrament of marriage. The Church is rather clear on this, as are the Scriptures. You must resist temptation until that time."

"I'll try harder, Father. Can't deny that it's . . . rather difficult, in a city full of lonely women. It's like they throw themselves at me."

"Women appreciate good conversation, too, my son. Try to leave it at that. And consider what might happen if she became with child. You certainly aren't doing her any favors."

"Oh, I take precautions."

A pause. "That too is a sin, as I'm sure you know."

"Yes, Father. I know. I am a sinner, and I'm seeking penance before the Lord."

"My son, you sound a bit cavalier. Might I inquire if this is a regular transgression?"

"Pretty much."

"Then, among other things, I think you should marry the poor girl. Perhaps that can be your absolution."

"Well, she's already married. They usually are."

Another pause. "Adultery, then. And did you say 'they'?"

"From their perspective it's adultery, but not mine, right? It's just considered fornication on my end? I've always been confused about that."

"How many women are we talking about? Wait, no, don't answer that." The man of God sighed. "Young man, the fact that you're here tells me you realize your sins are serious. Despite your flippant tone. So I would advise you to spend more time with the Good Book and less time with women who are spoken for—women of any kind, actually."

"That is sound advice, Father. Thank you."

The priest led him in an "Our Father" and an "Act of Contrition." For absolution, the priest did not tell Devon to marry anyone, thank goodness, as that likely exceeded his ecclesiastical powers. But he did assign an hour of Bible reading each night, which would be difficult for Devon to work into his busy nocturnal schedule.

"Go in peace, my son."

"Thank you, Father Ryan." Yet Devon didn't move.

The priest waited, sensing there was more.

"I've always found this whole arrangement fascinating. The secrets you must hear. The sin, the crimes. Yet you have to keep silent about it all."

"The confessional is a sacred place, my son."

"It must wear on you."

"It's my duty to take the weight of sin off your shoulders. The Lord does the work. I'm merely his vessel."

"It can also work both ways, you know. Me keeping secrets."

"I'm sorry?"

This got tricky with no body language to read, but Devon imagined the priest was gazing at the screen in confusion.

"There's something else we need to talk about, Father Ryan. I thought you'd appreciate some discretion; that's why I'm doing it here. But some of the things you've been telling your parishioners, Father, like how the war is, quote, a thinly veiled attempt by our political leaders to bail out Jewish financiers in Europe, unquote. Or how, quote"—and he turned a page in his notebook, barely legible when he held it up to the dim light through cracks in the door, but he wanted the priest to hear the page turning—"we need to find the inner strength to exert pressure on our politicians to call everything off and let Americans worry about America again, before it's too late, unquote. Those sorts of sentiments, Father—they seem designed to spread defeatism about the war."

"You came here to tell me what to say in my own church?" Father Ryan's voice reached a volume never before heard in a confessional. "Who do you think you are?"

Devon kept his voice more appropriate to the setting. "I think I'm an agent of the Federal Bureau of Investigation, Father Ryan. I think it's my job to root out sedition and attempts to sabotage the war effort. I think we've investigated other people for walking down the road you seem to be walking, and some of them have landed in jail. Some have landed in even worse places. I'm sure you remember Father Tobias."

Tobias, from a parish in Quincy, had been relocated by his bishop to Paraguay last year, after the FBI found evidence that he had helped a group of Fascist Italians establish a beachhead in Boston. Some of the other agents had wanted to prosecute, but the Church proposed banishment to avoid scandal, and Director Hoover had quietly approved it.

"Tobias?" The good father seemed stunned. Or maybe chastened. "I hardly think the content of my homilies . . . rises to the level of what he did."

"The Bureau prefers to nip things in the bud before they can rise to that level. Some of what you said, Father, sounds awfully similar to what I've read in some official Nazi publications. Eerily similar language. Word for word, in some cases."

"I'm sure that's . . . just a coincidence."

"I hope these rooms are lightning-proof, Father. It wouldn't do to lie in church."

Devon could hear the man breathing. Fuming.

"Are you even Catholic, young man, or is the blessed sacrament of reconciliation merely part of your cloak-and-dagger routine?"

"I am Catholic, yes."

"So you spy on your own leaders for your Yankee employer?" His voice thick with scorn. "How can you look yourself in the mirror? I hope you beg the Lord's forgiveness each night."

"Now that is the wrong tack." Devon wished he could stare the man down. "You don't seem to understand that I'm the one who can condemn you or let you off. I'm the one who decides whether I report to my superiors exactly what you said last Sunday, how you were pretty much quoting *Social Justice*."

That Fascist magazine was published by radio personality Father Coughlin, longtime lionizer of Hitler and Mussolini. Coughlin was based in Michigan but had followers all over the country, with an especially enthusiastic audience in the Northeast. His paper had been banned from the mail by FDR since shortly after Pearl Harbor, but distributing it by hand was still legal, and that seemed to be happening a lot in Boston.

"Or instead," Devon continued, "I could go to my superiors and selectively remember some things. I could say, 'Well, sir, while that priest might not have sounded gung ho about the war, I have no reason to suspect he's been reading Nazi literature or spreading Fascist propaganda to the good parishioners of Dorchester.' So, Father Ryan, I can either elevate this matter or let it drop."

Another, longer silence.

"I apologize," the priest said. "I shouldn't have said that to you."

"It's what you say to your parishioners I'm more worried about. Think you can rein that in, or do I need to pass your file on to the sorts of people who can send you to a parish with no running water?"

Devon could feel the priest biting back, hating the way he had to play along with someone he no doubt saw as a heretic, or worse. "I can rein it in."

"Good. I don't enjoy errands like this, Father, but when we get tips that a priest is quoting Goebbels, I need to check it out. Now, I'm sure your parishioners would appreciate your guidance on things like raising children and helping the poor, and you can leave the politics out of it."

"Of course."

"Thank you, Father."

After a moment, Devon asked, "Aren't you going to tell me to go in peace?"

Very long pause.

"I bless you in the name of the Father, and the Son, and the Holy Ghost. Go in peace." Devon wasn't sure if he heard irony or just residual bitterness. "And may you resist the temptations that surround us in these trying times."

If asked, Devon would have admitted that yes, of course he believed in the existence of divine intercession. He did not attend mass as regularly as when he'd been a schoolboy (and altar boy), and not just because his job kept him busy on certain Sundays. Like many of his peers, those weekly duties and rituals proved surprisingly easy to shrug off, at least temporarily, when not yet encumbered by wife or children.

Still, he would have *said* he believed in all he had been taught. But he would have said so to avoid controversy. Whether he actually, truly believed was something he wrestled with.

So it came as more than a shock when, not more than an hour after his confessional warning to Father Ryan, he crossed paths with Sandra Poole.

He'd recognized her the moment she stepped out of the small grocery. He'd spent only one night with her, but it had been a memorable one. Her husband was in Britain, he recalled, some sort of engineer working on airplanes.

He remembered they'd shared a bottle of beer after he'd finished interviewing her for a background check he'd been doing on one of her work colleagues. Then a second bottle.

He remembered she'd admitted her full name was Cassandra, but she hated it.

He remembered she'd had quite a lot of freckles on her chest and breasts, surprising given her complexion.

He remembered she'd laughed hysterically after they'd finished, which at first he'd feared was a criticism of his performance but which turned out to be her delayed reaction to the transgression she'd just committed.

He remembered she'd said he couldn't spend the night, but she'd cushioned the blow by doing it with him a second time before kicking him out.

He also remembered she'd been quite thin, but she certainly wasn't anymore.

"Devon," she said, frozen in place, holding a small paper bag to her chest.

"Sandra." He smiled. "Fancy meeting you here."

"I'm just on my way to a friend's for dinner," she explained. She lived in Cambridge, he recalled.

The bag she held was not big enough, nor was her blue dress quite loose enough, to disguise the bump in her belly. He quickly flipped a calendar in his head, did the math. It had been December or January, he remembered, and frigid out. Her apartment hadn't been much better, though they'd kept each other warm.

She might be five months pregnant, or six (Devon had five sisters, at least one of whom was with child at any given time, so he was good at guessing).

The math did not bode well for him.

"Your summer off to a nice start?" he asked, starting to panic but hoping not to show it. He felt his mouth go dry.

"Yes, thanks. Obviously, some changes are coming my way," and she smiled awkwardly, touched her belly with her free hand.

"Congratulations," he managed to say.

"Thank you." Her smile seemed forced now too.

He didn't often bump into his one-night stands. This was only the second time.

"So, ah, has your husband been back on leave recently?"

A brief pause. "Not recently. But a couple of weeks after you and I met."

Thank God. He tried not to look too relieved. "Well. That must have been nice."

"Yes. It turned out to be . . . very well-timed."

He never gave out his phone number or address, but women usually knew where he worked, which meant he wouldn't be hard to find should it come to that. If she'd wanted to pound on his door, he told himself, she would have done so by now.

"I, ah, I should be going," she said, flustered. "Don't want to be late. Good seeing you."

"You, too."

He watched her cross the street and exhaled, then lit a cigarette.

Father Ryan's warning about chasing women echoed in his head. Maybe Devon *did* believe in divine intercession. He would ponder the question all night, alone, in his apartment, because he sure as hell wasn't going on the prowl after this.

Chapter Ten

WORKERS, UNITE

As Lydia had predicted, plenty of the men at the Dockworkers Local 107 had indeed shown up to their meeting after a pint or two. They met at the Oddfellows Building, a few blocks from the docks where most of them worked. Though the meeting was supposed to be closed to outsiders, Elias had invited her along, clearing it with his "brothers" in advance. A bachelor in his early thirties, Elias was an immigrant who had made it out of France only a few years before Hitler invaded.

Nearly a hundred men sat and slouched in creaking chairs. Anne was the only woman in attendance.

"I keep getting funny looks," she told Elias.

"They think you're pretty, that's all."

She'd received a few leering glances, but many of the men conveyed more suspicion than desire. These fellows were wary of outsiders.

"Actually, one of them asked me if he could ask you out."

Oh, God. "Which one?"

"Freddy, the one with the beard."

She followed her cousin's eyes and saw a man who looked like he had recently been dredged from the bottom of the ocean: sweaty hair a mess, beard greasy, eyes fuzzy as if not used to seeing on land.

"I gave him our number and said he could call you."

"You *didn't*," and she punched him in the ribs.

"Ow," and he laughed at her. "I kid. I told him you were all but engaged already and not to waste his time. Of course, it will be easier to fend them off once you *are* engaged to someone."

"So you've said, many times."

Her editor Larry had told her that she had "an agenda," and perhaps he was right. Anne had developed her anti-fascism early, long before the rest of America finally accepted the fact that madmen like Hitler and Mussolini were threats to civilization. Because of relatives like Elias who had fled Europe in the '30s, she'd heard the horror stories long before her peers or even the local papers had realized what was happening. Even now, when American troops had taken North Africa from the Axis, she still overheard people talk about how the Nazis were unbeatable, how we should stay out of Europe, how we had been hornswoggled into a war we had no business fighting.

And yes, her agenda ran even yet deeper.

She had gotten involved in labor politics partly through Elias. As an immigrant, he had spent years trying to get decent work, and the stories he told of his mistreatment at various factories had radicalized her. Anne's mother, Millie, was a seamstress at a factory, a job she'd taken after the unexpected death of Anne's father when Anne was a teenager. Millie had never been one to raise a fuss, but at Elias's urging she'd joined the Seamstresses Union and taken part in a strike three years ago. Anne had started attending labor meetings while still a college student—thanks to a full scholarship at Radcliffe—initially writing about her mother's experience for school classes, then for movement papers. Within months, Anne became a full-fledged convert—picketing, soliciting signatures for petitions, shouting at cops who roughed up strikers, even sitting in, undercover, on speeches and rallies given by Nazi sympathizers. Things had calmed down, for the most part, since America declared war.

Finally tonight's meeting began, and once attendance was taken, Craig O'Neil, the local secretary, rose to the stage and, after a few minor announcements, began pressing the case Anne had heard him argue before, but with more energy this time:

"We need to strike, and soon. The longer the war goes on with us *not* striking, the more it sets a precedent." She liked O'Neil, who seemed the embodiment of a strong union leader: gray hair at his temples, relatively handsome, thick arms, and the kind of speaking voice that got other men's heads nodding. "If they start thinking we're too afraid to strike during wartime, they'll use the war as an excuse to up the quotas and cut our wages."

"And hire niggers and Jews," called out a man whose face she couldn't see.

Several people nodded at this. Anne stiffened and felt Elias doing the same. He had told her recently that he'd lied about his religion and background to get this job.

"Hang on now!" another man shouted, rising to his feet. "I ain't here to fuss against my fellow working man, no matter what the hell he looks like. We're in this together."

"Like hell," the unseen racist replied.

"The bigger point, gentlemen," O'Neil said, trying to retake the reins, "is that if we let Lloyd and Company get it in their heads that the war gives them free rein over us, we're cooked. We need to remind them that we know how to fight back, and soon."

"Public opinion'll be against us," someone called out. "They'll say us going on strike means their boys are going to the front lines with empty holsters. That won't look good."

"Then we'll say the boys' holsters are empty because the fat cats are hoarding all the money to themselves," O'Neil replied.

"Tell that to a grieving mum and see how far it gets ya."

A door opened. Anne and Elias were sitting in the back, all the better for her to jot down notes without making anyone feel too self-conscious. Several heads swiveled to see who was coming in. She knew labor meetings could get violent, after years of Fascists trying to rout unionists—and, to be fair, vice versa, as many left-leaning groups had attacked Fascists too. The debate died down for a moment as three newcomers entered the room.

Like everyone else here, they were big, men who worked with their hands and shoulders. In fact, two of them would have blended in perfectly if not for their fellow in the middle, who stood out due to his dark fedora, recent shave, and the smirk on his lips, like he thought he'd walked into a vaudeville act. His shirt bore French cuffs and his brown slacks were creased, his entire getup a cut or three above anything a dockworker owned, let alone wore to a union meeting.

"Sorry we're late," he said as he removed his fedora. "Don't let us stop you. Please, continue."

Anne picked up some grumbling, someone saying that this was supposed to be a closed meeting, what's going on here, others shushing that dissenter.

"Who are they?" Anne whispered to Elias.

"Bad news."

On the stage, O'Neil went on, "I'm proposing July twelfth. Enough time for us to rally everyone together, but not so far off that Lloyd and Company can tighten their screws. I'm willing to hear other dates as alternatives."

"July thirty-first," one man called out.

"When hell freezes over," said another, to laughter.

O'Neil folded his arms. "I'm trying to be serious here."

"It ain't serious when you're trying to railroad your idea and ignore everybody else's. I haven't heard a vote yet on whether we even should go on strike."

O'Neil nodded, looking part annoyed and part chastened. "All right, I rushed. My mistake. All in favor—"

"Folks, folks," called out the well-dressed newcomer in the back. The trio still hadn't sat down yet. "Sorry to interrupt, but there ain't gonna be any strike, and you know it."

"Is that a prediction or a threat?" O'Neil asked.

The man shrugged. "Just the way things are."

"Well, we're going to have a vote on it, and then—"

"There ain't gonna be any vote, neither," the newcomer said. "Like I heard one of you say, there are bigger things going on right now. There's a war to win. To the victor go the spoils. A strike now puts us on the wrong side. I think everybody here"—and he made a point of letting his eyes move from face to face in the crowd—"understands the way things are right now. I think everybody understands what he's got and what he stands to lose. Taking unnecessary risks like that, with their work. With their health. It's just very, very unwise."

Silence stretched out. The loudest thing in the room was Anne's pen on her pad.

"I still say we take a vote on whether to have a strike," O'Neil said, his voice slightly wavering.

"I think that would be very unwise, Mr. O'Neil."

"All in favor," O'Neil said after a pause, "vote 'Aye.'"

A few voices called out in favor.

"Opposed, vote 'Nay.'"

The victorious nays boomed.

Anne wasn't looking at him, but she could hear the stranger chuckling.

"All right," O'Neil said, deflated. "We'll move on to the next item on the agenda."

As he went on to address the latest work injuries, the three newcomers finally pulled up chairs and sat down. Anne heard the one with the fedora say to one of his friends, "I love democracy."

Anne had attended her share of testy meetings, and she could sense what was coming next. A certain harshness to people's voices, sidelong glances ricocheting everywhere. The fact that the room was too hot certainly didn't help, the fans in back doing nothing.

She kept checking her watch to make sure she wouldn't be late for the USO dance that Lydia had twisted her arm into attending, and with only fifteen minutes to spare, O'Neil finally adjourned the meeting. She folded her notebook into her pocketbook and stood with Elias.

"So who are those three men, really?" she asked him, quietly enough not to be overheard. "Are they Lloyd's plants?"

"They're something worse. Come on, let's go."

On the way out, they kept bumping into friends of Elias's who delayed them, *Hey, howya doing, and is this your sister?* Anne could tell they had all concocted phony reasons to chat with him when really it was her they wanted, and she parried them all with apologies that they needed to be going. *Sorry, we'll have to chat another time.*

By the time they made it outside, the narrow street was clogged with men, the voices even louder than at the meeting. It felt like everyone who'd left the building was still lingering. And arguing. Fingers pointed, faces red. She heard some of the usual insults, "red" and "collaborator" and "Nazi," plus rarer ones like "wop" and "mafioso," and she saw that the three newcomers were in the thick of it, and that they appeared to have many friends with them now.

The only way out was through the crowd, so Elias put a hand around Anne's shoulder. Usually she wasn't one for male chivalry, but this seemed a fine time to make an exception.

She didn't hear the first punch, but she felt it when a body bumped into her from behind. Whether it was the person who'd been hit or someone else, she wasn't sure, but suddenly the crowd shifted as if transformed into a choppy sea. Elias's arm tightened around her and the shouting grew louder and someone stepped on her right foot. She heard the dull thwack of blows against cheeks and noses and she ducked her head down to protect her face. Someone else's elbow or shoulder whacked her in the right side, but she pushed forward, she and Elias a tiny ship pushing against the current.

A hole opened up in front of her when someone fell down. She carefully stepped over him, Elias losing his grip on her now, and she was about to wade through more fighters when someone in front of her spun around, his eyes crossed like a cartoon character, and collapsed on her shoulder. She didn't mean to shout, but it happened, and she pushed his limp body off her. He landed in a heap on top of someone else.

She heard someone scream, "He's got a knife!" and by then she'd already seen a blackjack and two beer bottles swinging.

She put her head down again and pressed through the scrum, finally breaking free. Where was Elias? She ran a few steps, then turned and looked back. She saw men locked together, in chokeholds and strange wrestling poses, some throwing fists, others kneeling on top of fallen opponents and swinging, again and again. Finally she saw Elias break free of another man and run toward her. Two of his shirt buttons had been torn off and his hair was mussed but he didn't seem bad off.

"Let's go," she said, grabbing his hand and pulling. She had the feeling he was the sort who would have rather stayed in the fray, so she was glad that her presence helped bring him to his senses.

They walked the first block in silence, then heard police whistles and sirens closing in.

"This way," Elias said, taking a quick left so they stayed off Causeway. After another block, he asked her, "Are you okay? You get hit?"

"I'm fine." But her voice shook and she realized her hands were shaking too, adrenaline taking hold now that the panic had passed. "I've seen that at strikes, but not when *talking about* a strike."

"Everybody's on edge right now. And those folks make it worse."

"So they were"—she wasn't even sure of the right word, it sounded so Hollywood—"gangsters?"

"I think so. Fellows like that keep showing up at the meetings."

She thought of what Lydia had overheard the other day, something about gangsters at the Navy Yard. Perhaps that rumor was actually true?

They walked through Haymarket, the food stalls empty for the night, the smell of fish thick nonetheless. She realized Elias was walking toward the subway station, so she stopped and told him, "I need to catch a bus the other way, to Charlestown."

It took him a moment. "You're still going to the dance? After *that*?"

"I promised Lydia. She'll kill me if I back out. Why, is my hair very mussed?" She ran her fingers through it.

He appraised her for a moment and shook his head. "I already knew you were a tough cookie, but, wow. All right, kid. I'd tellya not to take any lip from any sailors, but I already know I don't have to. Have fun."

The swing band was loud enough to be heard a block away when she got off the bus. The ride had been short but still dragged, because it felt like people kept staring at her (maybe her hair was worse than she realized?).

Ladies didn't need to pay to attend the dance; they seemed to be the main attraction, a fact that rankled Anne, made her feel like she herself was an amusement.

Lydia wants me to be here and I'm being a good friend, she reminded herself. It just seemed strange to her, how anxious Lydia was to win some man's hand, get a ring on her finger, settle down. The world was on fire, no one had any idea what things might look like twelve months from now, yet Lydia's focus was so narrow and . . . *normal.* They'd been friends since high school, but she worried they didn't have as much in common as they used to. Anne had nothing against meeting men or having a fling, but something about dances like this left her cold, the way these young men seemed to feel owed, like it was her patriotic duty to show some leg and offer her hand for a dance or ten.

She wished she'd had a drink first. She could have asked Elias to take her to a bar on the way, but he would have been outraged. Male relatives could be so small-minded.

As she approached the building, she heard a roar and looked up in time to see two Civil Air Patrol planes swoop low over the city, keeping watch for German subs. The function hall was only a block from the Harbor, salt water thick in the air. She loved the smell, which made her miss her father again, all the times he'd taken her and her brothers fishing. Though they'd never had much money, he'd kept a small boat in the Harbor for years—his having grown up in Nova Scotia, being on the water was second nature to him—but after his passing the family had sold the boat. Anne hadn't been on the water in years.

Inside the dance hall, she signed her name in the book and smiled at some of the chaperones, of which there were many, stationed all over the dance hall. Most were elderly, but some of the lady chaperones looked younger than her mother.

"Annie! I was beginning to wonder."

She turned around right as Lydia walked up and hugged her.

"There are *a lot* of good-looking men here, Annie," Lydia said, just quietly enough not to be overheard by the chaperones, as the band finished a foxtrot.

"I suppose. Too bad they're all about to disappear."

"Well, they're here to*night,* and the night is young."

"You look smashing," Anne said, which was true. Lydia wore a blue sundress, cut just low enough to add some special fuel to the sailors' engines but just tasteful enough to avoid the chaperones' disapproval. It was good to see her long-mourning friend so excited again. "I love that dress."

"Why, thank you."

"Do you have anything to drink?"

The band started a Lindy Hop.

"Hard to get away with that in here. If we'd gotten together beforehand, we could've taken care of that."

Two sailors walked over, and once again Anne realized there was some subtle art to this that she'd missed, because she should have managed to attract a better-looking fellow than either of these. One had red hair and pale skin still marked with pimples; he didn't look a day over eighteen. The other had dark hair and eyes and was at least an inch shorter than Anne; realizing this, he was sidling up to Lydia.

"Ladies," the dark-haired one began, sounding like he'd been nervously practicing all night and needed his buddy for moral support, "may we have this dance?"

Before Anne could say no, Lydia had taken the other fellow's hand, so Anne felt she had to go along.

"I'm Roger!" her partner shouted over the music as they started dancing. She hollered her name back, and fortunately it was loud enough that they didn't need to talk anymore. He wasn't a terrible dancer, she had to give him that.

The next song was a slow number, and he pulled himself close to her before she could back away. *All right, one more song, then we're through.*

"They're saying we'll be off to Italy soon."

Anne frowned. "You know you're not supposed to talk about things like that."

"Jeez, it's hard *not* to."

The radio spots and movie trailers were nonstop: *Loose lips sink ships, never talk about troop movements.* She didn't know whether what he was saying was true or just a ploy to win sympathy and get her to spread her legs.

"But I'm looking forward to it. You can only do so much training, you know? Time for the real thing."

She wanted to roll her eyes at the bravado but managed to hold her tongue.

"You're real pretty," he said, pulling back just a bit so he could look at her again.

"Thank you."

Soon the silence began to feel even more awkward than the conversation, so she decided to see if he could serve a reportorial purpose.

"Say, I was wondering," she said. "I heard a rumor somewhere about Italian gangsters hanging out by the Navy Yard. It's probably bunk, but have you heard anything about it?"

"Gangsters, like *Scarface*? Not that I've seen. It's pretty busy down there, though. Maybe I missed it."

Normally she would want to find the source of a bogus rumor. But if this one was actually true, what did it mean? And what could she write about it?

"One thing I will say," he began, "is that . . ." Then his expression changed and he slowed his steps. "Say, is that . . . *blood* on your dress?"

Anne looked down. "Oh, dear, yes." So *that's* why she'd received so many odd looks on the bus. She and Elias hadn't noticed it on the dark streets, but apparently someone in the fight had left some blood on her clothes. She reached into her purse and took out a handkerchief and tried to blot it, but it was too late. "Don't worry, it's not mine."

He looked horrified, and possibly on the verge of nausea. He stepped back.

"Whose is it?"

"Long story. It's been a rough night."

Another sailor walked up, noticing that they weren't dancing anymore.

"If the lady is free, may I have this dance?"

"Sorry, I need to run to the restroom and see if I can get the blood out."

"Blood?" The newcomer glared at the first sailor. "Whatcha do to her, pal?"

"I didn't do nothin', it was already there!"

While they argued, she was honestly thankful for the bloodstain, as it had provided her with a convenient way to get away from her dance partner. In the ladies' room, other women were primping for the mirror and reapplying lipstick while Anne looked in vain for paper towels. The room only had one of those disgusting rotating towels, so she instead grabbed some toilet paper and ran it under the faucet, then tried dabbing at the stain, but she succeeded only in wetting her shoulder as the cheap toilet paper disintegrated.

"What happened?" asked the woman next to her.

"Too much marinara sauce, I guess," she lied.

"That's why I never eat Italian on dates."

"Italian *men*, on the other hand," said a woman on Anne's other side, "I could eat them all night!"

Laughter, and another agreed, "They know how to treat a lady."

Back on the dance floor, she'd made it only a few steps when she was intercepted by one of the elderly chaperones. He had white hair and the air of a high school principal.

"Miss, there's *blood* on your dress."

"Yes, but it's not mine. It's fine."

"No, it is not fine. We can't have something like that here."

"Are the soldiers and sailors scared of blood? That doesn't bode well."

"Miss, for gosh sake! You need to clean that up."

"Well, I just tried, and this was the best I could get it."

"Then I'm afraid I'm going to have to ask you to leave."

"Oh, *thank* you, you're giving me just the excuse I need," Anne said as she saw Lydia walking over. She turned to her friend. "Sorry, sweetie, I'm being kicked out. Are you all right on your own?"

"Kicked out? Of a dance? Why?"

Anne left it to the chaperone to explain, which he did in a tone of voice that made Anne's indiscretion seem quite a bit more severe than it was, in her opinion.

"I really *want* to stay," Anne lied, "but I appear to be violating Army regulation about bloody dresses. I'm terribly sorry."

Lydia folded her arms and gave the chaperone a suspicious look.

"Maybe you should try not to get in a fight next time."

"*I* didn't get in a fight. One broke out at the meeting."

"Of course it did, and of course you just had to go there so you can write about it later and of course you couldn't have just taken the night off and had fun with me." Lydia shook her head. "Well, I'm staying. Good night."

Lydia walked off, and before she'd taken three steps another man had asked for her hand, and off they went.

"Miss," the chaperone reminded Anne.

"I'm going, I'm going."

As she walked out, she felt like a bad friend, a bad activist, and a bad reporter all at once. The problem with playing too many roles, she realized not for the first time, was that it made you likelier to fail at all of them.

Chapter Eleven

AMONG THE LILLIPUTIANS

To Devon, Northeast Munitions always looked like it was on fire.
It wasn't that day, thank God, and it wasn't usually, though three small fires had broken out in the past year—most recently last week. Every time, he and Lou had been called in to investigate whether the fires had been attempted sabotage, and every time the fire chief had noted that if the fire had spread, and reached the ordnance warehouses, it could have caused an explosion that would have doubled the size of Boston Harbor.

Smoke constantly spewed from the two dozen stacks spread across the factory's massive roof—with workers on staggered shifts, Northeast hadn't been inactive in more than a year. The series of long hangars was located in Charlestown just past the sprawling Navy Yard, which was equally abuzz with activity. Devon could see at least two destroyer escorts in the dry docks, surrounded by scaffoldings brimming with workers, and beyond them floated an aircraft carrier that seemed as long as Boston's Esplanade. How something so enormous managed to float, he had no idea.

Devon and Lou drove along a secure road that cut between the Navy Yard and Northeast. Windows down, Devon could smell soot and grease and the weird metallic tang of something akin to gunpowder mixed with rubber cement. Steam hammers banged in asynchronous fury. It had rained late the previous night; as a few rays of sun peeked through the clouds, they released a fog of moisture from the damp wooden docks.

"We have two names," Devon recapped to Lou. "The ones Wolff's widow said he was closest to. McDonough says he'll have them ready for us."

The spire of the Old North Church was visible across the Charles, its whiteness poking out with historic importance amid the North End's brick tenements. In the opposite direction, it was possible to make out the Bunker Hill Monument looming to the north if the wind was right and there was no smoke, which meant that no one here ever saw it.

"Also, there was a fight last night at the Dockworkers Local 107," Lou said. "Maloney at the precinct called me this morning."

"Any arrests?"

"Yeah, five. Lots of other men needed medical attention but skipped the hospital."

"What happened?"

"Maloney says there was a vote to strike, and it lost. Sore losers, I guess."

Devon drove slowly as his path was crossed by welders and shipfitters, cutters and reamers, grinders and burners. Men, women, and some kids who lied about their age. Black goggles and gloves, steel-toed boots or makeshift approximations, old boots with thin sheets of metal wrapped around the end. Many of the workers had sunburns, or maybe they were actual burns. Devon spied a sign that read "The practice known as 'goosing' with air hoses can cause serious injury and is forbidden."

Cranes pivoted and wires crisscrossed and very large things indeed loomed overhead. A team of welders was perched atop a damaged landing-ship tank in the nearest dry dock, their torches aglow like magic wands as they crouched there surrounded by wiring. Devon pulled to a stop as a small railcar loaded down with scrap metal dinged along the rails. After it passed, he saw three men taking a smoke break atop an enormous, block-long pile of six-foot die-lock chains; they looked like Lilliputians atop the pocket-watch some giant had dropped before jumping into the Charles for a swim.

Devon let his government tags create a parking spot right by the front door to Northeast Munitions. He heard Lou make a small guttural sound of objection to this violation of vehicular decorum, but at least his partner didn't say anything.

As they walked toward the building, Devon noticed two cardboard boxes sitting by the door, their top flaps torn off. Inside each were two neat stacks of pamphlets, weighed down by rocks lest a breeze blow them away. He nudged a rock and picked up one of the pamphlets, an 8.5-by-11 paper sheet whose main headline asked *IS THIS PLANT EMPLOYING JEWS?*

"You seen these here before?" he asked Lou.

"No."

Devon skimmed it and flipped it over in hopes of finding information about the publisher, but didn't see anything. He'd seen similar literature back when America had been neutral, but not since Pearl Harbor.

And to answer the pamphlet's question: yes, this plant employed Jews. One of whom had just been murdered, hence Devon and Lou's visit today. He folded the pamphlet and was sliding it into his jacket pocket when out stepped Neil McDonough, Northeast Munitions' designated face man with the Bureau.

"Good to see you, gentlemen. I've pulled the three off the floor so they're ready, and of course it would be wonderful if you could make this quick so they can get back to work." McDonough had red hair and chalky skin that sweat an amazing amount even when he wasn't walking through the plant's smoky, humid, downright infernal work areas. His job title was "government relations executive," something Devon had never heard of before meeting him last year. "As you know, we have rather daunting productivity goals right now."

"Don't we all," Devon said, not making any promises. "Bring them one at a time, please."

As they made their way through the factory, they slipped into their ears the cotton that McDonough had handed them and then followed him down a long hallway, down two flights of alarmingly slippery stairs that descended to the factory floor, and through another subterranean passage. They passed men whose goggled faces seemed to gape eyelessly at them.

Inside, the agents made their way to their usual interrogation room, a small storage area filled with boxes, with a small table and three chairs in the middle.

As he always did in this building, Devon craved a smoke but didn't dare reach into his pocket.

They had little to go on so far in their murder investigation. The autopsy had been delayed, and the cops had lifted a partial print from the cocktail napkin in the victim's pocket. They'd confirmed it wasn't the victim's fingerprint, but that was all.

The first man McDonough brought in, Jaromir Zajac, was covered in soot and smelled like he'd been working inside a smokestack, which maybe he had been. Devon told him to sit. Tiny black clouds appeared when his ass hit the chair.

Dark mangy hair, a thick mustache that made him look like the secret third conspirator of Sacco and Vanzetti. Which he may well have been.

He belonged to the New Patriots League, an interracial Communist group active throughout New England. The Bureau had been tracking such organizations since at least the early thirties, when the Depression had made the idea of wealth redistribution particularly appealing to the masses. Four years ago, when Russia and Germany had signed their (brief) Non-Aggression Pact and divided Poland between them, the Bureau's concerns about Communists and Fascists merged together. But then in June of '41 Hitler double-crossed Stalin by invading Russia, and the bloodied Soviets crawled over to the Allies' side. That made it hard for the Bureau to justify spending much manpower on reds, as the reds were helping us fight a war against Nazis.

Still, Hoover wanted to keep some tabs on the godless Communists. Battle lines moved fast, on the killing fields and elsewhere.

Hands folded in his lap, Zajac eyed the agents with a thinly disguised hatred.

No, there had been no altercations at work lately, he claimed. No, Wolff had no enemies. No, we didn't socialize that much, just an occasional dinner here or there. No, we never went to bars. I told the cops what? Oh yes, we did go to a place that night, of course. Yes, sorry. Bucciano's, it's called.

"Was there any reason you went out that night, to that particular place in the North End?"

"Someone said it was good. Wasn't too long of a walk." Zajac shrugged.

"Who said it was good?"

Devon only asked to see if Zajac could come up with a name, which he did, and Devon wrote it down, though he didn't think this meant anything.

"You two lived in the same neighborhood," Devon noted. "So if you were drinking in the North End, a forty-minute train ride back to Dorchester, why didn't you head home together?"

Zajac looked like he didn't understand the question at first. "I was tired. He wasn't."

"So you left him out drinking alone?"

"He's a grown man. He was talking to some other men when I left. Was a friendly place."

"What men?"

"I didn't get their names. Just friendly men at a bar."

"Describe them."

Zajac did and Devon took notes, but the man's recollections were hazy and he admitted he'd been drunk by then. Devon could tell Zajac was holding something back, but he moved on.

"We know that you've been going to meetings of the New Patriots. Maybe that's why you got this job, because they want to have people at all the plants. Take over the unions, exert control over the war industry. That's the master plan, right? We also know that people like you love to disagree with each other about your little theories and dialectics, and you take that stuff personally. Maybe you and Abraham had a disagreement about some footnote Lenin scribbled twenty years ago?"

Lou coughed, not from allergies but because Devon was divulging more than he should. Lou believed it best to keep quiet about how much the Bureau knew about Communist infiltration into the unions, preferring to lurk quietly. *Talk less, watch more*, Lou often advised.

"I'm just here to work and work hard," Zajac said. "And I never hurt Abe."

"So what *did* happen to him?" Devon asked.

"He got robbed!" Zajac's shout took the agents by surprise. "He got robbed because people like you don't give a damn what happens to workers!"

Things went rather downhill from there. Devon offered a few half-hearted threats, but Zajac had nothing substantive to say.

Wrapping up, they asked if he'd mind letting them fingerprint him. Legally he could have said no, but they didn't tell him that, and the pressure of being asked at his place of work made it seem mandatory. He said yes, Devon doing the honors.

Then they dismissed him and sent McDonough to get the next man.

Devon told Lou, "You could at least fake a little interest."

"I'm telling you, he's right: it was just a robbery. Or maybe an anti-Jew thing. We're wasting time here and annoying McDonough, a man we want to like us."

McDonough brought in the only other man Wolff's wife had claimed he'd been friends with, Michal Baran. Short and stocky with a dark beard and thick hair, he had no known links to any red groups. They'd already known, too, that this was a fellow they could put pressure on: Zajac was a bachelor, but Baran was a father of three.

"You like this job, right?" Devon asked after a few unilluminating minutes.

"Of course, yes." His accent wasn't quite as thick as Zajac's.

"Feeds your family?"

"Yes."

"And it also helps us fight against the Nazis, which I assume you're in favor of."

"Very much, yes."

"So tell us the truth about Wolff." Devon waited a beat. "We know that your buddy Zajac there's been going to meetings of the New Patriots League. We know Communists have people at all the mills and factories, because the Soviets love to keep watch over their supposed allies here." Devon noted how Baran leaned back, shifted his feet, as if Devon had turned up the temperature in the room. "We know that Zajac doesn't want us to know what Wolff was really doing with his free time. And when we find out later that Wolff was involved in some sort of spy network and that's why he was killed, and when we realize you didn't tell us about it, you could go to jail. I've put fathers in jail, and trust me, it's unpleasant for everyone. But especially for them."

Baran scratched at his face in thought. Devon had initially thought the man was bearded, but finger streaks appeared on his cheeks and Devon realized that it was soot.

"I'm not involved in anything political. I love America and I want to crush Hitler. Some of the fellows here, they may be reds. For sure, don't know."

"I heard there was trouble at a dockworkers' union meeting last night," Devon said.

Baran shrugged. "I'm not a dockworker."

Devon leaned forward, knees on his elbows. "Look. I think we have a lot in common. Our interests aren't so different. But what about Wolff?"

Baran thought for a moment, then sighed and shook his head. "Something was funny about that night. He and Zajac, they both told me before they weren't doing anything after work, just going home. Then the next day I hear he's dead. Then Zajac tells me that they'd gone out that night, not home."

"You think Zajac's lying about something? I wouldn't want you to get in trouble for his lie."

Baran still couldn't quite find a comfortable position to sit in. "I think . . . there's something he didn't want me to know about that night. But I don't know what it is. Okay? That enough for you?" He held out his palms, pleading.

They got his prints too.

Next, McDonough sent in Patty Campbell. Unlike the other two, he was a native-born American, from Charlestown. Dark hair, athletic build, and bad smallpox scars that made Lou's look minor in comparison. Also unlike the other two, he wasn't a past associate of the victim.

"What's going on, Mulvey?" he asked without even sitting down.

"You heard about the murder of one of your coworkers, Abraham Wolff?"

"Yeah, but I didn't know the man, didn't even work with him. Different shifts, different jobs. Why'd you call me in?"

Campbell was one of several workers at Northeast that Devon occasionally met with to pick their brains about anything happening at the plant that a face man like McDonough wouldn't admit. The nephew of a priest, Campbell was very much not a Communist and had proven to be a trusted source in the past about things like thefts and a union-backed sabotage attempt a year ago. Devon hadn't expected him to be this defensive.

"Relax, Patty. You're not a suspect. Just wondering if you'd heard anything."

"Nah, nothing. I mean, people are talking about it, sure. That's why, you calling me in now, it doesn't exactly look good, you know?"

Devon typically met with Campbell for a drink, away from colleagues' eyes.

"Don't worry, Patty. No one thinks you did it. Although, if people do talk, you'll tell us what they say, right?"

"Of course."

"Tell me this, though. Wolff was Jewish. Did people know that?"

Campbell held up two very dirty palms. "Like I said, I didn't even know him. I've heard rumors there are Jews here, though. That they lied in their applications."

War plants weren't supposed to discriminate in their hiring. If Wolff had indeed "lied" about his religion, that meant Northeast Munitions was asking questions of applicants it wasn't supposed to. Devon filed this away for now. With a name like Abraham, Wolff wasn't exactly hiding who he was. At the same time, Devon had never seen anyone at the plant wearing a religious head covering or even a beard; workers here knew to assimilate for their own good.

"You hadn't heard any rumors about him in particular?" he asked.

"Nah, not a thing. Never even heard his name until a buddy mentioned the murder. *That* people are talking about, yeah. But any *details*? No. I'll tell you if I do hear anything, though."

A shift whistle blew, and Campbell glanced at the door. "That's my lunch. We good?"

"Yeah, we're good. But keep those ears open."

After Campbell left, McDonough returned and told them that Mr. Lloyd would like to meet with them briefly. The agents exchanged glances.

Matthew Lloyd was the owner of Northeast Munitions, which not long ago had been known as Northeast Machinery, manufacturer of boilers for homes and offices, engine parts for large boats. Like countless factories across the country, it had jettisoned and revamped its old assembly lines, reinventing itself for the government's insatiable new demands. It still designed some boat parts that came in handy for the Navy, but it mostly had moved on to artillery and firearms.

McDonough walked them into an office with a view of the busy Harbor, the sun glinting off the water. A young secretary smiled at Devon, pressed a buzzer and told Mr. Lloyd the agents were here, and the door behind her opened.

"Come in, come in," Lloyd said, smiling. Thick white hair, pin-striped suit, mild Brahmin accent. McDonough walked them as far as the threshold, then took his leave.

Devon had met Lloyd only once before, the businessman saying all the right things about cooperating with the Bureau. His office had two guest chairs, yet Lloyd was standing and hadn't invited anyone to sit.

"And how goes the daily battles of the intrepid FBI?"

"All seems to be going well, Mr. Lloyd," Lou answered first. He always seemed quicker on his feet around these old-money types than Devon, who found himself second-guessing his manners and choice of words. His years at Harvard had helped, but only so much.

On one wall hung a photo with Governor Saltonstall, the bland Republican who'd won office by defeating Irish hero James Michael Curley. On another wall, an on-field photo with slugger Ted Williams.

"Yet I hear you pulled three men off their lines today. These are busy times for us, gentlemen. Aren't there less obtrusive ways you could do your jobs?"

"We were just wrapping things up, actually," Lou said.

"I'm glad to hear it. We can't have these distractions if we expect to meet the rather staggering quotas the Army's put to us."

"We're done for today, Mr. Lloyd," Lou assured him.

"There may be more avenues to explore later," Devon added, shooting Lou a quick glance. "We'll do our best to be as . . . unobtrusive as possible."

The businessman sighed and leaned his derriere against his desk.

"Do you really have any reason to think this one man getting stabbed, outside a *bar*, has anything to do with what goes on here?"

Devon said, "We don't normally discuss the particulars of an investigation, Mr. Lloyd."

"Of course not. But, gentlemen, we play for the same team, do we not? Unless you've turned up something salacious that points to sabotage or espionage, which I just can't see in this particular case, I'd thank you to focus on some other matter and let us focus on getting these guns out the door. The boys on the front would thank you, too."

A buzz and the secretary's voice, telling him that he had a call from a "Representative Jeffers in Washington." Lloyd showed them to the door and thanked them for their time.

Devon waited until they were outside to tell Lou, "Boy, you bend over for the WASP big shots awful fast. What, are you afraid if you bother him, he'll revoke your country club membership?"

"I care about how the Bureau is perceived by men like that, yes. You should too. I'm ready to write up a report on the murder and close this. If you want to waste more time on it, do it on your own."

As Devon backed out of the parking spot, his eyes lingered on those two boxes of anti-Semitic sheets. The one he'd folded in his pocket seemed to stab at his chest, so he rolled his shoulders, as if the problem could so easily be shrugged off.

Chapter Twelve

THE CHALLENGE OF TEENAGE BOYS

Sammy, I was hoping we could talk about the night that, you know. When you were . . . roughed up."

Morning, their mother and Elias at work again. Sammy had been eating cereal when Anne finally got him alone.

"I don't want to talk about it."

"I know. But I've been thinking: if the police aren't doing anything about it, and it's not even in the papers, then maybe if *I* can help get a story out, that will finally get the city to do something."

The *Jewish Advocate* had reported on some of the worst assaults, but none of the other papers had. Anne had already reached out to an editor at the *Advocate* to offer her help for a more thorough, investigative piece, but he'd turned her down. As had everyone else.

"I don't want to be in some story about being beat up! C'mon."

"I'm not trying to embarrass you. But I can only help if people talk to me."

"No, thank you. No way." He shoveled more cornflakes into his mouth as if to preempt another question.

She'd expected this to be difficult, maybe even more difficult than asking him to talk about girls he had crushes on (why were boys and men so hesitant to *talk*?).

"What if I leave your name out of it, for now?"

Mouth full, he garbled, "'For now'?"

"For God's sake, how can I get other people to tell me their stories if I can't get my own brother to?"

"I don't care! I don't want to be in your story, Anne."

He tried to escape into his room, but she followed him. He sat on the bed and picked up a comic book, something about heroic FBI agents. Pretending she wasn't there.

Standing in the doorway, she tapped her pen on her pad. Two could play the obtuse game. If he wanted to ignore her, fine, she would just pretend she hadn't heard him.

"I already know the dates of the two attacks, as I'd noted them in my diary," she reported. "First let's talk about the most recent time: Mother said you told her there were three of them, right?"

"I thought I said I didn't want to talk about it."

Boys were so hard to get talking, about anything. She didn't even know if he had a girlfriend. She had noticed he seemed to be paying more attention to his hair and clothes, and a few times even wore cologne, but he hadn't been to any of the Saturday dances at the Hecht House or the Y.M.H.A. lately. Whether he had a crush on anyone in particular, she had no idea. He had grown rather handsome, and he wasn't nearly as shy as he used to be.

"I just need the basic facts. Like keeping a record. So, there were three of them?"

He sighed and put down his comic. Closed his eyes.

"Yes. Three."

"And if you had to guess, they were all a little older than you?"

"Yeah. One of them might have been in his twenties, the real big one. Short blond hair. Not like Army short, but short. He was tall."

"What did the other two look like?"

"Dark hair. One of them had a crescent-moon scar, on his right cheek."

"You mentioned that last time, in April," she remembered. "It was the same people?"

"No. I mean, yes." He sighed, desperate to end this. "Two of 'em were different. But the one with the scar was both times. I don't know his name, where he lives. Only that he has that scar. You don't forget a thing like that."

She asked him a few more questions but didn't get much out of him. She should leave him alone, she realized. But her heart ached for him. His bruises had faded, but not completely. He was lying on his bed, staring at the ceiling, his eyes set in that peculiar way of young men, where she couldn't tell if he was on the verge of tears or about to yell at her. Maybe both. Anne wasn't one to get tongue-tied, but she was struggling for the right thing to say to end this conversation gracefully, something that would buck him up.

So he surprised her by saying, "I can't wait till I'm eighteen."

"How come?"

He sat up and looked right at her. "So I can kill them. Why do you think? I'm tired of assholes like that having the upper hand over here. Over there, we can fight back. *Shoot* back."

His words chilled her. She'd never heard him talk like this. "Sammy, I don't think war is . . . something to look forward to."

His birthday was only five months away, he'd reminded her recently.

"Why not? You've spent all this time getting people excited for war. You do it with your typewriter, and I'm ready to do it with a gun. That's how war works, Anne."

Anne was not accustomed to losing arguments with him, but as she stood there in his doorway she realized she had no reply.

Chapter Thirteen

ON ISOLATIONISM

That night, Devon sat with his father in the old man's study, sipping Jameson after dinner.

"Dark times are ahead," John Mulvey said.

The second of Devon's five sisters, Jenny, was doing dishes in the kitchen with her eldest daughter, while Jenny's three other kids ran like hellions around the rest of the house. Since their mother had passed from cancer a year and a half ago, Devon's sisters had taken it on themselves to make dinner at their father's house once a week. The giant Sunday dinners their mother used to host had changed into weeknight gatherings designed to help Pop stave off loneliness.

Family meant never being alone. His mother had told him that, years ago. The remark had been intended as a positive, but at the time, teenage Devon had seen it as oppressive. For his parents and the previous generation, he understood the logic: recent immigrants drew from their family to stay safe, to look out for each other, to find opportunities. But for Devon, raised in a loud house with five sisters, being surrounded by countless cousins and now nieces and nephews, always celebrating someone's First Communion or birthday or birth, the concept of being alone had seemed like a luxury he could only dream about.

Moving into his own apartment after law school had seemed self-indulgent, bordering on antisocial—his mother had been hurt by it, having assumed he'd stay in her house until he married—but the freedom was intoxicating. He did make a point of having dinner with one sister or another, and his father, at least once or twice a week, when the job didn't get in the way.

Their father was alone a lot now, which worried all of them.

"I still can't believe we're waltzing into another European war," John said. "And after all I've done to try to stop it."

"Jenny's pretty worried about Philip." Jenny's husband had been sent to the Atlantic. She hadn't been the same since he'd shipped off, her voice tighter, her eyes often vacant, miles away.

"She should be," Pop said. "I'm worried about him too. And Joe, and Mike, and Mark, and all of the rest."

The youngest in the family, Devon was now uncle to six boys and nine girls, the youngest a wailing newborn and the oldest as tall as him. It also meant Devon had four brothers-in-law in the service. Jenny's Philip was in the Atlantic somewhere. Siobhan's Mike was in North Africa, where he'd seen combat. Julia's Mark was relatively safe, an engineer stationed in Britain, but who knew what might happen. Only Katie's David had been spared, as the forty-six-year-old had been declared 4-F due to his age.

At family gatherings, as in so many other situations, Devon often found himself the only male between the ages of eighteen and forty-five.

"I keep hoping something might happen to break people from their trance," Pop said. "Some catastrophe or political act that makes people realize what a horrible blunder we're about to commit."

"I think that plane has already flown." *And bombed Hawaii,* he wanted to add, but thought better of it. He'd learned that engaging his father in this subject never went well.

John Joseph Mulvey had been a vocal isolationist, cowed into relative silence only when Pearl Harbor rendered his objections moot. Like the recent U.S. ambassador to Britain, Joe Kennedy (a onetime business associate of his), Pop didn't see the point in wasting American lives to bail out France or Britain in their never-ending dispute with Germany. He despised the English for all the evils they perpetrated back in Ireland, and he still had cousins in the IRA. Equally bad, in his opinion, were the godless Communists in Russia.

Up until the morning those Japanese fighters streaked into Oahu, John had lobbied anyone who would listen—and quite a few people listened to John Mulvey—that the soundest strategy was to let Hitler take down Russia, which was the true threat. American boys should never again be asked to die to settle disputes between Europe's perennially warring tribes.

Devon had once shared his father's isolationism, having been raised on Pop's horror stories of trench warfare. Pop himself had been too young to fight in the first war but had lost two brothers to the trenches; a third, Devon's uncle Ray, had survived but had been driven near mad by the experience. Ray's empty stares and frequent benders had been an ongoing lesson in the folly of war, as had his early death from liver failure.

For these and other reasons, Devon's parents had been adamant that Devon not enlist in the Army. In late '40, he had just finished law school and had been applying to various firms when his father had approached him with some career advice. Some of Pop's friends in government knew FBI Director Hoover and had noted how the Bureau was expanding with various war-related tasks even though America wasn't yet at war. Hoover was a skilled bureaucrat who would surely find a way to protect his agents from being drafted, Pop figured. Landing a job at the FBI, then, would keep Devon from the slaughter of the battlefield while also protecting his manly reputation; he wouldn't be some yellow-bellied objector but a gun-carrying, crime-fighting federal agent.

How could Devon possibly argue with that? And so he hadn't, at least not out loud.

"Let's talk about something else, Pop." His father talked about the wrongheadedness of the war far more often than seemed healthy, Devon thought. He knew Pop missed his wife—her death had been sudden, shocking them all—and it seemed that, without her as an emotional bulwark, he worked himself up about politics and world events more than he once did.

"How's the Cadillac holding up?" Devon asked.

"Oh, it's great. Not that I can drive it much these days with the gas rationing."

Grandson of a potato-famine immigrant, John Mulvey had taken an accounting job for a small chain of grocery stores before, in his early twenties, talking his way into a job at Boston Financial, one of the city's biggest banks. By the time he hit forty he was one of the only Irish vice presidents in banking. The Depression had slowed the family's advancement up the social ladder only slightly, as he'd seen the crash coming and planned accordingly.

Pop was all but retired now. He still headed into the office but, at sixty-three, was treated more like a mascot. Which he resented.

"Is everything going well at the office?" Pop sipped his Jameson. He was so far unaffected by the awful whiskey shortage in the rest of the country, thanks to his connections.

"It's fine. Haven't made a big case in a while, but . . . I might have something." Part of him wanted to tell his father about the Wolff murder, but another part wondered if that might be a bad idea.

"Good. Father Boyle always asks me how your work is going. He's very proud of you. He's noticed, however, that you haven't been at mass the last few Sundays."

Devon wished his old man hadn't brought that up. "I was at a different church."

John watched him for a loaded moment. "I thought you told me you weren't doing that."

"I don't always get to choose my job duties."

His father loudly placed his glass on the table. "Honestly, I think I'd prefer hearing that you were forgoing mass altogether than knowing that they have you spying on the Church."

"It's not spying, Pop. They just wanted someone to listen to certain priests' homilies, fellows who've said a few things that—"

"*Priests* are not 'fellows.'" His father glared at him. "I wish they'd just send their Yankee agents to spy on the clergy and not force you to do it."

Devon should have lied and said he'd been skipping mass altogether. That sin would have been more forgivable.

"Look, it was all a big misunderstanding. A priest praises Father Coughlin or knocks FDR and it gets blown out of proportion, then Hoover wants an agent in the pews the next Sunday. I just go to mass and make sure nothing seditious is being said."

"And if there is?"

Devon stalled with a sip of whiskey. "You just said you wished they'd send some Yankee agent instead. But would you really? Wouldn't you rather it be someone you trust, someone who cares about the Church and can protect it? Wouldn't you rather have *me* filing the reports, deciding what should be in them? Give me some credit, please."

His father seemed to consider this. He picked his glass back up and took a sip, then shook his head. "Still. It makes me sick. The damned Yankees are using the war as an excuse to spy on us. And after it's over they'll manufacture a new one. Don't forget that, Devon."

"I seem to recall you lobbying me to take this job."

"And?"

"I thought you were glad I took it. Yet you act like it's tainted me somehow."

"I don't think that. That's not what I meant at all. I'm proud of you, you know that."

He hadn't known it, actually. It felt good to hear.

"But you still have to be careful. Never let the Yankees sink their claws into you too deeply, Devon. I know whereof I speak here: no matter how hard you work or how you might prove yourself, they'll never fully trust you. And you shouldn't trust them."

Chapter Fourteen

THE WAREHOUSE

The green-skinned-sailor rumor proved to be a rather easy one to report on, as Anne had expected. She had enough to write the piece now, but she slow-walked it, giving herself extra time to chase down the stories Larry didn't want her to write.

Larry said he had no desire to run a report on the attacks in Dorchester, and every other editor in the city had also turned her down. Her next idea was to lure a national journalist on to the story. She didn't have the connections to pitch a piece to New York herself, but maybe she could get another writer—someone with a bigger megaphone and a paycheck unaffected by Boston politics—to step up and work with her.

She knew a few New York journalists and placed calls that morning. Four turned her down outright; two sounded intrigued but didn't promise anything yet; she left messages with the secretaries for two more. She'd now run out of names and would soon run out of options.

Anne had told Flaherty the printmaker that she'd meet him at a Central Square diner at noon, wearing a yellow dress, so she wore a blue dress and sat at the bus stop a few feet from the diner. Smoking and wearing sunglasses, she tried not to be too obvious about the way she was staring at the diner's door.

At five past noon she saw a short, squat man in his late forties, in a driver's cap and short-sleeved white shirt with sweat marks in the armpits, hurrying to the door. He held a large cardboard box. She got only a quick glance at his face—gray hair, thin, hadn't shaved.

She wondered how long he'd wait in there for a lady in a yellow dress. She couldn't see inside the diner because of the glare on the windows.

A bus came and two passengers got on, but Anne shook her head at the driver.

Flaherty was a patient man. The midday sun had risen above the buildings and Anne was covered with sweat when the door to the diner opened and she finally saw him leave. He headed the way he'd come, south on Mass Ave.

She gave him a half-block head start, then followed. She'd arrived early enough to snag a parking space right by the entrance to the subway. But he passed the entrance to the train and kept going.

She got into her dingy Ford. Like most Bostonians, she rarely drove, using the streetcars and trains to get around. But her family had bought an old, used Ford from a relative a few years ago, and she used it sometimes when her reporting took her to hard-to-reach places.

She eased out of her spot and onto Mass, following him down Pearl, where he got into a tan Pontiac sedan and passed her going the other way, back down Mass.

She swore, pulled over, and managed a three-point turn to get back on Mass. She sped up and saw him ahead.

What exactly are you doing, here, Anne? she asked herself. She'd trailed a few Fascists to meetings in the past, but on foot—never in a car. She wanted to laugh at herself. But her heart was racing and she felt like she was *doing* something. Chasing a story. Where it would lead, she couldn't be sure. But she wanted to know who was printing those awful leaflets and working so hard to stir up hatred in her city. What she'd do next would depend on what she learned.

This was her best plan. At least it was fun.

After fifteen minutes they'd passed Harvard Square, packs of summer students looking carefree, as if their textbooks might protect them from the front lines. She drove with her windows down, the air hot in her face.

Soon they were in a rather bleak stretch of Somerville, three-deckers clustered closely together, few trees. She was a couple of car lengths behind Flaherty when they reached Powder House Square, near Tufts University. He turned right, up and then down a hill, then turned again onto a dead-end road.

She pulled over, lest she drive too far down and give herself away. It was a strange block, with four modest houses on each side and, at the end, what looked like an old warehouse, which is where Flaherty parked.

An out-of-the-way space like this would be a good spot for a hate-spreading printing press. The only windows in the building were high, but she might be able to see into some of them if she were to get out and walk around. Not while he was inside, though.

She checked the rest of the block and saw two men painting the last house beside the warehouse. Another reason for her not to skulk around the building, at least not now. Maybe they'd be finished in a day or two.

While she was considering this, Flaherty emerged from the building, carrying not the box but what looked like a large envelope. He locked the door and walked back to his Pontiac.

He tossed the envelope onto the front seat, then did something curious: he walked around to the trunk, opened it, and took out some items. A screwdriver. A license plate. He changed plates, tossing the old one in the trunk.

She lay down across her seat to hide from view as he got in his car. As he approached, she worried for a moment he might spot her, that he would pull beside her and confront her. But she heard the car drive past her.

She sat up and looked back just in time to see which direction he was going.

Why not? She'd gone this far. She pulled another quick three-point turn, drove out to the next street, and fell in a hundred yards behind him.

Minutes later, they were approaching the shopping district of Watertown.

At a red light, she jotted down his license number. Wishing she'd thought to do so earlier, when he'd been driving with a different plate. Whatever he was doing now, he clearly didn't want anyone to be able to trace it back to him.

He pulled into a gas station.

How close to get? How did real detectives do this? Making it up as she went along, she pulled over on the side of the road, well before the gas station. It was on the left, and she could see him walk into the small building, carrying the large envelope, but once he was inside she saw only the glare of the window.

She decided to creep closer, and parked by a phone booth. Got out, sunglasses still on, and walked into the booth. God, it was hot. Phone at her ear, she spoke to herself as though in conversation while she watched the gas station.

Flaherty was chatting with the proprietor. No one came out to pump his gas.

No more than two minutes later, Flaherty emerged without his envelope.

Were even gas stations distributing hate sheets nowadays? Given gas rationing, it didn't seem the wisest method of distribution, but these weren't wise people. She turned her back in the phone booth as Flaherty returned to his Pontiac.

She decided to let him drive away this time. She had a hunch.

Hanging up the phone, she got back in her car and pulled across the street into the gas station. Out the attendant came, greeting her with a smile. "What can I do for ya?"

Tall, thickset, forties, curly dark hair. The name badge sewn onto his shirt read "Arnie." The name of this establishment was Gold's Gas. She wondered if that could be short for Goldberg or Goldman. Either way, this was hardly a place she'd expect to find hate sheets.

She asked Arnie to fill it up. She barely had enough money on her, she realized. He asked her for a ration stamp, and she fished in her stamps book for the right one.

This must be a mistake. Why would an Arnie Gold be handing out anti-Semitic pamphlets? She'd heard of self-hating Jews, but this seemed a bit much.

She asked if she could use his restroom.

"Sure. Inside, door on the right."

She went into the restroom, which wasn't hideous for a gas station. She locked the door and stood there. Killing time. Staying long enough for him to finish his job, get hot in the sun and tire of waiting for her out there, then come back into the office. If another customer drove up, her plan wouldn't work. Due to the rationing, though, gas customers would be hard to come by, she figured.

Eventually she heard the bell of his office door. Waited another twenty seconds, flushed. Washed her hands.

He stood behind his counter and nodded at her. Even if he was suspicious, a man certainly wouldn't ask why she'd taken so long in the restroom.

She spied no crosses on the walls, no Christian-themed illustrations on the calendar behind him, both of which tended to be rather prevalent in Boston.

He told her the price and she reached into her purse. She saw, on the counter behind him, a fat envelope. It looked like the same one Flaherty had brought.

She realized she'd missed what he'd said. "I'm sorry, how much was it?"

"One-ten. You really didn't need much."

"Oh, you know, I never like it to get too low."

"'Course, these days, we're supposed to."

Great, so now she looked like an unpatriotic gas hoarder. "I've been having trouble with the gauge," she lied, "so I don't entirely trust it. I thought it was emptier."

"I could look into the gauge for ya."

"Oh, thank you, but I don't live around here. I have a local mechanic I use."

"Okey dokey. But you should have something like that looked . . ."

His voice trailed off as he reached out with her change. He seemed to tense up.

Her hand was extended to take the coins, but still he held on to them. Looking at her carefully now. Friendly smile gone.

"Where did you say you live?"

"In Brighton." Another lie, but hopefully a believable one, as it was just over the river.

He'd seen her glancing at the envelope, she realized. And he put it together with the fact that she'd pulled in right after Flaherty. And hadn't really needed gas.

She smiled awkwardly, and the moment seemed to last a very long time.

"Anything you wanted to ask me?" His face oddly blank.

She shook her head and said, "No." Hoping another customer might arrive.

Finally he extended his hand and dropped the change into hers. She thanked him and wished him a good day and tried not to run to her car.

What's going on? Why would an apparently Jewish man take hate sheets from Flaherty? She realized she'd made a mistake coming here, then another by glaring so obviously at that mysterious envelope.

She started her engine. As she pulled away, she looked in her mirror and saw him standing in his office doorway, watching her go.

Chapter Fifteen

STRANGE BEDMATES

People kept talking about "the duration."

We would work hard and go without for the duration. We would use ration cards and check the paper each day to see which cards could be used on which products for the duration. We would decline to grumble or complain and would consider it our patriotic duty to sometimes go without, for the duration.

Women would work jobs that men usually filled for the duration. We would cease taking pleasure drives, and therefore preserve both rubber and gasoline, for the duration.

Factories that had once built sedans or refrigerators or merry-go-rounds would instead design gun parts and tank gears for the duration. In certain neighborhoods we would pass signs that read "QUIET! WAR WORKERS SLEEPING!" and we would indeed be respectfully quiet for the duration.

We would join Civil Defense Leagues and would religiously patrol our blocks during blackouts to make sure no one had left a light on, and if we saw a light burning in apartment 4-B on the top floor across the street, then by God we would break into that building and climb three flights of stairs and turn the light off for the duration.

We would write letters to our loved ones and pray for the duration.

We would watch a staggering amount of war movies for the duration, although honestly we were getting rather tired of them, all that ultrapatriotic sloganeering and whatnot, so we wouldn't mind a good gangster movie, even one about immoral American bank robbers and liquor barons killing without regret, regardless of the propaganda that might provide to the Nazis and Japs, so therefore Hollywood wouldn't actually be making any such films for the duration, but it was nice to think about.

We would move back in with our parents while our newly married husband was off at war (unless we were a particularly bold sort of gal) for the duration. We would endure and toil and defer our dreams for the duration.

But how long exactly would the duration last? And who would we be when it ended?

If we were left to our own devices again, if we could freely inhabit the selves we'd left behind, what would those selves feel like on our skin after we took them out of the closet and brushed off the lint? Would we feel as good and strong as we'd remembered feeling, or was that just nostalgia? The headlines were alarming, the news bleak, the fear so constant that perhaps the duration would go on for many more years, longer than we could stand. Even so, people were peering into their closets now and then, daring to look for their past selves and wonder if they might fit again. Wondering if they should try them on, at night, when no one was around to judge. Gazing at our old selves in the mirror, fearlessly envisioning a new world to conquer, to cherish, and to love.

Would we ever be those selves again?

The next afternoon, Devon walked from his office to the North End.

It was a short trip to Haymarket, then he walked past the fishmongers and produce sellers, salt thick in the air, different accents and languages. The market had grown since the start of the war, thanks in part to government spending and all the busy factory workers nearby, the throngs of sailors who stopped off in Boston for destinations classified.

The bar where Zajac claimed he and Wolff had caroused on the night of the murder was called Bucciano's. A block south of it, Devon passed the alley where Wolff had been stabbed to death.

Lou had given up on this investigation. But the way Mr. Lloyd had all but warned them away from his workers rubbed Devon the wrong way.

Questioning three men for less than an hour hardly dented Northeast's productivity; why did Lloyd really want the feds to back off? Devon still hadn't found a match for the prints on the cocktail napkins, and he was running out of leads. He knew the cops had already questioned the staff here, and everyone on this block, but he decided to check it out himself.

Bucciano's was empty at that hour but for one old man reading the newspaper, sunlight pouring in through the window. It wasn't really a bar, Devon noticed, but more of an all-purpose restaurant, its hours 7 a.m. to 11 p.m. The dark wood paneling was freshly cleaned, the white tile floor spotless. Devon noted photos and paintings of the Tuscan countryside, Roman architecture, the Pope. A small American flag hung in a corner where, he was willing to bet, an Italian flag had hung until Pearl Harbor.

He walked up to the barkeep, a thin, thirtyish man with light brown hair, and introduced himself, showing off his badge. The barkeep, who was smoking, reached out and offered a firm handshake, introducing himself as Gabriele Bucciano.

"You're the owner?"

Bucciano spoke with a mild accent. "Her son. She's not here now. Everything okay?"

"Were you working here the night of the twentieth?"

"Yes."

Devon put a file folder on the bar, opened it up to reveal a photo of Wolff, taken back when he was hired at Northeast Munitions. "Did you happen to see this man?"

"This is the dead man?"

"Yes. Do you remember seeing him?"

The barkeep shrugged. "We were busy that night. Saw many people."

"Think a little harder. He probably spoke with a German accent." He moved the photo to reveal one of Zajac. "They might have been together."

"I don't know. Maybe. We get many accents here. Men sometimes come after work in the Charlestown factories and shipyard."

"So you do get a mix of people here? Real melting pot?"

"Sometimes. And that night, yes, I think so." He looked down at the photo again. "Like I said, we were busy."

Devon closed the folder and kept his eyes on the man. He wasn't sure he believed him. "Any fights break out that night?"

"Fights? No, not here. This is a clean place. Happy people."

"Happy drunk people sometimes get in fights, too."

Bucciano smiled. "True. But no fights here. We are not that sort of place. And fights are for Europe, these days. You don't want a drink?"

"I'll take a coffee."

Bucciano hollered at an aproned boy, maybe twelve, "*Nicò! Fa nu caffè a sto poliziotto.*" The kid hopped to it.

"Where are you from?" Devon asked.

"Salerno. Left twenty years ago."

American forces, including one of Devon's brothers-in-law, had seen their first major land combat the previous winter in North Africa. Trying to take land from the Italians and Germans in Tunisia, Morocco, and Algeria. It had not gone well at first, and the home front had seemed to hold its breath as people read the dreary headlines.

The Allies' fortunes had improved over the spring, though; Italy's North African forces had surrendered in May, the Germans retreating from the continent. American and British generals were now free to shift their focus north, bombing Italy. If the Allies landed ground forces soon, that big Italian boot would become the next killing field.

Devon asked, "Much family over there still?"

"Some."

The boy handed a demitasse cup to Bucciano, who slid it over to Devon. The coffee was black and bitter and delicious.

"And you—Mulvey, you said? People in Ireland still?"

"Some. Going back a ways now."

"Not very nice to the Irish over in Britain, are they?"

"No, they're not."

"Yet here we are, fighting for the British. War makes strange bedmates."

"Bedfellows. The expression is 'bedfellows.'" Although he had to admit, bed*mates* did sound a lot more appealing.

"I am no fan of Mussolini," Bucciano said. "Crazy man. Only got into war because he was jealous of Hitler taking so much land. We Italians aren't so good at war. Better at love. And this." He poured himself a glass of prosecco. "I am American now, like you. I would do what I can to help you. But I don't know those men."

Bucciano took a sip, then motioned to Devon's espresso. "Good, yes? Be careful, much stronger than American coffee. No sleep for you tonight!"

"Then I'll have to do something else with my evening."

He'd walked halfway to Haymarket station when he saw a face he recognized.

Elena Wolff.

He turned, lit a cigarette while facing a shop window that offered him a reflection of the widow. *Why are you in this neighborhood, lady?* She passed him and he gave her a block, then followed.

He already knew where she was going.

He watched from a distance as she retraced the path he had just taken, right to Bucciano's. He felt jittery, not only from the espresso but from the realization that he'd been lied to a moment ago. There was a chance she was only stopping by to ask questions herself, but that didn't seem likely.

He wished he could see what was happening inside, but standing across the street would have been too obvious—the barkeep would spot him. He lingered at the end of the block, smoking in the shade.

One cigarette down—hell, have another.

Ten minutes passed. The caffeine and nicotine coursed through his veins, and if he stood still much longer he feared he'd explode.

Finally Elena emerged, tears down her cheeks, with Bucciano a step behind. He looked angry. She turned, put a finger in his chest, and screamed in what sounded like French. Then she turned again and walked away. Devon ducked into an alley so he wouldn't be seen. He heard Bucciano close the door. After a moment, he stepped back out, saw that Bucciano was gone, and followed Elena again.

He could take her aside now, tell her he knew there was more to the story she hadn't told him yet. But the tears in her eyes made him wonder how badly that would go, plus she barely spoke English. He needed to think first, plan this out. He could tell Lou what he'd seen, but his partner would only roll his eyes and say Devon was inventing a conspiracy to alleviate his boredom.

The next steps, he decided, he would take alone.

Chapter Sixteen

TARGETS

The woman at the door did not look happy to see Anne.

"Where did you get my name?" she asked. Thin and short, she nonetheless managed to project a certain ferocity as she stood in the barely opened doorway.

"The people I spoke with want to remain anonymous."

"And that's exactly how I feel."

"We could still talk, I just wouldn't use your name."

"No. We just want to be left alone."

Anne stood at the threshold of this modest house on a side street off Blue Hill Ave. A small mezuzah hung to the right of the door, the inscription in Hebrew and English. Anne had grown up only five blocks away, in what was still a mostly Irish section.

It was three days since she'd tailed Flaherty to the gas station, three days in which she'd finally managed to recruit a New York writer to help her on a story about the violence in Dorchester.

"Of course," Anne said. "We all do. But this keeps happening. And the only way it will stop is if we bring more attention to it."

"Then they'll only beat him up again."

"I promise, we won't write anything or say anything that gives away your son's identity. I'm only gathering facts. There are people who don't believe this is happening. If we present the authorities with all the evidence, they won't be able to deny it. Then, finally, some good might happen."

"What 'good'?" The woman scowled. "Our rabbi agrees with us: if we kvetch in public, all we'll be doing is putting a target on our back."

"I'm afraid that target is already there. If we stand still, we're only easier to hit."

The "we" felt awkward on her tongue, not fully earned. But the woman didn't seem to notice.

"I'm sorry, but no. We don't want to talk. Good luck."

She closed the door. Anne flipped open her notebook and wrote *Mother won't talk, scared* next to the boy's name. She jotted down what else she could glean, making a note to come back later, maybe, or find another way to get more details about this attack.

She walked down the steps and into the shade of a maple tree. Harold Meyer, the thirtyish magazine reporter from New York whom she'd finagled into helping out, watched her and shook his head.

"So the whole 'Women are more likely to talk to other women' theory didn't work out, huh?"

Ten minutes later, at another house, she and Harold sat in a small but well-appointed parlor, facing a nervous mother and her eleven-year-old son.

Harold was a writer for *PM*, a left-leaning newsmagazine. She'd met him a year ago, when he'd been reporting on the annual meeting of the American Federation of Labor. Of all the writers she'd called about the attacks in Dorchester, Harold was the only one who'd responded. In fact, he'd so loved the fact that the Boston papers were ignoring a major story that he'd jumped on an eastbound train the next day.

She still would have preferred writing this story herself, but she knew she needed his help to get it printed. Being second fiddle was better than screaming into an abyss.

Plus, loath as she was to admit it, having a man alongside her would make reporting on a case like this a bit safer.

"You don't have to talk to them if you don't want to, Jakey," said the boy's mother, Mrs. Ginsberg. She spoke with what Anne guessed was a Russian accent. Though close to the Irish neighborhood, this one was predominantly Jewish, its residents immigrants from Eastern Europe and what was now the Soviet Union.

"I *want* to tell it. I *want* them to get in trouble."

He was looking down into his lap. His mother had poured him milk but he hadn't touched it, or the plate of cookies that sat in the middle of them all, Anne and Harold with their notebooks, Mrs. Ginsberg with her hands clasped tightly.

Jake had a large bandage on his left cheek and his right arm was in a cast and sling.

"We can't promise they'll get in trouble," Anne admitted. "But the more we know about what happened, the more we can help."

"Why don't you just start at the beginning?" Harold asked.

"Me and Oscar and Joe were walking back from the grocer's." The kid spoke in a monotone. He was a few inches shorter than Anne, his voice still childlike. "We'd gone together on purpose, like Ma said. Safety in numbers and all. It wasn't even dark out yet. We were each holding a paper bag, so we had our hands full. We were halfway home, right by the deli, when these four fellows walked out."

"What did they look like?" Harold asked.

"Big. High school, at least. You know, they had to shave and all." The kid twitched with his left hand, like he wanted to grab a cookie and then reconsidered, like he didn't trust his stomach. He described the four attackers as best he could, Anne taking notes. The only unusual-looking thing about them was that one had a semicircular scar on his cheek, like a crescent moon, as if he'd once been hit dead-on with the mouth of a pipe. Anne recognized the description from Sammy's attacks. "And one of them had a baseball bat."

"What happened next?" Harold asked.

"They just surrounded us and stood real close. The one with that semicircle scar asked us if we were Jews." He breathed. Still not making eye contact with anyone. His mother sat beside him and looked like she was doing all she could not to hug him to her, trying to let him finish s⟩ this awful moment could be over with. "None of us said anything at first, so they asked again. And . . ." He sighed. "I said, 'Yes.'"

His mother finally reached an arm around him, pulling him close. He flinched as she grabbed the shoulder of his broken arm.

"It's not your fault," she said.

"I know." He was scowling to ward off tears. A battle he would likely lose. "I was just so mad. I'd heard what they'd done to Josh and I know it should have made me scared but right then I was *mad*, too. That they keep doing this and getting away with it. It's not right that we should be ashamed to say who we are. So I said it. Then they started swinging."

Over the course of the day, Anne heard stories of swastikas painted on front stoops, painted on shop windows. Anti-Jewish leaflets poking out of the mailboxes of entire neighborhoods. Windows shattered at a synagogue, a kosher butcher, a Jewish bookstore.

And countless attacks from marauding gangs of Irish teenagers and young men. Young Jake Ginsberg was only the third victim, and the first minor, who had agreed to speak to them on the record, even if it meant his name appearing in print. The other two were a sixty-two-year-old man who had been blackjacked from behind while walking to a diner and a thirty-year-old man who had tried to chase off a pack that had been beating a young boy, only to have the pack turn on him and beat him with brass knuckles. He'd spent two days in the hospital with broken ribs and a concussion.

Several people told Anne they feared that the violence would only intensify now that school was out. Several parents admitted they were trying to keep their kids indoors at all hours, a tall order in summertime, with boredom and blistering apartments conspiring to drive everyone out into the newly dangerous world.

"How could the police not know about this?" Harold asked as they walked to her car after they'd been turned down yet again. They'd managed to convince people at three households to go on the record, though, so they decided to call it a day.

"I'm sure they *do* know. But they're all Irish, too. Why should they care?"

In the midday heat, all looked normal on Blue Hill Ave. She saw a trio of boys in Sox caps walking toward the Oriental Theater, saw women (some with their heads covered by scarves, some not) running errands to the kosher butcher, the grocer, the bakery. The streetcar heading south, the herring man standing with his barrel in the shade outside a cheese shop.

"And you think a magazine story will make them care?" Harold asked.

"The one thing that's guaranteed to make Bostonians angry is being looked down on by New York. A New York–based piece about Boston police ignoring attacks will get the mayor's attention."

She hadn't yet told Harold about tracking hate-sheet pamphleteer Flaherty to that warehouse. She knew it was all connected—those sheets all but quoted Nazi talking points—but she wanted to keep some of this to herself for now. Maybe if they wrote this piece on the attacks together, she could establish enough pull to write her own story on the hate sheets. She knew no good could come of being too reliant on a man, so she had to keep some of this scoop to herself.

As she took out her car keys, Harold asked her, "I meant to ask you before. You said you grew up around here, but weren't too specific. The Jewish part of the neighborhood, or the Irish part?"

She laughed. "That's a *bit* more polite than just saying, *What are you?*"

"Reporters don't need to be polite. What are you?"

"French-Canadian is the short answer. The long answer is, my father was Catholic and my mother is Jewish, though us kids didn't know it." She got into the car; he did too, and she explained further. "We were raised Catholic, not far from here, in one of the corners of the Irish section, where they tolerated Canucks like us. We were outsiders, but acceptable. Then my father passed away when I was thirteen. About a year after that, my mother announced that some relatives from France would be staying with us for a while. When they got here, not many of them spoke English, and my mother was the translator. And I couldn't help noticing they didn't have any Bibles but did have a Talmud."

She pulled onto the road.

"So, Mother explained. Turns out I was a Catholic girl who suddenly learned she was half Jewish. Just as I was entering the awkward years. Apparently Mother had given up her faith when she married my father and they moved from Down East."

"Down East?"

"Sorry, Nova Scotia. What we call it. I've never been there myself, but my father and his brothers would go up, usually once a summer, to see family. Bring back fresh lobster and a big box of blueberries. I never really knew my mother's family growing up; she'd been an only child, and her parents passed away shortly after she married. Then my father died, and Mother's French cousins moved in, and suddenly we had a house full of immigrants who didn't speak English."

"How did that go over with your friends?"

"About as well as you'd expect. We moved within a year."

She drove them through neighborhoods she still knew well, past stores she'd patronized, even saw some faces she recognized. Anne's mother, whether from the grief of losing her spouse or the influence of her suddenly reunited relatives, or a sense of kinship in response to what was happening in Europe, started going to synagogue within a year of her husband's death. Their new neighborhood had several to choose from, many of them Orthodox, though the one her mother and her cousins attended was Reform.

Those had been hard years. Missing her father, barely scraping by financially (Anne took on a job at a laundry at night), being shunned—sometimes immediately, sometimes gradually—by her friends. And living in a new neighborhood among people with different customs. Looking back, the fact that she and her brothers learned that their mother had hid part of her identity for years, and was now inhabiting it once more, wasn't remotely the most jarring thing about that time.

They'd all dealt with it in different ways. Joe and Sammy started going to synagogue too, having been only five and seven when their father died. Anne had argued with her mother about it—she'd received Confirmation just a month before her father died—and her mother had decided not to push it with Anne. The boys had attended Hebrew school for an hour each afternoon, plus three hours on Sundays, and had modest bar mitzvahs. The stories they heard about Europe had lit a fire in Joe; he'd enlisted in the Navy even before Pearl Harbor.

Anne had accompanied them to synagogue a few times, but it never became a habit; she'd been old enough by then for joining a new religion to feel somehow wrong. She'd resisted her mother's attempts to get her to learn more about these traditions that she hadn't realized were hers; it had felt like too much, mourning her father and also learning that her very culture was different from what she'd been told before. She felt guilty about that now.

She didn't attend mass anymore, either. If going to synagogue felt false to her, like something she was somehow unqualified for, the Church felt poisoned, by the priests who, upon learning of Anne's ancestry, told her (shortly after her father's death) that maybe she'd be more comfortable worshipping somewhere else.

Being a part of two worlds had a cost. She wasn't fully of either, so she constantly felt like she didn't belong. Forever apart from the first group, an unwelcome stranger in the second. She lacked the comfort others had of simply not thinking about such things, just blending in, natural as breathing. Sometimes she suffocated on her difference, felt it catch in her throat.

She wasn't even sure if she technically was *passing* as Gentile since she'd been raised thinking she *was* Gentile.

The one benefit was that she could move between the two worlds. Her upbringing meant she could insinuate herself into places where Jews were often barred. And her surprise heritage meant she had a currency that could get her into places a typical Gentile might not be welcome, like the homes they'd been visiting all day.

What an insane time.

She had actually stopped by a church on a weekday recently and prayed, something she hadn't done in a while. She'd prayed for her brothers— Joe somewhere in the Atlantic fending off U-boats, and Sammy here in Boston, where she now worried about his safety just as much. She had realized the irony of praying to the same God as those hoodlums, sitting in possibly the very same pews they did on Sundays.

"I have to believe," she told Harold now, "that some good will come of this."

"We'll light a fire under them, don't worry."

"Yet I still find it depressing as hell."

"That's why reporters drink."

"Oh, I drink."

"Glad to hear it. How about later tonight?"

"I'm sorry, I have plans." She added a white lie that it was one of her girlfriends' birthdays. The truth was, she didn't want to muddle this project by leading him on.

"Another time, then," Harold said.

Stopped at a red light, she was lost in thought when Harold yelled, "Look out!"

Movement to her right. A tall boy standing too close to the road, another behind him. Something else that her eyes couldn't focus on because it was moving.

The windshield shattered.

Anne screamed as shards stung her cheek, caught in her hair. She shut her eyes and opened them again, saw Harold lying across the seat, head down. Glass everywhere.

She looked up and saw the kids running away. Saw the brick in her rearview mirror, resting silently in the backseat like an evil passenger they hadn't invited in.

Harold sat up, glass falling from his shoulders. "Are you all right?" he asked. She heard voices, laughter, soles tapping on the sidewalk, getting quieter.

She nodded, no words available at the moment. Harold threw open his door and ran out onto the street, turned the corner, disappeared from view.

A car honked. Someone behind her, who'd only just arrived here, with no idea what drama he had barely missed out on. Anne pulled over to the side of the road and put the car in park. Looked around for other hidden assailants, saw none.

Got out slowly and carefully, lest she slide over glass and cut herself. Touched her face, saw blood on her fingertips, but only a little. Put that same hand on the roof of the car, steadying herself.

No one had yet walked up to ask if she was okay. She wasn't sure if that was because no one had seen the incident or no one cared. She wasn't even sure how many people were out, the world fuzzy right then, her responses slow.

Footsteps running toward her. She looked up and saw Harold returning, slowing to a jog. He shook his head, which was bleeding, a cut just below his hairline.

"Lost 'em." He put his hands on his hips for a moment, catching his breath.

She offered him her kerchief even though she too was bleeding. He took it and stared for a moment, confused. "Your forehead," she said.

"Thanks." He dabbed at himself hesitantly.

"I suppose," Anne said, still mostly in shock, her voice flat, "this is another reason why reporters drink."

Chapter Seventeen

COFFEE AND A TIP

R ise and Shine Coffee on Mass Ave was one of Devon's favorite places for meetings with his spies, for reasons demographic and culinary. A few blocks south of Boylston, it catered to professionals on their way to offices in the Back Bay or downtown, but was just south enough to get local foot traffic from the black working class of the South End and Mission Hill. Meaning it was one of the few places in town whose customer base was sufficiently mixed that Devon felt he could meet with a Negro contact without arousing suspicion.

The other thing Rise and Shine had going for it were the sweetest muffins in town; the bakery got around the sugar-rationing rules due to some vote-procuring favors the owner had performed for a councilman. Devon's inside knowledge of the city's ration breakers and black marketers allowed him to indulge his sweet tooth, one of his many vices.

It was nearly lunchtime yet he bought his usual blueberry muffin and coffee, resisting the temptation to flirt with the young woman at the register, as he sought not to be memorable here.

In the very back sat James Clark, alone with a newspaper. Devon took the second-to-last seat, opposite Clark. First he took a bite of the muffin and started his second coffee of the day while reading the front page, which he'd removed from his briefcase. *ALLIES REACH NEW GEORGIA IN SOLOMON ISLANDS.*

"So what's the word, Clark?" Devon was still facing his paper, Clark staring at his.

"Folks I work with, they're not happy about what went down in Somerville last week."

James Clark was forty-two years old, born in Springfield, moved to Boston with his folks when he was ten. A World War One vet, too old for this one. Devon had plenty of white informers within the various unions at the local war plants, but he needed a few men like Clark, whose race excluded them from most unions, so he could hear any scuttlebutt outside those camps. Also, because Clark's duties at Northeast Munitions mostly consisted of janitorial work, he had a handy excuse to wander into different parts of buildings with a broom or mop, accidentally overhearing things.

It took Devon a moment to follow. "You mean that work stoppage?"

"You call it that. We call 'em 'hate strikes.'"

Whatever one called it, what had happened was that a formerly moribund textile mill that had been resurrected by the military's need for thousands of uniforms had recently hired several Negroes. In response, every white worker who'd been stationed near those Negroes had walked off the job.

Management then faced a problem: fire the Negroes and risk getting unwanted attention from the Fair Employment Practices Committee, the federal agency FDR installed to ensure equal access to war jobs, or keep the Negroes but lose all its white workers during a time of war.

It responded by assigning the Negroes new roles that would keep them out of view of the white workers, who then returned to the line.

"Well, that was unfortunate," Devon said, "but it's under control now."

Clark made a grunt that didn't sound like agreement.

"You know a guy at the plant named Abraham Wolff?" Devon asked.

"Doesn't sound familiar."

"He was stabbed to death a week ago, in the North End."

"That I did hear about."

"What did you hear?"

"Only that he got himself stabbed. Didn't get any details."

"You still going to those New Patriots meetings?" The interracial Communist group organized against hiring and housing discrimination in the city, among other things.

"When they happen. It's become a bit irregular. Seem to be dealing with burnout. Maybe people are too busy working."

Devon had encouraged Clark to join the New Patriots a few months ago, in case the group started trouble at any of the plants, but it had proven to be most untroubling in military matters and was far more interested in whether Filene's or Macy's had hired any Negroes for jobs beyond elevator operator.

"Was Wolff ever at one of those meetings?"

"Not that I know of. Got a picture?"

Devon had placed a file folder on the table between them when he sat down. Clark opened it, took a look, closed it. "He looks familiar. Maybe I just saw him around the plant."

"Anything else I should know?"

"You mean, other than those missing guns?"

"Excuse me?"

"You didn't hear about that, huh?"

This got damned difficult when you couldn't look at a man's face. Devon figured the place was empty enough, so he dropped the clandestine pretense, lowered his newspaper, and made eye contact with Clark. "C'mon, spill."

"Happened to overhear some of the suits talking about a missing crate of M-1s." Clark kept his eyes on his paper.

"When was this?"

"Talk I overheard was on Monday. I don't know when exactly they went missing, though. They definitely said the word 'crate,' not 'crates.' They said it'd gone missing, that someone had taken it. So it's just the one, I think. But that's upward of ten rifles. Management didn't mention that one to you, did they?"

If Northeast Munitions believed someone had stolen a crate of rifles, they were obligated to report that to the FBI. They hadn't.

Devon asked for more details, but that was all Clark knew. Still, it was major news.

"Let me know if you think of anything. And keep your ears open."

"Wouldn't know how to close 'em."

"Till next time," Devon said. He had already slipped his envelope of cash between the first few pages of the newspaper. He stood up, dropped the paper closer to Clark, and left, failing to resist the temptation to take another glance at the pretty young woman at the register.

Located off Charles Street at the edge of Beacon Hill, the Boston branch of the FBI was close enough to the river for its agents to smell salt and oil when the wind was southerly, and close enough to the Harbor for them to smell salt and rotting seaweed when the wind was northerly. On windless days, they mostly smelled the cigarette smoke they exhaled as they typed reports and manned the phones.

As soon as he got to his desk, Devon called McDonough and launched right into it: "So tell me about these missing guns."

"Er, excuse me?"

Devon's cigarette was burning to nothing in his ashtray while he gripped the phone, his undershirt sticking to his skin. He hoped McDonough was feeling even more uncomfortable.

"The missing guns. A crate of M-1s. I heard a rumor."

"Well, ah, you know. In times of war, there are lots of crazy rumors."

"Neil. This little relationship isn't working the way it's supposed to. I think you've made some mistakes already, but you certainly don't want to go down the path of lying to a federal agent."

"Okay, ah . . . Yes. We seem to have misplaced a crate of M-1s. We can't say definitively that they were *stolen* as such, but—"

"Did you check your closet? Under your bed? Yeah? Then I'd say a missing crate of military rifles qualifies as stolen. A theft you failed to mention to me."

"Agent Mulvey, please. I apologize. We would have gotten around to it once we were definitively sure, but—"

"I am definitively sure. When did you first notice?"

Devon heard papers shuffling. "Ten days ago."

Jesus. Devon checked his calendar and noticed something. "The day after you had that fire?"

"Yes, that's correct."

"Would someone like Wolff have been in a position to make a crate of rifles disappear? Or his pal Zajac?"

"I don't know. It wouldn't be impossible, but it would be . . . bold of them."

"Well, it would have been easier if he had a buddy start a fire as a distraction, wouldn't it?"

McDonough sighed. "In theory, yes. But as you recall, we all ruled out arson that day."

"Have you questioned your workers about the rifles?"

"When we noticed the discrepancy, we started looking into it. But we haven't gotten very far. We've redoubled our security efforts in the meantime, I assure you."

Devon questioned him about some other names he'd been monitoring, then said, "You've now had a fire, a stolen crate of rifles, and a murdered employee, all in two weeks."

"There's no reason to think any of that is related."

"Oh sure, you're just running a factory that has an *un*related crisis every few days."

Devon hung up just as Lou was walking into the office. Devon gave him the scoop.

"Huh," Lou said as he sat at his desk. He sounded almost disappointed as he admitted, "So there *is* something going on over there."

It was too much of a coincidence that Wolff had been murdered the same week that some rifles went missing. *Maybe* the events were unrelated, but at the very least they both needed to be investigated. Devon refrained from saying *I told you so,* and Lou refrained from congratulating him for doggedly pursuing the truth.

Instead, they talked out what they knew so far, Devon telling Lou about his visit to Bucciano's, and Elena Wolff's surprise appearance there. Next Devon called his contacts at BPD and made sure everyone knew that if an M-1 rifle turned up anywhere in town that wasn't a factory or an Army base, the FBI was to be called immediately.

"We should question Zajac again, now that we know about the rifles," Lou said.

"He doesn't seem the type to fold that easily. I say we get a better look at what he's up to first."

They flipped a coin to see who'd get to fill out the paperwork to have Zajac tailed to and from work every day. Devon lost, but he felt like he'd won.

Chapter Eighteen

SOBER DECISIONS

Hours after having her windshield shattered, and after filing a police report with cops who didn't even pretend to care, and after having her car towed to a shop and going to the emergency room to have her chin cleaned up (no stitches, so maybe she needn't have bothered, though Harold needed three across his forehead), Anne took the streetcar home. Ignored the looks she received from people due to her bandage. Walked slowly from her stop toward her apartment, then took a detour to Lydia's place.

Lydia's eyes were saucers. "Oh my God, what happened to you?"

Somehow Anne hadn't thought far enough ahead, hadn't considered what she'd tell Lydia, or tell anyone. The truth just came out, as did a few tears.

Lydia hugged Anne tight. "Annie, that's awful! I'm so sorry that happened. Those bastards."

Anne hadn't wanted to cry about this yet; she wanted to press those emotions away, tamp them down. Fascists preyed on weakness, expected silence. She would give them neither. But here, finally, she let go a little.

"I'm all right," she said after a moment. "It was a long day. I filed a police report, though they don't care. The car's at the shop. It should be ready in a couple days." As if the windshield were the point.

"Can I get you something to drink? You need a drink. We're both drinking. That's nonnegotiable."

Lydia lived with her parents, both of whom were at work. She fixed two gin and tonics while Anne sat on an old sofa, the same one the family had had since she and Lydia were in high school. It felt good to be fussed over, yet somehow it made her feel worse. Lydia's reaction made her realize how bad things were, how dangerous this had become. She couldn't let her mother know about the brick, would have to lie and make up some story about debris from an overpass shattering the windshield. She wanted to shrug this off, be as tough as Martha Gellhorn reporting from wartime Spain, showing her boyfriend Hemingway how it's really done.

Sometimes she did feel that tough. Other times she had to fake it.

Lydia handed Anne her drink. It was light on tonic.

They were on their second round when Anne told her about her discovery of the pamphleteer's warehouse in Somerville.

"I need you to go on an errand with me. Since my car's in the shop. I need to break into that warehouse."

"What? *No.* Are you kidding? After this happened to you?"

"*Especially* after this happened." She pointed to the bandage on her jaw. "They did this to me. They beat up my brother, and they're stirring up hate all over Dorchester. All over the damn city. Whatever son of a bitch is printing those pamphlets, he's the source of the problem—or one of them, at least. If I have a chance of shutting him down, you're damned right I'm going to do it."

Lydia was silent. Anne got up to fix a third drink.

"You don't have to come with me," Anne said as she poured. "I know that's not fair of me to ask. But tomorrow night, with or without you, I'm going."

Chapter Nineteen

THE LADY VANISHES

It was nearly evening when Devon paid another visit to Elena Wolff. She clearly hadn't told him everything her husband had been up to before his murder. Devon needed to find out what else she knew, and why she'd dropped by Bucciano's. He probably should have brought Lou on this errand, but Lou had barely spoken the last time they'd questioned her, only sneezed, a lot, and Devon sometimes felt he could get more done without him.

The neighborhood seemed unusually quiet. Minutes before nine, some women and a few men were walking home from the train station, but a strange pall seemed to hang over the street. No kids out playing, no loud radios blasting from open windows.

The inside of the building still smelled of mold. He knocked on her door. No answer. Knocked again. Called her name.

Nothing.

He tried the knob. It turned. Revealed a room that appeared emptier than he remembered. No dishes on the table. Or in the sink. No smell of food.

He closed the door behind himself and stepped in.

"Mrs. Wolff? Hello?"

He didn't smell a body. Yet. He put his hand inside his jacket, unsnapped the holster. Walked in slowly, checked behind doors.

It didn't take long to search an apartment this tiny. She wasn't here.

He tried the dressers. Some men's clothes. No women's clothes. Looked for a jewelry case or makeup, found none. Opened the enormous chest from which she'd shown him all her papers the other day. A few knick-knacks lay at the bottom, but it was mostly empty, the paperwork gone.

She'd vanished.

The neighbor lady who'd translated for him, Lucja, had said her apartment was the "second door on the left." He knocked hard and called her name.

The door opened, chain attached.

He held up his badge in case she didn't remember him, which he doubted.

"FBI. Open up, please. Do you know where Elena's gone?"

"Gone?"

"Looks to me like she's flown the coop."

She closed the door, unfastened the chain, opened it freely.

"What happened?"

"I was hoping you could tell me. When did you see her last?"

"His funeral. Two mornings ago. You sure she's gone?"

"Pretty sure. She didn't say anything about it to you?"

She shook her head. He was angry at himself for letting two days pass from the time he'd seen Elena visit Bucciano's till now. He should have come here sooner.

"How well did you know her?"

"We talked, we had tea. She worked, I work. We don't see each other too much. But I like her."

He asked her more questions, about any hints Elena may have dropped about having somewhere to go, other relatives or friends in the States, but Lucja didn't have any ideas.

He folded his arms. "The other day, when I asked you if she ever felt unsafe, the two of you said a lot but you didn't tell me what exactly she said."

"She said . . . Abraham never say he felt unsafe at work."

"But he felt unsafe somewhere else?"

She was looking at him like he was a dim-witted child and she needed to figure out the least unpleasant way to explain an unfortunate truth.

"Of course. Here."

"What do you mean, here? Her apartment? Did they fight with each other?"

"No, the neighborhood." She threw up her hands, indicating the world around them. "Here. The attacks."

"What attacks?"

"All over neighborhood. The Irish boys."

Devon felt heat rise to his face. "I don't know what you're talking about."

"Gangs, they come beat up boys, beat up old men, chase women and girls."

This was the first he'd heard about it. "How long has this been going on?"

He wondered if she knew that Mulvey was an Irish name, if that's why she had been hesitant to mention this the first time.

"Weeks. Maybe months. Some people afraid to leave houses. Just go to work, come home, that's it. No one goes to park anymore. Or to movies. Only shop in groups, go to synagogue in groups."

He thought about the empty streets outside. "Have you gone to the police about this?"

"One man did, but . . ."

"But what?"

"Police beat him, too."

Jesus. "Do you know the name of the man the police beat up?"

"No."

"Was he friends with Abraham? Did they know each other well?"

"I don't know."

"Could you find out?"

She thought for a moment, then meekly said, "I don't know."

Meaning, she didn't want to be the one to find out. She had learned that the police were to be feared, in Boston as across Europe, so why would she want to inform on them? And why would she tell anything to this government agent, a glorified cop himself? No wonder the women had seemed so nervous in his presence.

He wasn't sure how to cut through that fear. If it was at all possible to win her trust.

If he even deserved her trust.

He unfolded his arms, tried to soften his voice. "Is there anything else you can tell me about the two of them? How did they get on? Did they argue much?"

"Not good to talk bad about the dead. But . . ."

"But?"

"He wasn't good husband."

"Was he rough with her?"

A sigh. "One time I think I heard them fighting, yes. He wasn't a good man for her. I didn't understand it. She beautiful, I tell her. And smart— she speak five languages! Him, he was serious but . . . I didn't like him."

"Wait, she speaks five languages? Does she speak English?"

Lucja looked down, ashamed. "Yes."

"She acted like she didn't the other day. *You* acted like she didn't."

"She was nervous to speak to police. Said it was hard to remember right words, so I help her. Please."

He decided to let that pass, but it amplified his suspicions of Elena. He'd thought she hadn't known what he was saying that day, but she was just using Lucja as a buffer, giving herself an extra few seconds to feign ignorance while she invented the right false answers for the G-man.

"Did it look like Abraham was running around on her?"

"No. But . . ."

"But?"

"Maybe *she* was."

Elena was getting more and more interesting. "You saw her with an-other man?"

Clearly she didn't want to talk about this. He waited for a moment, then he pointed at what used to be Elena's door.

"I understand you not wanting to talk behind someone's back, but look, she's gone. Your friend took off and didn't even say goodbye to you. If you know anything else that'll help me figure out who killed her husband, now is the time to say so."

"Abraham work many nights." Her voice quieter now. "One day I come up stairs into hall, very early, see man leaving her door. She sees me see him leaving and she says, oh, he's a delivery man, or something. But her face . . . I think she was lying."

"You only saw him the one time?"

"Another time I might have . . . heard. Noises." She looked embarrassed. "When Abraham wasn't there."

God bless nosy neighbors. "How long ago?"

"Maybe three weeks before he died."

"But she never told you anything about having a man on the side?"

"No. But I could tell."

All right, this was something. He didn't know what it meant or whether it had anything to do with Wolff's job—and if it didn't, then this officially was none of Devon's business, and Lou had been right all along. But it felt good to uncover something.

Lucja said, in a quieter voice now, "And I think Abraham up to no good."

"No good, how?"

"Elena say . . ." She exhaled, as if about to take a giant leap. "Elena say they going to move to better place soon. Because of Abraham making more money. She say it in a way that I think . . . maybe not a good way to get money."

"Like they were stealing something?" His mind immediately ran to the "missing" crate of rifles Clark had just brought to his attention.

"I don't know."

"Did she say anything about him stealing from the factory?"

"No."

"Did she ever say anything about rifles?"

"No. She just . . . hint that better times coming soon. That he knew people who would help him. Help them pay for relatives, to get to America. But," and she sighed, looking down the hallway at their door, "look like better times not come."

Later that day, as Devon left the office, he was walking down Beacon Street when he heard someone call his name. He turned around and saw a uniformed cop he recognized, the older fellow who'd ribbed him when he'd arrived at the alley to see Wolff's body.

"What's the rumpus?" Devon asked. The cop's name plate read "DUGGINS."

"I heard a rumor you were at Bucciano's the other day."

"And where, pray tell, did you hear this rumor?"

"You aren't the only fella with eyes on the street."

"Maybe I stopped by. Maybe I like their, what do you call them? The cannoli."

"Their cannolis are terrible, actually."

"Good to know. And why are we talking about desserts, again?"

"I guess I figure I deserve to know why a fed is messing with them."

"'Messing with them.' That's what I was doing? According to your 'eyes on the street'?"

Duggins held a poker face for a moment. Then he looked Devon up and down. "That is a mighty nice suit. Just as nice as the one you had on the other day. Good shoes, too. Florsheims, right? Quite the hat, while we're at it. That whole getup, gee, it'd take a dumb cop like me three or four months' pay to buy an outfit like you got on."

They'd moved from desserts to fashion, and Devon was starting to understand what this was really about.

"I wasn't there for a shakedown, if that's what you're asking. I was there on official business."

"Must be nice to get that fat federal paycheck. Must be nice not to need an occasional kickback to support the family. Must be nice to look down on guys who take a little grease here and there."

Devon held his stare. Duggins was basically admitting he took bribes from Bucciano, and he was either afraid that Devon was there to interfere with his meal ticket or he was annoyed because Devon's mere presence at the place sent a message to Bucciano that Duggins wasn't protecting him the way he was supposed to.

Devon didn't care to involve himself with the petty corruption that kept the cogs in this town turning. Most cops distrusted him anyway for being a Yank-loving fed; he hardly needed to give them a new reason. But it made him even more suspicious about Bucciano's, and why Wolff might have been drinking there of all places. And what was Bucciano making payoffs for?

"Look," he said. "I've got my job to do, you've got yours. I don't much care how you go about it. If you have to get some 'grease' from businesses here and there so that you can look the other way when it comes to some things, fine. I was there to check an alibi about a murder."

"The one in the alley?"

"Yeah."

"Bucciano's family has connections. The kind that people need to be wary of, you get me? Like Leo Marcuso."

Devon was intrigued, but also insulted. "I hear you. But the FBI doesn't get scared away from a murder case because some damned gangster might have been involved."

He was hoping to sound tougher about this than he truly felt. And he was annoyed to realize this late that the owner of the restaurant was connected to the local Mafia don Marcuso. If Devon had better relationships with BPD, he might have already known this. But the FBI had never prioritized organized crime, as Hoover preferred to focus on radicals and subversives, insisting that gangsters were merely the product of Hollywood and overactive imaginations.

"I wasn't saying you should be scared off." Duggins looked left and right. "I'm saying, Bucciano's in with Marcuso, and when you're connected like that, you wouldn't waste time knifing some hebe who was in the wrong part of town. The victim was killed in an alley around the corner, right? He probably hadn't been in Bucciano's at all. I'm saying, it can't be related."

Unless someone did something stupid because they figured they could get away with it, Devon thought, since they pay off the local cops and feel untouchable.

"The victim worked at Northeast Munitions," Devon said. "What do you know about the mob messing around with the unions?"

Duggins shrugged. "I haven't heard anything like that around here. In New York, yeah, that's their new play. Getting the union dues to make up for all the money they ain't making anymore from bootlegging. But here, nah. Those wops know not to try that kind of thing in Boston. Too many of us." He chuckled confidently.

Devon didn't buy it. "Irish and Italians were in the same unions last I checked. If the mob tries to muscle in, then it becomes my problem. Since it looks like the cops aren't putting up much resistance."

Duggins folded his arms. "You want to go that route, Mulvey? You want to pick a fight with the department and find out how easy it is to do your job when the cops hate you?"

"The cops do hate me. Don't pretend otherwise." He reached into his pocket, lit a cigarette, neglected to offer one to Duggins. "I have no desire to interfere with your little sideline, whatever it is; knock yourself out. But if someone at that restaurant has anything to do with the murder of a war worker, then it'd be better for you to get in front of it than to have it look like you're covering something up. If you hear anything, you know where to find me."

He turned and let Duggins see what this fancy, expensive suit looked like walking away.

Chapter Twenty

THE CROOKED TIE

A new windshield ran Anne twenty-five dollars she could hardly afford, along with the wrath of her mother.

She wasn't shocked by the violent reception she and Harold had received, but the speed with which it had happened was surprising. The hooligans had heard about her reporting within hours—either that, or the brick was unrelated to her story and was just thrown by cruel teens preying on her because they'd guessed right that she and Harold were Jewish.

She wasn't sure which explanation was more alarming.

Carless but undeterred, she took the streetcar to meet Harold the next day. He had only a few days before he was due back in New York, so she wanted them to get as much reporting done as they could. Waiting for Harold, she stood at a street corner a block from Blue Hill Ave, by the Beth Shalom synagogue.

A man who was about to pass her on the sidewalk said, "Beautiful day, isn't it?"

He wore a half-smile that fit him as well as his gray suit and fedora. His tie was rakishly askew, the top shirt button undone, a subtle sign of independence. He seemed to know he was handsome enough to get away with it.

"Yes, it is."

He stopped in front of her. "I know you from somewhere, but I can't remember where."

"I've heard better lines." She wanted to roll her eyes but found herself smiling instead.

"No, I'm serious: you grew up around here, right?"

"Lucky guess."

"No, not lucky, we knew each other somehow. I'm going to figure this out." He held her gaze for a silent moment, which felt uncomfortable and set her heart beating faster. Then he snapped his fingers. "I got it: your brother Joey went to Saint Ignatius, right? So did I."

She nodded despite herself. "You know Joe?"

"It's been a while, but yeah, I knew him—and you. We used to have those bang-out snowball fights in Franklin Park, remember, you and your brothers and half the neighborhood? As I recall, you had excellent aim."

"I still do."

His half-smile had grown. He seemed in possession of some secret joke that lightened the edges of an otherwise dark world. It was like he was asking her if she'd like to hear it.

"I knew I recognized you. I'm Devon Mulvey." He tipped his hat. "I think you were friends with one of my sisters, either Katie or Jenny or Julia or Rebecca or Siobhan."

She vaguely remembered some of those names. Theirs had been a social neighborhood, crowded with large families, kids running everywhere.

"Anne Lemire."

A trio of men in yarmulkes walked by, one of them holding hands with a little boy whose other hand gripped a red lollipop.

"You don't remember me at all, do you?" Devon sounded a bit wounded.

"It was a while ago."

"And I wasn't that memorable. But I remember you. And Joey, I remember the time he accidentally popped one of the deacons with an ice ball, or maybe it wasn't so accidental, and then we—"

She laughed, as if he'd thrown open a curtain she hadn't realized was there and now the sun was shining on her face. "I do remember that."

"We were certain he was going to hell for it. I mean, at the time it was hilarious—I'd never heard a man of the cloth say 'Shit!' before—but then that night I asked my mother if little Joey would really be going to hell. And she *dodged the question.* Which was very alarming to an impressionable kid. I said an extra prayer for your brother that night. How is he, by the way? I don't remember him being in high school, now that I think of it. Did you move?"

"Yes. Our father died and we wound up moving in with some relatives in Ashmont." Not entirely true—the relatives had moved in with them—but she wasn't about to go into detail now.

He nodded and opened his mouth like he was going to say something, then didn't. She wondered if he was remembering even more about her family now. There was an awkward pause that she didn't know how to fill.

"Are you waiting on someone?" he asked, breaking the silence. "Any man who'd make a lady like you wait needs a serious lesson in manners."

She was used to parrying a few Cyranos when she was out reporting, but this felt different. It was that look in his eyes, the secret joke he still hadn't told her. And that damn tie. She was a perfectionist; she preferred order. She felt a strong compunction to reach out and straighten his tie, fix the top button. It was as if he knew this about her and had left it undone just to bother her.

And though part of her wanted to shoo him away, the other part of her heard Lydia's admonishments ringing in her ears. *Lighten up, Annie. Have some fun.*

"Just a work colleague," she said.

"What do you do?"

"I'm a reporter, working on a story."

"What's the scoop?" If he was at all surprised that she was something other than a schoolteacher, typist, or secretary, he didn't show it.

"It's about the violence in Dorchester. The attacks on Jews."

Finally his expression turned serious. "Really. What do you know about it?"

"I know an entire neighborhood is living in fear and the police don't care one whit. People have been put in the hospital, and I'm afraid things are only going to get worse if the damned police don't finally do their job." She thought for a moment; they weren't that far from the Irish neighborhoods where she'd grown up. "Do you still live around here?"

"No, I'm on a work errand too. I've heard a little about this, but only recently."

"Stick around after it gets dark and you'll see how bad it can get."

"That sounds like a swell date, but I can think of better things to do if you're interested."

"I really don't think it's something to joke about."

"I'm sorry, you're right. Joking is my default expression. Keeps me sane in dark times." He made a show of looking around. "Your colleague has a punctuality problem, though. If you don't think this area is safe, why are you standing out here alone?"

"There hasn't been any trouble on this particular block. Walk a few blocks south and it's a different story. I had a brick thrown through my car window the other day." She hadn't meant to bring that up at all.

He touched his sharp chin, indicating the small bandage on hers. "Is that how you got that? Are you all right?"

"I'm fine. But I'm angry. And out twenty-five bucks for a new windshield."

"Did you go to the cops?"

"Yes, and they seemed quite uninterested as they told me to have a nice day. They only took down the report when I insisted, and I bet they threw it out when I left."

"I'm sorry to hear that. Do you remember the officers' names?"

She told him. "Why do you ask—do you know them?"

"I do know a fair number of cops, but not them."

He clearly wasn't going to leave her alone until Harold showed up, out of either chivalry or the desire to talk her into a date, or both. And in truth, she didn't mind talking to him—even if she seemed to be telling him more than she meant to; he had that effect on her. She asked, "You said you were in the neighborhood for work, too. What do you do?"

"I work for the FBI."

She waited an extra beat to see if he'd laugh, admit he was joking. "Really?"

"Yeah, they let a few Catholics slip in now and again."

She felt flustered. Was there any chance this wasn't a random encounter at all, but something he'd plotted? She'd had mixed experiences with the Bureau. She'd passed them many tips about extremist organizations over the years, some of which they'd followed up on, but plenty of which they'd ignored. And some of the labor groups whose meetings she attended were being watched by the feds—more than a few union men had confessed to her that the Bureau leaned on them to provide tips and gossip. Perhaps her work or some of the meetings she'd attended had set off an alarm within the government, and *that* was Devon's secret joke?

"That sounds like . . . important work," she managed to say, uncharacteristically tongue-tied.

"Well, a lot of people are doing important work these days. You too, apparently."

She wondered if she should be worried about him. No, she told herself. Surely this was just happenstance. Perhaps she could even play it to her advantage.

"Maybe the Bureau could do something about the violence here?"

He looked uncomfortable for the first time. "Neighborhood fights aren't exactly the sort of thing a federal agency gets involved in."

"It's more than just neighborhood fights—it's an organized effort to attack one group because of the war. If someone doesn't do something to stop it soon, people are going to get killed."

He seemed lost in thought for a moment. "Maybe that's already happened."

"What?"

"No, nothing, sorry." He shook his head, like he hadn't meant to say that. "I do know my share of cops. I may have some ways of motivating them to help."

"Thank you."

Silence for a moment.

"And if you'd like to give me more details about what's been going on, maybe you could tell me all about it over dinner some time."

"You are amazingly persistent."

"Well, I assure you, I *can* take no for an answer. It just seems like such . . . an unnecessarily negative answer, doesn't it?"

"'No' is indeed negative, that's correct."

"And there's so much negativity and worry in the world right now, we could use a little more positivity in our lives."

Again she smiled despite herself. She'd never met someone so unflappable. It must be nice to be so carefree; maybe that could rub off on her. If she wanted it to.

"So, what, by saying yes to your dinner proposal, I can help make the world safe for democracy?"

He pointed at her. "That's exactly it." Then he retracted his finger into a fist. "No, wait, that's terrible. I take it back."

"You take back the metaphor, or the offer?"

"Was it a metaphor? I'm not sure. The offer still stands, though. Just in a less grandiose kind of way. Whether or not you have dinner with me will have zero effect on geopolitical events or worldwide happiness. I think. But I also think that, for a lovely woman like you to have a candlelit dinner with a gent like me, who happens to have inside information on the few restaurants in town that find ways around the sugar and liquor rationing and still manage to cook a decent meal, how can that possibly be a bad idea?"

She pretended to need an extra moment to consider this. "Well, since you mention it, I *do* have a sweet tooth that's gone unsatisfied lately."

It was possibly the flirtiest thing she'd said in her life.

He put a hand to his heart. "I would love to remedy that."

They made plans and she told him her address, again wondering if this was a terrible mistake. But this was a fellow from her old neighborhood, and he seemed harmless. Maybe she could get something out of him, both for her cause and her ennui.

Finally she saw, over Devon's shoulder, Harold rushing toward them, a block away.

"My colleague is finally here, by the way."

Devon noticed the bandage on Harold's forehead. "Geez, he got it worse than you, huh?"

"I'm afraid so."

"This is my cue to leave you alone now, right?"

She smiled. Really, she'd started smiling a while ago and hadn't been able to stop. "I think so."

"Good luck with your story, and be careful." He tipped his hat again. "I'm looking forward to dinner." With that he walked off, whistling a tune she recognized but couldn't name. It would be stuck in her head all day.

Chapter Twenty-one

THE GRENADE GAME

The day felt the slightest bit sunnier, the breeze tastier after Devon's impromptu meeting with Anne from the old neighborhood. He realized later that he'd skipped his afternoon coffee and hadn't even missed it, as there was no buzz quite like flirting with a pretty woman.

He realized he'd come on a bit strong, bordering on the obnoxious, but he'd liked the way she shot him down at first. He reflected on that later, honestly wondering how much of the attraction was due to the fact that she hadn't swooned for his badge and fine clothes the way so many other women did. She wasn't lonely or desperate, as his other conquests had been. She'd all but brushed him off at first; she had better things to do than be with a man like him, which he took as a challenge.

He was excited about their date, even though he knew it wouldn't turn into another one-night stand. Maybe *because* he knew. She seemed too sharp for that. Sharper than him, maybe. He honestly wasn't used to chatting with women like her—she seemed to be some sort of rabble-rouser, an intellectual and maybe a radical. The Bureau would not want him to date that kind of woman.

Which, again, only made her more desirable.

So he felt an extra charge as he and Lou made their way through a few hours of mind-numbing background checks across Dorchester, Boston, and Cambridge, then returned to the office to type their uninteresting findings.

After work, Devon drove back through Dorchester, east of where the

Wolffs used to live. Nearly in the Harbor now, although it was funny how you could grow up in those neighborhoods and not realize just how close the ocean was. He drove down Dorchester Avenue past the same five-and-ten stores he'd patronized as a kid in search of candy, and later he steered beneath the elevated tracks where he'd once allowed other kids to dare him to place quarters on the rails just to see what would happen. Answer: Devon almost got killed, which his friends found hilarious.

Another Catholic church appeared every ten or so blocks, and as he drove he passed many whose masses he'd attended as his family had neighborhood-hopped its way south, away from the city. Work still compelled Devon to visit here often enough, so he wasn't flooded with nostalgia so much as the comfortable sense that the past would always be exactly where he left it, some of the storefronts different and a few three-deckers repainted but otherwise the same sights he remembered.

Devon had several cops in his extended family, with cousins and uncles in stations everywhere from Worcester to Fall River, Danvers to Brockton. Officer Brian Dennigan was one of a handful of his cousins employed by the Boston Police Department. Devon was dropping by unannounced to ask him a few questions.

Devon parked in front of the white three-decker that Brian had bought a few years back. Brian's family occupied the bottom floor and rented out the other two in the time-honored manner of Dorchester-ites. Just as residents of other lands might have used timber or mineral deposits as their tickets to prosperity, in Dorchester they used the three-deckers and all the tenant income they could bring. From here he could smell the confectionary goodness of the Baker Chocolate plant on the Milton line, that wondrously thick miasma a maddening distraction during Devon's childhood, until his family had moved south of the Neponset River.

To his surprise, the door was opened not by his cousin but by Devon's sister Siobhan.

"I didn't know you were coming for dinner," she said, hugging him. She looked tired as usual.

"I didn't either."

It turned out Siobhan was there with her four children; she'd grown close to Brian's wife, Patricia, over the years. Brian worked the night shift while his wife did her patriotic duty as a painter at a shipbuilding factory in Quincy, so Siobhan had dropped by to help out. Which meant a total of eight kids were on the premises. The two older ones were listening to the radio and playing chess in the parlor, which was a mess of toys and clothes and abandoned plates, while the younger ones sounded like they were trying to kill each other in the backyard.

"Patricia's at the grocer's and Brian had to get something at the hardware store. Let's talk out back. Wine?" He accepted.

They stepped into the backyard, where it wasn't exactly quieter due to the kids, but at least they had space.

"Finally feels like summer," Siobhan said. "Too bad we can't head out to the Cape." They'd canceled the annual family trek for the second year in a row; being on a narrow slip of land surrounded by potentially U-boat-harboring waters, far beyond the city's protections, seemed an unnecessary risk.

"Next summer, hopefully."

She told one of her sons to stop throwing rocks at his cousin. The middle son switched to pinecones, which Siobhan deemed acceptable with her silence.

"I ran into someone from our old neighborhood today," Devon told her. "Anne Lemire. Remember her?"

"I think so. Bit of a tomboy?"

"Yes. Not so much of one anymore, though."

She gave him a look. "Oh really?"

"Couldn't help noticing." He grinned, looked away.

One of Devon's nephews fell down, hurt, and Siobhan lifted him to his feet and assured him he was fine. He ran off again.

"Anne mentioned her father died when we were kids, and they had to move to a different neighborhood, right around the time we did."

"Wait, I remember that. They're the family that—"

"Yeah." He hadn't been one hundred percent sure his memory was accurate, but now he was. "Kids can be cruel."

"That's life for you." Siobhan had been watching the boys, but she turned to Devon. "Wait, did you ask her out?"

"Yeah."

"Careful."

"What, because she's Jewish? Do you really feel that way?"

She sighed. "You can run around with whoever you want to, Devon. Chase that forbidden fruit. I'm just saying, if you're thinking of settling down one day, you'd be asking for trouble if you did it outside the Church."

"It's a date, not a wedding proposal."

He knew she was right, that Pop would be stunned to hear he was taking a "Christ killer" to dinner. But he hated that backward way of thinking.

Still, it made him wonder how much of his attraction to Anne was because, as Siobhan noted, she was forbidden.

They watched her little hellions in silence for a moment.

"Any news from Mike?" he asked.

"He's fine," she said. It was as though someone was pulling at the edges of her lips with great force, keeping them perfectly straight. It looked painful and he felt bad for asking.

He'd once thought of Siobhan, the third of the Mulvey girls, as the funny and wild one, but her brood had changed her personality considerably, as had the absence of her husband.

She held the stem of her wineglass with both hands as if it were attached to a balloon that might lift her away from the madness of her children, who were running in circles and screaming. She changed the subject. "Why Pop doesn't give you heaps of guilt for not settling down yet, I have no idea."

"He just sees that I'm perfect in all other respects, figures he shouldn't press."

"That must be it. You know Mother would be nagging you about it."

"And you're doing a fine job for her."

He knew she was right, though. His mother, deep into her illness, had told him one of her regrets was that she wouldn't live to see her only boy wed. He found himself thinking of that remark now, a tiny memory he'd done his best to push away. He'd assured her that he would be fine, that she shouldn't worry, but he wondered now whether he'd maybe missed her point.

He looked at his sister, saw that her expression had darkened even more. "Is everything okay?"

Long pause as she considered this.

"Mike's last two letters, Devon. They made no sense." Not looking at him. Jaw set, neck stiff. "Pure gibberish, like someone had torn out a couple of pages from the diary of a . . . a mental patient."

Mike had seen combat in North Africa, though they didn't know many details.

She was whispering, for her kids' sake. "I have no idea how a military censor let them through. Maybe they thought he was joking, I don't know . . . There wasn't even a 'Hi, darling, I miss you, and how are the boys?' Just pure . . . raving."

Devon watched the boys as they chased each other through the yard, tossing pinecones. One of the cones hit Devon in the chest.

"You're dead, Uncle Devon!" screamed Timmy, age seven—one of Devon's three godsons.

"I sure am."

"Sweetie, don't throw things at Uncle Devon."

"But we're playing the Grenade Game. If you're hit, you're dead."

"That sounds like a really great game," Devon said.

"You're supposed to lie down, Uncle Devon. When you're dead."

"Really." He wasn't about to get this suit dirty. "Well, it so happens that Uncle Devon has a special suit of invisible armor that protects him from grenade blasts."

"Oh." Timmy looked disappointed, like he'd very much been looking forward to seeing his uncle writhe on the ground in agony.

"I could have told you that, sweetie," Siobhan said to her son. "Nothing ever affects Uncle Devon."

Devon rode that out for a few seconds. Maybe Siobhan had meant it as a compliment, but it didn't feel that way. The remark stung.

Other men go to war, other men fight and get dirty, suffer and sacrifice and die. And then there's charming, two-dimensional Devon Mulvey, to whom all things are given. Everything just rolls off his back.

He wanted to tell his sister she was wrong as Timmy wandered off in search of additional grenades for his more vulnerable siblings and cousins. But he didn't know how to say it.

And maybe she wasn't wrong.

First the insults from the widow outside Christina's apartment. Then crossing paths with a very pregnant Sandra, whom he found himself thinking about a lot lately (being surrounded by little ones didn't help). And now his own sister, all but calling him shallow.

Bumping into Anne the way he had, it was as if Someone was trying to tell him something.

"Mike'll be okay, Siobhan. Probably wrote it after a bad day. He'll have all that out of his system by the time he gets back. I'm sure Dad got letters like that from his brothers in the last one."

"That doesn't help. *Jesus.*"

That had been the wrong thing to say, he realized too late. All but one of his father's brothers had died in the Great War. "I'm sorry."

"If I even brought up the subject with Pop, he'd just say, *I told you so.* As if it's our fault there's a war that some people actually have to fight."

The kids had picked up sticks and were now playing the Bayonet Game.

"Mike will be okay. He's a tough son of a bitch."

She recoiled again. "Watch your mouth around them."

"Ah, they can't hear me over all the stabbings."

They stood for a moment in what passed for silence, surrounded by rampaging children as they were.

"I'm scared he won't come back. Then I'm scared he'll come back as . . . someone else. You're so lucky you weren't sent over there."

Devon put an arm around his sister and squeezed her shoulder, wondering why he didn't feel so lucky.

Chapter Twenty-two

NOCTURNAL REPORTING

With darkness falling, Anne rode shotgun as Lydia drove them back to the Somerville warehouse where she had tracked Flaherty.

"Maybe this is a bad idea," Lydia said when they were only a few blocks away. She'd said that when they first left, too.

"Look," Anne said, annoyed at the late-stage vacillating, "if you didn't want to come, you could have just let me borrow your car."

Anne would have done this alone if necessary, but she'd figured it would help to have a lookout. And moral support. Lydia's constant worrying, however, was having the opposite effect.

They reached the dead-end street and Lydia parked at the corner. Even with the headlights still on, Anne could just barely see the warehouse. There were no house painters next door at this hour. And no car parked in the warehouse driveway.

Lydia killed the engine, killed the lights.

A few house windows were illuminated, but not many. This was as good a chance as she would get.

"So I just sit here?" Lydia asked.

They'd been over this already, but Anne repeated her instructions. *Sit in the driver's seat with the engine off. Keep watch. If a car approaches and parks anywhere near the warehouse, honk the horn twice. I'll hear it and sneak out the back door.*

They heard a dog barking, but not too close by. Anne wore black slacks, a long-sleeved black top, and her quietest pair of shoes, ratty things she'd once worn quahogging. Inside a large knapsack she carried a notebook, a flashlight, and a camera.

Her heart was pounding. She thought about the brick those hooligans had tossed at her. Could have decapitated her. They would have laughed if it had.

"If I'm not out in ten minutes, beep the horn twice."

Finally she would get something done. Her day had been disappointing and unproductive thus far. She and Harold had spent a few more hours knocking on doors, with little to show for it. They'd been without Anne's car so couldn't cover as much ground, and had been extra mindful of their surroundings, proceeding more cautiously than before. They didn't seem to be followed, but they'd got only one young man to agree to speak to them. Everyone else declined to go on the record or outright refused to talk. After the third person in a row had explained that her rabbi had instructed her not to talk to journalists, they decided to visit the synagogue and hear it from the man himself.

"I appreciate what you're doing," Rabbi Horowitz had told them in his office at Congregation Beth Jacob. He was a portly man with gray hair, a closely trimmed gray beard, and the measured tone of one who chose his words carefully. "I see that your heart is in the right place. But I think you should reconsider this whole enterprise. It will do more harm than good. What I am thinking about, from the moment I get up in the morning until the moment I fall asleep at night, is how to do good and alleviate harm for my people. And I believe calling greater attention to these troubles would only make us a bigger target and create more harm."

Because Anne had been expecting that, she'd had her retorts ready.

"With all due respect, Rabbi, we've met with people who tell us they're too afraid to leave their own homes. We can't just expect people to . . . put up with this."

"Which is why we're organizing a neighborhood protective association. Some men who have been serving as air raid wardens and auxiliary police are going to be walking the neighborhood at night, in pairs or in groups. As bad as these incidents have been, it's mostly been teenagers causing the trouble, and I think they'll reconsider when they see us out in force."

Anne had friends at various Jewish organizations, like the American Jewish Congress and the Anti-Defamation League; she'd worked with them often when she'd run the Boston Center for Democracy. She'd never met Rabbi Horowitz before and had heard he was reluctant to get involved in what he called "politics."

"That's good to hear," she said. "But I still think it's important to get the word out that things here have deteriorated to the point where—"

The rabbi held up a hand, smiling slightly to ease the sting as he interrupted with, "I appreciate that *you* think it's important, but I don't agree. And to be frank, it's easy for you to say things like that, less so for us. We are living in a very delicate situation, miss, not just reporting about it."

She had been expecting that too, but it didn't make it any easier to hear. She'd noticed that the local Jewish paper, the *Advocate*, had reported on some of the attacks, but in a matter-of-fact way, as if they were random muggings.

"I have skin in the game too. My brother's been beaten up, twice. We only live a mile away. And although I was brought up Catholic . . . this affects me too."

"Someone threw a brick through her car window yesterday," Harold added. He too was Jewish, but as he wasn't local he didn't seem to feel it right to play that card here.

"As I said, I appreciate the fact that you think you're doing the right thing. And that you're willing to shoulder a burden. But I am asking you, on behalf of this community, to stop."

She'd felt dispirited after the meeting, not least because they had almost exhausted their list of names to visit. Without help from someone who knew more about the attacks, they'd never be able to write their piece.

"Let's call it a day," Harold had said, just past noon.

"The rabbi doesn't call the shots for everyone," Anne said. "I'll call my contacts at the AJ Congress and the Anti-Defamation League and see if I can find someone else who wants to be more helpful."

She'd spent the afternoon on the phone, leaving messages and getting nowhere.

She also used the time to pursue the next piece she'd pitch to Larry, the rumor that Italian gangsters were swarming the waterfront and preventing our ships from safely leaving Boston Harbor. She hadn't turned up much there either, but surely it was only a matter of time.

Hours later, Anne's feet were silent and no guard dogs gave her away as she crept toward Flaherty's warehouse. The occasional bird told his friends to go to sleep. Brahms emanated from an open window somewhere.

The warehouse itself was silent, its lights off. She tried the front door, found it locked. She thought about shining her flashlight in through the windows but was afraid she'd be spotted, so she slowly walked around the building.

It seemed some old mill building for an industry that had moved to another part of the state. The land around it was untended and in need of clearing. The grass and some shrubs made noise as she pushed her way through. When she felt hidden from view, she shined a light into a side window, but she could barely see anything.

Around back was a decaying loading dock. A few old crates lay in heaps. She reached the back door and turned the knob. Locked, too. Damn it. Break a window with a rock? How loud would that be?

Before taking that step, she checked the far side, which faced not another house but some woods. More windows. One of which wasn't shut all the way. At the bottom were two inches of space, either for ventilation or because it was busted. She tried to push it higher. Didn't work.

Back to the loading dock. She carried a crate to the side window. Standing on the crate, she had better leverage. She took a breath and pushed until the window gave. She got it open just enough to crawl through.

She'd put herself in odd and borderline-dangerous situations before, but this was something else. A story to tell, if only to the right people. A crime, technically. Which made it more fun.

Before climbing in, she shined her light. Mostly the space was empty. More crates here and there, and two card tables with thin wooden chairs around them. But in the rear was what she was hoping to find: two printing presses.

She climbed in, landing hard, as the ledge was high. It felt spooky to be in a dark and strange place at night, more so because it was so filthy she figured rats or possums must make their homes here. But she didn't want to turn on a light and give herself away.

By flashlight, she inspected the printing presses. The first was an older model, nothing like what she'd seen even at some of the small fly-by-night local newspapers she'd worked for in college. She smelled ink and oil and cigarette smoke. Also chlorine, which was odd. And alcohol.

The second press looked newer, a different shape than she'd seen before. Beside the presses sat a number of boxes, some of which held pamphlets she recognized. Even in the ones that were new to her, the headlines and cartoons carried the same sentiment. She propped her flashlight on a card table and tried to angle it like a mini spotlight, then she took a couple of pictures, hoping they'd come out.

On another folding table she found stacks of papers of a different shape than the pamphlets. She stepped closer and shined her light. Stared for a moment, confused.

Ration stamps. Sheets and sheets of them.

She picked one up, felt the tackiness on the back side in the humid air. Looked hard, tried to tell the difference between these forgeries and the real thing, couldn't see it. She was no expert, but these counterfeiters seemed to know what they were doing.

Anne wanted to scream. The same people who printed hate sheets about Jews, and spread rumors that Jews wouldn't fight, that Jews were war profiteers and got an unfair share of ration stamps—these same bigots were printing their own bogus stamps. Maybe they used them themselves, but more likely they sold them on the black market.

Beside another pile of papers sat a notebook. She opened it and saw names and dates, dollar amounts. The handwriting was poor, but she saw that they were business names: butchers, grocery stores, florists. One of the entries she recognized: Gold's Gas, the gas station where she'd tailed Flaherty the other day.

Wait—of course. That's why the man at the gas station had been so alarmed when he'd seen Anne glancing at the envelope. She'd gone there because she thought he was passing out hate sheets, when really he was involved with counterfeit stamps. One was legal but revolting, the other illegal.

She was surprised that anti-Semites would sell to a Jewish proprietor. Maybe they were too stupid to realize Gold was Jewish, or maybe simply willing to make money off anyone.

She turned to the start of the notebook and saw what looked like a series of slogans, as if some copywriter were testing his lines. *"The Christian Legion is dedicated to freedom and patriotism. The Christian Legion is united in fighting the dangers of Judeo-Bolshevism. The Christian Legion is our last chance to save America from destroying itself in a mindless war."*

She'd encountered various fringe groups over the years, and though "the Christian Legion" sounded familiar, she hadn't heard the name in a while; she'd need to check her notes later.

Beneath the notebook was a small stack of exercise magazines with various pieces of notepaper sticking out, on which someone had scribbled schedules for different workouts, running, and "drills." She knew this could be as harmless as someone's personal resolution to get in shape, but at its worst it looked like some sort of quasi-military training program.

"Don't move." Two words, spaces between them. Gritted teeth.

Anne jumped and let out a scream.

She turned and saw the shadow creeping toward her.

Then a click and light. A rope dangled in the air, attached to an overhead bulb he'd illuminated. Not Flaherty but another man, some Houdini who apparently could appear out of nowhere or walk through walls. Holding a gun aimed at Anne's chest.

Where had he come from?

"I'm sorry, I must have made a mistake."

"Yeah, you did." His eyes hard, his manner frighteningly blank. She could smell booze on his breath even from this distance. "Drop the flashlight."

He stepped closer.

"I'll scream again," she said. "Louder. Someone will hear me."

"Then I'll shoot an intruder and it'll be a short scream."

She could shine the flashlight into his eyes, hope to buy herself a second or two. But she needed more than a second to get out the back door. And firing a gun was so easy.

Anne dropped the flashlight.

He stepped back and motioned to one of the chairs. "Have a seat. I got a call to make."

Chapter Twenty-three

FAMILY BLUES

"What brings you to the neighborhood?" Devon's cousin asked after he'd returned from his errand and the men retreated to a tiny bedroom Brian had converted to an office.

"I was wondering if you might have some information that could help with a case. A worker at one of the plants I keep tabs on was stabbed to death in the North End." He outlined the when, where, and how. "Anyone in the neighborhood been talking about it?"

"Why would people around here know about a knifing in the North End?"

Brian was a few years older than Devon, meaning he had thrown elbows at his younger cousin on the basketball court and pitched baseballs into his back. By high school, Devon's family had moved to tonier Milton and he hadn't seen as much of his cousins except at the big holidays, like Christmas, when he and his sisters were warned by their parents not to comment on the relative largesse of Santa at different households.

"He lived in Dorchester. A few blocks off Blue Hill Ave."

"The kike part of town."

On the one wall that wasn't mostly a window, Devon saw a framed photo of a younger, thinner Brian with his arm around his former partner, both of them in their BPD blues. Danny McNulty, Devon had heard, had died in North Africa a few months ago.

"Yeah. He was a Jew. An immigrant."

"So you're wondering if someone from around here, what, followed him to the North End to stab him?"

"Just wondering if you'd heard anything. I've heard rumblings about gangs of Irish kids raising hell against Jews around here."

Brian's smirk rolled into a smile. "What of it?"

"Is it true?"

"Are you asking me if kids get in fights? Of course. Plus, there's a god-damn war on. You know, passions run hot."

"Except, we haven't declared war on the Jews."

"Maybe we should've."

Devon realized he'd handled this wrong. Perhaps a savvier questioner would have known a more oblique way to bring this up, taking Brian out drinking, asking him after a few.

It was depressing to realize just how entrenched his family's bigotry was. He too had been raised thinking that Jews were different, that they had betrayed Jesus and couldn't be trusted. It wasn't until Harvard that he interacted with Jewish students—many of them from hardscrabble backgrounds—and came to realize that the stories his father had told him were bunk. The few times he'd brought this up with Pop, he'd been accused of forgetting who he was, letting the Yankee establishment put silly ideas in his head. So he mostly kept his contrarian opinion to himself.

He wasn't sure whether such bigotries were getting worse because of tensions about the war and communism, or if he was just noticing it more because he felt he'd stepped beyond them. Pop was right that college had put ideas in his head, but Devon didn't feel that was a bad thing.

"The victim was named Abraham Wolff," Devon said. "You wouldn't know if anyone had gotten in a fight with him around here, if he'd tried to make a police report but the desk officer wouldn't do it? Maybe someone had him marked as a rat."

"We got more important things to do than worry about kids getting in fights, Devon. Who knows why some blabby kike got stabbed? We both know, no way in hell did some Irish kids go all the way to the damned North End to kill a Jew. They wanted to do that, they'd do it here."

"And have they?"

"What?"

"Have there been any killings around here I should know about?"

"I know how to police my beat, Devon. Jesus, why does this even concern you? Sounds like a BPD matter to me, which means *real* cops should be working on it. Not you college boys."

It always came back to that. Devon stood. "Sorry I bothered you, Brian. You're right, I should just talk to some real cops."

He had turned his back when he heard his cousin say, "They conned us into this war. A war for Hebrew bankers, like the last one." Devon turned back around and saw that Brian was looking at the photo of his departed partner. "They have Danny's blood on their hands, Devon. You know that, right?"

How do you contradict a full-grown man who suddenly seems on the verge of tears? Devon simply said, "Good seeing you, Brian." Then he exited through the parlor, where a group of unusually quiet kids surrounded the radio, rapt with attention as The Shadow duked it out with war profiteers.

He walked outside and stood on the top step, words ringing in his ears. *Some blabby kike.* Did Brian know Wolff after all? Had the man's mouth gotten him into trouble somehow? Or was that just another casual insult from a small-minded bigot, that Jews talked a lot?

As he stood there, a young man headed up the walkway. It took Devon a moment to realize it was Brian's eldest son, Johnny.

"I almost didn't recognize you." Devon marveled at his nephew. "You're nearly as tall as me now. That nonsense needs to stop."

"Sorry, Uncle Dev." Johnny smiled. The kid had nicked himself shaving, too.

"Soon you'll be able to grow a beard and cover up that scar."

"That'd be nice." Three years ago Johnny had been helping his father load junk into the rear of Brian's truck when a heavy pipe whacked the boy in his right cheek, nearly puncturing it and creating a perfect crescent moon of a scar.

"Just make sure you don't commit any crimes." Devon winked. "Makes you too easy to identify."

Chapter Twenty-four

THE TYPEWRITER

A nne sat in the chair as instructed.

At the table were cards, slips of paper, notebooks, a typewriter, ashtrays. The man kept his gun aimed at her heart as he stepped backward.

Her bag was a few feet away, where she'd put it on the floor before realizing there was another person here. Even if she could reach it, though, it held no weapons.

"Don't even think of getting up," he said when he was a good fifteen feet away. He reached the far wall, where a telephone sat on another small table. He picked it up, taking his eyes off her for a moment to see the numbers on the rotary as he placed a call.

Lydia was outside keeping watch and keeping time. She hadn't beeped the horn in warning because this man hadn't driven up—he'd already been here. Anne hadn't thought of that possibility. No car, dark windows, just a warehouse and not a dwelling. Why had he been *sleeping* here?

How long would it take Lydia to realize something was wrong?

The man said into the phone, "Hey, it's me. We got a problem . . . A Peeping Tom. Actually, a Peeping Sally . . . Yeah . . . No, not yet . . . Good news is, she's young and pretty. We could have some fun . . . Yeah . . . Something for a gag. And your handcuffs . . . Got it." He hung up.

Anne's mouth went dry as she imagined the horrors he'd hinted at.

Also, *handcuffs*? Who owned handcuffs but cops? Was his friend a cop?

He walked back over to her. "Shuffled" was more like it. He'd had a bit to drink, smelled of it too. She figured a door in the front must lead to an office of some sort; she wasn't sure if he had drunk himself to sleep at a desk or if he actually lived here.

He leered at her, eyes wandering all over her body. "What are you doing here?"

"I just . . . wanted some pamphlets." Usually she thought of better lies.

"Really."

"I didn't feel like buying them, felt I should just take them. I see that was wrong, and I'm sorry."

"Bullshit. What are you, really? A reporter? A Jew?"

She figured he wouldn't respond well to "Both," so instead she asked, "Who did you call?"

"Buddy o' mine."

"A policeman?"

"That's who you call to report a crime, ain't it?"

She wondered if he'd really called the police or if he was only trying to scare her. If it was the latter, it was working quite well.

She wanted Lydia to beep the horn, spook him into looking out the window or stepping outside. Lydia would honk twice at the ten-minute mark.

She wasn't even sure what Lydia could do. Call the cops? That would be a good idea, in normal circumstances, but not if one of these men *was* a cop.

"You don't have the right to keep me here."

"Sure I do. You're trespassing. Up to no good. Citizen's arrest."

"And you're printing counterfeit ration stamps."

"Who says they're counterfeit?"

"I thought it was only Jews who took advantage like that. Isn't that what your pamphlets say?"

"Yeah, you're a reporter, all right. You all think you're so damn smart. You never write the real truth, only this rah-rah stuff. You need us to set people straight."

"By 'us,' you mean the Christian Legion?"

"So you've heard of us."

"Not much, honestly. But I'm sure you're the same as the other crackpots that got put away."

"Tough talk, girlie. You'll see what we're like when my friend gets here. We'll show you what kind of fellows we are."

Anne didn't believe in miracles. But as the man backed up a step and lowered himself toward a chair on the opposite side of the card table, all the while keeping his eyes and his gun on her, he misjudged the distance between ass and chair. Or divine intervention caused his chair to move. Either it was a miracle or it was drunkenness.

He disappeared from view and she heard the chair hit the cement floor. Heard the gun land as well.

"Ow! Fuck."

Shocked, she sat there a full second—but only the one second—before realizing what to do.

She stood up, lifted the typewriter. One of Royal's smaller models, which she'd worked on many times. Narrow, but still heavy. She stepped around the card table. He was sitting, one palm flat on the floor and the other hand reaching for the table to steady himself.

She lifted the typewriter over her head and brought it down on his.

The Royal broke into pieces. Consonants and vowels flew off. The carriage return popped to the side and the entire contraption slipped from her grasp. It fell, as did he.

He groaned, still conscious. Maybe she hadn't hit him as hard as she could have.

She saw the gun on the floor. Farther away than she would have thought. On the other side of where he lay.

He must have seen it too, because he was crawling toward it.

Slowly.

She stepped around him, reached down, picked the gun up. He was still groaning. She'd never held a gun in her life, let alone fired one, but she knew you were supposed to thumb the hammer back, or at least that's what they did in Westerns. It clicked.

He was on all fours. The face staring at her already looked less than human. Forehead covered in blood, some of it dripping down the length of his nose. Greasy hair disheveled. She caught another tangy whiff of his breath and his white eyes were wide and he was only a couple feet away.

It would be so easy, she realized.

So easy.

A car horn beeped twice. Lydia—ten minutes were up.

Anne blinked, told herself to breathe. *Do not shoot him.*

The man's head seemed to constrict, as if he were a turtle trying to protect himself. Then he collapsed onto the floor, like she'd actually pulled the trigger.

She stared at him. Was he only unconscious? Yes: his back rose and fell, slightly. His lurch toward the gun had exhausted his energy. She couldn't see his eyes, only his hair and scalp and some of his bloody forehead. How hard had she hit him? Could she have broken his skull; was he dying right now?

She staggered back a few steps. Her entire body started shaking.

"Oh my God. Oh my God."

Two more horn beeps. Lydia impatient.

She heard another car, closer. Tires on gravel. Just outside the warehouse.

That's why Lydia was honking. The man he'd called. Maybe a cop. A dirty cop.

She needed to run. Out the back door. Wait, where was her bag? Her flashlight? She looked around the room as she heard a car door close. There, her bag. She ran toward it, picked it up. The flashlight too, turning it off and dropping it into her bag.

Her camera? There, over by the phone he'd used. Closer to the door leading to the front. Meaning closer to where the man in the car might be entering at any moment.

She ran to the camera, slung the strap around her neck. Missed somehow. Jesus, she was shaking so hard the camera strap felt complicated, impossible. She needed to put the gun down before she shot herself. She stuck the gun in her bag and this time got the camera strap around her neck.

Footsteps on gravel. *Hurry.*

She ran toward the back door. Surely they wouldn't be coming through the back. How many were they? Had she heard a second car door shut? She couldn't remember, had been too flustered.

Nearly at the back door now.

Thinking: escape, survive, get to tomorrow.

Thinking: I may have just killed a man and my fingerprints are all over this room.

Thinking: Lydia, please don't drive away without me.

She turned the knob. Leaving more prints. It turned but the door wouldn't budge. Wait, that's right, she'd come in through the window. The back door was still latched, stupid.

She unlatched it. Stepped into the night. Closed the door as quietly as she could.

Listened. Crickets. Faint Brahms like before. Otherwise nothing.

A creaking door. The man was inside the warehouse now.

Shining her flashlight might have helped, but it would give her away.

She took a few steps, trying to remember her way, but realized she couldn't go the way she'd come, as that would have led her to the front of the building. Too close to where the newcomer was. If there were two of them, one might even be waiting outside.

Deeper into the woods. Her eyes weren't adjusting to the dark fast enough, as if the dark was adjusting back. The night had turned cloudy—no natural light. She was a nosy child in a fairy tale approaching the bloody climax. Thorns tore at her arms.

She stopped, listened. Didn't hear anyone giving chase. Yet. She moved to her left now, making her way not on any trail, just walking through shrubs and beneath tree boughs. Soon the woods ended and she was in an untended area between two backyards. Hopefully no one could see her. She kept moving, crouched down, the camera bouncing against her side, the gun still hidden in her bag. Keeping her head lowered, she made her move, through the yard of a dark house, then down its driveway.

Across the street: Lydia's car. Lights off. Lydia's silhouette just barely visible at the wheel.

She ran toward it. Tapped on the window, more loudly and furiously than she'd meant to.

Lydia screamed. Hand at her heart. Then she leaned over and unlocked the passenger door.

"What the hell happened?" Lydia whisper-shouted as Anne got in.

"Just drive and I'll tell you. Quickly!" Her own hands shaking.

Lydia started the engine. The headlights shined all the way down the street, to the warehouse. In front of it sat a parked car, not a police car but a black sedan of some kind. She would later wish she had made note of its license plate, but she didn't think of it then, she simply thanked God that she didn't see someone standing out there, didn't see another man with another gun.

"Don't turn around down there, just do a three-point turn here. *Quickly.*"

"All right, all right." Lydia did as told. "Annie, what happened?"

"There was a man in the building. I didn't see him at first. He . . ." She shook her head.

"He *what*?"

There: a police car coming toward them on the other side of the road. *Jesus Christ.* No flashing lights at least, just driving like normal. Too dark to see the men inside it, nothing but two silhouettes. Anne realized she wasn't breathing as the car passed them.

"Annie?"

"Just keep driving but don't speed." She turned around to watch the squad car drive away—it didn't turn to follow them. But it did drive down toward the warehouse.

Somerville scrolled by, not quickly enough.

"Is anyone following us?" Lydia asked a moment later.

Anne kept turning around, again and again, risking vertigo. "No."

Mass Ave, and eventually Harvard Square.

It was ten long, long minutes before she felt confident that the cops wouldn't be coming for them, that they were out of danger.

"Are you going to tell me what happened?"

"There was a man in the building. He snuck up on me. He tried to keep me there." She spat the sentences out quickly, not even believing them herself. "Then I . . . I got away. Hit him over the head and he passed out."

"Oh my God, Annie! Are you . . . Are you hurt?"

"I'm okay." At a red light, she looked into her bag and wondered what she should do about the gun. She reached into the bag, took the weapon out.

"Is that a gun?!" Lydia scooted as far away as she could. "You brought a gun?"

"I didn't bring it. He had it."

"How did you . . . ?"

Behind them a horn honked. Anne told Lydia the light was green.

Lydia hit the gas. "I'm going to pull over. Then we can talk and think this out."

"No! We need to get as far away as we can. Then I'll throw this in the Charles."

Silence for a block. Then two blocks.

"Why do we need to throw the gun in the Charles? You didn't . . . use it, did you?"

"No." She hadn't explained that she'd clocked the man with a heavy typewriter. She didn't want to voice it aloud, and she was afraid Lydia would be even more horrified to learn Anne had possibly killed a man.

She felt a sudden wave of nausea as that reality hit her. She forced herself to breathe.

Reaching into her purse again, she took out a handkerchief and started rubbing at the gun. Was that all it took to remove prints? She hoped so.

"Jesus!" Lydia screamed again as she slammed on the brakes.

Anne slid in her seat and nearly bumped her forehead into the windshield. The light was green, but four young men in sailors' whites were crossing Mass Ave. Judging from their wobbly gait, they were loaded. Two of them stopped in the middle of the road at the sound of Lydia's screeching tires. They didn't look afraid, just curious. When one of them realized two women were inside, he waved and puckered his lips. The others stopped too.

Anne leaned out the window, letting her gun hand dangle. "Get the hell out of our way!"

"Fuck!" one of them yelled, and the four sailors split up, running pell-mell to opposite sides of the road.

Lydia hit the gas again. "Was that a good idea?"

Anne didn't answer. Because she didn't want to admit that, *No, that wasn't a good idea, in fact it was quite stupid.* But the sailors had seemed drunk enough that they wouldn't remember her. Hopefully.

She rubbed the gun again, hoping she could so easily erase all her bad decisions.

Chapter Twenty-five

THE CONTINUAL REFUGEE

There was a strange man smoking on the corner outside Elena Wolff's new apartment.

She'd moved to Lowell, less than an hour's train ride from Boston. The factories here desperately needed more workers, so it had been no trouble finding a new job.

She had arrived three days ago, staying at first with a cousin she barely knew. When Elena and Abe had first reached America, her cousin Marta had come into Boston on her one day off to meet them. After that, they had merely exchanged a few letters and never met up again. But when Elena needed a place to run—always running, always escaping— Marta's apartment was the only destination she could think of.

She wondered if she was safe here. Probably not.

She and Abe had listed Marta as their financial sponsor when they'd first applied for a visa to get out of France. Surely the American government still had those records; not her current address, as Marta had moved apartments twice since then, but Elena imagined government agents wouldn't have much trouble finding her. Assuming they were looking.

Did that explain this man smoking on the street corner? He wore a crisp white shirt and held a suit jacket draped over one arm. A finer outfit than on any other man in this neighborhood. He reminded her of that agent who had questioned her, though this man was different. Graying hair, glasses.

Surely he wasn't here for her. She was just imagining things.

She was on her way home from her second day of work, spotting him when she was two blocks away. She looked down, stopped. He hadn't seen her yet, she didn't think. She could always turn and walk away. Maybe at the next intersection.

Elena hadn't done anything illegal, had she? Something *wrong,* yes. Certainly. But not *illegal,* she didn't think. This was how she consoled herself, somewhat. Even though, in her heart, she knew it was her fault Abe was dead.

Maybe they *should* come for her. She deserved to be punished. Deserved to suffer.

She'd run here, fleeing from the memories of their life together, fleeing from the guilt, but she knew she couldn't escape it.

Her tears of grief had been genuine, even if she hadn't loved her husband in a long while. The feeling of sickness in her stomach, her inability to sleep, the sense that life was a series of doors that closed on her. The apartment had seemed even darker than before, the shadows outside more threatening. After the initial shock, she realized she was mourning her own past, her doomed childhood, her hopes that she could eke out true happiness somewhere. And yes, she mourned the man she'd once thought Abe was, the man she thought she'd married.

Theirs had never been a passionate love, never all-consuming. But he had seemed safe, and decent, and kind enough. In truth, how many options had she had? When he'd told her he had a way out of Germany, an opportunity near Paris, with extended relatives who could put them up for a time, it had seemed the smartest choice. It had meant leaving her widowed father behind, but he told her to do it, that he'd do the same in her shoes.

So she'd married a man she liked well enough, using him as her ticket out of Nazi Germany.

They'd lived in France for three years before he told her his new plan. America. She had made friends in France, had taught German to schoolchildren and liked her job, but he insisted they pull up stakes and start over once again. The Nazis were still coming; they hadn't fled far enough. America had more opportunity, he assured her. He had friends who had crossed the ocean, insisting life was better over there, and if they left now they could get out before the storm troopers appeared.

He'd been right, of course. Hitler invaded France only three months after they left, validating Abe's decision. Still, the fact that he'd *made* the decision for her rankled, another rift opening in the relationship. The few times that he noticed how unhappy she was in America, he would simply remind her of how they'd be so much worse off in France, sent to some work camp no doubt. As if him being right was all that mattered.

It *was* all that mattered, he said. They were alive.

But she didn't feel alive. Hadn't since arriving here.

Whenever she argued with him, he'd say she was taking out global concerns on him, as if the war were his fault.

Maybe the relationship would have had a better chance had it not been born of war and terror, flight and escape. She'd heard old stories and legends where the opposite was true, dashing tales in which danger heightened the romance, made life magical. That was not the case in the real world. War meant not having the luxury to relax into love. A poverty of the heart. Fear making you so focused on survival that anything else was extraneous.

She was glad she'd never gotten pregnant, even if that also worried her. The fear that something was wrong with her kept her up some nights. But at least she wasn't left to fend for a crying child alone, didn't have a piece of Abe along with her when she was finally rid of him.

She wasn't sure if this cold observation meant she was still in shock, or if a lifetime of shocks had made her too calloused to care for anyone else.

In Lowell she was stitching for the American Parachute Company, working with other women on a device that seemed beyond imagining. She'd never flown. Yet there were men who were flying all across Europe, all over the Pacific, and when things went wrong—as surely they often did?—this contraption would somehow save them. It seemed wrong for her to be paid for this, paid to make a device that couldn't possibly work.

She imagined all the men hurtling through the air, the parachutes opening above their heads and doing nothing, the men falling ever faster. Every death another mark on her soul.

Despite this, war paid. So many people making money. Even her husband, not only from his paycheck at the munitions factory but from his little scheme on the side. The scheme she knew was a terrible idea. She'd warned him, told him not to do it.

Perhaps she should have told that government agent the truth, what Abe had been up to. But then what? Might they have held that against her, too? Sent her away, or put her in jail? Even if she hadn't been the one who broke the law, they'd find a way to punish her, as the people in charge always did.

That, and the fact that she didn't want to impugn Abe's name. Despite how cold their marriage had become, she still didn't like the idea of telling anyone what he'd done. Didn't want people thinking of him as a lawbreaker, some *criminal*.

Better to let him be remembered as a victim instead.

She wished she had found a way to visit Zajac, tell off that son of a bitch. He hadn't even shown up for the tiny funeral. Other workers had pitched in some money for the burial, for a short ceremony, but Zajac hadn't even made an appearance. She hadn't liked him before—she blamed him for Abe's wrongdoing—but his cowardice made her hate him all the more.

The fact that she'd needed such handouts for the funeral was galling. So much for Abe's big moneymaking scheme. *What* money? Where was it when she needed it?

The strange man still stood at the corner. He was nearly finished with his cigarette.

She decided to stand at the intersection a block away, pretending to window-shop. Keep an eye on him. If he kept standing there in front of Marta's place after he'd finished his smoke, she'd know something was wrong.

So many things were wrong.

It was amazing how thin the parachutes were. Almost like silk dresses. And this was expected to save men's lives? They were fools.

She had to admit, the idea of parachuting into something new did not seem foreign to her. Paris, Boston, and now Lowell. She wondered how long she would stay. Maybe coming here had been a terrible idea, but where else? The city was disappointingly small and bedraggled. She'd known it was a lesser burg than Boston, but it was the most convenient escape she could devise. She knew so few people, had vanishingly few possibilities for true escape. She remembered the excitement she'd felt about moving to Paris, the glamour of being in the metropolis. That proved short-lived; she'd soon learned that being in a big city when poor was anything but exciting.

Now she was in a small city, and even poorer.

The other problem with moving again: if her father or any of her other relatives back in Germany wrote her a letter, she might not receive it.

She'd heard the stories of the roundups, the camps. She hadn't wanted to believe things would get *that* bad. But she hadn't received a letter in more than a year.

Her previous job had been at a grocery store half a mile from their apartment, and perhaps that meager position was what had doomed her.

She'd chosen it because a kindly, German-speaking neighbor had told her about it. Elena had been bored staying in the small apartment while Abe worked, and though they were surviving on his wage, extra money might help them get into a better apartment. The neighbor knew a grocer who'd been complaining about how hard it was to find honest workers. Elena nervously visited the store with her one day, met the voluble old man, also an immigrant, who needed help at the front register and someone who could do bookkeeping as well as random odd jobs.

The grocery only needed her for three shifts a week, just enough time to keep her occupied. Adding figures, double-checking accounts, stocking shelves. Learning more English as she went. She listened to the mothers who chatted with their children as they shopped, reading their shopping lists out loud, many of them so pleased to be buying items that

would go with meat they'd buy at the butcher's down the block, practically bragging about the cuts they could afford now that people were
working again.

And then she met him.

The strange man finished his cigarette, dropped the butt, stepped on it.

Elena had been pretending to be very interested in the flower ar-
rangements in the florist's window. Every so often she turned her head
just enough to see if the smoking man was still there, and he was. And
now he wasn't even smoking.

Who could he be? Another government agent tracking her down,
possibly. Or one of the Italians. Or someone else Abe had run afoul of.
She knew so little of Abe's scheme, realizing now that there must be
more tendrils than she could understand, so many ways her husband's
misdeeds could reach out and harm her.

It was her fault. She'd started things with the delivery boy. She'd slipped
off a stepladder and he'd caught her. The fall was an accident, but what
she did next wasn't.

She'd noticed him looking at her before. Eyes furtively darting away,
never wanting to admit he'd been caught. So young and foolish, but it
made her feel young too. Made her feel a way she hadn't in years, maybe
hadn't ever.

Mostly he cleaned the shop, stocked the shelves, helped out in the
alley when a truck was delivering goods. Their paths didn't cross much,
and when they did he usually just nodded, then looked away.

Eventually he greeted her in French, admitted he knew a bit of the
language and said he wanted to practice it on her, if she didn't mind. She
wondered what else he wanted to practice on her. He was handsome,
with rich brown eyes and perpetually messy hair that an older man
would have trimmed shorter, but that was part of his charm. So American, she realized. Unaware of how lucky he was, how blessed by his
birth. He seemed flustered, still making his way, not yet realizing that

so much was laid out before him if only he was ready to take it. Surely he had girlfriends his own age, which made Elena that much more surprised by how nervous he acted around her.

Until she fell off the stepladder. He had been stocking the shelves, right beside her of course, which is where she'd found him more and more often. They would talk about the weather, about the war, about his school (so young!) and his plans, about her experiences in Europe, or at least the parts she was willing to share. This time, though, they hadn't been talking, and his hands had been full of cans, but when she fell off the stepladder he'd dropped the cans and caught her.

He was a good six inches taller than her, taller than her husband. His arms were wrapped around her and the impact carried him into the shelves behind him, her leaning against him like that, and she steadied herself on her feet and looked up at those warm eyes.

"Are you all right?" he asked.

"Yes," she said, and it felt like one word too many.

He started to pull his hands away, and she reached down and stopped them before they could leave her, pressed them against her hips. She had to push herself up on her tiptoes to kiss him.

He kept his lips shut for a moment, like maybe he thought she was giving him an unusually friendly thank-you, something exotic and European. She pulled her lips back just for a second, giving him time to understand, then leaned in and kissed him again, and this time he was ready.

That look on his face when she finally pulled away. Stunned. Like he didn't realize a woman could make the decision for herself.

Or worse, she feared she'd misread him, that he was stunned because she was older, that she looked somehow asexual to him. This weird immigrant vagabond lady.

So she leaned in and kissed him harder this time, longer, trying to drown her fear that he thought that way about her, not let him come up for air.

He tasted like bubble gum. Sugar. Smelled like cheap aftershave that he barely needed, his cheeks so unblemished, and just a hint of sweat.

He moved his hands up her back, then down to her hips again. She'd been wearing a simple cotton dress and he inched his fingers lower until the bell chimed and a customer walked in. They were out of view, but the sound broke the spell.

She stepped back and smiled at him. Motioned for him to wipe the lipstick from his face. Then she headed to the restroom to clean herself up.

Two nights later, they worked late and closed the shop together, then spent an hour in the back office, the door locked.

It wasn't long before he'd convinced her to tell him when her husband was working the night shift, and he started showing his face at her apartment. It alarmed her—what if Abe came home early for some reason? What if a neighbor saw? But it also made this exciting. The affair had all the juvenile silliness of teenage love but all the risk of adultery. She and Abe were barely intimate anymore, only on the nights or mornings when he had the energy or was drunk and used guilt to get it out of her. This, however, *this* was something to savor.

She had known something so good would end, and badly.

Now the man who had been smoking, and who still stood right outside her building, looked at his watch and shook his head. Did he know when she got off work? Was he surprised she wasn't home yet?

Maybe she could find a pay phone, call Marta. Tell her she wouldn't be home tonight. But where would she go next?

Then a black sedan drove up and pulled alongside the man. He opened the front passenger door and got in. The other driver was an older man in a modest cap. A colleague, or perhaps his father?

The men spoke only for a few seconds before the sedan drove off, toward Elena. She turned to face the shop window again, saw the reflection of the sedan as it passed.

Maybe that man had nothing to do with Elena after all. Maybe she could dare to believe that she was safe.

Chapter Twenty-six

THE MORNING AFTER

Anne slept terribly, dreaming she was trapped in a box, or under water, or that her arms and legs were bound. She thrashed herself awake several times, worried she'd wake her mother, with whom she shared a bed.

Again and again she saw that drunk old man and his gun.

What if she'd killed him? She'd left her prints all over the building. Of course, her fingerprints weren't on record anywhere, but if she ever became a suspect, the police could take her prints, and they'd know. She could explain herself later, how she'd been kidnapped and had feared for her life, but the fact that she hadn't gone to the police right away would be held against her. She could see the case now: radical leftist breaks into right-winger's warehouse, kills him, runs off, then only after she's caught does she beg for mercy. No, that wouldn't fly.

Eventually her mother got up, but Anne faked sleep, pulled the covers over her head. With unpredictable wartime schedules, they were each used to sleeping while the other got ready for work, and her mother knew that Anne had been out late.

Now that Anne knew what this group was calling itself, the Christian Legion, and knew what they were doing, she considered her options. Going to the police seemed suicidal, as her kidnapper had hinted that his accomplice was a cop. She'd even seen a squad car pull down the road right as she and Lydia drove off. And technically Anne had broken the law by breaking into the place. Plus she didn't trust the cops to help on any case about homegrown Nazis. Plenty of people in Dorchester had already told her how the cops allowed those Irish gangs to run rough-shod over the neighborhood; she remembered the dismissive tone of the officer who'd taken down her report about her shattered windshield, as if she were some high-strung shrew who couldn't laugh off a prank.

What she wanted to do was write a story about what she'd learned, complete with her photos of the counterfeit ration stamps. But if she put her name in the byline, the Christian Legion would know who she was and where to find her.

She could farm the story out to another writer, like Harold again, but then she'd be putting *him* at risk. And she was tired of giving away her best scoops.

She could call the FBI.

Devon Mulvey from the old neighborhood was now an FBI man. And they were supposed to go out to dinner tonight! Jesus. She could tell him what she knew, but she wasn't sure she could trust him. The FBI had cracked down on Fascists, yes, but she'd heard it also kept close watch on socialists, Communists, and any other group that didn't neatly fall into Republican or Democratic party lines. Devon likely disagreed with Anne on a great many things.

An anonymous call, then? If the G-men didn't follow up, she could mail them some of the photographs she'd taken, assuming the pictures came out all right.

Finally, when she was sure her mother and brother had both left for work, she got up, fixed some breakfast. As she was finishing, Elias came home fresh off his night shift. He announced that he was going to shower and go to bed, so she was grateful he wasn't in a conversational mood.

She thought she should grab a newspaper, see if there was a story about an older man bludgeoned to death in a late-night attack. But no, it wouldn't be in the papers yet. She'd have to wait until evening at least.

While Elias was in the shower, she called the FBI.

The call was answered by someone other than Devon, which was good. Nonetheless she disguised her voice somewhat, just in case she wound up meeting this person one day.

"There's a warehouse in Somerville that's printing Nazi leaflets and counterfeit ration stamps," she said to the agent. She told him the address.

"How do you know this, ma'am?"

"I saw it with my own eyes. One of the men who prints them is named Pete Flaherty," and she read him Flaherty's phone number. "The group calls itself the Christian Legion. They might know they've been spotted by now, so I'd hurry if I were you."

She hung up before she might say something that gave her identity away. Realizing how ridiculous she'd sounded. Would they even believe her? They likely got false tips every day.

She didn't even know the name of the drunk she'd knocked out, only that he was linked somehow with Flaherty. If she'd had his name, she could have done more research, found out where he lived, if he owned any property, had a police record. For now, he was just a face, one that would haunt her dreams.

She'd showered and dressed and was nearly out the door when the phone rang. She hesitated, wondering if it could possibly be the FBI, calling her back after tracing her call.

She took a breath and answered.

"Annie Lemire, long time no see! Though I guess I'm still not seeing you. Which is terrible."

She exhaled with relief, hopefully not too loudly. "Aaron. Thanks for calling me back."

Her former neighbor Aaron Green was a year older than her; they'd met through their younger brothers. Aaron was working as a judicial clerk while trying to make it as a novelist. She'd given him notes on his most recent manuscript, a ridiculous murder mystery involving suspects who'd entered our reality through some portal in time or something (she'd barely followed it). Before Pearl Harbor, when he was a law student, he'd volunteered for the American Jewish Congress, raising funds for Jewish refugees and helping them navigate the thicket of immigration laws.

"So I hear you're writing a story for some New York glossy about the ol' neighborhood."

"How did you know?" She had only left her name when she'd called him yesterday.

"I've heard a rumor that some yenta's been schlepping all over the neighborhood, knocking on a lot of doors. I thought, now who does that sound like?"

She told him about her and Harold's discouraging lack of success in getting many people to talk to them. "We're running out of leads."

"Well, I'm a step ahead of you. Me and some friends at the AJ Congress have been doing the same thing."

"Really?" She wasn't surprised, though; it's why she'd tried to get in touch with him.

"We figured if we could get some of the victims to write out sworn affidavits, that'd finally get things moving. And we got a few, but then a couple of the rabbis got cold feet and asked us to stop. *Told* us to stop, really."

"Yes, I already spoke to Rabbi Horowitz."

"Most of the rabbis are pretty cautious fellows. Which I understand. So me and my buddies stopped doing the interviews. But I gotta say . . . it isn't sitting right with me. I guess I'm not as cautious as them."

"Does that mean you want to help?"

"It might get me in trouble, but yeah. We gotta get the word out. We'd recorded three affidavits when the rabbis put the kibosh on it, but I got a long list of other folks to talk to. Some probably won't, but a few I'm pretty sure will. I'll come along and help get folks to talk to you, if you promise you'll get that story run."

"That's the best news I've heard in a while, Aaron. You've got a deal."

Without a car, and not wanting to bother Lydia again—the poor girl was probably working at the diner anyway, if she hadn't called in sick due to nerves—Anne decided to take the streetcar to work. She feared her colleagues would see the guilt on her face, that she'd act funny, say something incriminating, and knew she needed to act as normal as possible today.

She caught the streetcar to Dudley Square, where she got off to transfer to a downtown car. As she walked toward it, she saw a flyer for a local Fourth of July parade stapled to a telephone pole. It noted that after the parade, there would be a few speakers in lieu of fireworks (which were forbidden, as they were last year, due to the small chance some very long-range Nazi bomber might be trolling the East Coast). One of the speakers was Michael Cavanaugh, a state representative who also happened to be an awful anti-Semite. One of the other names made her stop: "Charles Nolan of the Christian Legion."

She remembered Nolan. At a rally in early winter of 1941—shortly before Pearl Harbor—a number of groups had sponsored a pro-Nazi speaker at a downtown event near Scollay Square. She still had the event program in her office, and she remembered that it listed its sponsors; she wondered if the Christian Legion had been one of them.

Nolan, she recalled, was handsome and fit, what the Nazis would have considered perfect casting for their breed of virile manliness. And he was good at the podium; he'd introduced the speaker and had thrown in a few gratuitous lines about Jews and Communists. She didn't remember much else about him and didn't recall doing follow-up research on the group. Given the world-shattering events of that December 7, Nolan and his Christian Legion had fallen off her radar. Having never heard from them again, she'd assumed they'd been arrested or gone dormant.

Yet now they were back, not only printing leaflets and counterfeit ration stamps, but also planning to give speeches at a Fourth of July parade, no doubt subverting what was supposed to be a patriotic event into some kind of isolationist screed.

"Jesus Christ."

She needed to find out more about Nolan, and soon.

On her way to the office, she made a detour.

She got off the train at Park Street and walked along the Common, then a few blocks south on Tremont. On one particularly unsavory block, past two buildings that had been condemned and whose entrances were blocked by plywood, she entered the dirty vestibule of a four-story brick building that looked like it too fell afoul of various city codes. She buzzed number four, hoping it wasn't too early.

After her third buzz, a voice came on. "We don't want any."

"Marcie, it's Anne Lemire. Can I come up?"

"Annie? I'm not dressed, but it's nothing you haven't seen before." The door buzzed.

The stairs were no cleaner than the vestibule. Torn pages of newspaper, brown bags, an empty liquor bottle. Marcie usually had one boyfriend or another at her beck and call, but still Anne marveled at the fact that she lived here.

At the top floor the door swung open. "Look at you, working girl."

"Sorry, I know it's early."

Marcie's hair was cut pixie-short and she clearly had only risen from bed a short while ago. She'd thrown on a silk gown that looked altogether out of place in this dingy apartment.

Marcie Drummond was a friend from Radcliffe. She had outraged her wealthy parents by declaring that she wanted to be an artist, either a painter or a photographer, maybe both. As far as Anne knew, her family was constantly threatening to disown her; either they had yet to follow through, or her income from photo shoots for local magazines and ad agencies was just enough for her to afford her own place, run-down though it was.

Marcie invited her in and they caught up. How long had it been, three months? Her latest boyfriend was still asleep, but Marcie said not to bother whispering because the wake-up would do him good.

"I'm sorry to just drop by and leave, but I'm on my way to work. I was hoping you could develop some film for me."

"Don't you work for a newspaper?" Marcie lit a cigarette, and one for Anne.

"Yes, but . . . I'm not sure I want them to see this yet."

"Ooh, *that* sounds mysterious. Is it blackmail material? Catch anyone *in flagrante delicto?*"

She had rehearsed exactly how much she was willing to disclose to anyone, even trusted friends. "I'm working on a story, not for the *Star*, about all these hate sheets around town. I found out where they're printing them and took some shots of their hideaway."

"You broke in?" Marcie smiled wickedly. Anne realized too late that Marcie might have been a better accomplice to bring along than nervous Lydia.

"Well, sort of. And I would have taken better notes of all I saw, but I thought the owner was coming back so I had to hurry." She didn't like lying to her friend, but the alternative would have been worse. "I took pictures of some notes they had, but I didn't get a chance to read them. And the lighting was poor, so there's a chance they won't come out."

She fished the canister out of her purse and handed it to Marcie.

"I'll see what magic I can work." Marcie used one of the rooms in her apartment as a darkroom, Anne knew, and though she wasn't as politically active as Anne was—few people were—she was reliable. "Is it terribly urgent, though? I have to head out for a shoot soon and they'll keep me all day. But I can get to it tomorrow."

"That would be wonderful. And keep this between us, would you? The people who own that warehouse . . . I don't think they'd be very happy to know I took those pictures."

Marcie drew an imaginary zipper across her lips. "They're sealed, sweetie."

Chapter Twenty-seven

ROMANTIC INTERLUDE,
WITH WITNESSES

As Devon drove toward Anne's apartment to pick her up for their date, he wondered exactly how big a mistake he was making.

She was some rabble-rousing leftist and a muckraking journalist. Sure, she was pretty, but he'd never had trouble finding pretty women. Maybe he was attracted by the fact that she was forbidden, or would have been had Pop—or his boss—known what he was doing. Perhaps he needed to prove to himself that he didn't pick up only married women, that he was more than a cad out for a good time, more than the shallow rake everyone—even his sisters—thought he was. He could take a lady on a proper date, with maybe a kiss at the end if he was lucky.

And maybe he wanted to prove he wasn't as small-minded as people like his cousin Brian.

Still, he had looked up Anne's FBI file that very morning. And she indeed had one. Anne Lemire, age twenty-four. The file was scant when it came to her background or education, but he knew much of that already. What the file did note was that, despite her youth, she had become the founder a few years ago of the Boston Center for Democracy, an anti-Fascist organization that, prior to Pearl Harbor, had hosted a number of lectures about the evils of Hitlerism, had printed a newsletter, and had exposed local Nazi sympathizers. The file included several issues of their newsletter, which he flipped through, reading some of her pieces.

Most of the notes in her file had been recorded by an older agent who had been transferred to Detroit a year ago. Nothing had been added to the file in the last year, either because that agent hadn't passed the baton, or because Anne's group had been deemed unworthy of further monitoring or even gone defunct (notes indicated that their last two recorded meetings had been poorly attended, their fundraising minuscule). Anne had never actually been interviewed or questioned, as far as Devon could tell; the agent had instead used informants to keep him abreast of the group. A few Communists whom the Bureau had flagged had been at some of the BCD's meetings, though it wasn't clear if Anne herself was a red.

After he'd finished reading her file, he'd realized that the smart move would have been to call off the date. Any association with communism, even thirdhand, could be dangerous. Or he could keep the date but record it as if he were recruiting her as an informant. But he didn't want to do that, either. Didn't want to do it to her, or to himself. He wanted to believe he could just take the lady out, politics be damned, and that his employer didn't need to follow him everywhere.

He would keep the date, and keep it quiet.

Exactly on time, he parked in front of her building—it wasn't as hard to find parking spaces as it used to be, as so many older cars had broken down during the Depression and would not be replaced for the duration.

He knew, as he got out and approached the door, that he was dancing on dangerous ground. But he liked to dance, and he wanted to dance with her, and he was confident that he could find a way to sashay past any of the snares that lay about his feet.

And when he saw her smile as she opened the door of her third-floor apartment, he felt justified in his decision.

He'd been so preoccupied, though, that he hadn't noticed the occupants in a parked Olds half a block away.

The two men had been waiting outside the Lemire apartment for half an hour. She was a reporter, they had been told. Worked odd hours. That would make her somewhat harder to pick up, and they'd need to proceed very carefully indeed if she really did work for a newspaper.

At six o'clock, a well-dressed gentleman approached her building.

"Wait, I know that guy."

"Who, the suit?"

The driver snapped his fingers for a moment, trying to remember. "Devon Mulvey. He's a G-man."

"You mean, FBI?"

"Yeah. What the hell's he doing here?"

"Could be visiting one of the other apartments. There's six units in the building."

They sat and waited. Five minutes. Ten.

Then Mulvey walked out the door with Anne Lemire.

"What the hell. Are they an item? Or . . . related?"

Mulvey and Anne were smiling, chatting. If she had set up this meeting with Mulvey to report on what she'd seen with the printing press, the two men realized, they were fucked. Then again, she'd nearly killed ol' Frankie. She couldn't be so stupid as to implicate herself, could she?

Frankie was laid up in bed. They'd chosen not to take him to the hospital, which would have raised too many questions, jeopardized their operation. A shady doctor friend of theirs had given him some morphine and claimed he'd pull through.

Maybe the Lemire gal would keep quiet about her break-in so as not to get herself in trouble. But maybe not.

The driver drummed his fingers on the steering wheel.

"This is unexpected," he finally said.

"Think Mulvey's fucking her? Or is she a source of his, into the unions and reds? Or all of the above?"

"These are all excellent questions."

"So . . . what do we do?"

"Right now? We do nothing."

"I hate doing nothing."

"So do I. Which is why we won't do it very long."

For her part, Anne feared she was making an even bigger mistake going to dinner with an FBI agent after the break-in. She'd strongly considered canceling—what if she'd killed the man, and the FBI was looking into the murder? What if they'd uncovered some clue linking her to it? She was hardly in the mood for a carefree night out, but she was afraid that if she canceled with Devon she might rouse suspicions. She needed to live her life like normal, act as if nothing unusual had happened.

Maybe she was still in shock. She feared that once she got a glass of wine in her, she'd spill all her secrets.

When Devon rang the bell, she invited him in, introducing him to her mother. He was charming and polite, complimenting them on their beautiful apartment (so he was a good liar, Anne thought; interesting). She could see by her mother's smile that she too was smitten, giving Anne an approving look when Devon's back was turned.

She got him out the door before her mother could say anything to embarrass her.

On the drive to Beacon Hill, Anne commented on how rare it was to drive to dinner these days. The C sticker on Devon's windshield established him as the most essential of war workers, so the ban on "pleasure driving" did not apply. Part of her wanted to criticize this petty corruption—a government agent taking advantage of his position for a mere date—but another part of her felt flattered, and that part of her won.

"How old were you when you left the old neighborhood?" he asked.

"Thirteen."

She wondered how much he remembered of those days. He'd remembered her face, apparently, but perhaps that was all.

"So, Wellesley or Radcliffe?"

She laughed. "Am I so obviously a college girl?"

"Radcliffe, right?"

"Careful, Agent Mulvey. If you make too many correct guesses, I'll start wondering if you've read some file you have on me."

They were at a red light, and he looked at her. "Really, I'm not here as Agent anybody. Just a regular fellow who wanted to ask you to dinner. But if my clairvoyance about you is alarming, speak up now and we can go our separate ways. Honest."

Good though he looked, she wondered whether she should take this dis-invitation at face value and walk out now. Gracefully exit the dark world he represented. As if that might have prevented anything else from happening.

"Well, I wouldn't want to break the record for shortest date ever."

The light turned green and they went on.

The Italian place was dark and dimly lit, brick-walled, the ceiling thick with bougainvillea that hung low like out-of-season mistletoe. Even before the war, Anne had seldom ventured into a place like this. She didn't even have names for all the scents in the air.

The '37 Bordeaux he ordered was fabulous. She was impressed, almost shocked, by this luxury that had seemingly vanished from the world.

"The owner got in some trouble with the OPA for procuring black market beef a few months back," Devon explained. "I was able to help him out of the jam."

"I'll bet you have plenty of stories like that."

He grinned. "None I should be so quick to share with a journalist. We're off the record tonight, right?"

"Oh, I suppose."

"So what sorts of things do you write?"

"I write the Rumor Clinic at the *Star*, shooting down antiwar innuendo. And I'm trying to get some longer pieces placed elsewhere."

"What sorts of innuendo?"

"Everything from whether ladies with perms can work in factories—they can—to whether Jewish boys are cheating their way out of the draft—they aren't."

She still wasn't sure what to make of him, but he seemed to see this as a normal date.

"So you wanted to tell me what's been going on in Dorchester?" he asked.

She told him much of what she knew so far about the attacks. She didn't say anything that would have compromised the anonymity of the few victims who'd dared to speak with her, but she told him enough to make him understand how serious things had become.

"Isn't there something the Bureau can do about it?"

"To be honest, I don't think so. If I told my boss I wanted to investigate a bunch of Irish brats picking fights with Jewish kids, he'd laugh me out of—"

"It's not just kids," she interrupted. "These are full-grown adults in some cases, and they're causing serious harm. People have been hospitalized. Someone's going to get killed."

He thought for a moment. "Maybe someone already has been."

She shivered involuntarily. Was he talking about the man she'd escaped from? Did he know? Maybe he'd personally followed up on her anonymous call already; maybe he knew she'd been in the warehouse, had taken her prints from the scene and was about to take more from her wineglass.

"What do you mean?" she managed to ask.

"Nothing, it's just . . . I believe you that it's serious."

"You realize what's really happening in Germany, don't you? And everywhere else the Nazis have taken over? They want to . . . exterminate Jews. And every day that passes and we aren't in Europe fighting them, they get closer to their goal. Meanwhile, if we let people get away with demonizing and attacking Jews here, who's to say something similar couldn't happen?"

He waited before answering. "I suppose I choose to believe that Americans wouldn't do that."

"I'd love to agree with you."

"And to answer your earlier question, no, this is not the kind of thing the FBI would normally investigate. But . . ."

He gazed at the wine bottle, lost in thought, long enough for her to ask, "But?"

"I think there's more to it than that. I've seen the pamphlets and flyers. There may be something I can do to help. If I go about it very delicately."

He seemed to regret even saying that much. She couldn't tell if this too was an act, if he was just trying to score points with her by acting like he cared about her problems. Or if he was trying to get *her* to say or admit something she shouldn't.

"Why 'delicately'?"

"It's just . . . a complicated situation."

"Don't act like *the lady* can't handle whatever complications you're talking about. Look, before we joined the war, I used to sit in on some pro-Nazi rallies, when they could spout that nonsense in public. I was in the back taking notes, then writing stories about them."

She wanted to ask if he knew anything about the Christian Legion, but she was afraid that if she did, he'd link the question to her anonymous call, and then to the man she might have killed. So she kept the name of that group to herself.

"Now that we're at war," Devon said, "the worst of those groups have gone quieter. They know that if they set up some pro-Hitler rally, they'd be going to jail."

"Maybe they don't know that, actually. I just saw a flyer for the Fourth of July parade in Dorchester—some of the speakers are anti-Semites, and I think some of them are tied to pro-Hitler groups. The fact that they're allowed to talk at a parade turns my stomach. It would be nice if the Bureau took this more seriously."

"We do. I do. But going after religious groups has some constitutional hurdles."

"It's not 'religious' to say that Jews are to blame for the war."

"I agree with you. And I think I'm in a position to help. I just . . . can't tell you everything."

Anne motioned to the table. "Is this all just an elaborate ploy to distract me and get me to back off?"

He seemed surprised. "No, it's not. Look, you know I'm Catholic. But that doesn't mean I like the fact that some people use the Church as a shield for them to do some very unholy things. I'm going to get to the bottom of this, but I can't telegraph all my moves to a reporter. You'll have to trust me a little."

Just like that, the serious look on his face snapped away and he smiled. "How about another splash?" He poured more wine. It was like he realized he'd just allowed her to see something he didn't want to reveal, and now he was back to being Charming Devon again.

The service was not fast and they chatted for a while—about the war, the President, and the latest scandal in Boston politics: the aftermath of last winter's Cocoanut Grove fire, in which nearly five hundred people had died, partly because the owner of the nightclub had bribed city officials to look the other way when it came to compliance with fire codes.

They had just finished a dark chocolate torte, which they'd split, trading bites in what felt like a contest to see who could get the most, when Devon said, "Seeing you the other day, it got me thinking about a few things. I never felt good about how you were treated, back in the neighborhood."

She felt a step beyond tipsy at that point in the evening—the wine bottle was nearly empty—and she didn't know what he meant at first. When she realized what he was saying, she wasn't sure she could handle it.

"Okay," was all she said.

"We were . . . terrible to you. I know it. I mean, I wasn't the worst of them, but still, I just . . . We completely ostracized your family, and it was wrong."

She didn't want to be thinking of this. Of the names the other girls called her at school when they found out. Or the things the boys said. What her own parish *priest* said, the next time she'd tried to attend mass after the news had spread, when he'd met her on the front steps, arms folded.

Completely ostracized. The writer in Anne wanted to edit Devon's unnecessary adverb. That's what ostracism was, after all: a complete cutting off. You are the Other, you are leprous, you must be removed.

"Why are you bringing this up?"

"I just . . . thought that I should. That it would be wrong not to. It's long overdue, but I wanted to say that I'm sorry."

She felt anger overcoming all the other emotions, and the alcohol, inside her.

"So this evening was just to make you feel less guilty?" She had been wary that this FBI man was manipulating her, yet she'd missed his ulterior motive all along. "You bought me dinner because of your *conscience*? So you wouldn't have to *feel bad* anymore?"

He stared at her for a moment.

"No. I bought you dinner because you're beautiful." Said so matter-of-factly that she felt her cheeks go red immediately. "Is that better? I think you're pretty and smart and gutsy, and I wanted to take you out.

Because I'm a selfish bastard and I like being able to look at a beautiful woman for two hours. And you're fun to talk to."

She hated the fact that she was blushing. She didn't consider herself beautiful, maybe pretty enough, and had only ever heard words like that from one man, whom she hadn't taken seriously anyway. She never wanted to put stock in terms of endearment like that, yet despite herself she felt her anger turning into something else.

He continued, "Is that better than feeling guilty? I'm asking, because I'm honestly not sure."

Finally she managed to take her eyes off his. The truth was, she liked looking at him too.

She picked up her cloth napkin, wiped cocoa powder from her lips, balled it up, placed it on the tablecloth. Watched as it slowly unfurled itself.

"I guess I'm not sure either."

And there they are, walking along the sidewalk, her apartment building in view. They're framed perfectly between these two old maples that somehow haven't fallen dead despite the laying of the streetcar rails a few decades back and the demolition of an old road and the relaying of a new one. It didn't rain today, yet the surfaces of the city seem to shine, almost with dew, as if it weren't late at night but approaching dawn, the world birthed anew. The gentleman chivalrously walking between her and the road, their footsteps in synch. Even from behind, a viewer can tell from the way her hair dances that she's laughing at something he said. He's a funny one; it's clear even from this far back, across the street. They turn profile now, the couple (they're definitely a couple, anyone could tell) still standing on the sidewalk because if he were to take a step into the building then that would establish this as an altogether different sort of evening, and establish her as an altogether different sort of gal, which she's not. The viewer can tell from her eyes—the glimmer that perfectly matches the shininess of the city on this summer evening—that she is tempted, that she can feel already the incipient loneliness, and a very physical loneliness at that, of stepping into her apartment unaccompanied. But, again, that's not the sort of gal she is, tonight at least. She's saying something, and smiling, the viewer can see that now, it's a radiant one, the lady has clearly had a wonderful evening. Can't fake that smile. And then she leans in for the kiss that she was probably kidding herself about being able to abstain from, it's so obviously something to be craved and, in this moment, seized, as if it's the last one around. Because maybe it is. There's a war on. No one else on this street is kissing, one can just tell, even though the viewer wouldn't know, since he isn't aiming his camera at those other people. Other people don't matter. His camera is aimed at Devon and Anne, the couple so very helpfully placed here beneath the streetlamp that wouldn't be illuminated if they were a mile closer to the water, due to the government-implemented dimouts. No, the lamp is on, the subjects are lit, and these pictures should come out perfectly.

Chapter Twenty-eight

LEADER OF THE LEGION

The next morning, before taking down more witness statements with Harold and Aaron, Anne paid a visit to Charles Nolan, putative head of the Christian Legion. She took the streetcar with Harold, having decided, after some hesitation, not to keep this part of the story from him after all. She didn't want to visit Nolan alone.

He worked as an attorney, running a modest office in the South End. She'd looked up his home and business listings, so she could have just called, but once again she wanted to look a liar in the eyes.

His office was in the basement of a brownstone, beneath a seamstress and next to a deli. The sign read "OPEN" but the door was locked, so Harold knocked. Inside, they saw a receptionist's desk but no receptionist.

A moment later a man emerged from an inner doorway and walked through the small waiting area. Light brown hair parted on the side and slicked back, brown eyes, and a narrow face. Average height and build for a thirty-some-year-old man who took care of himself. Your completely average ordinary attorney, down to the white shirt and blue tie.

"That's him," Anne said quietly, recognizing him now from that rally two years ago.

Nolan opened the door and gave them a professional smile. "Can I help you?"

"Are you Charles Nolan?" Harold asked despite Anne's comment, ever in need of official confirmation.

"I am indeed. You folks in need of legal counsel?" He stepped back to let them in. "My girl's out sick today, but I have time to chat."

The waiting room was a bit shabby, complete with a moldy smell coming from the carpet. Anne was willing to bet he'd already lied once: he probably couldn't afford a receptionist.

They walked in, and as Anne passed Nolan she handed him one of the pamphlets.

"Anyone who prints these must be good with the law," Anne said.

He chuckled, "I like to think so, yes." He closed the door behind him.

"Because he seems to know exactly how much he can get away with saying legally before getting himself into quite a bit of trouble."

The smile faded. He stuffed the pamphlet into his pocket and left his hand in there too. "Excuse me?"

"So am I correct in assuming this office doubles as headquarters for the Christian Legion?"

"Who are you?"

"We're reporters," Harold said, flashing Anne an annoyed look. He didn't seem to approve of the fact that they hadn't explained themselves from the start. He'd lectured to her before about proper journalistic ethics; for that reason, she hadn't dared tell him about her warehouse break-in, only that she'd heard from "a source" that Nolan and his group were behind the hate sheets. "Writing a story for *PM* about the attacks on Jews throughout Dorchester. We thought we'd give you a chance to explain yourself for the record."

"Are you Jews?"

"And what if we were?" Anne demanded.

"If you were, I wouldn't trust a thing you have to say. And even if you weren't, but you've just taken up their cause for some foolish political reason, I still wouldn't trust you."

"I am Jewish, Mr. Nolan," Harold said, "and I don't care if you trust me. I do care that you're spreading these lies throughout Boston and that they're responsible for men and children being attacked and hospitalized."

"I haven't attacked anyone. Or lied. As your girl here says, there's nothing in those pamphlets that's illegal."

She wouldn't bother correcting him about her being Harold's girl, instead countering him with, "What about printing counterfeit ration stamps? That's illegal."

Nolan stared at her for a moment. "I don't know what you're talking about."

She felt Harold looking at her too—since she hadn't told him about the warehouse, she hadn't mentioned the counterfeit stamps, either. She hadn't meant to say anything about it, but Nolan's haughty attitude had incited her to blurt it out and catch him with something.

Her heart was racing as she felt both of them staring at her, but that's not the only reason she was convinced Nolan was lying. He knew about the counterfeiting; she was certain.

She wished she could see his inner office and whatever other back rooms this place had. She wondered if he had more pamphlets stashed here, if the Legion was clearing out their warehouse now that they knew it had been discovered, in which case they'd need another place for it all. No printing press would fit in a South End brownstone, but plenty else could.

"So you *are* part of the Christian Legion, then?" Harold asked, ever dutifully seeking confirmation.

"The founder, in fact. I don't have to say a thing to you about those pamphlets. What matters is, we're a patriotic organization and we love our country." Harold scribbled in his notebook as Nolan ranted. "We're doing our best to protect America from the threat of Judeo-Bolshevism, which has only grown since President Rosenfelt agreed to pal around with Stalin. Communists like ol' Joe burned priests alive and slaughtered nuns in Spain before right-thinking people fought back. And yes, I am allowed to say that out loud, believe it or not."

"And you're actively encouraging the attacks in Dorchester," Anne said, more as a statement than a question.

"I'd be very careful about what you put into print, young lady. This country still had libel laws last I checked. As I said, we haven't attacked anyone."

God, she hated him. How a man could print and distribute lies by the thousand but then bring up libel laws the moment he was exposed; she couldn't believe his gall.

She was on the verge of telling him off when Harold asked, "So you say you're not involved in the attacks. Do you have any other comment on them?"

"What attacks? Kids getting in fights? That happens. And if people are angry at Jews for roping us into this war, can you blame them? Actions have consequences."

"Most groups like yours," Anne said, barely able to restrain her anger, "got put away or went quiet after Pearl Harbor. I would think you'd be worried about the same fate."

He folded his arms and grinned at her. "I'd like to see someone try it. We have thousands of supporters, not just in Boston but all over the Northeast. Worcester, Fall River, Portland, Providence. New York. And as you said, I know the law. I can say what I want."

"Not if Hitler's paying you for it."

"We're not spies and we're not on the take. We're patriotic Americans, as I said. People like you just can't stand that we know the truth."

"And what truth is that?" asked Harold, pen at the ready.

Nolan simply chuckled again. "Fine, go ahead and write your little story. No one will care. No one cares about you people, don't you see? We're only at war because of Pearl Harbor—it's the *Japs* everyone hates. The fact that they're allied with Germany is the only reason we're even *considering* going to war in Europe. If you think it's because we really love the Bolsheviks and the Jews, you're kidding yourself." He opened the door. "Now, if that's all, good day."

Anne stared him down for another moment, then walked out, Harold behind her.

As they walked toward the streetcar stop, Harold said, "I honestly expected him to deny everything. These people are so delusional they don't seem to realize how much trouble they could be in."

"Or," Anne said, thinking about the police officers who had driven to the warehouse that night, "he's not worried about being in trouble because he knows people are protecting him."

In which case, it was Anne and Harold who should be worried.

As they got in the car, Harold asked, "What was that about counterfeit ration stamps?"

"Oh, just a rumor I heard."

Chapter Twenty-nine

STAKEOUTS ARE BORING, UNTIL THEY'RE NOT

The next night, it was Devon's turn to tail Zajac. Agents had been trading shifts, solo, and this was his second time since he and Lou had put in the request.

He still didn't know what to think of the Wolff murder. He was worried Wolff had been killed for being a Jewish immigrant; the last thing he needed was to find out that some Irish kids were responsible. He could already hear his fellow agents gloating, reminding him yet again how backward the Irish were. He felt a need to defend his tribe's reputation, or at least find a way to manage the situation.

The stolen rifles worried him even more. Thefts from military factories were endemic all over the country, but the disappearance of a crate of rifles was unusually bold. If Wolff had been involved in such a theft, the next question was who had the rifles now and what were they planning to do with them.

He sat in his car outside Zajac's sad apartment building for an hour. Zajac had come home straight from work, according to the agent Devon had relieved. The lights in his second-floor apartment were still on.

Time passed. He realized how tired he was. This could be a damn boring job sometimes.

Eventually he got out of his car and walked to a pay phone, from which he still had a perfect view of the building. He rustled up some dimes and made calls. To Jimmy Moore at BPD Homicide, to see if the long-delayed autopsy had revealed anything interesting (answer: no). To Siobhan, to check on his sister (she said she was okay but didn't sound it; thanks for calling, but she was tired, she needed to go, good night).

And to Anne. Calling a lady the night after a first date wasn't his normal MO, but he didn't care. He liked that this wasn't another one-night stand, liked how sharp she was. He wasn't used to dating someone so opinionated. She'd granted him only a kiss their first night, which was another change of pace for him.

He liked her. Even more than he'd expected to.

She was difficult to impress. The women he was used to romancing were ever so flattered by his attentions, by this gentleman who was happy to listen to their thoughts and worries. Someone as left-wing as Anne was less inclined to fawn over his law degree and good job than a typical Financial District secretary might. He felt unmoored by her, the usual rules of no help.

The phone was answered by Anne's mother.

"Hi, Mrs. Lemire, this is Devon Mulvey. I hope I'm not calling too late?"

"Oh, we're all night owls over here these days."

"Yeah, these wartime work schedules are a bear, huh?"

He asked how her day had been, careful to show his manners. (Mothers loved him.) They chatted for a moment before she put Anne on.

"You sound like you're on a pay phone," she said. "Where are you?"

"I'm on a stakeout, actually."

"How exciting. Who are you following?"

"I really can't say."

"You're not following me, I assume?"

"Now that *would* be exciting." He smiled. Then he decided to have some fun. "Actually . . . look out your window."

He heard her gasp. Then the sound of her moving to another room, as far as her cord would allow, perhaps. She said, "I don't see you."

"That's because I'm good."

"But . . . where?"

"See that tree over to your right?"

"Yyyyes. Are you . . . under it?"

He laughed. "No. I'm not in your neighborhood at all. But I made you look."

"Ha, ha." The laugh was fake, yet he heard her smiling. "I don't usually think of myself as gullible."

"Yeah, you reporters are supposed to be skeptical."

"I am, thank you. But I suppose it's fun to believe in something far-fetched every now and then."

He almost didn't notice Zajac's window go dark. Maybe Zajac was going to bed?

"I wanted to say that I had a lovely time last night. And since I won't be doing stakeouts every night this week, I was wondering if you were free on Friday?"

Just as they were making another date, he saw the building's front door open, and out Zajac came. He looked newly bathed, wet hair combed, wearing a short-sleeved shirt and light slacks. Devon turned sideways to avoid being spotted head-on.

"Great, I'll see you then," he said, hoping she wouldn't wonder why he'd lowered his voice. "Good night."

He hung up and listened to Zajac's footsteps. Gave him a one-block head start, then followed him to the train station.

Devon braced himself for another boring meeting of reds, more talk of poor working conditions and the inevitability of their triumphant revolution, et cetera. He didn't share some agents' obsession with the red menace—these uneducated foreign bumpkins were hard to take seriously, to be honest, and their meetings were interminable. At best, perhaps he'd see some new faces or discover a new group they hadn't known existed, and he'd be able to take credit for putting it on the Bureau's list.

Unless this was something else.

Not many people out and about at that hour, so Devon kept his distance. Dropped his token and waited by the turnstiles for a while, then slowly made his way to the platform as a train approached. He watched Zajac board a car in the middle, then he hustled aboard the last one.

Back to the city.

Transfer to the Green Line.

Zajac got off at Haymarket.

They walked toward the North End, Devon the unknown caboose of this little train. As they wound their way through the North End's narrow, labyrinthine streets, he figured he knew where they were going.

As expected, Zajac was walking past the very alley where his supposed friend had been stabbed to death. He walked into Bucciano's, just as the widow had done a week ago. The restaurant's windows were open and a few patrons sat inside, but the place was quiet. Devon stayed on the opposite side of the street and stood in the dark entrance of a closed deli, and he watched as Zajac spoke to the same bartender Devon had chatted with, Gabriele Bucciano.

No drink for Zajac, no food. He sat there and waited as the bartender disappeared. Then an older woman—possibly Bucciano's mother, the establishment's owner—emerged from a back room. They did not talk long. She did not seem pleased to see him. She used her hands and arms a lot. Zajac pointed at her. The bartender returned to enter the fray, but she held up a hand and blocked his path. She pointed at Zajac and Devon wished he were a lip-reader, assuming they were speaking English.

Zajac nodded. The bartender nodded. The old woman folded her arms and offered the final word with a look of satisfaction. Zajac stood up and walked toward the door. Devon crouched behind a parked car.

He listened to the footsteps. Zajac was walking north, not back toward the train. Devon peeked from around the tail of the car, saw Zajac turn right onto the next street.

Again the delicate dance of shadows, staying just far enough away not to be spotted. Eventually Zajac reached a small park, where he sat on a bench. Devon had to linger at a street corner. Was Zajac waiting to meet someone? Zajac lit a cigarette. Devon envied him—he'd give himself away if he did the same.

Minutes passed. The cigarette was a memory now, ash on the ground. Was Zajac falling asleep? Devon felt ready to. He fingered the rosary that he sometimes carried in his left pants pocket, not praying so much as fidgeting.

After fifteen minutes, Zajac stood. Doubled back. Devon had to scamper into an alley to avoid being spotted. He watched as Zajac passed, waited a few seconds, then followed again.

He wondered if they were headed back to Bucciano's, but no, Zajac took a turn Devon hadn't expected. For ten minutes they wound their way through the twisting streets, toward Boston Garden, where Devon's father had brought him to a few big fights when he was a kid. Eventually Zajac stopped to smoke yet another cigarette, this one from beneath a streetlight in front of an auto body shop called Murray's Repairs. Devon retreated into the shadow of a building while Zajac stood there, smoking alone.

Then, the sound of a door opening. Zajac walked out of sight and a door closed.

Devon gave it a few seconds, then stepped back out. The lights at the auto shop were still off. Had Zajac gone to a back room? But the front was all glass, and Devon would notice if a light was on inside.

Voices to his left. The building next door had appeared vacant, the windows boarded up. A wooden sign above the door had cracked, the left half fallen off, the right half saying "ROCERY." Light emanated out of the wood slats.

He peered into a gap in the boards and saw an empty room, the shell of an old shop. The only light came from a bulb hanging in the rear. Zajac stood with his back to Devon, facing two men in light linen jackets and ties. Shiny shoes, sharp hats. They hadn't gotten the memo that Communists had no style.

Or they weren't reds.

Devon looked behind himself, checked both sides. No one on the sidewalks, but he felt conspicuous out here. He stepped into the side alley and found a window, also boarded up but providing just enough of a gap for him to peer inside. From this vantage he couldn't see Zajac's face but he got a better look at the other two.

"I'm telling you, we had nothing to do with that," one of the men said in a mild Italian accent. The taller of the two, he needed a shave. "And we don't appreciate being called out here because you're seeing ghosts."

"Why should I believe you?" Zajac asked.

"Why should we care what you believe?"

The other stranger was standing by a sawhorse on which some wooden boards lay. On the floor near him were a few cardboard boxes, but the place was otherwise empty.

"Our business is through," the second man said. Less of an accent, deeper voice. Then he said something in Italian to his friend.

"What are you saying?" Zajac demanded.

Devon heard a weird popping sound to his right. He turned that way, distracted. Waited a second, saw a white blur, another pop. Two kids must be out, he figured, playing catch with a baseball, bathed in the streetlights. In the middle of the night.

Devon returned his attention to the ex-grocery.

"Stay away from Bucciano's," the taller one said, "and stay away from us. Okay?"

"I don't trust you," Zajac said, stepping toward them.

"That's good!" the taller one said, smiling. "You shouldn't. Have a good night and see you never again."

"No! I want to know what you did to Abe and you will fucking tell me!"

Sudden motion to Devon's right. He looked that way and saw a baseball bouncing into the alley. *Shit.*

"I'll get it!" he heard a kid yell, then two seconds later a twelve- or thirteen-year-old kid ran into the alley. Eyes low, searching for the ball, till he noticed Devon standing there.

"Oh!" he blurted, startled. Devon put a finger to his lips. The kid no doubt thought he was a thief, or worse.

More words in Italian coming from the building, and the sounds of shoes scuffing. Did they hear the kid out here? Did they realize now that they were being watched?

The kid looked down at his baseball, which was halfway between him and Devon. He looked unsure if it was worth picking up.

"Take the damn ball and go to bed, for God's sake," Devon whispered to the kid. Who obeyed and vanished. Devon heard him and his buddy scampering off.

What he heard next was a hell of a lot louder.

Automatic gunfire, from inside the building. Several rounds in barely a second. Deafening sound, then silence.

Devon ducked. He waited, his heart pounding. So confused it took another few seconds for him to realize he should be drawing his gun now.

Being an FBI agent on anti-sabotage duties wasn't all that glamorous. Or dangerous. He'd never so much as heard a gun fire while on duty before.

He pulled his revolver out of its holster.

He heard angry Italian syllables being thrown back and forth. Finally realized the shots hadn't been aimed at him. Dared to stand back up and look through the wood slats again.

The shorter Italian was holding a very large gun. Smoke trailing from its barrel. Zajac lay flat on the ground several feet behind where he'd been standing before.

The men kept snapping at each other in Italian. The tall one sounded displeased that the other one had killed Zajac. Or maybe he was just mad that he hadn't been warned in advance, or that a quieter method hadn't been employed. The shooter casually propped the smoking rifle against his shoulder, then held up his other palm in the universal gesture of *Who fucking cares?*

Zajac's face was staring to the side, toward Devon, his mouth open. Zajac coughed, twice. His right foot twitching, each twitch shorter and slower than before. A pool of dark blood was already spreading around him.

This was new to Devon. He had seen only a few dead bodies, and they'd all been dead several hours.

Devon leaned against the wall for a second. *Good God.* Took a breath. Looked to his left, but the alley ended in a solid wall—no access to a back door. He realized what he was supposed to do, overwhelming though it was.

Holding the gun with both hands, barrel pointed up at ninety degrees, he ran out of the alley and to the front of the building. Stared at the wooden door.

He kicked it open, aimed, and hollered, "FBI! Don't move!"

Saw them stare at him wide-eyed for just a second. Saw the man with the rifle lowering it into position again.

Devon fired twice.

He saw the taller man pulling a pistol out of his pocket and maybe Devon could have kept his feet planted, maybe he would have had time to fire more rounds, maybe it would have worked and he would have been quite the hero, but he realized in that split second that he was unwilling to gamble his life on it.

He ducked out of the doorway, leaning against the building as the other man fired twice, three times, four.

Devon took a breath, waited. Then he leaned back out, gun-first. A back door that had been closed before was now open.

The man who'd been holding the rifle lay on the ground. Devon must have hit him. But the rifle was gone.

Devon stepped into the room, his revolver seeming to guide him forward. *Good God, this is happening.* He realized the second man could be waiting behind that back door, waiting for Devon to step closer until he was in range with nothing to hide behind.

Devon took a few more steps and wasn't shot. He ran the rest of the way forward, toward the back doorway. A quick glance at the fallen man told Devon he wasn't a threat anymore.

Next was a small room, also empty. It had taken all his courage to make it this far, but now this room had another goddamn back door. Likely leading to another alley.

It did. He checked that the alley was clear, then he stepped into it. Took another breath. Ran down the alley. After a block, it ended at a narrow street. He leaned against a brick wall and looked both ways, saw nothing. Heard a car horn, some laughter from far off. He expected another shot to ring out at any moment, but none came.

He peeked around the corner, stepped out.

Then it came. Deafening again. The sheer brightness from the rifle's barrel startled him as much as the sound. He felt something biting at his neck as he reached out to aim his gun, but before he could squeeze the trigger something big reached down and knocked the black sky on top of him.

Chapter Thirty

POSTMORTEM

There he is."

"Welcome back to the land of the living."

Sinuses on fire. Eyelids like sandpaper. Dizziness despite lying down. The sense that his head had been fused to the ground.

"Can you talk?"

Someone removed the smelling salts and stepped back. Devon blinked despite the pain and realized he was on the alley floor.

Darkness intercut by flashlights weaving this way and that. The vague awareness that people were chatting nearby. Their soles tapping on the ground sent pain through Devon's skull.

"I'm guessing this means I'm not dead."

"Au contraire. I am St. Peter and these are my gates. We need to talk about your sins, young man. They are legion."

Okay, that voice was old pal Detective Jimmy Moore. Tired of the ribbing, Devon tried to sit up. Moore offered a hand.

Devon leaned against the brick wall. He was pretty sure someone had urinated on it not long ago.

"What happened?"

"You weren't shot, which is amazing given how goddamn many shell casings we found at the other end of the street. So maybe despite your sins, an angel did intervene. Judging from all these shattered bricks on the ground, I'd say someone let loose on you with a very powerful weapon that they weren't too skilled at aiming. Tore some chunks out of the wall, one of which hit that hard head of yours."

"Better that than a bullet, I guess."

Devon tried to move again, then felt dizzier. He leaned over.

"You gonna puke? If so, aim away from my shoes."

An hour after the shooting, an ambulatory Devon was joined in the vacant grocery by Moore, four BPD uniforms, and a police photographer, as well as Lou and their boss, Special Agent in Charge Reynolds Gardner. *Snap-snap* went the camera as the photographer crouched by Zajac. *Snap-snap* as he stood over the dead gangster.

Devon had already explained everything to Moore and the uniforms, and he did it again for his late-arriving FBI colleagues. Everyone wanted to smoke but no one did, Gardner decreeing this a cigarette-free environment so they could check any found butts for prints.

The cops were very displeased about the lack of smoking.

Moore took a look at the dead gangster.

"Not bad, Devon. Dead center in the heart. Your first, right?"

"Am I supposed to keep score?"

"Yes."

Hands in his pockets mainly to keep himself from lighting up. "My first."

SAC Gardner was crouched on the floor, looking very intently at a faint footprint left in some dust. Devon had already checked and he didn't think it was nearly enough for a match or even a shoe size, but Gardner stared at it as if by concentrating he could make its outline clearer. Gardner had been in Boston less than a year, having transferred after the previous SAC moved to Chicago. Devon didn't know him well, only that he, like most SACs, was a stickler for rules, etiquette, dress codes, and painstaking research, arguing that only through a scrupulous and scientific application of investigative technique could the Bureau do its job.

Moore caught Devon's eye and smirked at the SAC. Gardner's Sherlock act could play thin in the office, but in the presence of city detectives it seemed even more square.

"How many you fire?" Moore asked Devon.

Devon checked his revolver. "Four."

Moore chuckled, as if to say that hitting the man only once seemed less impressive now.

"You know the guy?" Moore asked.

"No. You?"

"Based on his attire, I would say it's likely he made his living in some illegal trades. Christ, those *shoes*. Wish they were my size. And this other fella, Zajac, you say he was buddies with that other victim you've been looking into?"

"Yeah, Abraham Wolff."

"Detective," Gardner said with an officious air, "we want all your intel on this gangster and whoever he runs with."

Moore snickered again. "My 'intel.' Got it. Oh yeah, because *you* don't know anything. You G-men always have acted scared of the mob."

"We're not scared of anyone," Gardner huffed. "We have bigger fish to fry these days. But it looks like those fish are swimming with some other sharks."

Devon felt seasick amid the aquatic metaphors. "This is what I know so far," he said. "Zajac told me he and Wolff had been drinking at Bucciano's a few blocks from here the night Wolff was killed. He told me they'd picked that place randomly and had never been there before, and the bartender there, the owner's son, later told me he didn't know them. But tonight I tailed Zajac to that same joint, and he had a heated conversation with the bartender and the owner. Wolff's widow visited the place, too, before she vanished."

Devon removed his pack from his pocket out of habit, then remembered and put it back. Goddamn it.

He continued, "I also heard from a source, and later got confirmation, that someone swiped a crate of M-1 rifles from Northeast Munitions, where Zajac and Wolff both worked. Now tonight, Zajac comes back to Bucciano's, talks to the bartender, kills time in a park, then shows up here to meet these two—whom I've never seen before—and asks them what happened to his friend Wolff. They claim not to know, he gets angry. So they open fire on him with an M-1."

"You sure it was an M-1?" Moore asked.

"Pretty goddamn sure."

"Our ballistics boys will check."

"*Our* ballistics will, thank you," the SAC said.

"However you like it." Moore shrugged. "Bottom line, sounds like munitions workers were swiping guns and selling 'em to the mob. Maybe Zajac here didn't like how much they'd paid him or something, and this is how they handle their disagreements."

"I didn't think the mob would try to touch Northeast," Devon said. "I thought they knew well enough to stick to loan-sharking and whores and drugs. Why would they mess with a federal munitions plant when they know how hard we'll come down on them?"

Moore shrugged again. "Maybe they don't know how hard you'll come down on them. Maybe people aren't as afraid of you G-men as you think. I guess they haven't read those comic books."

While the SAC walked off to take a closer look at the shell casings, Devon leaned against the alley wall again. Moore discreetly reached into his jacket and emerged with a flask.

"You need this."

Sweet Jesus, yes. He took a snort and handed it back before the SAC could see.

"You know, if you were a real cop, and this was your first shooting," Moore explained, "I'd be obligated to take you out for some Jameson. We have our traditions."

"That would be nice of you. If I were a real cop."

Gardner, not hearing any of this, stood up and walked over. In his hands was an evidence bag with the dead man's wallet. "Let's get to the office, Mulvey. We've got some paperwork to do."

Moore winked at Devon as the SAC walked off. "Drinks tomorrow night, then."

The dead man's name was Gustavo Celini, age twenty-nine. Back at the office, Devon and Gardner made calls and got what they could from BPD. Celini had a long rap sheet: bootlegging in '30 when he should have been in high school, possession of an unregistered firearm, assault and battery twice. He'd done short stints in Waltham but had seemed clean for the past two years.

As far as BPD knew, Celini was part of Leo Marcuso's gang, which operated out of the North End and had tendrils as far north as Maine and as far west as upstate New York. The hour was late and Devon was drinking coffee he didn't really need, he was so wired from adrenaline.

Past three in the morning, he called the home number of Officer Duggins, the cop who'd told him to steer clear of Bucciano's. The phone rang for more than a minute before Devon heard a very tired "Hello?"

"Hiya, Duggins, this is Agent Mulvey. This a bad time?"

"Jesus, it's the middle of the night!"

"Yeah, I'm awfully sorry about that. You know a guy named Gustavo Celini?"

"What?"

"When you're taking payoffs from the local mob, have you ever run across a Gustavo Celini?"

"You smart-mouthed son of a bitch. You wake me up so you can insult me?"

"I'm calling you so I can find out everything you know about a guy I just killed because he tried to kill me first. I'm doggone sorry about your beauty rest."

"Wait, slow down, slow down."

Devon recapped his night for the no-doubt bleary-eyed officer. "Now I told you the other day I didn't much care about your little grifts. But I *really* don't care for mob hoods making off with military rifles on my watch and then firing them at me."

"I don't know anything about stolen rifles, Jesus. Haven't heard a thing, I swear."

"Good. I'll be asking Leo Marcuso next."

"You're *what*?"

"How do I reach him? I noticed he's not listed in the book."

Perhaps if he wasn't overtired, wired, and still mentally unwound from his near-death experience, he might have been less cavalier about a mob boss. But his mouth seemed to be going faster than he himself could control.

"Mulvey, Jesus, you don't just call up a man like that! Not if you care about your health."

"The FBI is supposed to be afraid of a gangster? Is that how *you* operate?"

"Oh, you're just full of piss and vinegar, kid. You want to waltz your way to an early grave, you go right ahead and—"

"Duggins, I'm giving you a chance to side with the mob or side with the United States government. That shouldn't be a hard fucking decision. Now, you find out how to get me in front of Marcuso as soon as you get out of bed tomorrow morning, or you can find yourself dealing with an anti-corruption sting the day after."

Duggins was still insisting Devon was crazy when Devon hung up on him.

Chapter Thirty-one

THE LIST

"I hear you had a date," Elias said as Anne poured her morning coffee. He was eating cereal at the table. No sign of her mother or brother, both at their jobs already.

"I did."

"And I wasn't here to make sure he deserved you."

"Does anyone deserve me, Elias?" She sat down at the small table.

"*Pshaw.* But your mother tells me he's a policeman? That does not seem your type."

"An FBI agent, actually."

He raised his eyebrows. "Seems even less your type."

"We knew each other as kids."

"Agent or not, he gets fresh with you, he sees me later," and he smacked a fist into an open palm.

"I can handle myself, thank you."

He exhaled sadly. "I know this. But I have to say it anyway, it is required. Family tradition. Your father, rest his soul, would be angry with me if I didn't say it."

She couldn't decide what to make of Devon. She liked him, maybe too much. Which worried her. He'd said he would help her, but over the years she'd sent tips to the Bureau that they seldom seemed to follow up on. Perhaps a personal connection would make a difference.

He could simply be trying to stall her, even though he denied it. Or maybe he was only doing her a favor so she'd sleep with him. She was wary of being used, in more ways than one. But he was a damn good kisser, and something about his casual, happy-go-lucky attitude made her envious, made her want to linger in its glow a little longer.

Everyone always called her serious, told her she needed to have more fun. And here was a man who seemed to be having a lot of fun, even in the midst of a tough job in a trying time. Part of her wanted to write that off as him being pampered, just another fortunate man insulated from the worst aspects of the world. But part of her wondered if his carefree attitude was something she needed more of, if only she'd welcome it into her life.

Elias spotted her daydreaming. "Your mother said he was good-looking."

She felt herself blushing, so she stood up to fix herself some breakfast. Elias chuckled.

He added, "Your mother told me to remind you, the baby-naming for Jessica Gilman's daughter is tomorrow." The Gilmans were neighbors; Anne had always been friendly with Jessica, but she wished her own mother would make fewer comments about how wonderful it was to see a young woman like her married and with a baby. "You said you'd be there."

"Of course."

She thought of the way Devon had brought up, during their date, how her family had been treated years ago. She'd been angry at first for his spoiling the mood, but she realized later how accurately he'd diagnosed her, how he'd zeroed in on the one moment that had recharted the rest of her life.

She didn't like to admit how important it was. Her activism may have been informed by her mother's and Elias's experiences with unions, but she knew in her heart it mainly came from the way her family had been treated when people learned they were Jewish. She had been hurt so many times, and she'd smothered that hurt with righteous anger, with hard work, with the stories she wrote and the truth she pursued.

At the same time, she didn't want to be defined by this. She didn't want it to be all she was.

When she sat back down, she said, "I haven't had a chance to ask you. But that fight at the union meeting—what's going on?"

He leaned back in his chair. "What's going on is criminals want to control the docks, which means control the unions. Want to take their cut of everything. Take their cut from our dues, from our pay, from what the companies ship. Steal from everyone."

"But unions vote. Can't you all just vote against—"

Elias laughed. "Did you not see what happened? The fight? Yes, we can vote. Then we can get beat up for voting the wrong way. Can lose jobs for voting wrong way. Can see apartments burned, families hurt. You are good with the politics, but politics don't always work against fists and knives. They saw that in Germany and in Italy, and they'll see it here too, I'm afraid."

She'd been picking up more rumors about mob involvement with the docks. She knew it was a stereotype that Italians were criminal-minded, so she had of course assumed the rumors she'd been hearing were false, just like all the rumors she killed. But now she wondered if she'd been too skeptical.

Supposedly false rumors were turning out to be true lately.

She knew the Italian stereotype was due to the fact that recent immigrants were often shut out of legitimate work, so that some had no choice but to resort to crime and the black market to feed their families. That's how it worked: an entrenched economic system forced people into roles, and once you were forced into your role, everyone else said it was your nature, who you truly were. Negroes are lazy. Irish are drunks. Italians are criminals. Jews are bloodsuckers. Whereas the economic truth was so incredibly obvious to her, she still didn't understand why so many others didn't see it.

She stepped into her bedroom, found her notebook and brought it to the table. As she ate, she read through some of the notes she'd jotted down recently, finding a small chorus about this subject amidst all the other gossip. A bartender at a Southie bar popular with dockworkers had overheard rumors of some wild plan to send American mafiosi on an advance mission to Italy, in hopes that they might assassinate Mussolini and save our troops the trouble of an invasion. A woman who ran a restaurant in Charlestown with a view of the harbor said that an unusually well-dressed man with what "might've been an Italian accent" had been dining alone at a quiet afternoon hour and had taken photos of the waterfront before she shooed him off. "He'd been wearing real nice shoes," she'd added, as if this were damning. And Anne had seen with her own eyes the roughnecks who'd crashed the dockworkers' union meeting.

She thought again about Devon and his role protecting war industries. Back in the kitchen, she asked Elias, "How could the police let the mob take over the docks during a *war*?"

Elias looked at her like she was a fool. "Because they're crooked, why you think?"

"But . . ." She shook her head. She was the last person anyone could accuse of being naïve, yet still this surprised her. "It's a matter of national security. If crooked cops let the mob interfere with shipping during a war, surely there would be consequences."

He swallowed some cereal, then shook his head. "I wonder what kinds of conversations other families have at breakfast table. Anyway, no, mob won't mess with shipping. That's their whole point. They *won't let workers strike.* They want to take our dues, but also our power. That makes national security people very happy, I think."

"So the government actually *approves* of the mob taking over the docks?"

He sighed. "I don't know. I just think, it's complicated."

She decided to change the subject. "How do you think Sammy's doing?"

"He's fine."

"I'm worried about all the fighting in the neighborhood."

"I know you are. I worry too. But he's smart, he'll stay out of trouble. And I'm gonna start walking at night when I'm not working, part of the new protective association. My first shift is tonight, actually. Those Irish boys will back off when they see us out on patrol."

She didn't share his confidence but decided not to argue. "Has Sammy ever talked to you about having a girlfriend?"

"No. But I wonder. Think maybe he works with a girl he likes, and that's why he didn't mind working so late that night?"

She'd wondered the same thing. "He told me the other day that he's looking forward to enlisting. Can't wait to turn eighteen and put on a uniform."

"It will happen, Anne. Soon enough." Then he stood, leaving his dishes on the table for Anne to clear, as usual. "Off to work—day shift today. Stay out of trouble, young lady."

She rolled her eyes. He had no idea.

Her car finally repaired, Anne picked it up from the mechanic. The destroyed windshield meant she didn't have her gas sticker anymore, so technically she had to go to the DMV to pick up a new one or she'd be ticketed. She decided to run that risk for now, swinging by Marcie's to see if she'd developed the prints yet.

"Hello?" Marcie's voice over the intercom was groggy, as expected.

"Don't tell me *this* is too early—it's past noon."

Anne heard Marcie sigh through the speaker, then the buzz as the door unlocked.

When Anne reached the top floor, the door was already opened. Marcie and a young woman Anne didn't know were making eggs and bacon, the kitchenette's windows open.

"Anne, this is my friend Jeanette. Jeanette, Anne."

They both wore sleeping robes, hair disheveled as if they'd just rolled out of bed. Jeanette was strikingly tall and blond, her eyeliner smudged from the night before. Something about the way Marcie's hand lingered on the small of Jeanette's back told Anne they were more than friends. She found herself remembering certain comments Marcie had dropped over the years. Anne had always assumed Marcie just liked to sound risqué, but perhaps there was more to it than that.

"The writer friend." Jeanette smiled. "Good to meet you."

"You too. Sorry to interrupt breakfast."

"I developed your pictures last night," Marcie said. "Step into my laboratory."

Anne walked past Jeanette and followed Marcie into the second bedroom, which she had converted into a makeshift dark room. The bitter stench of chemicals was only slightly less powerful than the smell of bacon and cigarettes from the kitchen.

"God, Annie, your face."

"What?"

"For a radical, you can be a real prude."

"I didn't say anything."

"Not with your lips."

She didn't know what to say. She'd heard stories about women who did this but had never actually interacted with any, as far as she knew. She had nothing against it, just felt unmoored, and she realized too late she'd insulted her friend.

"Anyway, you were right, the lighting was terrible," Marcie said. "A few of your shots were utterly worthless, dear, try as I might. But I managed to rescue a few of them."

Hanging from a clothesline were half a dozen large photos, blown up eight by ten. Anne saw the printing press, the piles of hate sheets. The stack of counterfeit ration stamps was clear in at least one of the shots; again, she had no idea how to tell the stamps were counterfeit, but the fact that they were in some random warehouse rather than a government office was probably damning enough.

"You had a few shots of some notebooks, but this was the only one that's legible."

She remembered the notebook, the page on which she'd seen "Gold's Gas" scribbled down, only a moment before the man had startled her. Now she took a closer look at the page, which appeared to be a list of local businesses. A few of the names were crossed out, but the majority had checkmarks to the right of them, along with dates from the past two months.

Meyer's Meats. Al's Grocer. Brighton Ave Laundromat. Friedman's Flowers. Cohen Bakery. Gold's Gas. More.

"I know Al's Grocer; it's around the corner," Marcie said. "I'm pretty sure the owner is Jewish."

Every surname on the list was Jewish, and Anne was willing to bet that the businesses with generic names were Jewish-owned too.

It made a terrible kind of sense now: Flaherty and his accomplices were printing counterfeit ration stamps and selling them only to Jewish proprietors. That way, they made money *and* they snuck a bit of truth behind the rumors they themselves were spreading, that Jews had extra ration stamps. They were stacking the deck in favor of their lies. That's why the man at the gas station had been so alarmed when he'd seen Anne glancing at the envelope Flaherty had delivered. Anne had gone there because she thought he was passing out hate sheets, when really he was buying counterfeit stamps.

"Is this some kind of hit list?" Marcie asked. "Are they going to burn these places down?"

"Jesus, maybe. Or they want to burn their reputations down first, and then hope that someone else does the literal burning for them."

Chapter Thirty-two

FREE CROISSANT AND ESPRESSO

Bucciano's was doing a brisk morning trade when Devon and Lou walked in.

Gabriele Bucciano stood at the bar, making another of those fabulous espressos. He made eye contact with Devon and froze.

"Hello again," Devon said without a smile. His head was pounding from his adventure last night; he'd been up past four before collapsing into sleep at his desk, and his decision not to seek medical attention for his knock on the head was beginning to seem unwise. He wore yesterday's clothes and knew he looked like hell.

"Officer," Bucciano said. "Is there something I can—"

Devon ignored him, stepped toward the tables, and held his badge high over his head.

"Federal agents!" He slowly weaved between the tables. "Ladies and gentlemen, this establishment is now closed! Please leave the premises immediately. No need to pay your server, please just take your things and make an orderly exit."

Everyone was staring in shock, no one quite ready to be the first to move.

"*Now!*" He grabbed the forearm of the nearest man and gave him an ungentle tug. The fellow rose to his feet and so did everyone else, women hastily grabbing purses and men straightening hats.

Devon noticed from the look on Lou's face that his partner was not pleased with this little display.

As the customers left, Devon pointed at a waiter, then at the young kid who'd been helping at the coffee bar. "You two, take a fifteen-minute break. Your boss and I need to catch up."

Once the joint was empty, Devon marveled at the empty room, all the abandoned tables and half-full plates. He shook his head at Bucciano. "Say, that must have cost you an awful lot of money. Sorry about that."

He found an untouched croissant on one table and helped himself. Layers so thin and buttery they'd melt in sunlight. Crumbs cascaded from his mouth.

"What do you want?" Bucciano asked.

Devon stepped to the bar and took the demitasse cup Bucciano had just poured. Took a sip. God*damn* this was good stuff.

"You lied to me the other day. You said you didn't know the man that was killed right outside here, but not ten minutes later his widow walked in to talk to you. You also said you didn't know his buddy Zajac, but last night he came here too. And within an hour, he was dead."

Bucciano held out his palms. "Yes, okay, widow came here. Very angry. She ask questions like you did, but I have no answers for her. And I don't know a Zajac."

Devon finished the coffee, which was too small. "Another, please. You don't remember a man coming in here late last night, and talking to you, and you maybe arranging for him to meet with a couple of other fellows at an abandoned grocery store a few blocks away?"

Bucciano hung his head for a moment, then looked back up. The man was so demonstrative that, Devon reflected, he seemed unlikely to be a good liar. He wore his thoughts on his elbows, his shoulders, his eyebrows.

Bucciano sighed. "He didn't tell me his name. But he told me he needed to speak to a man I know."

"What man?"

He looked down again.

"Would you rather chat in a prison cell? Because that can be arranged."

"Dantana. Ricardo Dantana. We knew each other more when we first came here, but we are no longer . . . close friends."

Devon asked him to describe Dantana, and it sounded like the man who'd gotten away last night.

"He friends with a Gustavo Celini?"

"I do not know."

"Where's my coffee?"

Bucciano shook his head, muttered something in Italian, then stepped over to a complicated-looking contraption and started moving nozzles, adjusted a clamp. Devon looked over at Lou, who had his arms folded and was watching his partner with disgust. He hadn't said a word since they'd walked in.

"So you know how to get in touch with Dantana? You have his number?"

"No, but I know a man who does."

"Then I want that man's name and number."

"Are you trying to get me killed?" Bucciano threw up his hands again as the espresso machine made a racket without him. "If we pay those men, we do it so they don't burn our *ristorante* down. We do it to protect our family. I want no part in whatever other business they conduct."

Devon would feel guilty later for what he was doing. Bucciano had been easy to hate from a distance, but the longer they spoke the more Devon saw that he was what he appeared to be: an innocent businessman trying to keep his operation afloat in a mob-controlled neighborhood.

An older man in a tan straw hat and linen suit opened the door. Devon called out, "They're closed, sir. Come again tomorrow."

"Huh?"

Bucciano spoke to the man in high-speed Italian, and the fellow eventually nodded and walked off.

While they were conversing, Lou stepped up to Devon and said, quietly, "This is wrong on multiple levels."

"I don't know, I think I believe him."

"I mean *you* are wrong. This is not how we operate, and you know it."

"Sorry, Lou, I'm having trouble hearing you. My ears are still ringing from being shot at last night. Fix the sign at least."

He kept his eyes on Bucciano, who was making the coffee, and heard Lou's footsteps to the door, heard Lou flip the sign from "OPEN" to "CLOSED" and slide the dead bolt so they wouldn't be interrupted again. Bucciano passed the demitasse cup and saucer to Devon, who took a sip.

"*Mm.* Now, call your friend and tell him I want to meet with Marcuso."

"Marcuso? Are you crazy?"

"Do it or I get OPA to shut you down for ration violations."

"What violations?"

"Whichever ones I feel like making up." He downed the rest of the espresso in one gulp. "Let's go, Lou. Mr. Bucciano has some work to do."

Chapter Thirty-three

FRAME JOB

The news Marcie had revealed by developing Anne's photos felt so hot Anne shared it with Harold and Aaron immediately.

The trio had spent the previous day doing more interviews in Dorchester and neighboring Roxbury, and their plan was to do more today. Yesterday they'd gotten two teenage boys and one adult to write out affidavits about the beatings they'd suffered (in two of the instances, the victims had gone to the police, but the police hadn't taken down a report and had instead threatened to arrest the *victims*). Once they had enough statements, Anne would arrange to have the affidavits notarized. With these statements part of the official record, that would help Harold's story and hopefully goad the city into action.

Today she met them outside the same corner bakery they'd chosen as their meeting place, which happened to have the best bagels in town (it never hurt to be well fortified for a hard day's work). Harold caught a cab from his hotel and Aaron walked from his house; as Aaron had done yesterday, he brought his German shepherd, Marley, along with him. For protection, he had explained. Anne wasn't a fan of dogs, and this one was a giant. Dark brown, wolflike ears. Fortunately, Aaron kept him on a tight leash, and the beast seemed controllable, but she decided Aaron would wait outside while Anne and Harold conducted their interviews.

"Before we start, there's something I wanted to mention," she said, telling them about the list of Jewish business owners. The more she'd thought about it since coming from Marcie's, the darker that list became.

Of course, telling them about the list meant telling them about the warehouse, which meant explaining her break-in. She left out the part about the man who held her at gunpoint, still not sure how badly she'd hurt him.

"Shit," Aaron said. "Sounds like a hit list." He offered a piece of lox from his bagel to Marley, who eagerly snapped it up. "What are they gonna do to those businesses?"

"It also sounds like they've been selling those businesses counterfeit ration stamps," Anne explained. "We keep hearing that cops aren't taking this seriously—what if cops are actually involved?" She hadn't told them how the man at the warehouse had said as much, since she was afraid to mention him. "What if this group has cops with them, and they're entrapping Jewish businesses in a counterfeiting ring? They're selling them stamps now while accusing Jews of being cheaters—next, they're going to go public, maybe even arrest them, as a way of proving their point."

"When were you going to mention this warehouse?" Harold asked.

"Honestly, I wasn't. I didn't think it had to be a part of this story. It was something I was hoping to . . . cover myself."

Marley's enormous head moved from speaker to speaker, as if he were following along.

"Look, if we're working together, you need to be honest with me. I can't have you holding important information back," Harold said.

Easy for him to say, she thought. *The story's going to run under his byline.* He didn't seem to appreciate the sacrifice she was making, giving him the fruits of all her research so he could win all the credit. She wanted the news out there—that was the most important thing—but it was still galling to see how this man would get all the praise, and just because he had more connections and was based in a city whose editors weren't so cowardly.

"All right," she said, not liking it.

"We need to make the ration stamps part of this. Which means we should talk to those business owners."

"Not just for your story but to warn them about what's coming,"

Aaron said. "They may be crooks, but we gotta warn them they're being led along here. Before something even worse happens."

First, more witness statements.

They worked for three hours, at the end of which Anne felt drained, the stories depressing and at times unbearable. Some people only agreed to speak with them off the record, but four more agreed to write out affidavits. Their list of other names to follow up with was growing longer, too.

As it neared four, they called it a day. Aaron walked home with Marley, whose tongue was hanging out from the heat, and Anne drove Harold to his downtown hotel. She felt exhausted as usual, her to-do list never-ending. She'd meant to spend some time that day writing an angry letter to her town councilman, demanding to know why Dorchester was going to use city funds for a July Fourth parade at which an avowed anti-Semite would be giving a talk, using tax dollars to fund Hitlerism. Maybe she'd get to that tonight.

"You mentioned the other day that your brother got roughed up too?" Harold asked her.

"Yes—Sammy. He's only seventeen. It's happened twice, actually."

She drove with the window down, her hair getting bigger by the minute, but it was worth it for some air.

"Why don't we get an affidavit from him? Should be easy enough."

"It's not. He doesn't want to."

At a red light, she noticed Harold watching her quizzically. "His sister is running all over town getting statements from strangers, but he won't give one?"

"I think he's embarrassed. Trying to be a tough guy."

"So are most of the kids we're talking to, but they still manage to talk to us. Look, I don't mean to pry into family matters, but if this had happened to one of my relatives, I'd damn well be taking their story down."

The light turned green and she hit the gas harder than she needed to, annoyed.

"Are you sure he's telling the truth?"

"Why wouldn't he be?"

"I don't know."

She thought for a moment. "He described some of the attackers, one of whom is the same one we've heard about several times, with the crescent-moon scar. Look, my brother's a lot of things, but he wouldn't be making this up for attention. And trust me, I saw the bruises."

"Okay." They were a block from his Tremont Street hotel when he asked her, not for the first time, "How 'bout a nosh and a drink? That was some tough work; we deserve it."

"I wish I could, but my tough day's not over yet."

"C'mon, even you can blow off some steam a little."

"Not today. Sorry."

Maybe a week ago, she might have joined him. They had a lot in common. She realized she was turning him down due to loyalty to Devon, but was that a mistake?

After she pulled in front of the hotel, Harold reached for his door handle and paused.

"Something else I wanted to ask you. Are you sure you're prepared for what'll happen when I publish this story?"

The "I" in that sentence grated on her, even if he was technically correct. He would be writing the story, and it would run under *his* byline in *his* magazine. But everything they'd done so far was collaborative—if anything, she'd done more of the work. She told herself to let it go. She'd been swallowing her pride during this entire project and couldn't afford to jeopardize it now.

"Of course I'm sure. I can't *wait* until it's published. Then the public will be outraged and demand that City Hall does something about the attacks."

Now that they weren't in motion, the humid air felt stifling. Or maybe it was the conversation.

"That's our goal, but it might not pan out. It might just make the cops really, really angry. And when that happens, I'll be safely back in New York, but you and Aaron live here. And so does your brother."

"What are you saying?"

"I'm saying you're great to work with and I admire your chutzpah, but don't kid yourself about what happens next. The cops will hate you for this. The mayor may just shrug and ignore everything. We might be kicking a hornet's nest, with all of those negatives and nothing positive to go along with it."

"Well . . . I hope you're wrong."

He told her he hoped so too as he got out.

On the way home, Anne stopped at the kosher butcher's and bought some chicken to cook for the family. Her family didn't strictly keep kosher, but much of the neighborhood did. A few years ago another butcher had tried to open a shop that sold both kosher and non-kosher meats, claiming that he would keep the two separated; this only provoked outrage, and his shunned business was closed within a month.

Anne planned on making more calls to follow up on the mob rumors after dinner; she'd found that people were easier to reach on the phone in the evenings anyway, even if it annoyed her mother for her to use their home line for work calls.

The apartment was empty, but soon they'd all be back from work. She turned on the oven but decided that maybe she could put off cooking just a bit, long enough to make one call.

She looked up "Gold's Gas" in the yellow pages, then dialed the number. A man answered. Remembering the name sewn on his shirt, she asked, "Is this Arnie?"

"Speaking."

She wasn't sure whether he himself was the proprietor or not, so she asked, "Arnie Gold?"

"Yeah, speaking. Can I help you?"

"Pete Flaherty referred me to you."

"Can't say I know the name, but I'm happy to help you, miss. You having car trouble?"

"Pete Flaherty, the printmaker."

Silence for a beat. "Mmm, like I said, doesn't ring a bell. But I work on a lot of folks' cars and I don't always remember their names." Self-deprecating chuckle. "What's going on with your car, miss?"

He sounded too natural to be lying, and he was trying hard to win her business. He had no clue as to her real reason for calling. Which meant either Flaherty hadn't given Gold his name, or Flaherty had used an alias.

"I'm not calling about my car, Mr. Gold. I'm calling about the ration stamps."

"We accept ration stamps, of course. You can't always use gas stamps on repairs, though, if that's what you're asking."

"That's not what I'm asking." She paused. "I'm asking you about the extra ration stamps. The ones you're selling on the side."

His voice sounded different when he said, "I don't know what you're talking about. You have a good d—"

"You're going to be in a lot more trouble if you hang up on me."

Silence. He finally asked, "Who is this?"

"I'm not going to answer that right now."

"You were in here last week. Jesus, you were following him."

"Whatever he told you his name is, it's actually Pete Flaherty and he has a nice little printing press that makes those ration stamps, among other things. So how did it work—he came to you and offered you a deal you decided was too good to pass up?"

"What are you, a reporter? You working with the cops?"

"What you don't realize is, you played into their hands. The people who are printing those counterfeit stamps call themselves the Christian Legion, and they're also printing hate sheets, all about how evil Jews are and how we're conning the U.S. into going to war with good Christian Germany."

"Look, I don't know anything about all that. And you think I don't already know that I do business with folks who call me a kike behind my back? Lady, if I had skin that thin, in *this* town? I wouldn't make a buck."

"It's not about having thick skin, it's about not giving them extra ammunition to fire at everyone else."

"Like I said, I don't know anything about that. Or him, really. He came to me to make me an offer and maybe I said yes, maybe it helps me pay the bills during hard times. That's all it's about, okay?"

"Oh, just a fun little way to make a buck, huh?"

"You know how hard it is running a business right now? You want to judge me, lady? You married? How's your husband earn his living, or your daddy? Ask them how well they play by the rules before you judge me."

It wasn't worth correcting his many assumptions. She bit back what she wanted to say and waited until he sounded done.

"You need to open your eyes, Mr. Gold. People like the Christian Legion love to say that Jews are liars and cheats, that Jews don't enlist, that Jews get extra ration stamps, and meanwhile *they're* the ones selling you extra stamps. They're using you to prove them right."

A pause, and his tone changed. "Lady, I'll fill up your tank on the house, anytime you need. I'll do free repair work anytime, okay? Don't call OPA on me, please. I got three kids."

He still didn't get it. "They're setting you up, Mr. Gold. They *want* you to get caught. That's why Flaherty didn't tell you his real name. He even changed his license plate before driving out to see you, just in case you wrote it down. *They're* going to call OPA on you, or the cops, and when you get *arrested,* they'll get to point to you as a perfect example of what they've been warning everyone about: another dirty Jew cheating 'regular Americans.'"

Silence as he seemed to ponder this.

"If I were you, I'd burn any of those stamps you have left, right now. Burn any evidence you ever worked with him." She wasn't sure how Harold would feel about this, whether she was stepping beyond journalistic ethics here, but she felt she had to help Gold protect himself. "Assuming you sold those stamps to other people, it might be too late. Once the Legion rats you out, they'll try to find people you sold them to."

"Fuck," he said, his voice quieter than before.

"What *do* you know about him?"

"Nothing. A hell of a lot less than *you* seem to."

"How did he first approach you?"

"Just . . . came in for gas one day, asked if I'd be interested."

"And you thought you could trust him? A stranger offers you black market stamps and you just said yes?"

"There was a cop." He said this blankly, like he was in shock, flipping through an old memory and marveling at what he'd found. "That was it. He didn't come for gas at all, it was a *cop* that drove up for gas. Then this other fella comes up, chats with the cop, shakes hands and all like they're old friends while I'm filling up the tank. Then the cop drives off, and this Flaherty follows me into the office and gets to talking." He paused. "They timed it that way on purpose, so I'd trust him. Showing off how he was connected. I'm such a sucker."

The man in the warehouse had hinted to Anne that he had cops as allies, and this confirmed it.

"Do you remember the officer's name? Did you get his car number or license plate?"

"Lady, I wasn't checking license plates, c'mon."

"Do you remember what the cop looked like, whether it was Watertown police or Cambridge, anything?"

He sighed. "He was wearing a uniform, all right? I wasn't taking down notes like you are. I can hear you scribbling."

Yet when they hung up and Anne read through her notes, she wasn't sure she'd learned anything helpful, and anyway, it was all bad news.

She'd barely started cooking dinner when the phone rang.

"Oh, Anne, I'm glad I caught you there."

It took her a moment to recognize the woman's voice. "Hi, Mrs. Doherty." Lydia's mother. "How are you?"

"Well, not too good." Her voice quivered. "You wouldn't happen to know where Lydia is right now?"

"I don't." She had been so busy she hadn't called Lydia or dropped by the restaurant the last couple of days. "Is everything all right?"

"Well, George and I were out of town for a couple days, and when I tried to call she never answered. Now we're back and it doesn't look like she's been here. We called her work and they say she hasn't shown the last two days. Are you . . . are you sure you don't know anything about where she'd be?"

Anne sank into a kitchen chair, the room beginning to spin a bit. She hadn't seen or heard from Lydia since the night at the warehouse. And they had used Lydia's car to drive there. They hadn't thought the car had been spotted. But maybe it had been?

She opened her mouth but realized she didn't know what to tell Mrs. Doherty, didn't know whether the many bad ideas racing through her head could possibly be true.

Chapter Thirty-four

THE IRON NAIL

Devon was back at the Bureau office late that afternoon, shaky from caffeine and lack of sleep, when his phone rang.

"Agent Mulvey, this is Leo Marcuso. I understand you wanted to speak to me."

Marcuso was in his sixties and had less of an accent than Devon had been expecting. He did not sound alarmed or concerned.

"Yes." It took Devon a moment to gather himself. He waved over Lou, who picked up a phone linked to the same line. "There's a man who works for you, Gustavo Celini. You won't be seeing him anymore because he passed away last night, and when he did he was holding an M-1 rifle that had recently been stolen from Northeast Munitions. He was with a man named Ricardo Dantana, and maybe you will be seeing him again, and in fact I'd very much like to see him again too."

"I'm sorry, Agent Mulvey, I don't know these people. I'm puzzled as to how I can help you."

"Look. I know you have friends with BPD, but, as I'm sure you can imagine, stealing rifles from a military plant runs afoul of several federal laws. And you don't have any friends in this office."

"If you're suggesting I am in any way involved in the theft of military rifles, I can assure you, you have been misinformed."

Devon ignored him, continuing, "And when it comes to federal laws, we have all kinds of interesting tools at our disposal now. You've heard of custodial detention?"

"I have not."

"Interesting thing, custodial detention." He saw Lou shaking his head. "It sounds like what happens to a bad kid who has to stay after school and clean the place, but no, what it is, see, is it's a new law that lets us lock up people even if we don't have what used to be called 'probable cause.' On account of the war and all, sometimes there are people who we decide are dangerous even if we don't have ironclad evidence against them yet. So we put them in custodial detention, which is basically jail. And they can stay there for a very long time, without us having to go before a judge or all that rigamarole. We're using it on the Japs in California, and it seems to me we can certainly do that with some Italians in Boston who are stealing from the military."

Marcuso said nothing. Lou was staring daggers.

"A fellow like you, I'm sure you're very smart and you've been very careful about keeping your hands clean. All the illegal shenanigans you have your boys do—they do it, you keep far away from it, there are no fingerprints or paper trails that would ever get *you* in trouble, right? You can just laugh at the cops and us feds who try to build a case against a smart, careful fellow like you."

Still nothing.

"But now there's a war on and we can lock you up if it's in the best interests of the country, and I'd say that's looking increasingly likely right now."

Devon heard the son of a bitch laugh.

"Agent Mulvey, I'm not the man you think I am. I'm also not accustomed to being insulted and accused of terrible deeds. But, as you say, this is wartime and perhaps manners and old ways are changing in our country. Yes, *our* country, Agent Mulvey. I'm an American too, and I'm on your side. I had nothing to do with any military rifles, and I don't believe I've ever met this Dantana fellow. But because I am so patriotic, and because I want the good FBI to stay focused on our true adversaries in this trying time, I will prove myself to you. I will find this Dantana. I will find him for you and I will have him by tomorrow night."

That was a better offer than Devon had expected. "For someone who says he doesn't know the man, that's awfully fast."

"When I set out to do something, Agent Mulvey, I do it, and to the fullest extent. So, let's say tomorrow night at nine. In front of the Old North Church. I'll have this Dantana ready for you there."

After they hung up, Devon said, "Not bad, if I say so my—"

"You can't go threatening custodial detention on someone like that! You know full well there are channels we need to go through."

Lou still seemed furious at him for his display at Bucciano's, and this didn't help.

"It got him moving, didn't it? I'd say that's progress."

"Go home, Devon. Take a nap and when you come back, make sure your head is screwed on straight."

Devon didn't care for how Lou put that, but it seemed like good advice, so he left.

After waking up in the afternoon, he made a call to the *Boston Star* to see if Anne Lemire was available. Her phone rang six times before another reporter answered; he decided not to leave a message. But he called his local florist and ordered an arrangement for her, saying to put it on his tab.

It was early evening when he returned to the office and put in a few hours. At eight, the sun setting, he got a call from Jimmy Moore, much raucous noise in the background. "We're still on for drinks, right? The Iron Nail in Charlestown. Come on, we're here already."

Two hours later, Devon, Moore, and two cop buddies of Moore were finishing their third round at the Iron Nail.

The bar sat a mere six blocks north of Northeast Munitions, part of the row of Monument Avenue taverns that deadened the pain of factory workers and longshoremen. Devon, like most people who did not live in Charlestown, had never set foot in the place before tonight. In fact, he'd seldom ventured to Charlestown until he'd started this job.

Even though "the Town" sat just over a short bridge from Boston, it was its own world, with little to recommend it to outsiders. Elevated trains cast much of it in shadow. Sugar factories and the Schrafft's candy plant exhaled smoke and odd chemical flavors so very different from the sweets they were creating inside. The state prison loomed in the distance, if not physically then spiritually, haunting the area with an occasional dip in electric power when an inmate was executed.

The neighborhoods of cramped three-deckers were not so unlike those in Dorchester where Devon's family had once lived, but the Mulveys had moved beyond such places long ago. All the more mystifying to Devon was the fact that most Townies had such pride in their hardscrabble, blighted spit of land, expressing deep love for a place everyone else scorned. The phenomenon was not so unlike the loyal Sox fans who stood by their losing team season after season, but at least Sox fans were hoping that the team would actually, one day, somehow, win again. People in the Town, as far as Devon could tell, either enjoyed losing or assumed it was a natural by-product of life itself.

Or of being Irish.

Which, to Devon, wasn't pride at all, but something worse.

The Nail had a buzz and clamor that felt just short of spontaneous fistfight. It made even a drinker like Devon realize what a refined and civilized fellow he was in contrast. Sawdust on the floors, sweat in the air. Riveters and welders and painters and other assorted Yardies lined the bar and stood around tables, draining bottles and glasses and growlers. Curved steel cargo hooks hung from longshoremen's belt loops, a work tool earlier and a possible weapon later. There was no music, as no one would have been able to hear it anyway over the hollered conversations, though on occasion the shouts and yells coalesced into old Irish ballads and fight songs. So really there *was* music, but intermittent and bad.

"How's that bump on your head?" Moore asked.

"The more I drink, the more it flattens out."

The other two cops were uniforms named Hoskins and O'Meara. Hoskins was thin, wiry, and chatty, older than forty. O'Meara was a younger fellow who barely spoke but laughed loudly at everyone's jokes, happy to be invited.

Moore had mentioned during the first round that BPD had searched Zajac's house and found two hundred dollars in cash, likely paid by the mobsters who'd bought the stolen rifles from him.

"So what war dirt can you give us?" Hoskins asked Devon.

"War dirt?"

"C'mon, you feds must know something. What's happening next?"

"What, you want me to tellya all about my briefing with the President?" He rolled his eyes. "I watch the factories, boys. That's it."

"But you know how to read between the lines," Moore said. "Devon here's always been good at that."

Devon took the compliment, which went to his head, which he knew was the point. But it worked anyway and he said, "Something big's coming soon, that's all I can tell."

"How soon's soon?" Hoskins asked.

"Imminent."

"Hoskins here can't spell 'imminent,'" Moore said.

"I know what it means, though."

So odd to be out with the local cops celebrating his first kill. He knew it was a stupid ritual, knew they were doing it to take his mind off the enormity of the event, but he appreciated the gesture all the same. He wasn't really their colleague, though; he was a fed, and he knew damn well that his fellow agents, including Lou, would never have offered to do something like this.

It made him realize just how isolated he was at the Bureau. *These* were his people.

Which also made him sad, because he wasn't one of them, either.

Which made him finish his beer and crave another.

Hoskins wandered over to the bar, his turn to buy. O'Meara got up to hit the john. Moore slid closer to Devon.

"Now, I know I'm just a dumb cop and your boss doesn't want me to know shit. And in fact I'm so dumb and drunk that I won't remember this conversation tomorrow."

Sure, Devon thought.

"So, tell me. Since we got wops robbing the plants so they can outfit themselves with military weapons. They gonna try to blow up the Harbor next, or machine-gun City Hall? I need to know what's happening in my city, Devon."

"I'm working on it, Jimmy. I'll tell you more when I know it myself."

Moore took a sip. "If someone as powerful as Leo Marcuso is gathering military weapons like that, I don't think he's using them to shake down gamblers and bar owners."

Devon tried to make sense of this. "No, but I don't think a new front in the war is about to open in Boston."

Jimmy reached forward and playfully tapped at Devon's skull. "You got a red mark here tells me otherwise."

Devon pushed Jimmy's hand away.

"You know I like you, Devon. And maybe this is the wrong time to say it given what happened to you last night, but I'm gonna say it anyway: I'd feel better if I thought you and your college boys were being a hell of a lot tougher about what you do. Because if you can't lock things down, we can."

"We'll lock things down." Devon held his stare for a while.

Devon didn't care for the insult, especially coming from a cop at a department that was rife with corruption. He wanted to ask if Jimmy could crack down on other cops taking cuts from the mob, but he knew that was all but impossible, and he didn't want to put that on Jimmy in front of these other two cops—who, for all Devon knew, were on the take themselves.

He got up and walked toward the men's room. Walking past the bar, he realized he was still holding a crumpled napkin in his hand. He'd picked it up and made a fist, still angry at what Jimmy had said. He unballed his fist and took a closer look at the napkin.

He'd seen one like it before.

He stopped walking.

In the center of the napkin, a very small logo of an iron nail had been embossed. A minimalist design, barely two centimeters, and just slightly three-dimensional. So small, in fact, that the first time he'd seen one like it, he hadn't realized what it was. Because someone had drawn over it.

The swastika on the napkin they'd found on Wolff.

He was sure of it now. The swastika had been drawn on one of these napkins. The axis where the lines of the swastika intersected had been drawn right over the iron nail. He'd noticed it before but hadn't realized it was a logo, had thought only that something funny had happened with the ink from the pen.

He stood there staring, thinking.

Trying to make sense of the various revelations from the past few days.

Wolff was a Jewish German immigrant war worker who had swiped military rifles and apparently sold them to low-level Italian mobsters. And at some point the night of his murder, either he had been drinking in this Irish pub, or his killer had been.

Everything made less sense than before.

Devon made it to the bathroom, then returned to the table. Moore was in the middle of a story about a man who had tried to escape the scene of a robbery without wearing any pants, for reasons Devon missed. Everyone else loved the story. Laughs all around.

Moore looked at Devon and asked if he was all right. Apparently Devon hadn't been smiling.

Chapter Thirty-five

PANIC

The next morning, Anne called in sick to the *Star*. Panicked about Lydia, she had called every mutual friend she could think of the night before. It didn't do any good—no one had seen Lydia since that terrible night.

It was within the realm of possibility Lydia had met someone and run away for a few days. But that seemed too convenient. Far likelier: someone connected to that warehouse had done something.

Anne had met Nolan, looked him in the eye while he lied to and insulted her. He'd seemed capable of a lot, she'd felt, but had he and his colleagues actually abducted Lydia? He had seemed so confident, so sure that he'd found every legal loophole that allowed him to preach hate and encourage violence—he'd said over and over that his group hadn't actually *committed* violence, as if this made everything else okay. But maybe they'd done something to Lydia, and he'd known about it even as he smiled at Anne?

Her fear for Lydia was compounded by her guilt, the sense that *she* was the reason Lydia was in trouble.

In which case, why hadn't they come for Anne too? Was *she* being followed?

She called the restaurant where Lydia worked; the last shift Lydia had shown up for was three days ago, the owner explained. She'd clocked out at two. That was the day following their misadventure at the warehouse, just a few hours before Anne's dinner with Devon.

Moments after she hung up, a sleepy Elias slowly walked into the kitchenette and poured himself a coffee.

"Hard at work already?" he asked, eying her notebook and the phone.

"Not exactly." She wasn't sure if she should tell her family about Lydia.

"Listen, I need to tell you," he said as he sat down at the table with her. "Something strange happen last night."

Elias had worked the day shift yesterday, then after meeting a friend for a quick supper at a bar, the two of them had walked the neighborhood that night as part of the new protective association.

The good news, he explained, was that it had been mostly uneventful. He and his friend Gregory had been out from the hours of seven until eleven, walking nearly the whole time but sitting on a few stoops to rest their feet now and again. Gregory had carried a baseball bat, something that could be a weapon if needed but also explained away as a harmless prop in case anyone questioned what they were doing: *just coming back from the park after some practice.*

A hot night, they'd expected to find trouble somewhere. Windows were open all over town, the kind of evening kids would have been out playing late. But they'd seen no kids or teenagers. Parents weren't letting kids out. They passed a few people here and there, returning home from work, often walking in pairs but sometimes alone, moving quickly, keeping their heads up.

No roving hooligans, no one out spoiling for a fight. At least not on the blocks they walked.

Finally, at midnight, their job was over. Hopefully what they'd done had helped, simply being a presence. Maybe they had stopped trouble from breaking out without realizing it. There would be other nights, other shifts.

Gregory lived just down the block, and as they were nearing the building where the Lemires lived, Elias spotted something they seldom saw: a police car.

It was parked directly across the street from his building. And as he got closer, he realized the cop was looking at the building, maybe even at their third-floor window.

"Good evening, officer," Gregory said, as the cop's window was rolled down.

The cop glanced at them, startled. He hadn't heard them coming, and he seemed unnerved to be addressed.

"Good to see you out here," Gregory added. There had barely been any police presence in the neighborhood during these weeks of violence.

The cop didn't say a word. Instead, he started his car and pulled away.

"I don't know," Elias told Anne. "Maybe he was just on break and resting and he felt like we'd caught him goofing off. Maybe he had just been called for something in the neighborhood, and was finished. Maybe just coincidence we walk up then. But . . ."

"It felt like he'd been out there watching our building, and only left because you spotted him?"

"Yes. Maybe he know I was part of neighborhood patrol? Or maybe what you are writing about, he's not happy about it."

The man at the warehouse had said he worked with cops. Anne hadn't wanted to believe him, but it was feeling more and more likely.

Last night, when Lydia's mother had called Anne, she'd said she and her husband were going to call the police next. Anne feared that wouldn't do any good—maybe cops themselves were responsible for this—but she hadn't been able to think of a way to tell that to a worried mother.

"You need to be careful, Anne," Elias said. "Especially at night. Protective association can maybe keep Irish boys away. But not police."

She told him she'd be careful, then he retreated to his bedroom to change.

She wondered if she should call Devon. The feds weren't the cops; if a band of dirty cops was helping the Legion, surely the FBI could shut them down? But she didn't like the idea of running to a man for aid, and she still wasn't entirely sure she trusted him. God, it was possible Lydia had disappeared at the same time that Anne had been out on her date. Was *Devon* connected with her disappearance?

Had his date with Anne been nothing but an alibi?

She still hadn't seen anything in the local papers about the man she'd hit with the typewriter. Nor had she seen a story about the FBI raiding the warehouse to find anti-Semitic leaflets and a printing press with counterfeit ration stamps. Had the G-men not bothered to follow up on her anonymous tip?

She needed to figure out how much she really trusted Devon.

That morning her family went to the Gilmans' house three blocks away for the baby naming ceremony. Despite the festive atmosphere, the blessings and the mazel tovs and the coos at the tiny, week-old babe (they really do look funny at that age, Anne realized), she found it impossible to relax. Only a couple of the families here knew Lydia, and when Anne discreetly asked if anyone had heard from her recently, no one had.

As soon as the brief ceremony was over and people were descending onto the buffet, Anne walked up to Aaron Green.

"I'm sorry, but I won't be able to do any interviews this afternoon. You can meet Harold and go on without me."

"Everything okay?"

"I'm not really sure. I'll tell you later."

Before he could ask her any more questions, she found her mother, who had just loaded her plate, and told her she needed to run.

"Already?" Her mother lowered her voice. "Annie, don't be rude."

"I'm not trying to be, I just have to make some urgent calls." She didn't want to explain her fears about Lydia, which would only make her mother try to keep her from reporting. "I'm sorry."

"Come on, Anne. You can take a break sometimes."

She apologized again, knowing that she was disappointing her mother yet again and hating herself for it, but feeling like she had no choice. She hoped no one else noticed her early exit.

Back at the apartment, she made a few futile calls to people who might have heard from Lydia, but got nowhere. She decided she couldn't limit her search to phone calls anymore. Regardless of how dangerous the outside world had become, she needed to do something.

She had Peter Flaherty's address. Maybe if she drove out to his residence in Watertown, she could learn more about him. Maybe they even had Lydia there? She picked up her car keys and left a note for her mother and Elias, telling them exactly where she was headed, just in case.

Chapter Thirty-six

CHEWED OUT

Being called into the SAC's office first thing in the morning never augured well. Doing so with a hangover made the chore particularly unpleasant.

Yet there Devon stood beside Lou, called by their boss into his too-small office only moments after Devon had arrived at the office.

"Close the door," the SAC told them, another bad sign. As soon as Devon closed it, the SAC began, not even giving them time to sit. "Would you mind telling me what on earth you two think you're doing, arranging an audience with Leo Marcuso?"

Normally Lou did most of the talking with the SAC, but Devon sensed his partner wasn't eager to excuse Devon's methods, so he replied, "Sir, as you know, we have mobsters running around town with stolen M-1s, so I figure Marcuso knows about it."

"You know darn well we have certain ways of doing this, Mulvey, and that's not it." Devon hated the SAC's aversion to cursing as much as he hated his rules. "If you suspect Marcuso is involved, there are a dozen more careful methods of finding that out without tipping him off the way you did."

"Sir, I merely thought—"

"Being shot at does not give you carte blanche to make things up as you go along, Mulvey. We don't 'wing it' here. Building a case against someone like Marcuso would take months, at the very least, and we don't have those kinds of resources at the moment."

"Well, that's why I figured an expedited approach might get us—"

"I'm tired of hearing you talk, Mulvey. I'm not interested in your excuses or your opinions. I believe you have plenty of work to do, so you will not add mob-hunting to your duties. Under no circumstances are you to meet with Marcuso or anyone in his organization. Is that understood?"

"Yes, sir," Lou said, ever eager to please.

Devon couldn't bring himself to agree yet, instead asking, "Even if they're stealing military rifles?"

"First of all, I thought your theory was that a few factory hands were stealing them, then maybe selling them to gangsters. So that's different." It seemed like splitting hairs to Devon, but before he could object, the SAC continued, "Second of all, we are not investigating the mob. Good God, we have enough to deal with at the moment, and our remit is clear: preventing espionage and sabotage, protecting the war industries, keeping tabs on anyone and everyone who might try to disrupt the war effort. Organized crime falls far, far down on the list."

"But what if the mob is disrupting the war effort?"

The SAC made a show of folding his hands together on his desk. "Agent Mulvey, are you having trouble hearing my very clear orders?"

Devon took a breath. He knew he'd handled Bucciano and then Marcuso the wrong way yesterday, but he still hadn't expected this.

"No, sir."

"Good. Stay away from Marcuso, stay away from the mob. Now, I believe you both have a mountain of background checks you should be getting to."

"Yes, sir," Lou said again, practically jumping at the chance to open the door and walk out. Devon reluctantly followed.

When they were closer to their desks and out of earshot of the other agents, Devon said, "Jesus, Lou. You ratted me out to the SAC?"

"No, I didn't. You think *I* enjoyed that?"

Devon didn't know what to believe. It was possible Lou had in fact told the SAC about Devon's call with Marcuso—Lou was such a Boy Scout he would have been inclined to do so, even if it meant suffering through those last few minutes. But if Lou was telling the truth, and he *hadn't* told the SAC, then how did the SAC know?

Had Marcuso gone to the SAC himself and told him to call off his agents? That seemed absurd. The FBI did not take orders from the Mafia, as far as Devon knew.

He was starting to realize just how little he knew.

Lou sat at his desk and started looking through his stack of background-check files, which indeed seemed much taller than yesterday.

Confused and angry, Devon also felt hurt. Jesus, he'd been shot at the other night. If that had happened to a cop, half the BPD would be storming the homes of the shooter's known associates. It would be personal to every cop in the city, a goddamn vendetta. *You don't fuck with a cop.* He had expected his fellow agents to respond the same way, but no one was rallying around him. Would this be different if he was a WASP? If *Lou* had nearly been killed, would the SAC be telling them all to declare war on the mob? Once again he felt that disrespect, that he'd never truly been accepted into this particular boys' club.

Devon asked Lou, quietly, "Why do you think he really wants us to stay away from the mob?"

Lou made a show of opening the top file and seemed to be quite absorbed in reading it. "I don't know. And I don't care. I like my job and I plan on keeping it. I don't need the SAC angry at me. I don't need to barge into businesses and raise hell. I also don't need to question suspects alone without my partner. I don't need to make up my own rules because I think I'm special."

He finally looked up at Devon. Still whispering, but he sounded furious: "You, however, seem awfully anxious to get fired. And then you'd be drafted, Devon. *Then* you'd get to play hero all you want. Boy, wouldn't that be swell. Maybe that's your master plan all along. Maybe you think you can sabotage yourself here and get to salvage your precious self-esteem. Well, count me out. Count me out of *all* of it. I said from the beginning that that case shouldn't involve us, and it shouldn't. Ruin your life over it if you need to, but don't mess with mine."

With that, Lou shook the file in his hand. "Now, how do you want to divide these up?"

Chapter Thirty-seven

THE PROBLEM WITH NEW WINDSHIELDS

Flaherty's house sat in the middle of a modest block, much like Anne's in Dorchester. Two- and three-story homes, most of them subdivided into apartments, based on the multiple mailboxes outside each. Narrow lots, the front gardens well-tended. Flaherty's was a yellow building, in good repair, with two mailboxes in the front.

She slowly drifted past the house, trying to see if the windows were open or if a lamp was on, but that wasn't as easy as she had hoped. The summer light reflected off the windows, so she couldn't see through them, couldn't tell if anyone was home. She didn't see Flaherty's car parked on the road, but his building was one of the few on this block that had a garage behind it, so possibly it was inside.

At the end of the block she turned, then drove around so that she could return to the street and park in a way that she faced the apartment door. Her car windows were rolled down and she was getting hot; with the sun beating in through her windshield, she realized she hadn't thought this through very well. She spotted a shadier spot up ahead so she moved the car, realizing that by now if anyone was keeping an eye out, they'd surely notice her odd behavior.

Sitting out here was only marginally better than sitting in her apartment.

What was she doing here?

She felt powerless, and she realized as she sat there that she worked so hard in life partly so she could avoid this very feeling. There was so much in life that was beyond her control, but the harder she worked, she'd figured, the more she could trick herself into thinking she was more than just a pawn in a larger game.

Her job was to chase down stupid stories and disprove them. Even if life was increasingly feeling like a stupid story. The author of world events a deranged madman. People believed the damnedest things nowadays, yet Anne had believed that if she could stamp out at least some of the worst fictions that floated about, if she could starve the fires of hatred of some of their oxygen, then she would be doing some good.

She feared now that she'd only been kidding herself.

What good did her Rumor Clinic column really do? And what good would her and Harold's coming story do? If something terrible had happened to Lydia, no story could undo that. No magazine article, no byline, no press release could save her friend from danger. Maybe people like her who believed in the power of the pen were deluding themselves, and the only power that mattered was guns and tanks and bombers.

She had been sitting there for nearly an hour, feeling increasingly despondent, when another car drove up. A green Cadillac, shiny and recently washed. Out stepped two men wearing suits and straw hats. She didn't get a good look at their faces, only a bit of hair color to determine that one was much older than the other.

They knocked on the door to apartment A. A moment later the door opened and she caught a quick glimpse of Flaherty. Then they were all inside.

She jotted down the license plate number of the Caddy.

Only ten minutes later, the two men emerged from the house. They stood outside for a bit and this time she could see their faces clearly: one of them was Charles Nolan. The older one took off his hat and mopped at his forehead with a kerchief.

He looked familiar. In his late fifties or sixties, but barrel-chested and fit, with thick white hair. Where did she know him from? An attendee at some pro-Hitler meeting she'd sat in on a couple of years ago, most likely. But she wasn't certain. A local pol whose name she was forgetting, maybe.

Nolan and the mystery man got into the Cadillac, Nolan in the passenger seat. She leaned over so she wouldn't be spotted as they passed.

Sitting alone in a car on stakeout for unclear reasons was torture, a strange mix of boredom and potential danger. She was only here because she felt like she had to do something, but this wasn't getting her any closer to finding Lydia or to putting these bastards in jail.

Finally she admitted defeat, started the car, and drove off.

She was only a mile from home when she heard the sound of a police siren. She glanced in her mirror and saw a squad car right behind her, lights flashing.

Her heart started pounding as she pulled over. The squad car pulled up right behind her.

"Oh, Jesus." She hadn't been speeding. She told herself to stay calm as she reached into her purse for her driver's license.

The cop stayed in his car for what seemed an unusual amount of time, not that Anne had any experience with this. Finally he got out and slowly made his way to her.

"License and registration, please."

She complied. "Is everything all right, Officer? I couldn't have been speeding."

"This vehicle doesn't have a gas rationing sticker, miss." He looked about forty, with hard brown eyes and a sharp chin. "You should know that's against the law."

Damn it, she knew she'd been risking this. "I had one, but I'm afraid my windshield was shattered the other day and I haven't had a chance to get a new one."

"We're not big for excuses right now, miss. There's a war on and we can all do our part. Wait here."

She was tempted to tell him that she'd filed a police report and could prove that her sticker-bearing windshield had been destroyed, but if he was anything like the cop who'd taken that report, he wouldn't care.

Elias's warning from this morning rang in her ears. Could this even be the same cop who'd been outside their building last night?

He carried her papers back to his car.

He seemed to keep her waiting longer than necessary. Minutes passed and the late-afternoon sun was baking her through her newly installed, sticker-less windshield. She felt sweat all over her body and was desperate for a shower or at least a cold drink.

Finally he walked over again. "Step out of the car, please, Miss Lemire."

Anger spiked to panic. "What? Why?"

"I can't allow you to drive this vehicle without a sticker. It will be impounded and you'll have the opportunity to reclaim it once you've paid your fine and purchased the appropriate sticker."

"That's ridiculous! I need this car to do my job!"

He put his hands on his hips, his right hand close to his gun. "Step out of the car. Now."

She felt she was nearing some breaking point beyond which the ramifications of her actions would be greater than she could pay. Tears welled in her eyes but she told herself to stay calm, breathe slowly. He didn't deserve to see her snap.

She got out and closed the door. He roughly handed her papers and the ticket to her, pressing them into her chest.

"Call the station in a couple hours and they'll be able to tell you which pound it's at. Would you care for a lift back to your house?"

"No, thank you. I can walk."

"It's hot, you know. Only gonna get hotter, given all you've been up to lately."

". . . Excuse me?"

"Someone like you goes looking for trouble, doesn't she? Doesn't care how hot it gets, how unhealthy it is. Someone like you, Miss Lemire, should think awful hard about what's she's doing. Or things could get a whole lot hotter."

She glanced at his name plate: "DUFFY." At least she had his name.

"Where's Lydia?" she demanded.

"Who would that be?"

"It makes you feel real big to threaten women, is that it?"

"Way I see it, you're the one's been making threats. Always trying to get other people in trouble. That's what you Bolshies love, ain't it? You just want to tear people down. Tear the city down, tear the country down. Well, lady," and he leaned just a bit closer to her and whispered, "we ain't gonna let you."

"I'm not a Bolsh—" But no, she stopped herself. She would not give him the satisfaction of hearing her explain herself.

If he was referring to the hate sheets and the warehouse, and the old man she'd clocked, she would need to watch what she said. But no, if he was a Dorchester beat cop, he was likely referring to the reporting she and Harold were doing; he didn't want see-no-evil cops like himself to be implicated in her story.

"The only thing I'm trying to tear down," she said, trying to keep her voice calm but already feeling herself shake, "are the thugs who are beating up boys and old men. In a neighborhood that people like *you* are supposed to patrol."

"Watch who you're calling thugs, lady. You ain't seen nothing yet."

Chapter Thirty-eight

POLITICKING

Devon had just finished having lunch with a source at Hibernian Hall in Roxbury when he was surprised to hear his father's voice.

"Pearl Harbor was terrible, yes," his old man was saying from another room. "But if the choice was between losing some far-off island of dark-skinned Samoans or fighting another European war, then I'd have been happy to say sayonara to Hawaii."

"Agreed," another man responded.

The Hall was a four-story brick building where, for generations, Irishmen had been gathering for hatching business plans, hosting fundraisers, arguing over which politicians to support, and launching whatever other schemes they wanted to occur out of the Yankees' sights. And out of women's sights, which was one reason Devon seldom dropped by (the appeal of all-male spaces was lost on him). He'd come today only because a well-placed source at a local factory had wanted to meet here; their chat finished, he'd been walking down the second-floor hallway to leave when he heard his father.

He stood there for a moment, listening as Pop continued, "Let the Japs have Honolulu-lulu. That's no reason for our boys to be sent to Europe."

Devon wasn't thrilled to realize his father was out spouting his frustrated isolationism in semipublic, and maybe he should have just walked away. But he decided to pop in and say hello. He gave a quick knock, then pushed the not-quite-closed door the rest of the way open.

"Devon," his father said, as surprised as his son had been. He hastened to his feet, as did the three men with whom he was sharing a small conference table. Devon had the sense he'd interrupted something more delicate than his father's too-loud voice earlier had indicated. "I didn't know you were here."

"Sorry to interrupt; just heard your voice and thought I'd say hello."

"By all means. A happy coincidence." As his father spoke, Devon recognized one of the other men. His heart jumped a beat. He realized too late that he shouldn't have walked in.

"Devon," Pop proceeded with the introductions, "this is Father Ryan, from St. Luke's on Blue Hill Ave; Charles Nolan; and I assume you know Michael Cavanaugh, our state representative."

Father Ryan was the very priest whose mass Devon had attended several times to take notes for the Bureau. Their one conversation had been in the darkened confessional, with a screen between them, so Father Ryan had never seen what Devon looked like. He would recognize Devon's voice, though—maybe not right away, but surely he'd make the connection if Devon's job came up.

So Devon laid the bonhomie on thick, keeping his voice far from the somber tone he'd used before, as he smiled and shook Father Ryan's hand. "Pleased to meet you, Father. I hope you're not trying to woo my old man away from St. Joe's—Father Boyle wouldn't like that!"

Father Ryan smiled back. "I wouldn't dream of it."

Devon's mind raced. Had his father known it was Father Ryan whose homilies Devon had been monitoring? Devon hadn't even realized the men knew each other, but still he'd been careful not to tell Pop the name of the priest or the parish. Maybe Father Ryan had complained to Pop about the pesky FBI, and his father had put one and one together? Or, hopefully, neither Pop nor the priest had made the connection.

Regardless, it worried him to see his father palling around with this particular cleric.

Devon shook hands next with Nolan and Cavanaugh. He'd never met either before, though of course he knew Cavanaugh's name, and knew his father was excited about the ambitious young pol's prospects. Cavanaugh looked to be in his mid-thirties and wore the smart suit of a downtown executive, a silver watch, and shoes Devon made a note to ask him about later if the opportunity arose. The third man, Nolan, was a stranger to Devon, fortyish with a serious brow, his attire more rumpled than Cavanaugh's.

"Michael was just telling us he'll be giving a speech at the Fourth of July rally in Dorchester Park next week," Pop explained.

"That's swell."

"Normally it would be our congressman's privilege," Cavanaugh said, "but he's quite ill and asked me to do the honors."

"I think the man should just step down," Pop said, "since he's clearly too ill to do his job. Let the next generation take over."

Cavanaugh smiled. "Well, I'll get my chance in November. He's said he won't run again."

The state rep, Devon recalled, was as much an isolationist as Pop. His name had popped up among the attendees of certain Nazi-sympathizing meetings the Bureau had helped shut down a couple years ago, but he personally had emerged unscathed from that dragnet. Politicians had been much less likely to face charges, as the Bureau tread warily around them.

Devon knew that Pop had become more involved in local politics, that it helped him quell the widower's loneliness. He clearly enjoyed the influence that his wealth and connections bestowed, taking pride in his ability to promote upstanding young Irishmen. But Devon didn't think Cavanaugh qualified.

"And what is it you do?" Cavanaugh asked.

"Munitions security," Devon answered. Lying somewhat. He cut his eyes to Pop and hoped the old man wouldn't feel the need to brag about his FBI agent son. "Preventing industrial sabotage; not as interesting as it sounds. How about yourself, Mr. Nolan?"

"Please, call me Charles. I'm an attorney, and I suppose you could say I dabble in politics. I'm doing what I can to get Cavanaugh here to the next level, and I help coordinate like-minded candidates all over New England."

They chatted a bit as Cavanaugh told them about his campaign plans, the allies he'd made and relationships he'd developed, with Nolan adding a point here or there. Devon could tell this meeting had been set up by Cavanaugh, hoping to loosen Pop's wallet. The talk was far too isolationist for Devon's taste—at one point, Cavanaugh mentioned finding ways to "turn things around" on the war. It was like they were still hoping to win an argument that most of America thought had already been decided against them.

"Everyone's become so war-crazy," Pop lamented. "I made the mistake of seeing *Casablanca* the other day. It was absurd. All these pro-war Hollywood movies—financed by Jews, no doubt—trying to make it seem like this war is democracies versus dictatorships. *Please.* We're allied with Joe Stalin, for God's sake!"

"Yet people fall for it," Father Ryan said.

"I may have to see it anyway," Devon said, trying to change the subject. "That Ingrid Bergman's quite the looker."

"My son here," John Mulvey said disapprovingly, "always has liked to elide the seriousness of certain subjects."

"There's no sin in being entertained, Pop, especially during wartime." With that, he apologized again for interrupting and bid them good day.

He was halfway down the hall when his father hurried after him, alone. "Devon. Why the subterfuge about your job?"

Devon stepped closer so he could keep his voice down. "Pop, you need to be careful with people like that. No one is going to 'turn things around' on the war, all right? Even *trying* to is asking for trouble."

"Well, you never know. We may have some ways of pulling it off yet."

We? Devon felt a creeping nausea. "Pop, you saying things like that . . . it puts me in an awkward position."

"I'm just talking to my son, aren't I? Or are you taking notes for the Bureau?"

"You do realize that talking about trying to stop the war—"

"I'm an American citizen, correct? Endowed with the right to free speech? I can criticize this damn-fool war all I want."

"Criticize, yes. But . . . are they actually *doing* something? Are you?"

His father looked away. "There's no industrial sabotage afoot, Devon. Nothing that affects your job duties, I assure you."

"What aren't you saying?"

"Well, use your head, damn it! You just said you didn't want to be put in a difficult position. So, I'm not going to put you in one. There's no reason for you to know certain things. No reason for you to have to be troubled by whatever trifling ethical dilemmas you seem to fear. Best you don't worry your head about it. And bear in mind: we're trying to *save* people. Save more Americans from getting killed in a damn-fool war. Save your brothers-in-law. And so many others."

Devon had always understood that his father had wanted him in the FBI to keep him from the front lines. Now he feared there was more to it.

He wanted to insist that the old man explain what the hell he was talking about. But he was afraid of the answers, and what he'd have to do once he heard them.

He'd been back at the office only for a few minutes when Anne called.

"Hello there," he said with a smile. She was calling about the flowers, no doubt.

"Would it be possible for you to come over? I need to talk to you about something, but not over the phone."

"Is everything okay?"

"No, it's really not."

Chapter Thirty-nine

COMING CLEAN, MOSTLY

Anne was sitting in the front room when she saw Devon park. She'd been keeping watch ever since calling him, partly to see him coming but also to see if any cops were staking her out.

A moment later he knocked on the door and said, "It's Devon."

She undid the latch and let him in. Hat in hand, he smiled at her, as if perhaps his mind was on other things, being with her unchaperoned like this. But his smile faded as he noticed her worried expression. She closed the door behind him, redid the locks.

"Can I get you anything, a coffee?" She stepped into the kitchenette, nervous. She knew it was risky having a man visit her—would the neighbors see him come or go? What would they think? She'd have to explain something to her mother, who was still out with Elias. Meeting Devon in public would have been more practical, but not when discussing a subject like this.

"Thank you, I'm fine. Are you okay?"

She sat down at the small table and he did the same.

"I'm afraid that a friend of mine is in trouble." Realizing that sounded like a euphemism for pregnancy, she decided to be more direct: "She's gone missing."

"For how long?"

"Two days now. She hasn't been home or to her job."

"Maybe she met some sailor and they're painting the town red? That sort of thing tends to happen these days."

"No, Devon, I think it's serious. I think . . . I think someone wanted to hurt her."

"Have you gone to the police? Or have her parents?"

"I think they have, but . . ."

"But what?"

She had been afraid to tell him anything, and she still was. He was a federal agent and surely had friends who were cops. Even cousins and uncles. She couldn't predict what his reaction might be. But every extra minute that passed while Anne vacillated was another minute that Lydia's life might be at risk.

"I'm afraid it could be policemen who have done something to her."

His brow knit, and she couldn't quite tell if he was skeptical or was taking her seriously. "Why would you think that?"

She ran a hand across the back of her scalp, looking down, and then back up at him. "I can trust you, right?"

"Of course." He reached out across the table and she did the same so he could clasp her hands in one of his. "Tell me."

So she did. She explained how she'd been trying to find the distributor of the hate sheets, told him about the warehouse, the counterfeit ration stamps, even the drunk man who'd held her at gunpoint, and how she'd clocked him. At some point in her story, he released her hand and leaned back, as if her tale was on the verge of knocking him from his chair.

"When he called some friends of his on the phone, he told them to bring *handcuffs.* And he told me they were *policemen*—I suppose that could have been a bluff, but when I got back to Lydia's car and we drove away, we passed a squad car headed down that same street."

He was very still as he asked, "So he'd called the cops to arrest you for breaking and entering?"

"No, Devon. That's not what it sounded like at all."

She held his gaze for a moment while he took this in. He rubbed at his jaw in a nervous tic, looked away from her for a moment, then back at her.

"So the anonymous call to the Bureau the other day about the warehouse, that was you?"

"Yes."

"Why didn't you just tell me?"

"I wasn't sure how badly I'd hurt that man. And I can't prove that he'd had a gun on me, and I *had* broken in. I was hoping if my call led you there, the Bureau would be able to put a stop to them without me being involved."

"I've been meaning to check out that warehouse."

"I left that tip three days ago—I wish you'd acted on it."

"I've been a little busy." He sounded insulted, so she didn't press it. "And honestly, most of those calls tend to be bunk. If I'd known it was you . . ." He shrugged. "The squad car you saw, was it Somerville police? Boston, Cambridge?"

"I . . . I honestly didn't notice. All I know is, it was a squad car. My point is, what if they'd taken note of Lydia's license plate as we drove past? They were expecting to find me hostage in the warehouse, so when they saw a car with two women in it, they didn't think we were important enough to turn and follow us. But they still might have noted the license plate."

"In which case, you're afraid they tracked her down and arrested her?"

"But if she's been arrested, she would have called her parents by now, wouldn't she?"

She was afraid to say out loud what she was really afraid of, but he seemed to follow her. He ventured, "This . . . isn't the sort of thing cops usually do, you know."

"But if cops are part of some . . . group that's pushing out hate sheets, and looking the other way when thugs attack people all over town, then maybe they're breaking plenty of other laws too. Especially if they're afraid they're about to get caught."

He thought for a moment and exhaled slowly.

"Which night was it you went there?"

She told him, and he seemed to flip through his mental calendar for a moment.

"The night before we had dinner? I wish you'd told me all this then."

"Like I said, I wasn't sure what to do. If dirty cops are involved, then, you being a federal agent, I just wasn't sure . . ."

"If I was dirty too?"

She hadn't wanted to say that, and hearing him do so made it even worse. She folded her arms and looked down, not so much ashamed as wanting him to think she felt ashamed.

"Okay," he said after an awkward pause. "The man you KOed with the typewriter—you're not sure if he survived?"

"He had a *gun* on me, Devon! What was I supposed to do, just sit there and wait for his accomplices to show up?"

He held up his hands. "I'm just trying to get all the facts. Like whether he's alive. How badly did you clock him? Did you notice if he was breathing?"

"I don't know. But I haven't seen anything in the papers about a suspicious death."

"They might have taken him to a hospital that night. I'll make some calls." He tapped his finger on the table, thinking. "You took a hell of a risk going to that warehouse instead of just reporting your suspicions about this Flaherty fellow."

"Reporting to who, the police? Good thing I didn't. And I suppose I could have called the Bureau about him, but then my tip would've just sat there without anyone doing anything about it for three days."

He didn't seem to appreciate that, but he nodded. "I'll find her."

"And what if they come after me next?" She mentioned the cop Elias had told her about, the one who'd seemed to be watching her building.

"Maybe he was sitting there because they're finally trying to crack down on the fights," Devon said.

"Elias didn't think it felt that way."

He thought for a moment, then he peppered her with more questions: when exactly had she last seen Lydia, who else might have heard from her, did Lydia have any male acquaintances Anne was suspicious about. What did she look like, height and weight, hair. He took it all down in a small notebook.

"Devon, I really don't think you should tell the police. I came to you so I wouldn't have to go to them. A cop impounded my car yesterday, and he threatened me." She told him about her stakeout of Flaherty's place, and Officer Duffy's warning.

"I hear you, but I can't track her down without at least some help from the police, and there's at least a few cops I trust. In the meantime, I don't think it's helping you to sit around and fret. Why don't we take a ride? Let's go see that warehouse."

Chapter Forty

COLDLINES

As he drove out to Somerville, Devon apologized again for not having followed up on this lead before.

"That's all right. I imagine you get a lot of calls." It sounded, he thought, like she was trying to talk herself out of blaming him.

True, the Boston field office had an anti-sabotage hotline, but it was more of a *cold* line, considering how infrequently it had been used lately. The Bureau had initially plastered the number around most war plants, factories, and ports. "See anything suspicious? Call this number and the G-men will investigate!" God, had people ever called, especially in those first few months. Devon had followed up on countless supposed U-boat sightings, reports of suspicious men walking slowly near fenced-off areas, and strange premonitions felt by elderly women in the South End.

The calls had never, not once, yielded anything of interest, though all the reports had been dutifully investigated and filed by Devon. The calls had slowed considerably over the months, owing to a slight lessening of fear among Boston residents, an apparent decrease in the number of supernatural premonitions suffered by elderly ladies in the South End, and the fact that many of the posters had fallen down and Devon had deliberately neglected to post any new ones.

He knew that he absolutely should not be bringing Anne along on this trip. This, Lou would say, was another example of Devon's bending the rules and doing things his own way. Well, fuck Lou. The sanctimonious bastard had all but said he didn't want to work with Devon anymore. If Devon didn't have a true partner, Anne could serve as his new sounding board, for some things at least.

"I've been trying to figure out who owns the warehouse," she said. "It's technically owned by a company called Cork Management Industries—I dug up the records at Somerville City Hall. But I'm still not sure who owns them—I need to scrounge up the records at the State House for that. All I know is, it's being used by a group calling itself the Christian Legion—have you heard of them?"

"Doesn't ring a bell."

"Their leader is an attorney, Charles Nolan."

"Nolan?" He'd just met a Charles Nolan. "What does he look like?"

She described him, and his heart sank as he realized it was the same man his father had just introduced him to. *Jesus Christ.* Nolan was helping to get Cavanaugh elected to the U.S. House, and his father was cutting Cavanaugh checks. What the hell else were they up to?

"Do you know him?" she asked, and he feared he'd given himself away.

He couldn't get into this with her, not until he'd figured out a lot more about what was going on. "His name *does* ring a bell—I'm just not sure from where. I'll do some digging."

He pulled into a gravel parking area in front of the warehouse. It was hard to tell whether anyone had parked there recently. He saw no business sign, no evidence that the place had been used recently.

"Are you okay?" he asked her. He'd hoped bringing her here might help her by giving her something to do, but now he wondered if it might only be bringing back bad memories.

"Fine." Arms folded, voice clipped.

"Wait here, please." He got out, looked around. Then he pounded on the front door. "FBI. If anyone's in there, open up."

No reply. He walked around the place, the windows too high to peer through. At the back, though, he noticed a shattered window by the back door. The door was locked, but he was able to reach into the broken window and unlock the door from the inside.

He hit the lights. A big empty room, nothing but a few folding tables and some old boxes. He called out again, but it was clearly deserted.

After walking through the place, he opened the front door, invited Anne in.

"Looks pretty empty," he said.

"I *swear* to you, there was a printing press right here. Look, you can see the markings on the floor."

He saw what she was pointing at, where the wood floor had been scratched by the feet of something heavy—recently, judging from the fresh fibers of wood poking out. And the smell, like new paper and some chemical he couldn't place. The building may have looked abandoned from outside, but something had been happening here not long ago.

"I have pictures, too," Anne said.

"You didn't mention that."

"I meant to," she said, looking away. It sounded like she was lying, making excuses. She still didn't trust him, he could tell. It made him wonder what else she was holding back, how much he could trust *her*.

"And may I see these pictures?"

"Of course. They're back at my place."

Next they inspected the small office in front, finding more nothing—an old desk, the drawers empty. Even the waste bin was empty.

"Looks like they were pretty thorough about clearing out. You must have spooked them."

"I wish we'd been faster."

I wish you'd *been faster,* he knew she meant.

They were halfway back to the city when Devon said, "I still think we'll find out that Lydia's run off and she's okay. But just in case, if you aren't feeling safe, I do have a second set of keys to my place in the Back Bay." He was at a stoplight, so he turned to gauge her expression. "I'm not trying to take advantage, honest. I'll sleep on the sofa. You can even lock the bedroom door. Honestly, I'll probably be making calls at my office all night anyway."

"Thank you, but—"

He didn't even let her finish. "Yeah, I figured. Just wanted you to know you have the option."

Minutes later, after an awkward silence, she broke it.

"Actually, I think I will. If you do take the sofa."

"I love my sofa."

"Just for tonight." She told herself this was the right decision, to hide out for a moment. She didn't think her adversaries would come after her family, but they'd likely be looking for her.

"I'll have Lydia tracked down by then anyway."

Not for the first time, Anne wished she shared Devon's sunny confidence.

He swung back to her apartment, waiting in his car while she ran inside to get some things and leave her mother a note claiming that she had to work late. He studied the street for any sign that some cops or anyone else was staking her place out, but he didn't see anything.

Back in the car, she handed him a folder with photos.

"I only have the one set, but the negatives are in a safe place."

"I'll get them back to you," he told her.

During the short drive to the Back Bay, he checked his rearview mirror but was confident no one was following them.

His spartan, third-floor apartment was a block off Commonwealth and a short walk from Copley Square. A small parlor, a kitchenette, a bedroom, and a bathroom. He was a rather neat fellow as bachelors went, though he imagined she was picking up on all sorts of hygienic shortcomings. He grabbed some spare sheets and threw them on the sofa for later. While she was politely inspecting the place, he double-checked that his desk drawers and file cabinets were locked—he wasn't giving her *that* key.

Again, if the SAC or any of his fellow agents knew he'd let someone like her into his apartment, he'd get a chewing-out that made this morning's seem friendly. Hell, maybe Lou was right and Devon *did* want to get fired—he knew he was taking stupid risks but couldn't stop himself. It was harder to stop when it felt like it was actually the right thing to do.

"I'd offer you dinner if I had anything, but there's a couple great spots across the street. Help yourself to anything you do find, of course."

She looked a bit nervous to be there, her eyes slightly wider than usual. He felt an added charge, too. He wanted to give her a goodbye kiss, but he felt that would make him look like he wasn't being a man of his word, so he hurried for the door.

"I'll probably be late, but I'll be quiet letting myself in. If I get good news before then, I'll call."

"You probably don't want me answering your phone, though."

"Good point. I'll call once, hang up, then call back. If that happens, it's me."

Back at the office, he called BPD and asked for the records clerk. No Lydia Doherty had been arrested in the last three days.

Then he asked for Jimmy Moore and was routed to Homicide. The cop who answered told him Jimmy was out at the moment.

"Have you had any Jane Doe victims in the last three days?"

The cop told him to hold on, ruffled some papers. There was indeed one female murder victim, he said, and one who had died in a fire the day before. Devon asked for details, his pulse quickening. Thinking, *Don't be her.* The murder victim was in her forties at least, and the fire victim was short and overweight, not a match.

"Thanks. Have Moore call me as soon as he gets in."

He did the same with Cambridge and Somerville police, again not turning up any murder victims who might have been Anne's friend.

He called local hospital emergency rooms. Again, no one who sounded like Lydia. As for the man Anne clocked, Devon did uncover a few cases of men with head injuries from the night of Anne's warehouse adventure, but they were all too young to be the man she had described.

After calling every emergency room within fifteen miles of the warehouse, he switched tack and called a source at WAAC's local office, plus the WAVES (the Navy's equivalent) down in Newport. He asked if it was possible to check whether a Lydia Doherty had enlisted in the past few days. His sources told him they'd check their records and get back to him.

While making his calls, he'd flipped through Anne's photos. Yes, he saw the ration stamps and the printing press, though the shots were grainy, the backgrounds black. There was no way to prove that these shots had been taken in that particular warehouse. A defense attorney would be able to say they could have been taken anywhere. The notebook with the handwriting about the Christian Legion—the words in that shot were nearly illegible, and he doubted a handwriting expert would be able to say who'd written them. He could still pass these on to OPA, but he doubted they could do much with them.

It was another photo that caught his attention. He'd flipped past it at first, but now he stared at it. Looked through his desks for his magnifying glass. Moved his desk lamp closer.

"I'll be damned."

She'd taken a picture of some crates and boxes along a wall. She wouldn't have known what she was looking at, but he recognized the crate at the bottom. It hadn't been there when he visited the warehouse earlier, but it was clear in the photo. He recognized the numbering system printed on its side; only the first few numbers were legible, but they were enough.

It was a crate from Northeast Munitions.

He dug out his notebook from his last call with McDonough and found the serial number of the missing crate, confirming it: these were the missing rifles.

So where the hell were they now?

Devon leaned back in his chair and lit a cigarette. Trying to make sense of the many threads he'd been pulling on lately. A German Jewish war worker probably helped steal the rifles, which he likely sold to the Italian mob, either before or after the rifles were routed through an anti-Semitic Christian group. Which made no political sense. Then the worker was stabbed to death, at a time when other Jews were getting beat up in Dorchester. That same anti-Semitic group, which might involve dirty cops, was distributing hate sheets and running a counterfeit ration stamp scheme, as well as stealing rifles or somehow winding up with stolen rifles. And a friend of Anne's, who'd been at that warehouse, was missing.

He'd nearly finished his smoke when Moore called him back. Devon asked him if the name Lydia Doherty meant anything to him.

"No. Should it?"

He'd known Jimmy for years, long enough to understand that Jimmy's record wasn't spotless. Still, he couldn't imagine Jimmy would be involved in a counterfeiting scheme, let alone the murder or kidnapping of an innocent woman.

He hoped the real problem wasn't that his own imagination was poor.

"She's a friend of one of my sources," Devon explained, "and she's gone missing. Two days now."

"You checked to see if she's been brought in?"

"Yeah, and she hasn't. But this source of mine, he"—changing Anne's gender to disguise her—"has reason to believe some cops may have taken Doherty. Off the books."

Silence for a bit. "What are you talking about, Devon?"

"I need you to keep this under your hat. But I'm working on a case that may involve counterfeit ration stamps, and I have reason to believe some of the people involved wear badges." He decided to keep to himself the fact that the rifles had shown up in the warehouse. "This Doherty gal may have gotten herself into trouble with them."

"Should I be insulted that you thought to call me?"

"I just want to know if you've maybe heard any comments, or anything at all."

"Counterfeit stamps?" Moore had lowered his voice. "Look, I know that goes on, and OPA deals with it. I would hope no cops are involved in anything like that, but I have no idea." He exhaled. "And what does this have to do with your job patrolling war factories?"

"Maybe nothing, Jimmy. I'll pass it on to the OPA boys. One more thing: you know about a group called the Christian Legion?"

"Yeah, I've heard of them."

"What have you heard?"

"One of those 'defend Christianity from the godless reds' groups. From what I can tell, it's part Bible study group, part athletic club. Working out to stay in shape for Jesus or something. You ask me, it's just guys feeling insufficient for not being at war, trying to save face by acting tough."

"But you don't know of them being involved in anything illegal."

"No. Hell, a lot of them are priests, or deacons at least."

"They're led by an attorney named Charles Nolan. Know anything about him?"

"I'm Homicide, Devon. All I know is, he hasn't killed anybody."

Devon refrained from saying "as far as you know," thanking Jimmy and hanging up. Thinking, *What the hell is Nolan's group doing with military rifles? And how, if at all, is it connected to local gangsters?*

He checked his watch: nine-thirty. Only thirty minutes until the meeting with mob boss Leo Marcuso, the meeting the SAC absolutely, definitely did not want Devon to attend.

For him to go to that meeting anyway would be extremely unwise, both for his career advancement and possibly his safety. The SAC might well suspend him. Lou would kill him. But he was still angry about being chewed out for doing his job. His boss didn't want him investigating the mob, even though gangsters clearly had wound up with stolen M-1 rifles? That made no sense. Lou wanted to do safe, boring background checks until retirement? No, thank you.

Maybe Lou didn't mind that there was clearly something the SAC wasn't telling them. But Devon wanted to know what it was, and he sure as hell wanted to find the man who'd nearly killed him.

If he were instead to go straight home right now, Anne would be waiting. That was tempting. Maybe *too* tempting, and he didn't want to do something he'd said he wouldn't. To prove, to himself at least, that he was more than that.

The hell with the SAC, and the hell with Lou. He needed to hear what Marcuso had to say.

On the drive toward the North End, Devon thought again about his conversation with his father. Which made him reflect on how he'd handled Father Ryan in the confessional a week or so ago. Back when he'd filed his report on Father Ryan, he could have chosen his words differently, could have encouraged the SAC to spend more resources keeping watch on the priest, but he'd instead made the judgment call that Father Ryan was a well-meaning old codger who'd simply let his emotions get the best of him and said a few things he shouldn't have.

Pop had been angry at him for spying on a priest, but he would have been relieved to know that Devon had actually protected the priest. Despite Devon's threats in that confessional, his less-than-completely-truthful final report could be seen as him having given the priest tacit approval to continue fulminating against the war effort, against Roosevelt and in favor of Nazi appeasement.

And worse.

Devon's father had talked him into taking this job. Was his father using Devon's position with the FBI as a hedge against ever getting in legal trouble? Maybe Pop knew he could travel in certain circles, attend certain meetings, join certain groups, all while confident that he would never get hauled before any court, because his son was there to protect him.

Maybe, Devon realized, he had been doing exactly what his father wanted all along. Maybe he should be worried about that.

Parking in the North End was impossible, so he pulled in front of a hydrant, his government tags saving him as always. This was another faux pas Bureau manuals strongly advised against, but he was breaking enough rules already, why not another?

He had driven past the Old North Church and not seen anyone lingering outside. His watch read 9:50. If no one showed, that might mean Marcuso knew that the SAC had told Devon to lay off. That alone would tell him something.

Darkness had slipped its way onto the city. Streetlights would normally be on by now, but on account of the war they stayed extinguished. He still didn't see anyone outside the church.

Ten o'clock. Maybe gangsters were hiding behind doorways or in parked cars. Maybe he was stupidly showing up at his own assassination, and Marcuso had never intended on helping him find Dantana. What had Devon really been expecting, that the head of the local mob would show up with Dantana bound and gagged, ready to be hauled off to the pen? That sounded ridiculous, he realized, but yes, it was what he was hoping for.

At ten past ten, he decided he was angry enough to chance it. He took his gun out of its holster and checked it, reholstered it. Got out, looked up and down the street once again, then walked to the front of the church. Salem Street seemed unusually quiet. He heard footsteps, saw an older man hurrying along with a paper bag in his hand.

A car pulled up. Black Ford, a lone driver. It stopped in the street, not even pulling over to park. Devon tensed, moved his right hand to his stomach, closer to his gun.

The driver's door opened and a man exited. Not tall, not big. Just a regular fellow, suit and fedora.

"Agent Mulvey," the man called out across the distance, then started walking toward Devon, leaving his car running. No accent. Unusually friendly voice despite the circumstances.

Devon kept his eyes on him but tried to stay aware of his peripheral vision, expecting someone else to leap out of a corner at any moment.

"I had a feeling you'd show up anyway."

The man was only a few feet away when Devon asked, "And you are?"

"George Ferris, Naval Intelligence." He extended a hand, which Devon hesitantly shook.

Then Ferris reached into his jacket, and Devon's hand flew into his own jacket, reaching for his gun.

"Whoa, whoa!" Ferris stepped back and laughed. Devon hadn't drawn yet, but almost. "Easy there, cowboy. I was going to give you my card." He slowly pulled his hand out and yes, that indeed was a business card. He handed it to Devon.

"You've got quite an imagination, Agent Mulvey. But this isn't a good place to set you straight." He patted Devon's shoulder in what felt like a demeaning gesture. "The man you thought you'd be meeting won't be coming. Drop by my office tomorrow at eleven. We have much to discuss."

Feeling a step behind, Devon read the card to verify it was legit as Ferris returned to his car and drove into the night.

Chapter Forty-one

TROUBLE SLEEPING

Anne wasn't entirely sure what was crazier—to be spending the night at an FBI agent's place or to be back home where some rogue cops might be hunting for her. She had chosen the former, telling herself it was a smart idea, but she couldn't help wondering if she'd made this choice for less rational reasons.

She sat on Devon's sofa—where he would be sleeping later, he'd promised—reading a novel, *Dragon Seed* by Pearl Buck, trying to keep her mind off things. It wasn't working. The stories of poor Chinese civilians whose lives were ruined by the Japanese invasion was hardly light reading under any circumstances, and it only reminded her of the high stakes of her job.

Past eleven, she was just realizing she should go to sleep, in the bedroom, and hoping she would be able to sleep through Devon's return, when she heard footsteps outside and a key in the door.

She stood just as Devon stepped into the room. "Hey, there," he said. He looked tired. He seemed to be making himself smile, but his face seemed pale. She braced herself for bad news, but he read that in her eyes and said, "I haven't found her yet."

He tossed his suit jacket on the desk chair and took off his tie. Undid the top button. The sight of him doing all that brought home the fact that she was in his private space, and that he was shedding some clothing without a second thought.

She had packed modest bedclothes but hadn't changed into them yet.

"The good news is, I called every hospital and emergency room in the area, and no one's reported a patient that matches her, and there have been no murders or bodies that could be her." He gave her some more details about whom he'd called, assuring her that he trusted Detective Moore at BPD Homicide.

"So, she's missing," he said, "but we have no reason to think any harm's come to her. I'm not trying to sound patronizing here, but the most likely answer is what I said before: she ran off with a man or she joined up with WAAC."

"I really hope you're right."

"Me too. I'm gonna pour myself a drink. Care for one?"

"No, thank you. I mean, yes."

He laughed. Her first impulse, again, had been to turn him down, because she was afraid where a drink might lead (all right, maybe not "afraid" exactly, but mindful of the fact that she didn't need to be sleeping with him right now). Then she realized that yes, she absolutely wanted a drink. She had already checked his liquor cabinet (a few bottles; not an alarming number) but had managed to hold off so far.

She had also checked his desk drawers and file cabinets, annoyed to find them locked. Was it bad of her to have looked? Probably, but she couldn't turn off her journalistic curiosity. He was an FBI agent and he'd granted her access to his place, so what did he expect? Well, he'd expected her to be nosy, therefore he'd locked everything. Smart fellow.

He opened a bottle of ginger ale, poured two glasses, and added a healthy amount of Jameson to each. He raised his glass in a silent toast.

"You weren't waiting up, were you?" he asked.

She sat back down on the sofa. He sat in the chair, even though there was plenty of room to sit beside her. He seemed to be taking pains to show that he didn't have any designs on her tonight.

"Please, I'm a night owl. And it was so nice and quiet, it was good to read. I'm used to a crowded apartment."

"Yeah, growing up with five sisters, I never had much space of my own. This place is small, but it's nice to have an escape."

She asked about his sisters, which eventually led to conversation about his brothers-in-law, and Anne's own brother, away at war.

"When did you hear from Joe last?" he asked.

"Two weeks ago. He'd said his next letters would be delayed; that's about as much as he's able to say and get through the censors."

Devon nodded. He'd already finished his drink, as had she.

"I'm sure he's okay. We seem to be getting a better handle on the Atlantic these days. And the Pacific."

They were silent for a moment.

He said, "It's strange, not being out there. My father lost three brothers to the last war. And me having three brothers-in-law in uniform, you gotta figure the odds are . . . one of them won't make it. I would never say that around my sisters, but . . ." He shook his head.

"My younger brother, Sammy, he's anxious to go. At first I thought it was just . . . youthful bragging or something. Talking big to look big. But now, I see it: he honestly, truly wants to get out there."

"I know how he feels. I like to think that I'm doing my part here, but . . . it's different. This is probably the biggest moment of our lives. And here I am in Boston, like always."

"So am I."

"But you're doing a lot to help, you know you are."

"And so are you."

"But . . . men are expected to do more."

"Do you really feel that way?"

He thought for a moment. "Yeah, I do. I mostly push papers and call people on the phone, Anne. Hardly heroic." He picked up his glass again for a sip, seemed to realize it was empty, put it back down again.

"I've been working for years to get people to realize how dangerous the Nazis are," she said, "but now I'm worried that all my work has really done is get my best friend . . . in trouble." She barely managed to get those last two words out.

"Don't think like that. She's going to be fine—she *is* fine. You aren't to blame for anything." He looked her in the eye when he said this, trying to convince her. She wanted to be convinced, and she liked being looked at that way, but she still wasn't sure she believed him.

"I think it's swell you've been working as hard as you have," he went on. "A lot of people I know didn't want us to get in the war. Hell, my own father . . ." He let the thought go as she waited. "Plenty of people needed convincing, and you're part of what did that. Look, honestly, *I* wasn't so into the idea a few years ago. Most of the people I know weren't, and I just parroted what they said. But I've seen the light, have for a while now. I'm no activist like you, but what you've done so far, all the people you've been spreading the word to, you should be proud."

"Thank you. But it's exhausting. The work never feels done."

"Hopefully it will be, maybe in a year or so. Knock on wood." Which he did, rapping against the small side table.

"I hate feeling like there's nothing I can do to change things." Maybe that's why she worked so hard; this need to show not just the world but herself that she could do something about the war, about the hatred, about anything at all in this mad time. "I hate feeling powerless."

"That is not a word I would use to describe you."

She felt herself blushing. She wouldn't have minded another drink, but she knew that would be a bad idea. Instead, she stood and told him she was going to go to sleep.

"It's been a hell of a day. Thanks for letting me hide out. Maybe I didn't need to, I don't know. Hopefully things will make more sense in the morning."

You're such a prude, Annie, she heard Marcie say.

He stood too. "You're welcome. Providing a safe house isn't usually one of the services I offer, but I'm happy to do it. And we'll find her tomorrow, I know we will."

"Good night," she said, feeling very awkward indeed to be standing there now, this moment so charged, and she took a quick step to him to give him a kiss, which he gladly accepted, and if perhaps she'd meant it to be a short and cursory kiss, it wasn't anymore; it progressed as of its own volition to something entirely different, and better, and warmer, she with a hand behind his head and he with his on her shoulders, and it didn't seem so wrong to be standing here doing this, not at all, but maybe she should stop—she should, shouldn't she?—so after some very long seconds of thinking that, she managed to stop.

"Good night," he said, and she turned and walked to the bathroom feeling like her feet weren't quite touching the floor.

* * *

Sleep, of course, was impossible.

She was a rough sleeper in even the best of circumstances, which this was not. An unfamiliar bed, though rather luxurious compared to the cramped quarters she shared with her mother. The window open but the air not moving, because she had closed the bedroom door, and even locked it, which had felt strange to do, but at least she could tell herself it was the right decision—it was, wasn't it?—even if it made the room stuffy and almost unbearable.

Every now and again a car horn. Someone shouting outside at some point, a drunken argument. The siren of a fire truck. Dogs barking.

How long had she been lying here?

The irony of having this big bed all to herself while he was on the other side of the wall was not lost on her. She thought she should be proud of herself for resisting him earlier, but now she wondered if she was a fool, winning a bet she never should have taken.

At some point she slept, but not well, and not for long.

Devon loved this sofa, true, but as a sofa. And all it symbolized: his independence from his family, his status as a bachelor. Still, it made a lousy bed.

He could not get comfortable no matter what position he tried. And why was this room so warm? Having all the doors shut kept the air from circulating, and he felt miserably hot. It did feel strange to have Anne in the other room, like it was some weird slumber party, so that wasn't helping.

He'd been behind on sleep ever since the shoot-out, plus the late night at the Iron Nail, yet his mind wouldn't shut off. Earlier tonight, he had thought, for a very brief moment, that the man who turned out to be from Naval Intelligence was about to draw a gun and shoot him. His mind kept replaying that one moment.

He may have fallen asleep eventually, but then he was awake again, and Anne was standing there asking if he was asleep.

It was neither impulsive nor premeditated. Or maybe it was both. She climbed on top of him and he sat up to meet her there and they kissed, her kneeling with one hand on his chest and the other behind his head, he holding himself up with one hand and rubbing her back with the other, and they kissed for a while until she pushed him down on the sofa and lay on top of him.

He tried to roll her over a few times but she insisted on being on top, even laughed about it. He'd pulled off her nightdress and she'd gotten him out of most of his clothes before he said, "At the risk of stopping the momentum, I'd like to mention that my bed is much more comfortable."

"I thought it was very *un*comfortable," she said, kissing his neck, "but maybe that's because I was alone."

She got up and hurried to the bedroom.

Afterward, they knew there were things they could not or should not talk about, so as not to dispel the mood.

They found themselves talking about what they'd thought when they'd reconnected, only a few days ago now. She couldn't remember which of them had brought it up. She still didn't know what time it was, but she could hear birds chirping, which wasn't a good sign.

"You were so damned serious," he said.

"You certainly didn't seem repelled by that."

"You were doing your best to repel."

"Well, you were trying *so* hard."

"I'm a tenacious bastard, it's true." He kissed her neck.

"And your tie was crooked."

He stopped kissing her neck. "My tie is never crooked." He sounded offended.

She laughed. "And the top button was undone."

"You must have me confused with one of your other suitors." Kissing her shoulder now. "Some slovenly ape."

She laughed again, wondering if he really hadn't realized it that first day. His lips moving down again, as if seeking to prove just how tenacious he could be.

Chapter Forty-two

SCOOPED

Feeling better?" Cheryl asked.

"Oh, *much* better, thanks," Anne said, remembering that she'd called in sick yesterday, half a lifetime ago. "I ate some bad chowder, I think."

She put her bag on her desk, feeling only slightly concerned by how easy it was to lie to someone she liked. She wondered if she was smiling too much, if she was giving herself away, if Cheryl was perceptive enough to notice. Surely she wasn't actually physically *glowing*, but it did feel that way.

Larry came striding across the bullpen, newspaper in hand.

"Good thing I didn't let you cover the rumor about Jews getting extra ration stamps," he told her without a hello. "Turns out it was true."

"Excuse me?"

He handed her the morning edition. "Page one in Metro."

She pulled out section B, saw the headline above the fold: *SEVEN BUSINESS OWNERS ARRESTED FOR RATION STAMP VIOLATIONS.*

The glowing seemed to stop in a heartbeat. "Goddamn it."

"Yeah, I hate being scooped," Larry said, misconstruing her anger. "I would have liked to write that one myself."

So this was the story that the hate sheet pamphleteers had wanted to get into the press: that Jewish store owners had extra ration stamps. They'd manufactured their false reality, then they'd gotten coverage in a legitimate paper. She had hoped to find a way to stop them before their story broke, and she'd failed.

She read the piece quickly, then went back over it a second time. It was a rather breathlessly written crime story about cops raiding eight local businesses; with only one exception, each raid had turned up varying amounts of counterfeit ration stamps that the owners had been selling. As she reread it, a few things registered: number one, the writer at least hadn't pointed out that the proprietors were all Jewish. He did name the seven guilty businesses, though, which included Meyer's Meats, Friedman's Flowers, and Cohen Bakery, names she recognized from the photos she'd taken in the warehouse. Gold's Gas wasn't listed, so apparently Mr. Gold had followed her advice and burned the evidence.

She had meant to call the other business owners and warn them, too, but Lydia's disappearance had taken priority. She felt drowned in guilt, wishing she had done more to stop this.

According to the story, the police had been "acting on an anonymous tip" when they raided the businesses yesterday afternoon and evening. The story quoted the lead officer, a Sergeant Dunleavy, and noted that the case had been the result of local police forces working together, as it involved wrongdoers in Boston, Cambridge, and Watertown.

Anne tried to tell herself that the story could have been worse, but the damage was still done. People would read it, see the names, connect the dots, draw their biased opinions.

"This is bull," she said, slamming the paper on her desk. "The reporter got played."

"What are you talking about?" Larry asked.

The byline was Patrick Kielty's. "Do you know Kielty?" she asked Larry. "Where does he sit?"

Same floor, other end of the bullpen, by the windows with a decent view of the towers downtown. One man stood leaning against his desk, a smile on his face, telling a story to three other fellows. They were all laughing as she strode up and addressed the one leaning on the desk: thirtyish and thin, sleeves rolled up, hair prematurely vanishing.

"You're Kielty?"

"I am. What's up?"

The other three men backed up just a step but hovered, perhaps intrigued by Anne's barely contained rage.

"You got played in that ration stamps piece."

"Excuse me?"

"You wrote that the cops were acting on an anonymous tip. Really? An anonymous source claimed to know about all eight businesses, even though they were spread across town? One or two, maybe, but seven? That didn't strike you as odd?"

He folded his arms. "Real reporters don't talk about our sources, sweetheart."

One of the others opened his mouth to say something, but before he could she charged ahead with, "You didn't write that your source was the tip, you wrote that the cops said they got a tip. So which is it?"

Kielty shook his head and chuckled nervously. "Who are you, again?"

"Anne Lemire. And you haven't answered my question."

"I don't have to answer a damn thing, hotcakes. But because I'm feeling charitable, yeah, the cops said they got an anonymous tip about all eight businesses. Must have come from someone who knew the counterfeiters, obviously, but the cops tested it by sending some undercovers to all eight, and they managed to buy black market stamps from all of them but one. A cop who's always given me the straight dope told me about this two days ago. He offered to take me along on the raids yesterday so I could write it up, and I did. So what the hell is this about me being played?"

God, she hated him and his circle of admiring chums. She wanted so badly to take him down a peg in front of them.

"You don't even realize it, do you? You're just giving oxygen to the sorts of people who want another Kristallnacht here in Boston."

He held up his palms. "I didn't write a damn thing about Jews."

"No, you just named all the businesses and let the readers draw their own conclusions."

"Yes, that is exactly what real journalists do. It's not my fault if all the crooks involved were Jewish."

"And it didn't strike you as the slightest bit odd that the cops raided eight businesses and they were all Jewish-owned?"

"Unfortunate, maybe, yeah. But that's how it shook out."

"And you let the police lead you by the nose so you could write exactly what they wanted you to. So who's your source in the department, was it the one you mentioned, Sergeant Dunleavy, or someone else?"

"Like I said, none of your business."

"It's my business because I work here too and I don't like seeing our paper get played. It was all planted. The police were in on it—*they* sold the ration stamps to those businesses themselves, all so they could bust them for it and look like heroes in the paper."

"What?" one of the others said. They were looking at her like she was crazy.

Kielty smiled uneasily and shook his head. "That's a load of bull."

"I have photographs of a notebook with all of those businesses listed in it, along with the dates and the amounts they sold the stamps for, plus piles of anti-Jew hate sheets. And I know cops were involved in it."

She knew she shouldn't be saying this, but her need to win this argument and see that smug expression wiped off his face was too strong.

"What?"

"You heard me. The same people that were selling those stamps have been passing hate sheets all over town—you can see the notebook and the hate sheets in the same photos. They were selling stamps to Jewish owners only, all so they could publicly bust them for it and make the good Christians of Boston see that Jews are dirty cheaters. All they needed was a stupid, gullible reporter to put it in a reputable paper for them. So, bang-up job, Kielty."

He opened his mouth but nothing came out.

"Where are these photos?" one of the other men asked. He was older, with a gut and gray hair in an unfortunate comb-over.

"I have them. I've been working on a piece for the Rumor Clinic, I just needed a few more things to come together first."

"The Rumor Clinic?" he scoffed. "That's a gossip column. This is the hard-news section you're standing in, girlie."

"Well, this girlie got the straight dope while your man here was being spoon-fed bullshit by the same cops who look the other way while people are being attacked all over Dorchester. Or is that another hard-news story you don't know anything about, since it would require actual reporting?"

She turned her gaze back to Kielty. "Just tell me if your source was Dunleavy or someone else."

He told his fellows, "Excuse us," then grabbed Anne's left forearm and tried to steer her to an empty corner of the office. She shook her arm free and told him she could walk her goddamn self.

Once they were out of earshot, Kielty said, "I don't know how you know all that, but if you're accusing some cops of running a dirty racket, you'd better have solid evidence and be goddamn careful even if you're right."

"I am being careful. And they may be even dirtier than I've let on, which is why I need to know who exactly passed you that tip."

He watched her for a moment. "How much dirtier?"

"I've had cops threaten me, and someone I was working with has . . . disappeared. I think they had something to do with it. And so does a source I have at a federal agency."

She knew she was speaking beyond what she could prove, and Devon had never claimed to agree with her on Lydia's disappearance. But she needed some leverage to get Kielty to open up.

He shook his head again, more marveling at her than disbelieving. "You said you write the gossip column?"

"No, that's what your chum over there said. I write the Rumor Clinic, which means I disprove bullshit. And I know you don't like printing bullshit any more than I would, so tell me who planted this bullshit story and maybe I can help you dig your good name out of it."

"Why should I trust you?"

"Maybe you shouldn't. Look, I won't put the cop's name in print unless I find something on him and unless I'm certain, like you said. But I need to know who it was who told you about the ration stamps. Then at least I have a better chance of finding this person who's missing."

He thought for a moment, then sighed. "It wasn't Sergeant Dunleavy. It was an officer under him, Brian Dennigan."

"Thanks."

As she was walking away, he called out, "When do I get to see these photos of yours?"

She turned. "When I finish writing *my* story."

Chapter Forty-three

DEVIL'S BARGAIN

Maybe Devon just wasn't going to have a solid night's sleep ever again, and he'd have to accept it. If the reasons were the same as last night, there were certainly worse things in the world.

Anne had to be the most surprising woman he'd ever known. He had tried so hard not to seduce her last night, to act gentlemanly, help her out, and expect nothing in return. It had felt damned awkward, contrary to nature almost, yet it also had felt like the right thing to do. Maybe that was the trick?

He barely made it to work on time, then couldn't wipe the smile from his face, not even when one of the other agents tried to get a rise out of him by loudly complaining about former mayor James Curley "and all those damned Irish."

He was due at Naval Intelligence at eleven. He needed to show Lou the pictures Anne had taken, proof that the Christian Legion at least had something to do with the stolen rifles. But he was still wrestling with how exactly to tell Lou he'd procured the photos without revealing the fact that he had just slept with his source.

Lou was out, giving Devon time to ponder what to do. Then the mail girl dropped a long manila envelope on his desk. He noticed his name and the office address written in unusually careful block letters; there was no return address. He tore it open, emptied the contents onto his desk.

Photographs, blown up eight by ten. The first appeared to be a couple embracing, though he couldn't make out much of it.

In the second photo, he recognized himself. And Anne.

What the hell?

The photos were taken during their date the other night. In some of them he and Anne were outside the restaurant, in others outside her apartment. They were kissing in two of them. In the margins of the last photo, someone had scrawled a caption in the same block-letter handwriting.

A FED LOVES A RED?

He felt his heart rate quicken, his armpits go damp. He flipped through the shots one more time to make sure he hadn't missed anything. No other note in the envelope, no letter or hint at who had sent this.

He could dust the envelope and photos for prints, sure, but he had a feeling the sender had been careful. And Devon certainly wouldn't send this to the lab boys.

He slid the photos back into the envelope, checked to make sure no one was looking at him, and placed it in his bottom drawer. Locked it. Then he headed out.

He couldn't believe someone had tailed him and Anne to dinner. What the hell was going on? Goddamn it, he was an FBI agent. *He* was supposed to follow other people. It hurt to realize he was so bad at his job, and apparently so unthreatening, that someone would try to blackmail him.

He tried to think of his options. He could fess up: admit to the SAC he'd taken Anne, a journalist and leftist activist, out to dinner without making any reports about it. And why hadn't he, the SAC would ask. Because it had just been a date and not officially in a work capacity. Of course, he'd also taken her out because he'd wanted to learn more about the Dorchester attacks she'd mentioned to him. So why hadn't he made a report about *that*, that SAC would ask. *Well, sir, because it sounds like the attackers are all Irishmen, and I'd rather find a quiet way of defusing things so as to avoid an embarrassing scandal, if that's all right with you?*

He could only imagine how that would play. He'd look like he was putting loyalty to clan above the Bureau. Putting kinship with his fellow

Irish Catholics ahead of his job duties. That kind of admission could get him fired. Deservedly, perhaps.

The crate of rifles escalated everything. What the hell was Nolan's group planning? The Bureau had to come down on them, hard and fast—and Devon could lead the charge. But exactly how tied to Nolan was Devon's father? And how could he explain Anne's photos without explaining their relationship?

He had only himself to blame for getting into this jam. Surely he could figure a way out.

The Naval Intelligence office sat on the second floor of a nondescript four-story building in the Navy Yard, not far from Northeast Munitions. Despite his FBI badge, Devon was detained at two different checkpoints until proper escorts could be found. He tried not to act insulted.

When he reached the right office, a secretary in a khaki uniform asked him to wait. The office felt stuffy, the windows only slightly open and the blinds drawn all the way, just in case Axis lip readers with powerful binoculars were spying somewhere.

He sat reading the newspaper for ten minutes before two men came out to greet him. The first was the man from last night, Sergeant Ferris: a few years older than Devon, trim with dark hair. His superior officer, Lieutenant Chalmers, was another ten years older, with the belly, height, and broad shoulders that would make him a bad candidate for submarine duty. Both wore their uniform of crisp white shirt, white jacket, black tie, and a few medals that didn't mean anything to Devon other than the fact that maybe they were a big deal.

They invited him into a back office with no windows. They all sat around a circular wooden table. FDR watched them from a wall.

Chalmers seemed to give his subordinate a signal, and Ferris said, "We need to talk to you about your little shoot-out the other night. This is a very sensitive matter, as I'm sure you understand, so everything we're telling you is strictly confidential."

"I play by those rules too. What's the rumpus?"

"The man you shot, Gustavo Celini. He settled in Providence ten years ago, moved to Boston in '39. Bit of a hothead, as you learned. We're assuming the other one was this man, Ricardo Dantana?" He slid a folder across the table. Devon flipped it open and saw a single photograph, recognized him.

"Yeah, he's the one who got away."

"Celini and Dantana are pretty much fused at the hip. Well, they were, anyway."

Devon returned the folder. "Why do two men from Naval Intelligence know so much about gangsters?"

"In times like these," Chalmers spoke up, "war can make strange bedfellows."

"You're the second person to tell me that this week," Devon said, recalling his first chat with Bucciano. "Who are you saying you're in bed with, exactly?"

"You understand the importance of the Mediterranean," Chalmers said. "People with inside knowledge of the political climate in Italy, not to mention maps and photographs of the ports and cities over there, are coming in very handy. And so, we have developed . . . certain relationships."

"We spoke to your superior, Special Agent Gardner, about this," Ferris explained. "He was supposed to set you straight, but apparently the message didn't get across."

"Tell me again the message I didn't get?"

"Agent Mulvey," Chalmers said, "we invited you here to politely ask you not to interfere with our relationship, as many thousands of lives are at stake. Hundreds of thousands."

It took Devon a moment. Jesus, they were telling him that Naval Intelligence was working with the Mafia in New England. The gangsters must be giving the Navy tips on which Italian ports to hit, Devon figured, or other scraps of information that could help lay the groundwork for the coming invasion of Europe. What was the Navy giving the gangsters in return—free firearms?

Devon leaned back in his chair, unafraid to hide his anger. "I would hope they're giving you some excellent information for you to be turning a blind eye to what they're doing over here."

Ferris held up a palm. "We aren't turning a blind eye. No one's given La Cosa Nostra carte blanche to raise hell in Boston. It just happens that some very senior people in that . . . *organization* are providing us with helpful information. Maybe in return for reduced prison sentences, maybe in exchange for leniency on a case over here, that sort of thing." He shrugged, as if those were little details that didn't matter.

"And what, you threw in a crate of M-1s as a bonus?"

"No, that's not—"

"Jesus Christ. A man was gunned down in front of me with one of those rifles, and I nearly was too."

"Plenty of men are being shot at right now, Mulvey," Ferris snapped. "It's them we're worried about, not some whining FBI agent."

Devon stood up, eyes on Ferris. "Excuse me?"

Chalmers stood too. "Hold up, goddamn it," he said to both of them. "Look, Agent Mulvey, we have nothing to do with the rifles. That was someone freelancing."

"What exactly does that mean?" He was as angry over their coded speech as he was over their questionable ethics.

"To be clear, no one has given the mob a green light to do whatever they want, in Boston or anywhere." Chalmers paused again. "What we are doing is working with certain highly placed men, and in return they've put out word in their organization that they shouldn't do anything that negatively impacts the war effort. In fact, they're even making sure the workers don't go on any harebrained strikes."

"But that organization," Ferris took the baton, and took the opportunity to stand up as well, "isn't known for having the greatest rule followers. It looks like Celini and Dantana figured this was a great time for them to buy stolen rifles off some war workers and get away with it, even though their bosses wouldn't have condoned that. From what we can tell, these two low-level hoods had some connection with Zajac, who sold them the guns. Just two crooks taking advantage of what they saw as an opportunity. Now one of them is dead, and the other, we've been assured, has been punished internally."

"What does that mean, some Mafia enforcers slit his throat?"

Chalmers waited a beat, as if mentally sanitizing what he wanted to say. "We have been assured that individual is no longer a problem. And we received a call last night that the missing rifles would be waiting in an abandoned grocery just a few blocks from here, and there they were."

"So Marcuso had Dantana rubbed out for disobeying orders," Devon de-sanitized it, "and he tracked the rifles down for you. Which means we're party to mob hits now. Great."

Chalmers held up his hands. "Honestly, we don't know what Marcuso did to Dantana, and we don't want to know. We just know that this has been taken care of, and we have the missing rifles, and nothing like this will ever happen again."

"How many rifles did they return?"

Chalmers looked down at a piece of paper. "Six."

"There are ten in a crate."

"Well," and he seemed flustered, "we've been assured those were all that were stolen."

"Assured, by a gangster."

"The bottom line is, the factories you've been watching over are safe, Agent Mulvey," Ferris added. "And now even the lowest man in the mob knows that if he ever tries to steal from a military factory, his punishment will be severe."

Devon shook his head and tried to replay what they'd said and hadn't said. Mob boss Marcuso, after getting off the phone with Devon the other day, had called his new friends in and told them to get Devon off his back. Naval Intelligence had then called SAC Gardner, who yelled at Devon to stand down. It all made sense now, in a morally ambiguous, nauseating sort of way.

"Meanwhile, what, you expect me to file a report saying that everything is fine, no harm done?"

Ferris shrugged. "The rifles have been recovered. We're happy to send them your way for inspection so you can get them back to Northeast, or we can send them over ourselves."

"*Most* of the rifles have been recovered, you *hope*." He debated telling them about the photographs, the crate stashed at the Christian Legion's warehouse. But he held this back for now.

"We understand the type of people we're dealing with here," Chalmers said. "But they hate Mussolini as much as we do. Maybe even more. He tried his damnedest to wipe out the Mafia over there and nearly succeeded, which is partly why so many wop gangsters came to our shores. I'm sure Hoover will gladly unleash you and your fellow agents to shut them down, when the time comes. But for now, the fact that mobsters are so anti-Fascist is a good thing for the United States. As is their detailed knowledge of the Italian coast."

"So we are asking you, again, very politely," Ferris said, "to let this matter drop."

And if Devon were to say no, he understood, they would find some other way to force him away from their embarrassing little relationship.

"And Wolff? The other war worker who was killed last week?"

Chalmers shrugged. "We assume Celini or Dantana killed him, too, some disagreement about how much he was paid for smuggling the rifles out of the factory. But who knows?"

"Yeah," Devon said, "who knows. That's one of the reasons it would have been nice for me to actually question Dantana, instead of just having the mob rub him out for you. But I guess we do things differently at the Bureau."

"Frankly, who killed Wolff is not a concern for us. And it needs to not be a concern for you, either."

Devon's recollection of the brief conversation between Zajac and the two gangsters rang differently. They had been telling Zajac they hadn't killed Wolff. Of course, they weren't the most honest and upstanding of people, so maybe that was just their way of trying to get Zajac off their trail, and when Zajac pressed the matter they'd decided killing him was easier. So quite possibly they *had* killed Wolff.

Devon asked, "Do you have any reason to think the Christian Legion was involved?"

They both looked confused by the question.

"I don't even know who that is," Chalmers said. "Again, it was two small-time hoods mistakenly thinking they had their superiors' blessing, a mistake that will never happen again."

"And you're absolutely sure Dantana and Celini bought the rifles from a war worker, that there was no middleman involved?"

"Yes."

So either the gangsters had bought stolen rifles from Wolff and Zajac, then resold a few to the Christian Legion, or the workers had sold a few rifles to both the mob and the Legion.

The Navy men didn't care about the rifles, they only wanted Devon to go away and leave the mob alone. That was one of several things that nagged at Devon. Christian Legion pamphlets were circulating at Northeast Munitions; he'd seen that for himself. They'd passed the security gate. Most likely meaning that someone from the Legion worked at Northeast.

And Devon still didn't understand why, when Wolff died, he possessed a bar napkin, from an Irish tavern, with a swastika scrawled on it.

"Well, thank you for your time, gentlemen. Are you in bed with anyone else I should know about?"

"If we were," Chalmers said, "we wouldn't be able to tell you. Look, let's remember that we're at war here, and we're on the same side."

"With friends like these," Devon said, and took his leave without another word.

Chapter Forty-four

THE PAPER TRAIL

Part of Anne wanted to thank Kielty for writing his bullshit piece and for being so condescending to her. He had made her *angry* again, which felt so much better than being scared and worried, as she'd been ever since Mrs. Doherty had called about Lydia. Fear crumpled you, made it difficult to move, to plan ahead, to think rationally. Whereas anger propelled you forward, put the rest of the world on notice.

There was safety in anger, even if it was an illusion.

She needed to finish putting this puzzle together. The fact that Kielty's story had come out was a problem, yes, and untold numbers of people would be swayed by it. She couldn't change that now, but what she could do is learn everything possible about the plotters and shine an even brighter spotlight on them.

Step one was finding out who owned that warehouse.

After putting in a couple more hours at her desk, she told Cheryl she had an errand to run and headed to the State House. The secretary of state's office was not as grand as it sounded, just another overcrowded and musty room with too many files and not enough windows.

At least the clerk here, a very Irish redhead in her thirties with pale skin and an exacting manner, seemed competent. "What can I help you with?" she asked.

"I'm with the *Star*," Anne said. "I'm hoping to find out who owns a certain business. It's called Cork Management Industries, but I'm afraid I don't know when it was founded. Is that a problem?"

"No, it just means I'll have to pull a few years. Have a seat."

Anne watched as the woman ventured into the adjoining room, pulled files from boxes, flipped through them, put them back, found more.

"Here we are," the clerk said as she approached her desk again. She laid a file out so that Anne could read it, her finger indicating the entry. "It was formed in '37."

Anne read the line the clerk was pointing to and saw the name of the company's owner.

"Oh my God."

"I'm sorry?"

Anne put a hand to her chest. "Oh, nothing."

She tried to smile her comment away, as the clerk regarded her with suspicion. Anne thanked her, then stepped back and turned around, tried to gather herself.

It was the man she'd seen visiting Flaherty yesterday morning with Nolan, she now realized, the one she remembered from somewhere but hadn't been able to place. The leonine white mane, the blue eyes. Before yesterday she hadn't seen him in years, but yes, she realized now, his was the name she'd just read.

John Joseph Mulvey. Devon's father.

Chapter Forty-five

A TIP

Devon was back in his office an hour later, making painstaking progress on the mountain of background checks, and trying to make sense of his last meeting. If the Navy men were right, and Wolff had likely been killed by the gangsters he'd sold the stolen rifles to, then everything was now wrapped up nice and neat. *Almost* everything: the swastika napkin still didn't make sense. And neither did the suspicious way in which powerful people—first the owner of Northeast Munitions, then the SAC, now Naval Intelligence—were telling him to back off, that there was nothing to see here.

And there was the matter of Anne's photograph of a Northeast crate in the Legion's old warehouse. Either the mob or Wolff and Zajac had sold some of the rifles to the Legion. What was the Legion planning to do with them?

He knew he could file a report and be done with the murder case, which maybe he should have done two weeks ago. But he felt there was too much he didn't understand. He needed to figure out how to tell his colleagues about that crate without implicating Anne—and himself—in inappropriate behavior.

His phone rang.

A whisper on the line: "Is this Agent Mulvey, red lover?"

He paused and turned in his chair, addressing the wall so he was less likely to be overheard in the office. "This is Agent Mulvey. Who's speaking?"

"No, the better question is: why, oh why, would an FBI man be bedding a Bolshevik?"

"What do you want?"

"You get any interesting pictures in the mail today?" The man sounded like he was from Boston, and definitely not a Yankee Brahmin.

"Maybe I did."

"Do you want anyone else to see them?"

"I already asked what you want."

"I want you to stay away from the Christian Legion."

"And who would that be?"

"Don't play dumb. Whatever that Bolshie broad has been telling you about the ration stamps, you need to keep it quiet. Understand, Mulvey, that we can send those pictures to your boss anytime we want. And to the newspapers. How long you think Hoover'll let you keep that job once he knows you're bedding a red?"

Devon took a breath, thinking. The caller had mentioned the ration stamps but not the rifles. Interesting.

He said, "I don't think you know the first thing about how the Bureau works."

"You thinking about calling our bluff? Try it. The moment you do, you're out of a job. Maybe even thrown in jail for being a Bolshie spy."

The mystery man was right, Devon knew.

Damn it, why the hell *had* he met with Anne? Maybe Lou was right and Devon didn't know how to "turn it off" around pretty women. But that wasn't the only reason. He'd wanted to prove to himself he was better than some members of his family. And he'd been worried the Wolff case and the missing rifles might implicate his community, so he'd been hoping he could find a way to defuse things without causing yet more problems. He'd told Anne this was complicated because it was; he needed to believe he could solve the case quietly, without putting a spotlight on the worst elements of his people.

Now that very discretion made him look suspect.

"You honestly expect me to stay silent about you making off with military weapons?"

For the first time, the caller paused. Maybe he hadn't known Devon knew about the rifles. "We expected you to be a friend," the caller finally said, "but you're making yourself an enemy. If you keep that up, we will ruin you. Remember that. You will become an ex-agent very, very fast."

The caller hung up.

Minutes later, another call; this time it was Clark, his lone Negro source at Northeast Munitions.

"Are you still looking into that murder you told me about? Abe Wolff?" Clark asked.

"Why, did you hear something?"

"I did. You know about the FEPC hearing?"

"No."

"Wolff was scheduled to be a witness against Northeast Munitions."

Devon leaned back in his chair. "That's news to me."

The Fair Employment Practice Committee was the federal agency in charge of enforcing Roosevelt's Executive Order 8802, which prohibited discriminatory hiring in war industries. Such work had often been restricted to white people until '41, when A. Philip Randolph threatened to hold a massive "March on Washington" in protest, and FDR finally gave in, banning all-white workforces in military-related factories.

"I guess I'm not surprised the powers that be at Northeast didn't see reason to tell you," Clark said.

"How do you know about the case?"

"I have friends with the NAACP, and one of them has a friend down at the FEPC in Washington. Bunch of us were talking the other day, and it came up. Story is, Wolff was one of the employees willing to testify that he'd overheard managers at Northeast talking about how to get around hiring more Negroes."

"You're saying someone at Northeast maybe killed the guy so he wouldn't testify against their *hiring practices*?" It sounded preposterous to Devon.

"I'm not saying anything. I'm just telling you what I heard."

Devon had the feeling he'd disappointed Clark with his reaction.

"The FEPC barely has any power," Devon said, trying to explain himself. "I haven't heard of them so much as fining anyone yet. Why would Northeast care that much about a hearing?"

"Well, someone's gotta be the first to get fined. Or lose a war contract. Maybe they didn't want to risk losing the case. Maybe they didn't want the publicity. Want to show how patriotic they are, obeying all the rules and regulations. An FEPC case wouldn't have been good for them."

Devon drummed his fingers on the table. Part of him wanted to write this tip off as gossip, conspiracy theories. But the more he considered it, the more sense it made. Devon knew from his own conversations with factory managers that, while they understood their bottom lines were being fattened by war work, they wanted to avoid looking like profiteers. What might a company do to prevent the good times from ending, or even slowing down? An FEPC case, at the very least, would have been a black eye for the company. It could possibly cost them lucrative contracts down the line, for however long the war lasted.

Devon found himself remembering his cousin Brian's words: *some blabby kike.* If word had gotten around that Wolff was going to testify against the company, he might have become a marked man. Then again, Patty Campbell, one of Devon's sources at the plant, had told Devon he'd never even heard of Wolff until the murder, so word of the hearing must not have spread very far.

Unless Campbell had been lying.

"So what's happening with the case against Northeast now?" Devon asked. "Is it dead?"

"What I heard was, there were a few folks going to testify against Northeast. Three of them are Negro. Wolff was the only white man who'd come forward so far."

The implication being, Wolff's word might have carried more weight.

"Some of the bosses," Clark said, "had been talking about the case, buddy of mine said. Said he'd heard people talking, that if this Jew gets to testify, the plant could shut down and we'd all lose our jobs."

The government would never shut the plant down during wartime, Devon knew, but paranoid workers who'd barely survived the Depression might not realize that. They might have truly feared their jobs were at stake.

If someone at Northeast had killed Wolff, Devon thought, he should pass it on to Jimmy Moore. It shouldn't be Devon's case, as it didn't involve sabotage or interference with the war effort. But the idea that the suits at Northeast might have been responsible for this sparked an anger in him, that the same fellows who smiled while shaking his hand and talked a good game about their patriotic bona fides were putting out hits on their own employees.

"Thanks for the tip, Clark. I'll look into it."

He hung up and wondered whom he knew who might have contacts at the FEPC.

Chapter Forty-six

FAMILY TIES

Anne returned home to her apartment that afternoon. Perhaps it had been silly to stay with Devon for the night—she'd thought she was doing it out of a need for safety, but now she looked at herself and saw how her motives had been muddled by desire. Had she made a terrible mistake?

She walked cautiously down her street, seeing no signs that her building was being watched. But would she know it before it was too late? It was awful, how nervous she felt to be on her own block. She almost wished she had Aaron's giant German shepherd with her.

She made it safely home. The apartment was empty, everyone at work as usual.

After sitting down and double-checking much of her research to make sure she hadn't gotten anything wrong, she called Devon at his office.

"How's your day going?" he asked, sounding distracted. "I imagine it's been all downhill since this morning."

"Yes, actually, it has been. I'm back at my place. Could you come over again? There's something I need to tell you, in person." She knew she sounded stiff and even cold, almost like she was calling to break things off already. She felt bad about what she had to tell him and still wasn't sure how to do it.

"All right. I can be there in an hour. In the meantime, I just got some good news. Your friend's okay—she enlisted with the WAVES, in Newport."

Anne was shocked. "Are you sure?"

"I haven't spoken to her, but yeah. My source at WAVES just called; a Lydia Doherty of Dorchester, Mass, enlisted two days ago."

Anne felt profoundly relieved. But also confused. She and Lydia had discussed WAVES a few times, but Lydia had always seemed against the idea. She'd said she never wanted to leave Boston. If she'd had a change of heart and wanted to enlist, why hadn't she joined the WAAC, which was closer to home, instead of moving two hours away to Rhode Island?

"That's . . . so odd."

"You don't sound happy."

"I guess I'm just . . . surprised."

"It looks like the simplest story was the right one. She caught the patriotic fever and joined up. Why don't you try calling her now." He read her the phone number for Lydia's barracks. "I'll be over in an hour."

Anne hung up and called the number, but the line was busy. She tried again five minutes later, with the same result. And ten minutes later. If it was a barracks phone, perhaps it was a popular line. Devon had sounded so proud of himself for finding her, but had he really?

She was sitting in the front room when she saw Devon's car pull up in front of the building.

He knocked and she let him into the apartment. She reminded herself that letting a man visit her when all her relatives were away was risqué, but this wasn't the kind of conversation she could have over the phone. He stepped in for a kiss, which she granted, but she broke it off quickly, not wanting to lead him on before hitting him with the bad news.

Was it really only a few hours ago that they'd made love? This whole day felt like a blur.

After their kiss, he walked straight to the living room and peered out the windows, just as she had done earlier.

"What are you looking for?" she asked.

"I wasn't followed, and I didn't see anyone on the street. But it never hurts to take an extra look."

She got right to the point: "There's something I have to tell you."

"What is it?" He took off his fedora and, noticing the lack of a hat rack, laid it on the kitchen table.

"I went to City Hall and found out the owner of the company that owns the warehouse." She took a breath. "It's your father."

A few seconds passed as they stared at each other. He blinked. "My father."

"John Joseph Mulvey. And I saw him the other day. Leaving Pete Flaherty's house with Charles Nolan. Flaherty's the printmaker, and Nolan runs the Christian Legion."

He frowned and said, harshly, "You spied on my father? And didn't tell me?"

"I didn't know who he was then—I recognized him but couldn't place him, until I saw his name in the ledger today. But the larger point here is that your father is mixed up with something illegal. And reprehensible."

He shook his head and exhaled. Thought for a moment. "My father knows a lot of people. Too many for his own good, and maybe a few of them are . . . shadier than he realizes. He's always been the kind of fellow who gets along with everyone, and I know—"

"Certainly not *everyone*."

"—he's invested in properties here and there, going back years now. Sounds like he had an old warehouse he wasn't using, and maybe a friend of a friend asked if he could use it, and Pop has no idea what's been going on there."

She hadn't expected him to take the news well, but he didn't seem to want to take it at all.

"I think that might be wishful thinking, Devon. Based on what I remember of your father . . . this seems very believable to me."

"What's that supposed to mean?"

She folded her arms. "You know what I mean. Or are you conveniently forgetting what his reaction was when the neighborhood learned that my family is half Jewish?"

"Look, I know he isn't the most . . . open-minded of people—"

"That's putting it rather nicely."

"—but he wouldn't be involved in any harebrained counterfeiting scheme. He's a banker, for God's sake, and a successful one. He doesn't need to break laws to make a buck."

"I don't think he's in it for the money. Some of his accomplices may be, but I think his main goal is to make Jews look bad so he can blame us for the war."

Devon shook his head, but he didn't refute her theory. She had the feeling, once again, that there was something he wasn't saying.

She told him about the ration stamps story that had broken in the paper that morning. Told him that his father, Flaherty, and whoever else they were working with had already accomplished at least part of their aim: making a group of Jewish business owners look like unpatriotic cheats, getting them arrested by telling their story to a cop named Dennigan, *and* getting the story in the papers for all to see. That was galling enough, but what was next in their plan?

Devon looked sick. "Brian Dennigan?"

"Yes. You know him?"

He nodded. "I'll talk to my father."

"Devon, I think this is more serious than a little father-son chat. He's involved in something illegal and dangerous."

"This is my father we're talking about."

"I know, and that's why I'm telling you first before writing a story about it, but we have to—"

"You wouldn't do that." His tone of voice sharp, like throwing an elbow.

She took a breath. "I admit, I don't know exactly what to do with all this. But hushing up the fact that your father is in bed with Nazi sympathizers, and counterfeiters, is not one of the options I'm considering."

He watched her for a moment. Her heart was pounding, her nerves on edge, and she had no idea what he might do or say next. She wondered if she'd made a horrible mistake by opening herself up to know him, by ever inviting him into her life.

"He's not a Nazi," he said, his voice calmer than a moment ago. "He just hates the war and . . ." He shook his head. "He's been in a bad place since my mother passed away, so maybe some of his new friends have gotten him involved in something stupid."

"It's not just stupid, it's illegal and dangerous."

He looked at her again, and for a moment it was like a shadow was cast across his face. "I don't think I should be talking about this with you."

"Devon, you are . . . uniquely positioned to be able to stop him, stop whoever he's working with."

He shook his head again. "Has this been your play all along? Get me to do your work for you? Has this all been some honeypot scheme to blackmail me into doing something I shouldn't?"

"What are you talking about?"

"I don't know why I didn't think of this sooner. But one night you break into that warehouse, and the very next night someone photographs us on our date. How do I know it wasn't someone *you* work with, trying to get an FBI agent in a compromising position and using that to get me to do God knows what?"

"'Compromising'? Wait, what photographs? You didn't tell me about any of this. What's going on?"

He sighed. "Just this morning, someone sent me pictures of the two of us outside that restaurant. And walking home afterward. Kissing. I don't know who it is, but it's someone who wants to hold over my head the fact that, supposedly, I'm dating a red."

"I'm not a Communist."

"Close enough, in most folks' eyes."

"And I'm not a blackmailer. In case you're forgetting, *you* came on to *me*."

He ran his fingers through his hair and looked away.

This conversation had veered in too many directions already. She said, "Some of the counterfeiters are clearly cops. Maybe it's this Officer Dennigan, the one who passed the tip on to the reporter, or Duffy, the one who impounded my car. If they're trying to blackmail you, too, what is it they're asking for?"

"Someone called me today and told me to lay off the Christian Legion. And that if I didn't, they'd send those pictures to my boss and I'd be out of a job. Or worse."

She thought again about the photos she'd given him. They showed the hate sheets and a notebook with the names of the same Jewish-owned businesses that were in the *Star* piece; that was proof that the Legion was distributing both the sheets and the counterfeit stamps. Which would be very bad for his father, as it would prove the elder Mulvey's property was involved in both activities. What was Devon willing to do to protect his father?

What a mistake she had made with him, all week, and last night.

"Call Lydia," he said after a pause. "You'll feel better when you hear that she's okay."

She didn't like the patronizing way he'd said that, as if the whole problem here was that Anne needed to *feel* better.

"I've tried, several times, but the line's busy. I can't help but wonder if it's the right number you gave me."

He was looking at her like he had no idea who she was. "Of course it is. Try it again."

She walked over to the phone, dialed the number for the fifth or sixth time. It finally rang.

A young woman—not Lydia—answered on the third ring.

"Hello, can I speak with Lydia Doherty, please?"

Devon nodded in triumph. He walked past her and to the bathroom, to give her privacy, perhaps.

"She's on shift right now," a young woman said. "This is the dorm. Want to leave her a message?"

"Yes," Anne said, her mind racing. Was Lydia really there? Or was this all an elaborate con to trick Anne? Jesus, she didn't know what to believe anymore. One moment she's unfairly suspicious of everyone, and the next she's being conned by the man she's falling for.

She glanced at the bathroom door, which Devon had shut. She heard the toilet flush. "Could you tell me exactly where I've called, please?"

"This is Dorm 3A," the woman said, sounding confused. "In Newport. Rhode Island."

"And you're with the WAVES?"

"Yes. Lydia joined us just yesterday. No, the day before, I think. Anyway, who should I tell her called?"

"Can you describe Lydia to me?"

"Excuse me?"

"I just want to make sure we're talking about the same Lydia Doherty."

Devon stepped out of the bathroom, walking away again, this time stepping into Sammy's tiny room. She would tolerate his being nosy for now.

"O-kay," the woman on the line said slowly, as if realizing she was talking to a crazy person. She proceeded to describe Lydia quite accurately. It really was Lydia down in Newport, then. She'd enlisted, like Devon said. She hadn't been killed or abducted.

Unless this was a false number Devon had given her, and the woman on the line was some plant? Maybe Anne was crazy to think that a possibility, but she didn't know what to believe anymore. She wouldn't completely buy this story until she heard Lydia's voice. She left her name and asked the woman to have Lydia call her as soon as she could.

As Anne was speaking on the phone, Devon stepped into a closet that appeared to have been turned into a makeshift bedroom. *Christ, this must be where her younger brother sleeps.*

He noticed a comic book lying across the unmade bed. *Stories of the Real G-Men!* He reached down and picked up the comic. He wondered what Sammy (that was his name, right?) would think if he knew his sister had just slept with a real-live "G-man."

He sat down on the bed, flipped through the comic. Something about it made him incredibly sad. The simple heroism, the easy narrative, the clear and obvious villains. Comics like this had been around for years now, but he'd been too old to read them when they'd first come out. Still, even as a young man he'd bought into the stories, seen the Hollywood films. He wondered if he was any less naïve than her little brother.

What the hell was his father involved in? Pop had all but admitted to Devon that he was wrapped up in something Devon shouldn't know about, given his job. Now his cousin Brian was involved too, according to Anne. He felt sick. He'd always known that some of his relatives—okay, many of them—distrusted anyone who wasn't Irish, and that they downright hated entire groups of people for various reasons, and he knew Pop despised the war. But Devon hadn't truly thought Pop capable of something so foolish, so dangerous. So cruel.

Devon understood how important kin was, the way his forebears had looked after each other when they came over here with nothing. From starvation to a hostile, foreign city. He'd heard the stories over and over again. The "Irish Need Not Apply" signs, the "lousy micks" slung about with abandon, the poverty of cramped quarters in the old North End and Southie and Charlestown. He understood how important family was, how vital it was to stick together. But how that had transformed into clannish hatreds was beyond him—this constant need for enemies, the joy of dishing it out to someone else.

Did Pop know about the rifles? What the hell were they for, anyway?

He remembered with some disquiet a comment his father had made a few nights ago, how he wished "some catastrophe or political act" would break people from "their trance" about the war. Jesus, was Pop trying to *create* such a catastrophe?

And what was Devon supposed to do? How could he stop Anne from turning his father into fodder for the headlines, another fiery Irishman whose bad judgment and backward thinking led him into a harebrained scheme, followed by, what, jail?

Devon needed to think.

He heard Anne leaving a message with whomever she'd reached at the WAVES. Not Lydia, apparently. Then, because Devon was a nosy bastard and wanted to learn more about her family, and because such nosiness was an occupational hazard but one he indulged in freely, he found himself opening the top drawer of her brother's bedside table.

More comics: *Captain America*; *The Phantom*. Did Devon miss being seventeen? Honestly, no. He'd been a virgin then, had yet to discover the joys that made the world go round. But a certain innocence, yes, he did miss that.

Beneath the comics were some barely legible notes scribbled on torn-out notebook paper. And a photograph, a small portrait. A portrait of a certain pretty woman, but looking even prettier than Devon had ever seen her; he'd only seen this particular woman looking distraught. That's why it took him a moment to recognize her.

What the hell?

He picked the picture up as if by doing so he could make sense of it, but he couldn't. He heard Anne wish her caller well and hang up. He walked into the kitchenette and held the photo up for her.

"Tell me you know her," he said. Realizing that the look on his face was grave, because he saw the severity reflected in her eyes.

Anne squinted, shook her head. "Who is that?"

"You don't know her?"

"No, I don't. Who is she?"

"This was in your brother's bedside table."

"Why were you snooping in his—"

"Her name is Elena Wolff. Someone murdered her husband a couple weeks ago, and she's disappeared." He let that sink in for a moment. "If you don't know her, how does your brother?"

"I don't know. I've never seen that photo before. And I'll ask it again: why were you snooping around in—"

"Because it's what I do, all right? I've been trying to figure out who killed her husband. Where is your brother right now?"

She was staring at him in horror. "You planted that."

"*What?*"

"Oh my God. You planted that. You brought it here. You didn't find that in his room."

"Are you kidding me?"

She let out a bitter, disgusted laugh. "I find evidence that your father's involved in crimes, so now you're going to frame my *kid brother*? Are you really that low?"

He couldn't believe this. Couldn't believe that *she* could believe him capable of such a thing.

"Anne, Jesus! I swear on my mother's soul, I just found this buried under his comic books."

"Bullshit!"

"I'll get it fingerprinted for proof if you don't believe me!"

"Oh, and I'm sure I can trust you to do that without faking the results!"

He'd spent hours trying to track down her friend, and this was how she thanked him? She hated him for being in the FBI. Maybe she was attracted to him too, wanted to have some fun, but the bottom line was, she believed all her fellow radicals' stories about feds planting evidence and trampling over people's rights. She just couldn't trust him, because he was a government man, and Irish, related to too many people who were assholes and loyal to them nonetheless.

He was a fool to have trusted her, and to have thought she might trust him.

She pointed at the door. "Get out. Now."

"Anne." He held out a palm, beseeching her to see that he wasn't the embodiment of all her worst fears. "I don't know what this picture means right now, all right? But it could mean that your brother is in serious, serious trouble. Now, do you want some random beat cop to haul him in for questioning, or are you going to tell me where he is so I can ask him to explain himself?"

She only shook her head, silent. Tears welling in her eyes.

He walked over to the door and she stepped back to give him room. He put his hand on the knob. Turned it, opened it.

He looked back at her. "Let me ask you a different question. Did your brother own a red plaid shirt? But the collar got torn off a couple weeks ago, so he threw it away?"

She opened her mouth, but still no sound came out.

Chapter Forty-seven

A WARNING

Half an hour later—half an hour of crying and pacing and screaming a few times alone in her apartment, and also punching some pillows, and swearing quite a lot, and not knowing what the hell to do next—Anne heard the phone ring, and answered it.

"Hi, Annie," Lydia said. "Sorry I worried you."

She felt dizzy. Part of her *still* hadn't believed Devon's story. Now that she heard Lydia's voice and knew this wasn't some elaborate ruse, that her friend really was alive, she felt so much relief that she sank into a kitchen chair and felt more tears well up in her eyes.

"I'm so glad you're okay." She laughed and cried all at once.

"Yeah. I'm fine." But her voice sounded strained. Maybe she was in a crowded room, self-conscious?

"Lydia, what happened? I thought you said you never wanted to sign up?"

"Yeah, you know, I suppose I had a change of heart. I'm, ah, I'm sorry I didn't get a chance to tell you first."

"Your parents didn't know either." She dabbed at her eyes with a tissue. *Thank God* Lydia was really okay. "You didn't even leave them a note?"

"I called them last night. It's okay."

But Lydia's voice still sounded odd, as did this whole situation.

"Lydia . . . is everything all right?"

A long pause. If not for some background noise, Anne would have thought they'd been disconnected.

"Not really, no. And I think you . . . you really need to be careful right now, Annie."

"Did something happen to you?"

Another pause. When Lydia spoke again, her voice was much quieter, and on the verge of breaking. "They told me not to say anything."

"*Who* told you?"

"I wanted to call you, but I was afraid. I'm sorry, Annie, I'm just . . . I'm not as strong as you. So I ran."

"What happened? Please tell me."

"You have to *promise* you won't *write* about this. Okay? You won't tell anyone."

"Okay, I promise." She wondered if these lines were monitored by military operators, if that's why Lydia was being so cryptic.

Lydia's voice became a whisper. "They were cops, Annie. Some of them, at least. Uniform and badge and everything. But they didn't . . . They didn't take me to the station. They took me . . . somewhere else."

Anne heard a loud bell in the background.

"They knew we had been at that warehouse. I thought they were going to *kill me,* Annie. They . . . tied me up. Manhandled me a bit. So when they asked who else I'd been with, I gave them your name." She started crying. "I'm so sorry."

"No, I'm sorry," Anne said. "I'm sorry I dragged you into this."

"They kept me in that room for a day. I think they were . . . arguing about what to do with me. Then finally they blindfolded me . . . and put me in some truck and dropped me off by a factory in Cambridge. They said if I told anyone, they would . . . kill me. And I believed them."

"Jesus, Lydia."

Lydia cried for a moment, and Anne waited.

"One of them said it would be safer . . . if I got out of town. They didn't have to ask me twice. I went home and packed a bag . . . caught a train to Newport. I was halfway here when I realized I hadn't even left my folks a note."

"Can you tell me what they looked like? Were the cops wearing name plates?"

"No, Annie! Didn't you hear me? They said not to talk. I shouldn't have even called you, but I got your message and didn't want you to worry about me. But for God's sake, stop all this. Write about something else and leave this alone."

A background bell again, this time two quick notes.

"I have to go. Please be careful, and please, please stop making these people angry, okay?"

"Lydia, we can't just let them get away with this. We—"

"Anne, stop this, please, please, please. Be careful."

Anne tried to keep her on the line, but it was too late—the background noise had gone quiet, as Lydia had already hung up and Anne was alone again.

Chapter Forty-eight

THE KID

Even from his parked car outside, watching Sammy stocking shelves through the store window, Devon could see the family resemblance. Sammy had his sister's eyes, the thick curly hair. A certain femininity to him still.

Devon sat in the car and waited. Soon it was five o'clock, and after another few minutes Sammy stepped out.

"Sammy Lemire," he said as he got out of the car.

"Yes?"

"I'm a friend of your sister's. Devon Mulvey. Maybe she's mentioned me?"

"Oh, yeah. Hello." With his right hand he brushed too-long hair from his eyes.

Christ, he was still a kid. Barely looked like he needed to shave, his cheeks so soft. But he was tall, had decent biceps from lifting heavy things at the store, and as Devon took a hard look at those brown eyes he saw how easy it might be for a lonely woman to fall for him.

"I'm going to drive you home. Hop in."

Sammy eyed him, motionless. "I can walk."

Devon pulled his badge from his pocket just long enough to see the kid's eyes go wide. "That wasn't a request. You're going to get in my car now. And you absolutely are not going to even think of running away."

"Why," and the kid managed to smile, a very nervous smile indeed, and quite fake, "why would I try to run away?"

"Get in the goddamn car."

Guilt all over his face. Finally he moved, nervously walking around the front of the car and opening the passenger door. Once he got in, Devon did too, and started the engine.

He let the silence play out for a full minute before pulling over and parking alongside Dorchester Park. He needed to face the kid for this.

"Tell me about Elena."

"Elena? Uh, she works with me. Used to, I mean."

"Why 'used to'?"

"She's left town or something. I mean, she just stopped coming in to work."

"How do you know she left?"

"I just . . . heard somebody say it."

"What somebody?"

"Mr. Henry, our boss."

"That's really how you know? Or do you know because you dropped by her place to see what had happened?"

"I don't . . ." He shook his head and looked away. "No, it's what Mr. Henry said."

"Why do you think she'd leave town, Sammy?"

"Am I . . . Am I in some kind of trouble?"

"Yes, you are. Why do you think she'd leave town?"

He took a breath. "Because . . . um . . ."

"Jesus, we haven't even gotten to the hard questions yet."

Sammy's voice turned quieter, but he didn't pause or stammer as he said, "She probably left town because someone killed her husband."

"Did you kill him?"

Eyes wider still. "No! I mean, gosh, no. *Kill* him?"

"Did you kill her?"

"*No!*" The thought of killing *her* seemed to bother him a lot more. "She's not . . . She's not dead, is she?"

"Not that I know of. You get along pretty well with her?"

He looked away again. "Sure. I mean, yeah, she's nice."

"Nice and pretty, huh?"

Sammy shrugged, nodded, acted like his head wasn't entirely sure what it should be doing on top of his neck.

"You take that picture of her, or she give it to you?"

Eyes back on Devon. "What picture?"

"The one in your fucking bedside table, Sammy. Stop playing dumb. I do think you're on the dumb side already; you don't need to overdo it. Were you fucking her? Or you just wanted to?"

He shook his head again. Devon could see tears welling in the kid's eyes.

"You own a knife, Sammy? Are you any good with it?"

"*No*. My cousin's . . . teaching me to box, but no, I don't carry a knife."

"We're sitting here in my car, Sammy. We aren't at a police station or my office. Like I said, I'm friends with your sister, so I'm treating you a hell of a lot nicer than I probably should be. So answer my questions completely, and don't leave out anything that a guy like me might find interesting. Were you sleeping with Elena Wolff?"

After a few seconds, Sammy nodded. A tear fell down his left cheek and he reached for it fast, like he was afraid it might explode.

"I mean, a couple times."

"And so you decided to take the husband out of the equation."

"I didn't kill him! Jesus, I'm not a killer."

"Where were you the night of June twentieth?"

Sammy exhaled loudly. Devon feared the kid might throw up in the car. "Answer me."

"Okay, okay. Let me explain it. I . . . I followed him that night. He'd been . . . rough with her. A few nights before. Choked her. She hadn't told me about it, but she wore this thing around her neck, this, I don't know what you call it, this thing ladies wear, to cover it up." Jesus, he was so young. "And she finally told me about it, and I . . . I wanted to tell him never to do that again."

"So you cornered him in an alley."

"I wanted to talk to him. Confront him, okay? I . . . I love her." His voice broke and he looked out the windshield and it took him a while to continue. Devon waited, and even with the windows half down it was getting very hot in the car. "I thought I could tell him to back off, maybe even to leave her. I know . . . it sounds stupid now. But I thought . . . I should do it. I was . . . nervous. I wanted to go up to him outside their building, when he was coming home from work, but . . . I chickened out, because he had a friend with him."

Devon described Zajac. "That sound like the friend?"

"Yeah. Anyway, I saw Abe come home, and he and his buddy walked right past me 'cause they didn't know me from Adam. And I chickened out. Stood out there like an idiot, knew I'd missed my chance."

Sammy took another breath. "I lit a cigarette so I'd have something to do, wouldn't just look like this idiot standing there, you know? Then a couple minutes later he and his buddy come back out. And they're speaking French, but I'm pretty good at it so I know what they're saying. I didn't follow everything, but it was something about them going to a place in the North End. And they're walking toward the train, so I figure, maybe I should follow 'em, maybe I'll get another chance to talk to him later, especially if he's had a few drinks. I know it's stupid, but I thought maybe he'd be easier to fight and scare then."

Devon listened while Sammy described tailing the two men, getting off at Haymarket, and following them to the North End. Sammy had watched them walk into Bucciano's, saw that there was a bench around the corner, wound up buying a newspaper and sitting there, waiting.

"I know it was stupid, but I was . . . trying to steel myself for it. I sat out there for more'n an hour and was starting to wonder if they'd be out all night, if I should just go home. If he and his friend left together then I'd just wasted the night for nothing, you know, I wasn't going to fight *two* men. But I figured if he was alone, and if he was drunk . . ." He shrugged. "I knew my ma would start wondering if I wasn't back soon, so I was about to give up, and that's when he came out. Alone."

Devon asked what happened next. Sammy closed his eyes.

"I went up to him and I said he needed to stop hitting her. At first he just stared at me like he had no clue what I was talking about. I guess it was kind of out of the blue for him. I said it again and then he put it together and . . ."

"And?"

"He grabbed me around the neck and started cussing me out. I guess . . . I guess he'd already been suspicious that she was cheating on him. Then it just . . . went wrong."

"Explain that."

The kid sighed, and Devon could see he wasn't anxious to relive a humiliation. "I knocked his arm away and threw a punch but I barely got him. Then he started on me. Hit me a few times, pushed me into the alley and . . . did it some more."

Devon remembered the corpse's bloody knuckles.

"My uncle's boxing lessons didn't help much, let's put it that way. Abe didn't look that big, but . . . he knew what he was doing."

That appeared to be all Sammy wanted to say. He seemed less scared now than embarrassed, the kind of shame that's hard for a kid to fake.

"He was beating you up and you had no shot against him, so you took out your knife and settled it that way."

"*No!* I don't have a knife—I've never had a knife. I didn't 'settle' anything. He won. I was on the ground and he kicked me in the stomach and he was gonna do it again before someone stopped him."

"Who stopped him?"

"I don't know, these two guys. I guess they heard the fight and they were laughing about it, telling Abe to lay off."

"They knew him? They used his name?"

"I don't . . . I don't remember."

"Think."

He looked away, his eyes inward. "Yeah, they did know his name. They said Abraham. One of 'em did, at least."

"Did you get a good look at them?"

"Yeah."

"What did they look like?"

He thought. "They weren't wearing hats. One had dark hair, scruffy. One had red hair, real short, almost military-short but not quite. He had a narrow face. The other guy, the dark-haired guy, had a lot of smallpox scars on his cheeks, real bad."

If only every witness were this sharp. That moment must have been so humiliating for Sammy that the visuals had been etched into his brain with perfect clarity.

"How were they dressed?"

"Like factory workers. Their hands were dirty. The redhead, his *ears* were dirty." He said that with surprise, as if just realizing it.

"His ears?"

"Like he had some kind of job that got his face all filthy, and he'd washed his face, but hadn't gotten his ears."

Sounded like half the men who worked at Northeast Munitions.

The description of the dark-haired one could mean a lot of people, but Devon's mind immediately went to Patty Campbell, one of his sources at Northeast. Who had said to Devon's face that he'd never heard of Wolff before, and who lived not far from the Iron Nail.

"Would you be able to recognize them if you saw them again, in a lineup?"

"A lineup?"

"Wolff died in that alley, Sammy. If it wasn't you who killed him, it was probably those two. If you don't want this pinned on you, if you don't want to go to jail for the rest of your life, you need to help me find them."

Sammy nodded, eyes wide. "I'll help. I'll do anything."

"What did the two men say exactly? You're on the ground and Wolff's kicked you and he's about to kick you again and what, they tell him to leave you alone, break it up, go easy? They cheer him on? What exactly?"

Sammy closed his eyes, steeped in his humiliation. "'Easy there, Abraham. Think you won this one.' That's what they said."

"They definitely said 'Abraham'?"

"Yes."

"Did they have foreign accents? Or sound like they're from around here?"

"They sounded normal. I don't remember otherwise."

"And Wolff was alive and well when you left that alley."

"I *swear* it."

"Good, because you'll have to, not just to me but to a judge most likely." Sammy nodded.

"And you were wearing a red plaid shirt, weren't you?"

"How'd you know?"

"He tore your shirt collar in the fight. We found it on the alley floor. Under his body. Where's the rest of that shirt?"

"I threw it away. I told my mom and Anne it got ruined at work. Am I . . . Am I gonna go to jail?"

"I'm thinking about it. I'm thinking very hard, and I'm thinking you may be okay but you need to be sure you aren't lying to me or leaving anything out. Then maybe I can help you."

Sammy nodded again.

"So you lied and told your family that you got jumped by some neighborhood bullies?"

"Yeah. I knew they'd believe it, because it's happened before."

"Jesus. You know your bullshit story got your sister off on a crusade against Irish kids for supposedly beating up Jews?"

Sammy's face toughened up. "There's no 'supposedly.' I made up a story about *that* night to cover my tracks, yeah, but that same thing happened to me a couple months ago, and it's happened to plenty of my friends. Our neighborhood's a goddamn war zone. I might not love how Anne's out there making it her business all the time, but at least she's trying to *do* something about it. I don't see anybody else trying."

Devon figured that was a shot at him, but he let it pass. They sat in silence as he ran different possibilities through his head, imagining the various endings he could lead the kid toward.

"Tell me about the cocktail napkin."

"What?"

"The napkin." He paused. "With the swastika."

Sammy looked utterly confused. "I don't know what you're talking about."

"We lifted a print from it. So you'd better not."

The kid held out his palms. "What napkin?"

"Ever been to the Iron Nail?"

"What's that?"

"Forget it." It had been worth checking, but Devon believed him—Sammy hadn't planted the napkin on Wolff.

The napkin meant the murder had been planned. Those two men hadn't just randomly happened upon Wolff in that alley. They'd been following him too. Sammy had merely beaten them to it.

Devon was realizing that the murder had nothing to do with the stolen rifles or the mob. Wolff had been a thief, yes, and some of those rifles had gotten into the hands of the mob and the Christian Legion, but that's not what had gotten Wolff killed. Sammy had tailed him to the North End, but what if someone else had too, or had known that Abe would be at Bucciano's?

Clark's FEPC story had seemed far-fetched, but it was making more and more sense. If word had gotten around that Wolff was going to testify against Northeast Munitions for only hiring white men, and then some managers had let a few workers know that there was a chance the company could run into trouble and maybe need to lay people off to make room for new hires with a different skin color, what might a couple desperate workers do?

Two men follow Wolff into an alley. They know his name. They'd been drinking at the Iron Nail earlier. They'd been thinking of doing something to shut him up. Maybe a few of them had their eyes out, hoping to catch him someplace unawares. Maybe a buddy had been at Bucciano's, had seen Wolff, had called his friends to come over.

Sammy had been hanging his head but now he looked up at Devon again.

"Can you find her for me?"

"What?"

"I just . . . want to know she's okay."

Devon shook his head at the kid. Sammy was heartsick, so mesmerized by this older woman—his first love, or so Devon imagined—that he couldn't think straight. Couldn't focus on the fact that he was *this close* to a jail cell, or worse.

At the same time, what Sammy had just said was a good reminder to Devon. After Elena had flown the coop, he'd placed some calls and had been trying to track her down, but he'd let the trail go cold after his shoot-out with the mob. Elena clearly knew more about her husband's unsavory activities than she'd been letting on; he needed to refocus on finding her so he could get the straight story from her this time.

"You let me worry about Elena, kid. Now, who else knows about you and her?"

"No one."

"You didn't brag to any friends? Your boss never caught you making goo-goo eyes at each other? You didn't tell your sister?"

"I didn't brag to *any*one. And I sure didn't tell Anne—she'd kill me if she knew I was with a married lady."

Again, Devon believed him. "Okay." He pulled a small notebook out of his pocket. "In all the time you've known her, I'm sure she said various things about her past and about her husband. And you're going to tell me absolutely everything she ever said about that, right now."

Chapter Forty-nine

CONFESSIONS

Anne sat by the front window, waiting anxiously for Sammy to re-turn from his shift. He was more than half an hour late. What had Devon done with him?

She didn't even know what she should be hoping for. Hope that Devon was lying and was trying to entrap Sammy in something he had nothing to do with? Or hope Devon was telling the truth, and Sammy was some-how mixed up with a married woman whose husband had been killed?

Her mother came home from work and they caught up a bit, though most of what Anne had done weren't the sorts of things she could share with her mother, at least not yet. She could tell her mother was still dis-appointed in her for leaving the baby naming early and then not even being home that night—what would she say when she learned about the trouble Sammy was in? When Anne looked at the last few days through her mother's eyes, she realized how bad she looked, and that's without her mother knowing she just slept with an Irishman. Her mother had never pushed Anne to embrace her rediscovered religion, but she'd clearly been hoping it would happen with time. She had never accused Anne of being on the wrong side, or even choosing sides. But Anne feared that her mother thought those things, and that maybe she was right. Hard as Anne had been working lately, she still felt like she was a disappointment, or worse.

When she finally saw Sammy walking home, she opened the door and waited on the landing, intercepting him before he came in so they could talk away from their mother. His steps up seemed unusually slow.

"Hey, Sammy," she said when he was half a flight down.

"Oh. Hi."

"So tell me what happened."

"Oh, just work. You know." He took three more steps; only two more to go. He looked like he'd been crying recently.

"What did Devon say to you?"

"Anne, I can't . . ."

It was all she could do not to have her knees give out. "Oh, Jesus, Sammy. Was that really your photo?" She had hoped and hoped that Devon had planted it; that too would have been terrible, but for different reasons. "Who is she?"

That's when Anne realized she could still be shocked, as her little brother explained that he'd had an affair with a married woman. His voice breaking and his eyes watering again, he told her the tale, and how the woman's husband had been killed two weeks ago—*that* was the murder Devon had obliquely referred to on their date, she realized. Sammy swore to her that he hadn't killed the husband, and that he'd told as much to Devon.

"He believed me."

"You *hope* he believed you." She grabbed the banister to steady herself.

"He said he might have to pick me up sometime soon, bring me to a police station and look at mug shots. Or a lineup." He sounded dazed, like he was relaying events that would have been interesting had they been occurring to someone else and he didn't quite believe they were happening to him.

"Don't go anywhere without telling me," she said. "We'll get a lawyer. We'll find out—"

"With what money?"

"We'll figure something out."

"I don't want to make a big thing of this. I just want to get back to my life."

"It *is* a big thing! Sammy, Jesus, if you're a witness who can place the real killers in an alley, then we need to figure out who they were before *they* realize what you know."

Clearly, that hadn't occurred to him yet. He looked like he might be sick.

"Devon probably didn't tell you that part, did he?"

Sammy ran his fingers through his hair. "I don't remember everything, all right? Jesus. What do you think I should do?"

"I don't trust the cops around here, but if Devon says they have an actual suspect you can ID, then you should try to do it. Otherwise they'll be back out on the streets."

"Okay, I will." He took another step. "Can I come home now?"

She didn't move. "So you lied to me, all this time."

"I know. I'm sorry."

"This is why you wouldn't give me an affidavit about the night you were attacked."

"I couldn't talk about it. All right? I'm sorry. I shouldn't have made you think something that wasn't true. But the time I got beat up in April, I've always told the truth about *that*."

"Then you'll happily give an affidavit about that time? Because the more testimonies we have, the better."

He exhaled. "Not happily. But yeah, I'll say whatever you want."

"What I want is for you to tell the truth. I can add you to our list of interviews for tomorrow. Then I'll type it up and you'll sign it. All right?"

"Deal. But, about this other thing . . . are you gonna tell Ma? About me and Elena?"

She knew it wasn't what he wanted to hear, but she told him the truth: "Yes, we both are, right now."

Chapter Fifty

PERSONNEL

Had any residents of Massasoit Street, a narrow one-block lane in the South End, happened to have been up very late on that stuffy weeknight, perhaps with insomnia, and stepped out onto their stoop or peered out their open window, they might have seen a shadowy figure briskly and silently walking alone.

They would have lost sight of the figure, however, when it ducked down the few steps leading to the garden level of the fourth brownstone on the east side. Had they been listening carefully, they might have heard the sound of metal files and other tools of the locksmith's trade being deployed in lieu of keys as the figure let itself into the building.

But no residents were awake at that hour, Devon was fairly certain. He had checked the block twice: once the night before, on the way to his apartment after work and before meeting Anne, to get a sense of the residents' nighttime routines, and once earlier this evening, only an hour ago. The lights were all out, the cars all parallel-parked along the street, and none of the few businesses here were the sort to be open this late.

Certainly not the office of Charles A. Nolan, Attorney-at-Law.

It took him less than a minute to get inside, having studied these dark arts as a rookie agent in New York, trained by veterans who had used such tactics to access the inner sanctums of various radicals, reds, and criminal suspects. Agents were supposed to obtain a warrant first, of course, especially if they were breaking in for the purpose of placing recording devices, but that wasn't Devon's aim here. Warrants took too long anyway, he'd been told, and weren't always granted.

Practical tips like these were never put in writing.

He wore thin black leather gloves, an annoyance in the heat but necessary. And once again he was without his partner. He couldn't let by-the-book Lou—or anyone else, for that matter—know what he was doing.

Once inside, he took out a small flashlight and inspected the desk by the front door. Nothing of note, just some bills and loose papers that didn't seem related.

The next room, farther inside and where he was less likely to be spotted, as it had only a small side window that looked out to an alley, was Nolan's private office. Diplomas on the wall, a desk, one very old guest chair, two filing cabinets, and a coffee table. In the closet, yet another filing cabinet.

This was going to take a while.

"So tell us about this FEPC hearing that's coming up."

The next morning, Devon and Lou sat in McDonough's office at Northeast Munitions. They hadn't explained what they were here for, had wanted to wait until they were in his office.

"Oh, it's just a bureaucratic formality," McDonough answered Devon. "One of many hoops we need to jump through for Uncle Sam to keep signing his checks."

"We heard that this one had the potential of being fairly difficult for the company."

"Where did you hear that?"

"We also heard that the higher-ups were worried about a fine, maybe the loss of some government business. That Uncle Sam might stop signing those checks."

McDonough rearranged himself in his chair a bit. "It's true that some . . . disgruntled people have accused us of unfair hiring practices, if that's what you're getting at. But we're confident those allegations are meritless."

"And did you know that Abraham Wolff was one of the people prepared to testify against the company?" Lou asked.

Slight pause. "That does ring a bell."

"Yet you didn't think to mention that to us when we dropped by last week to question his associates."

"I had no reason to think the two were connected."

This time Devon was the one who let some silence pass. He finally asked, "Did any managers here put out word that Wolff was talking to the FEPC? That his mouth was going to get you in trouble and possibly cost some men their jobs?"

"If you're asking if we made some official announcement, then the answer is no. I can't swear that word didn't spread somehow, of course, but it's not like this was discussed at the shift whistle assembly or anything like that."

In the day since Clark had alerted him to the FEPC case and Wolff's role in it, Devon had spoken to four different sources at Northeast Munitions. Three of them had heard rumors about the case, and one had even known that Wolff was going to be testifying.

"It really would have helped had you told us about this a long time ago," Lou said. Devon was ready to speak much more harshly to the weaselly bastard, but he knew Lou would criticize him if he did.

"Are you suggesting," and McDonough seemed to be horrified by this idea, or was pretending very hard to appear so, "that the reason Wolff was killed was because someone didn't want him to testify in a hearing?"

"It sounds like a motive to me," Devon said, "especially if any of the managers here were filling workers' heads with fears that they'd lose their jobs if the company had to hire more Negroes to keep Uncle Sam happy."

"And you're suggesting that a manager here, what, 'put out a hit' against Wolff?" The executive spoke that phrase as if it were almost too preposterous to voice aloud.

"Maybe no one here needed to spell it out in those terms," Devon explained. "All they had to do was, like you said, let word spread that the man was going to testify, and that if that happened, people would lose jobs. Just let the word get around and see what might happen."

"I assure you, we never would have done something like that."

"Well, that's awful good to hear, Neil." Devon gave him a broad smile. "In that case, to demonstrate your good faith and cooperation, I'm sure you'd be happy to let Agent Loomis and I take a look at your book of all the employees' headshots."

"Right now?"

"Unless you have something more important to do than assist in a murder investigation and clear your company's good name."

After McDonough left them alone in the office, Devon told Lou, "I never liked that son of a bitch."

"He's definitely lying," Lou conceded. Devon had needed to talk Lou into making this trip, but now his partner's curiosity was piqued.

Devon was still keeping quite a lot from Lou. The mob/Navy angle and his failure to follow the SAC's orders to stay away from Marcuso. The pictures Anne had taken, which showed a Northeast Munitions crate at the Christian Legion's warehouse. The fact that he was being blackmailed by the Legion. His break-in at Nolan's office and some of the paperwork he'd found.

If he played this right, he'd never have to mention any of it.

McDonough soon returned, pushing a rolling cart stacked with boxes of files. He explained that they contained the headshot and basic details for every employee, and that photos were taken on a worker's first day, so that some were several years old.

"Thanks," Devon told him. "Why don't you go grab yourself some coffee for a little while."

McDonough stood there blinking for a moment, realizing he was being dismissed from his own office.

After he left again, Lou closed the door while Devon reached into the bag he'd brought, removing a camera. He and Lou split the files in half, determined to find and photograph the files of every man with dark hair and smallpox scars, hoping Sammy Lemire would be able to ID him.

They were finally leaving when Mr. Lloyd, the owner, met them in the hallway.

"What's the idea here, gentlemen? Neil tells me you're looking through all our personnel files?"

As usual when they were dealing with big shots, Lou spoke first, sounding as accommodating as possible.

"We'll be out of your hair now, Mr. Lloyd."

"But it sounds like you're going to be 'in my hair' quite a bit." His voice had been loud but he lowered it to say, "You think someone here was involved in some kind of *murder*? We're trying to fight a war here!"

"No one's accusing anyone of anything right now," Lou said, stretching the truth.

"And *the FEPC*, Neil says? For chrissake," and Lloyd shook his head. "What would you have me do, gentlemen? If I went and started hiring more Jews and Negroes, what do you think would happen? Damn near every one of my workers would go on strike on the spot! They refuse to work with people like that! I'd lose every white worker I have. How would *that* help the war effort? You really want me to hire a few more blacks and take our productivity down to near zero?"

Lou didn't appear to know what to say, but Devon had had enough of the man.

"We're not telling you how to run your business, Mr. Lloyd. But we are trying to solve a murder, and we're going to succeed at that. And if you do anything that affects *our* productivity, then a little FEPC hearing will be the least of your problems. You have a good day."

He walked past the CEO and waited for Lou to follow.

Chapter Fifty-one

THE CENSORS

When Anne arrived at her desk the next morning, she saw through the window in Larry's office that he was sitting with two unfamiliar men. They both wore gray suits and looked too put-together to be fellow journalists. Clothes not rumpled, hair neatly combed.

Larry did not seem to be enjoying the conversation.

She placed her purse on her desk. Cheryl, with her back to Anne, was smoking and typing away.

"Who are the suits with Larry?"

"Oh, sweetie, I think you're about to find out."

Larry's door opened and he called out, "Anne! Can you come in here, please?"

Jesus, more bad news? Anne's stomach tensed. Strange men in suits. Government men. Did they work with Devon? Was this about Sammy?

Anne walked slowly toward Larry's office, trying to think. To make a plan. Prepare her story, marshal her evidence.

Larry closed the door behind her. His cramped office could barely fit two guest chairs in addition to his chair and desk, and the two men stood. They did not smile.

"Anne, this is Matt Sanderson and Mark . . . what was it?"

"Mark Grant. Please, Miss Lemire, have a seat."

Grant motioned for her to take a chair, but he and his comrade still stood. In such a tiny space, they were nearly leaning over her.

The good news was that they weren't *Agents* Sanderson and Grant, or

Officers, either. She saw no badges. They didn't look like cops: both were thin, unassuming, and middle-aged, their expensive-looking suits the most striking things about them.

Larry explained, "They're with the Office of War Information."

She felt relieved, somewhat, that she was dealing with the OWI rather than FBI agents or cops, but she was still on guard. She asked, "How can I help you?"

"Well, I'm afraid I have some bad news," Grant said, though his tone implied he didn't feel bad about it at all. "We're here to tell you that the Rumor Clinic is no longer running."

"Excuse me?"

"Unfortunately, we need to shut your column down."

"I don't understand." She looked at Larry. "I don't work for them, I work for you. Am I fired?"

Larry opened his mouth, then stopped, apparently unsure what to say. He looked at Grant, then back at Anne.

"Have I done something wrong?" she demanded.

"No," Larry finally came to her aid. "You're not *fired*."

"Well, that's semantics," Grant said. "The bottom line is, we can't allow your column to run anymore."

"'Allow'?" Anne asked. "I thought we had a free press in America."

"That's because we're a free country. But we won't be free anymore if we lose the war."

"What is that supposed to mean?"

"It means we need to tighten the controls on what goes to press for the duration. The federal government is the final authority on what information can and cannot be shared right now. We as a nation cannot afford to have disinformation spreading and causing hysteria."

She couldn't believe this. "Have you actually read what I write? Stopping disinformation and hysteria is exactly what I do."

"Miss, no, I'm afraid not." Grant picked up a folder that he'd apparently dropped on Larry's desk earlier. He read out phrases that Anne recognized as her own: "Negro baseball teams are altering their tour schedules so that they can plot troop movements. GIs are impregnating women of the WAAC, who are then sent to taxpayer-funded abortionists. Indians are attack—"

"Those are the rumors I *dis*proved! For God's sake, you have it backwards."

"What my colleague is trying to say," Sanderson said, "is that, while you may feel you're doing your readers a service by quote disproving unquote these rumors, what you're actually doing is spreading those rumors more widely."

"Sorry, if you think you're translating for your colleague here, you're doing a lousy job. Neither of you are making sense." She looked at Larry, hoping to find an ally in this insanity. "Do *you* understand this?"

"They're saying our readers are too stupid to get it," Larry quipped.

"Well, no," Sanderson said.

"Actually, yes," Grant admitted.

"I'm starting to feel a little stupid," Anne said.

"This whole conversation is stupid," Larry agreed.

"Look"—Grant held up a hand—"there are all kinds of crazy rumors out there; we get it. It's annoying; people do and say ignorant things. But it's all word of mouth. The spread of such rumors is slow. We've even conducted studies on this, so we know what we're talking about."

"Ooh, studies," Larry said, rubbing his hands together in mock excitement. "I'd be happy to read 'em, so long as they don't have too many big words."

"But Miss Lemire," Grant ignored Larry, "when you put those rumors *in print*, and when the *Star* distributes them to a wide audience, even though you think you're disproving them—"

"I *am* disproving them."

"—we're afraid what people really remember is the rumor itself, not the fact that it's false. You're telling people the rumor is a lie, but your act of telling them that is merely spreading the lie."

"That's ridiculous."

"No, it's proven fact. As I said, there are studies."

"Can I write a story disproving the rumor that the OWI is full of baloney?"

"Absolutely not," Grant said.

"Look," Sanderson added, "I know you were only kidding." (She wasn't.) "But our point remains. What you're doing here, you think it's for a good cause. And I applaud you for it, really. I think it's swell that a young gal like you has shown that kind of gumption. But the hard truth is, you're doing more harm than good. You're overestimating your readers."

"And you're hindering the war effort," Grant added.

Anne couldn't decide what was worse, their complete misinterpretation of her mission or their patronizing attitude.

"This is ridiculous." She pointed at Sanderson. "You're only saying this because you're jealous that I broke all those stories. And because I clearly hate Fascists more than you do, since *I've* been sounding the alarm about these people for years, well before the government decided to get on board."

Sanderson looked insulted. "That's not true."

"Now, c'mon, Anne," Larry chided her.

"Oh, you're taking their side? I thought editors had backbone and knew when to stand up to government censors."

Larry folded his arms. She realized too late that she had the entire room against her.

"I made some big shot angry, didn't I?" she asked the feds. "What was it, too many questions about the Italian mob at the docks? Or the way some Irish councilmen are buddying up with the Christian Legion? And now you're going to shut me down because you don't like the truth about what I'm saying?"

Grant and Sanderson moved toward the door.

"We are going to shut you down, yes," Sanderson said. "We have that power during wartime. We came here to be polite and tell you in person, and because we were under the impression you could act like a professional. Apparently, we overestimated you, too. Good day."

Then Sanderson nodded at Larry and said, "I trust you can control your other lady writers better than this one."

"Go to hell," she snapped at them as they headed out the door.

Larry shook his head after the government men's exit. "You don't make this easy, kid."

Jesus, was she going to cry now? No, no, God no, she would not cry. Everything in her life seemed to be falling apart in twenty-four hours, but she swallowed down the thickness in her throat and said, "I never expected it to be easy, but I still thought you'd back me."

"We can find some other pieces for you to work on," Larry said, softly. "Society pages, maybe a profile."

"I don't care about that bullshit," she said. "If I can't write *my* stories, I quit."

He didn't do anything to stop her as she walked out.

Chapter Fifty-two

BEARING WITNESS

Early in the afternoon, when Devon pulled in front of Anne's apartment for the third time in as many days, he did so with Lou sitting beside him. This would be an official visit, by the book, with his partner to vouch for him later should that be necessary.

He had told Lou only that he knew Anne because they'd grown up together, that they'd recently bumped into each other and had become friendly again. How exactly he'd happened to find the photo of Elena among her brother's possessions, he'd been vague, noting that Sammy was a minor and they'd need to proceed with care. Technically, this should now be BPD's case, but given the involvement of Northeast Munitions, Devon wanted to make sure that, when he handed the case over, the Bureau had gathered as much evidence as possible so the cops couldn't flub it.

The FBI could be fast when it needed to be: technicians had already developed the shots Devon and Lou had taken, fourteen in total. If Sammy could identify one of the men, Devon would pass it on to Jimmy Moore. Hopefully that man's fingerprints would match the partial print they'd lifted from the paper cocktail napkin; if it didn't, and if the suspect had any known associates with short red hair, they'd need to find that other fellow and get him in a lineup in front of Sammy, and hopefully *his* prints would match.

Spaces were few, so Devon parked a few doors down, then got out of the car, Lou right behind him. He'd made it halfway to Anne's building when a squad car approached. The driver's window was rolled down, a left arm dangling casually as the car slowed to a stop.

"Devon." His cousin Brian wore a crooked grin. *You son of a bitch,* Devon thought.

Yet he made friendly as he introduced Brian and Lou. Brian parked and got out, shook Lou's hand.

"What's new with the Bureau, gents?"

"Oh, fun-filled background checks." Devon flapped the envelope in his hand and hoped Lou wouldn't give anything away. "It's tough work, but someone's gotta do it. How 'bout you?"

"Another day, another dollar."

"Give us a minute, Lou. Got a quick family matter to discuss."

Devon tried to play it cool and ignore the sour look on Lou's face. *You're dismissing me? Who do you think you are, again?* Hopefully Lou would write this off to the strange rituals of Irishmen, which perhaps it was.

Devon kept his gaze on Brian and kept his fake smile firmly in place as he listened to Lou's footsteps fade, heard him light a cigarette to kill the time.

"Can I help you with something, Brian?"

"Yeah, I think you can. I think you can help quite a bit by staying the hell out of the way. Believe you got a message to that effect?"

Devon had suspected it ever since Anne told him an Officer Dennigan had been the source of the *Star*'s counterfeiting story, but it still felt like a punch in the gut to have it confirmed.

"My own family, huh?"

"Yeah, your own family, Dev. People who work hard and are trying to make things right. We don't need you and your Yankee colleagues fucking things up right as it's all coming together. That warning you got was something you should be taking seriously."

Devon took a breath. "I always knew you were a few cards short of a full deck, Brian, but I still never thought you'd stoop this low. If you've pushed my old man into getting involved in something that's going to tear down his name, I will make you fucking regret it, I promise you."

Trying to threaten his cousin while keeping his voice quiet enough for Lou not to overhear wasn't easy.

Brian kept on smiling. "You as a tough guy? The act just doesn't work, sorry. Whatever you learned in law school ain't gonna help you on the streets. And trust me, no one has pushed John Mulvey into a goddamn thing and you know it. You being a fed was supposed to make things easier for us, but you don't seem to be getting the message."

Devon folded his arms. "The message was to stay away from the Christian Legion. I'm not here about them, if you must know. I'm here about Abraham Wolff."

"Who?"

"The murder victim from the North End I asked you about last time we talked."

"I told you I didn't know anything about that, and I don't."

"Yet you referred to him as a 'blabby kike' the other day. How'd you know he was blabby?"

Brian just smiled, looked away, shook his head. Not remembering the comment but realizing he'd been caught at something.

"I'm here to solve a murder," Devon said. "I'm here to do my job, unlike some people."

He desperately wanted to punch that cocky grin off Brian's face, even though he was fairly certain that, if he tried, Brian would easily best him. His older cousin was taller and thicker and the sort of fellow who started fights for fun, possibly every day. He knew that when Brian looked at him, he saw a soft face, a nose that had never been broken, and manicured hands that were more accustomed to paperwork than working over a suspect.

"But since you mentioned the Legion, I thought I'd ask: what's your little Bible group doing with M-1 rifles?"

That changed Brian's expression: his eyes went cold, the smile a memory. "What rifles?"

"The ones you finagled out of Northeast Munitions."

After staring Devon down for a moment, Brian said, "Do whatever it is you're here to do, quickly, and then leave. From now on, stay out of this neighborhood. I don't want to see you or your partner tomorrow, or any other day."

"Why, what happens tomorrow?"

Brian looked even angrier now, realizing he'd given something else away. "Nothing. And fuck you."

"Everything okay, gentlemen?" an impatient Lou asked, footsteps approaching.

Tomorrow was the Fourth of July.

"Yeah, fine," Devon answered.

"Good to meet you, Agent Loomis." Brian nodded brusquely and got back in his car, then drove off.

"What the hell's going on?" The curse meant Lou was really, really mad.

"One thing at a time, Lou. Let's get the kid."

It took a while to get the photos in front of Sammy.

Mrs. Lemire had been told last night about Sammy's relationship with a married woman, apparently, but much time was spent explaining and re-explaining. There was a man also living in the house, one of Anne's French cousins, and he was alternately protective of Sammy, warning the agents that the kid had rights and they had no reason to be bothering him, and chastising of Sammy, telling the kid to do what the agents told him and get this over with.

Finally the Lemires all sat down in the living room while Devon, standing but trying not to loom over the kid, took the fourteen photos out of the envelope.

Sammy flipped through the pictures slowly, but at the fifth he stopped. "This one. It's him."

Sammy was pointing at Patty Campbell, Devon's occasional source of gossip at Northeast Munitions. Two weeks ago, he had told the agents he hadn't ever heard of Wolff. They hadn't thought to fingerprint him that day the way they'd fingerprinted Wolff's two friends, hadn't suspected him at all. Campbell had acted nervous, but Devon had figured he just didn't like talking to the feds at his workplace, afraid of looking like a rat to his fellows.

In truth, Campbell had been afraid the feds were on to him.

"Are you sure?" Devon asked, feeling like a sucker. "It's a picture of a picture, so it's not great."

"Yes. This is absolutely one of them."

* * *

Devon explained that he and Lou would pass this information on to Boston police, so the Lemires should expect a call soon from Detective Jimmy Moore. The cops would bring the man Sammy IDed in for questioning, and hopefully he'd confess. If he didn't, they'd see if his prints matched evidence from the scene—Devon didn't mention the napkin specifically.

It felt awkward to pretend he barely knew Anne in front of Lou, to pantomime formality around her and her mother. But now was not the time for Lou or anyone at the Bureau to realize he'd been with her, blackmail letter or not.

Based on the way he caught her glaring at him, though, the two of them would never be in a compromising position again. She seemed to blame him for all of this, as if he had anything to do with her brother's poor judgment.

He politely thanked the family for their time and headed out the door.

"Patty Fucking Campbell," Devon said once they were out in the hallway.

"He lied to us," Lou said, "unless the kid's wrong. But I don't think he is."

"Me neither. Campbell played us."

He and Lou had made it down a few stairs when the door opened and out came Anne.

"Devon, I wanted to show you this." She was holding some paper, and she walked down the half-flight of stairs, joining the agents on the landing. Devon avoided his partner's eyes, hoping Lou wouldn't ask exactly how familiar he and Anne really were. "I know Sammy lied at first when he told us he'd been beaten up that night, but I don't want you thinking he's an unreliable witness."

"What's this?" Devon asked as he glanced at the paper.

"It's an affidavit he gave about the time he was attacked in April." She addressed her next comment to Lou: "I've been taking down these statements so we can prove to the mayor and whoever will listen that there have been violent attacks targeting Jews all over the neighborhood, for months now. I haven't had a chance to get it notarized yet, but this is a copy."

It was two sheets of paper, signed at the bottom by Sammy and a witness, Anne. Devon read the story, an account of an evening when

Sammy and a friend were surrounded by four attackers, older teenagers and young men, who asked if they were Jews, then beat them up. He noticed, with a familiar sense of nauseating disappointment, that one of the attackers' description matched that of Brian's son, Johnny—the son of Devon's cousin, namesake to Devon's father. There couldn't be that many teenagers around here with crescent-moon scars on their cheeks.

"What are you planning on doing with this?" Lou asked Anne when it was his turn to read it.

"A reporter from New York and I are working on a magazine story. We're nearly finished with our reporting, and hopefully once this is in print, the city will do something. But because the cops are part of the problem here, I was hoping you two might be able to do something about it, too."

Lou looked at Devon to gauge his reaction, then said, "I'm sorry this happened to your brother, Miss Lemire, but it doesn't seem like a federal matter."

"We're at war with Germany, and the Nazis have their own little fiefdom right here in Dorchester, yet that's not a federal matter?"

"Right now we need to concentrate on getting this fellow arrested," Devon said, motioning to the envelope of photos in his hand.

"How can I trust the cops to do the right thing about a murder when they're letting all hell break loose around here?" Anne asked.

"I trust the homicide detective we're giving this to," Devon said. Realizing that didn't sound reassuring. And worrying that he was wrong. Everyone else he trusted seemed to be betraying him.

With that, he nodded to her again, hating how stiff they were acting around each other. Realizing they might not be that other way ever again.

"Good luck with your story," he said, and the agents left without another word.

Chapter Fifty-three

THE PRECINCT

Anne tried to make sense of the morass into which her brother had been dragged. He'd confronted the husband of his lover, challenged him, and lost. Then as he left the alley, beaten and embarrassed, two strangers had walked in. Moments—perhaps even seconds—after Sammy had stumbled away, those two men had most likely killed the husband.

That's all Devon had told her: nothing else about who the men were or what their motive had been. She'd been able to put together the fact that they worked at Northeast Munitions; the photos Devon had shown Sammy had all been personnel headshots from the plant. But she didn't know if it was some rivalry among workers, a workday spat that spilled over after hours, or something else.

It bothered her that Devon wouldn't tell her anything more, that he'd demoted her from Lover to a much lesser role: Sister of Witness, or, even worse, Journalist Around Whom to Proceed Warily. She told herself she should take it as a strange compliment, that she was so good at her job she made a G-man nervous, but she hadn't wanted that. Her heart ached and she hated herself for it, for letting her emotions get in the way of her job, but she also hated *him* for it, for trampling on the feelings she'd dared share.

This is why you should never make yourself vulnerable, she realized, too late.

She should have known better than to fall for a man like that. She *had* known better, but had gone along with him anyway. Because he was handsome and charming, because she wanted to believe that *she* could be as carefree as he always seemed to be. Because he had offered a false apology for the way his family had treated hers years ago, and she had wanted to believe he was better than he'd shown her in the past.

The way he was refusing to admit the truth about his father showed that he hadn't grown beyond those days at all.

That night at seven, she got a call from Detective Moore from Boston police, asking if Sammy could come in to look at a lineup.

With her car still impounded by that son of a bitch cop Duffy, she decided to spring for a taxi even though it would put a dent in her spending money—especially since she'd just lost her job. But she didn't trust the neighborhood enough to walk and take the train as night fell. It had come to this, she realized: feeling unsafe in her own home.

Elias and her mother were working. Her mother would be furious that Anne was taking Sammy without her—she had expressly said to call her at the factory if the police needed Sammy tonight, so Anne was disobeying. But she didn't want her mother to miss work, and she didn't want another family member to have to go through the indignity of dealing with cops. She knew she'd get an earful for this later, but it was worth it to spare her mother from the experience.

Sammy didn't say a word on the ride over. Usually Anne tried to draw him out of his moody adolescent silence, but not now.

As Detective Moore walked them through a bullpen of plainclothes officers, smoke thick in the air, she wondered how many of these cops had personally ignored the calls for more police protection in Dorchester. Whenever Anne and Sammy passed a uniformed beat cop in the hallway, she wondered if this was one of the ones who had even joined in on some of the attacks.

No one insulted her, at least. No one gave her a sidewise glance or sniggered after she passed. Maybe some of these men were decent people after all. That or, more likely, they just didn't realize who she was.

They'd certainly know her once Harold printed their story. She recalled his prediction, that the story might cause more harm than good, that it wouldn't goad the police into action but would enrage them, turning Anne and her family into even bigger targets.

She felt nervous being here. She stepped closer to Moore after they'd passed through the bullpen and said, hopefully quietly enough for Sammy not to hear, "Shouldn't you have brought us in through a more private route?"

"It's only cops in here, Miss Lemire. You're fine."

Surely he wasn't that naïve.

Finally they reached a small, narrow room with three chairs, a desk, and fake wood paneling on the walls, its main feature a long window offering a view into another, similar room lacking any furniture. She'd seen such things in films, but never the real thing.

Moore explained how it would work, and a minute later four men were walked into the room on the other side of the one-way mirror. They ranged between five-five and five-ten, according to the helpful markings on the wall behind them, and all had dark hair and some sort of scarring on their faces. She didn't think she'd seen any of these men before.

"Take your time," Moore said.

"It's number three," Sammy said without hesitation. "That's him."

Chapter Fifty-four

JUSTIFICATIONS

Devon drove out to his father's house in Milton that night, angry at nearly everyone he knew. So many people had been playing him, and he'd gone along with it like an idiot. Patty Campbell had played him, but that wasn't the worst of it by a long shot. Devon's own family was playing him.

He'd called ahead to make sure his father was home and alone, as he didn't want anyone else around. Pop called out that the door was unlocked when Devon rang the bell.

"I'm in the study," Pop called out. "Care for the usual?"

Devon stepped into the dark room, lit by a single lamp on Pop's desk. "No thanks, not right now. Look, we need to talk. About your friends at the Christian Legion."

"What's wrong?" his father asked. He poured himself a whiskey neat and sat down in one of his leather chairs.

Still standing, Devon said, "I need you to tell me everything you know about the Christian Legion and whatever Nolan's planning."

Pop watched him for a moment. "Am I being asked this by my son or by a federal agent?"

"Take your pick."

"Why don't you tell me what *you* know about the Legion."

Dodging questions, refusing to talk straight. So far, all Devon's worst fears—and all that Anne had alleged—seemed confirmed.

"I know that Nolan's helping Cavanaugh run for Congress; we both know that. And I know he also runs the Christian Legion, which has been printing the hate sheets that I see all over town. I also know—"

"'Hate sheets' is a rather biased name for them."

"—he'd been printing them, until recently, from a warehouse that *you* own."

"Devon, you know I own a lot of property." An awkward smile. "I can't claim to know about everything that's happening everywhere. Please, sit. You're making me feel interrogated."

Pop hadn't denied anything, Devon noticed. He folded his arms, still not sitting. "So are you saying you didn't know he was doing this? That he was using that warehouse without your permission?"

"And since when is printing needed information about the war illegal?"

"If those sheets are judged to be Nazi propaganda, then they're illegal. You know that. And I've read them, Pop. There are *reasons* they're being printed in secret."

"We both know very well," his father countered after taking a healthy sip, "that Roosevelt's been bending laws about free speech because he can't bear to hear criticism. The fact remains that many, *many* patriotic Americans are against our joining the war in Europe, and they have a right to express themselves. I've done well in life, so wouldn't it be the least I could do to help them out?"

Part of Devon hadn't wanted to hear his father admit to any of this. But part of him needed it.

"What if I told you that there's photo evidence that Christian Legion pamphlets were being printed right alongside counterfeit ration stamps? You going to rationalize that away too?"

For the first time, his father averted his gaze. His eyes found the floor, then the view out the window.

"I just read a newspaper story about counterfeit stamps," Pop said. "It was all Jewish business owners who were involved."

"Yeah, and they *bought* the stamps from someone else, someone I'm betting was connected to the cops or had access to an actual OPA printing press, which they somehow made off with, and that's why those stamps looked almost perfect—just perfect enough to convince everyone, but with a few carefully placed blemishes so they could be proven to be fakes."

His father grinned. Like it tickled him to see how this was all playing out.

"As I understand it, people are quite enraged about the situation. It's more proof that the Jews are playing us, profiting from the war and—"

"Your little group entrapped them, and you know it."

"'My' little group? There's nothing that could possibly tie *me* to any counterfeiting. I haven't set foot in that warehouse in years. It's practically condemned. If someone has . . . broken in and used it for their own ends, no one can prove I had any knowledge of it."

"Except this conversation." But there was in fact proof, which Devon hadn't mentioned yet: he had seen paperwork in Nolan's office demonstrating that his father had quite a bit of knowledge about what had been happening in that warehouse.

"And would you do that, son? Would you tell anyone about this? About your own father?"

Silence stretched between them.

"They had guns stashed at that warehouse too, Pop. Military rifles, stolen from a war plant. What do you know about that?"

"Nothing." Finally, his father looked surprised. "Rifles?"

"Yes, rifles I've been tracking. I need to know where they are, and what the Legion is planning to do with them, immediately." He hadn't found the rifles or any records of them in Nolan's office.

"I have no idea. Good God, why do you think they have rifles?"

"I don't think it, I *know* it. For God's sake, Pop. You've been palling around with crackpots and expecting that when things go south, I'd protect you."

"I don't need your protection. And these 'crackpots' happen to include priests, Devon. Leaders, men of honor and integrity."

"Priests with rifles?"

"Priests in Spain sure needed rifles to keep the reds away. You know how many priests and nuns the reds butchered over there before Franco won that war?"

"Enough, Pop." God, he was tired of hearing about the oppressed

Spanish clergy, and the oppressed Irish "back home," deployed as a justification for anything. "I know it's been tough for you since Mom passed, but that doesn't mean—"

"Don't you use her like that." Pop put his glass down on a side table, nearly hard enough to crack it.

"Why not? Are you going to tell me she would have approved of you financing a nut like Nolan? That she would have been fine with you spending time with thugs who are picking fights all over town? You think she would have gone along with all that? I don't. I'm trying to come up with *some kind* of an explanation for how you could've gone off the rails like this, and that's the only—"

"This has nothing to do with her!"

His father stood, his face red. Devon waited for the moment to pass, let his father gather himself.

He kept his voice calm as he said, "There are people in Dorchester who've been collecting signed affidavits from Jews who have been beat up. At least one of them mentions *Johnny,* describing him and that scar of his perfectly. "So someone in our family is a street thug terrorizing Jewish kids. The fact that his dad's a cop may have protected him so far, but at the very least he's going to be exposed for what he's done. I would think you'd at least be concerned with how that makes the family look."

His father sighed. "Brian and his family . . . have had a harder time with some things, you know that. They've never managed to move out of the neighborhood, and so they run with a . . . a coarser type."

"Brian's part of the counterfeiting ring, too—he fed the story to the press. And he threatened me, by the way. He said that if I try to stop what he's involved in, he'll get me fired."

"How could he even do that?"

"Don't worry about it." Devon certainly wasn't going to mention his relationship with Anne to his father; he'd probably already said too much. "The point is, you seem to be siding with people like Brian over *me.*"

"That's not true. I've worked to keep you insulated from this because of your job. I know it wouldn't do for you to be associated with . . . some of this, so—"

"Because you know damn well it's illegal."

"We are in a time of *war*, Devon!" His father pointed at the floor, on the verge of shouting again. "I am trying to *save lives*. You've all but told me an Allied invasion of Europe is coming, that it'll happen any day now. That's why we need to *act*, before one drop of American blood is spilled on that continent. You know as well as I do, once there are GIs in France or Italy or Greece, once we've joined the battles over there and have taken any losses at all, then we'll be in it till the bloody finish. There's no way we'd turn away from the fight once we've joined it in earnest. *This is our chance* to avert a disaster on a scale that you can't possibly imagine."

It was like the ghosts of Devon's dead uncles were here in the room, egging Pop on. No matter what Devon said, he knew, he would never be as convincing as the brothers Pop had lost.

"So what happens next?" Devon asked. "What exactly are you and the Legion planning?"

"The hope is that everything, all of it in concert, will convince enough people and get them to agitate for change. The pamphlets keep the message out there even though Roosevelt banned our missives from the mail. And things like those Jew business owners with their counterfeit ration stamps, that will further incense the public. They'll demand accountability. They'll elect the right leaders. Remove the wrong ones."

Devon rubbed at his face, as if he could erase all he was hearing. "'Remove' how? Do you not realize . . . how unhinged this sounds? This is where the rifles come in, isn't it? It's the Fourth, right? They're planning something for the rally on the Fourth?"

"I already said, I don't know anything about rifles!"

"Then who does? I've seen enough bodies this month—who's next?"

Pop shook his head and, for the first time, looked worried.

"It's . . . a large organization, Devon. I don't know everyone involved. And some of the men, I suppose, are more prone to violence. I've heard some people *say* things, but I just figured it was . . . all talk, jokes, that sort of thing."

"Jokes about what?"

"About . . . certain politicians. And how it would be best if we were . . . rid of them."

"Assassinations? They're 'joking' about assassinations while they're hoarding rifles?"

His father held up his palms. "I promise you, I never thought anyone was *planning* something like that."

Devon's mind raced through the possibilities.

"You're wrong about not being tied to this, Pop. There's a paper trail. I've seen some of Nolan's files. Your name comes up more often than you may realize."

No response this time.

"Is this why you wanted me to join the Bureau all along? So you'd have someone to protect you when you went off the rails?"

"I have not gone off the—"

"I could go to *prison* if it came out that I protected you!" Devon pointed at his chest and lowered his voice even though the house was empty. "Do you care about that at all?"

"We both know that won't happen." Pop's voice was calm, measured, like he was talking his child out of an overreaction to a loss on the baseball diamond. "We both know you're smart enough to get yourself out of any little jam. And we both know you'll do the right thing."

Devon glanced at the window, worried the neighbors could have overheard. But it was dark out, the window was closed, and all he could see was the reflection of a man who had run out of good options.

Chapter Fifty-five

ON OUR SIDE

Nearing midnight, Devon and Lou stood in an observation room at the Boston police headquarters, watching Patty Campbell stew.

Campbell had already been questioned for over an hour by Jimmy Moore and another Homicide cop. Thus far, he'd denied everything, but he'd visibly stiffened when Moore mentioned the fact that the killers had left something behind at the crime scene, and he looked almost sick when Moore had followed that up with the chuckling comment, "And you'd been drinking at the Iron Nail earlier that night, hadn't you?"

The detectives took a break, Moore stepping into the observation room with the agents.

"They're still looking at the prints, but I say we have our man."

"Looks that way," Devon said. "But if the prints don't match, then all we have on him is the kid's ID."

"That can be enough."

If Sammy's eyewitness testimony was the only thing putting Campbell at the scene, though, Devon didn't like how that would play out. The kid would be an obvious and vulnerable target until the trial.

He asked Jimmy, "Mind if I go in there next? Alone."

"Sure," Jimmy said.

"Why alone?" Lou asked.

"No offense, Lou, but I think I can get him to talk to me. We've known each other since before I was a fed. You two listen in."

Lou didn't look pleased, but he went along with it. Devon waited ten minutes so Campbell could steep in his guilt a little longer.

When he finally stepped in, Campbell gave him a guarded look. They'd always bantered with each other easily in the past, but the setting changed everything.

"This is bullshit," Campbell said. "How can they keep holding me like this?"

"It's a complicated process, Patty." He eased himself into the chair. For a few minutes he listened to more of Campbell's complaints and denials, nodding along as if he believed the poor fellow, playing into his sense of victimization.

Then he asked, "You're part of the Christian Legion, right?"

"What if I am? I'm a God-fearing man, aren't you?"

"And it's a big group, from what I understand."

"It is, thank goodness."

"And within a group that large, there are disagreements. Fellows don't always see eye to eye."

Campbell watched him carefully.

"Some fellows want to go about things one way," Devon continued. "Others have a different opinion. Especially when it comes to big things. Like trying to stop the war. And what they'd be willing to do to make that happen."

Devon paused.

"Tell me about the rifles."

"Which rifles? I work with rifles all day, you know that."

"Which is why it'd be so easy for a few of them to disappear. Maybe even a whole crate."

Campbell looked away for a moment. "What are you talking about, Mulvey? You trying to get me fired?"

Devon laughed. Stretched it out. Laughed so much that Campbell even grinned, as if he were being laughed with and not at.

"'Fired'?" Devon quit with the laughing. "Patty, do you understand, getting fired is the least of your concerns right now?" He leaned over and held his hand well under the table. "This is where getting fired ranks with your problems." He raised his hand until it was level with his chin.

"And this is where murder ranks." Raised his hand over his head. "And up here is sedition."

"What are you talking about?"

"Sorry, that's a big word. How's 'assassination'? That's big too, but I think you get me."

"I don't know what you're—"

"Enough with the bullshit." He slapped the table. "We both know there's a fifty-fifty shot your prints are a match for the murder. And if they're not yours, they'll wind up being one of your best buddies', and once we book him, he'll tell us you were right there with him. We also have witnesses. Patty, you're fucked. You are absolutely fucked, and you are not getting out of here anytime soon. Years. Decades."

He paused.

"Unless."

Devon waited again, until an impatient Campbell said, "Unless what?"

"Unless you bargain your sentence down by giving us something we want. Something bigger. Like who has those rifles now and what they're planning to do with them."

Devon knew Lou wouldn't approve of this; they couldn't officially of-fer Campbell anything at all, at least not yet. But Campbell didn't know that, and Devon wasn't going to tell him, and he hoped that Lou would refrain from stepping into the room to interject or do anything to kill the rhythm here.

"I don't . . ." And Campbell shook his head, his eyes darting every-where but Devon's face.

"It's war, Patty. And it wouldn't be fair for soldiers to go to jail while the generals walk."

More silence. Devon let it stretch awhile.

"Whatever the Legion is planning," Devon went on, "it's not going to work. They're going to fail, and then they're going to prison. The only thing to figure out is whether you're going to speed up that failure, in which case you help yourself out quite a bit. Or whether you're not going to help us at all, in which case, best-case scenario, you're behind bars for the rest of your life."

Campbell shook his head again. In a quiet voice, he mumbled, "This is bullshit."

"Yeah, you said that already. Maybe it's bullshit, but it's also real, and it's happening to you. Only to you. How is that fair?"

Campbell stared hard at the floor for a while, then he shot Devon a look. "You were supposed to be on our side."

He'd been hearing that a lot, and it still stung. Devon felt eyes on him from the other side of the two-way mirror.

"I'm on the side of people who obey the law, Patty. Not sure how you could have ever thought otherwise."

More silence. Then Campbell leaned back in his chair, as if belatedly absorbing a punch in the nose.

"What do you want to know?"

After Devon had invited the BPD detectives and Lou back in to take furious notes and ask more questions, Devon and Lou stepped back into the observation room.

"Nice job," Lou said. "But how did you know the Legion had those rifles?"

Devon still couldn't let Lou know about Anne's photos or his relationship with her. "Some photos showed up in the mail this morning, sent anonymously," he lied. "I meant to tell you about it, but things have been happening so fast."

"And what did he mean by that, you 'being on their side'?"

Devon shook his head. "I have no idea."

Chapter Fifty-six

INDEPENDENCE DAY

Early the next morning, on the Fourth of July, Anne got another call from Devon. He was on a pay phone somewhere—she heard distant voices and an occasional car horn.

He told her the police were still holding the man Sammy had identified, Patty Campbell, but that his prints apparently didn't match some item found at the crime scene.

"Which means it most likely comes from the other fellow Sammy saw that night, the redhead," Devon explained. "The police need to find him. Once they do, we have to hope *his* prints match, and I think they will. The cops are holding on to Campbell, because we've tied him to some other crimes."

She heard yelling in the background. "Where are you?"

"I can't say."

"Devon, I didn't care for the way your friend Moore paraded me and Sammy through the station. Plenty of cops got a good look at Sammy, and I'm sure at least a few of them are dirty."

"Sammy's doing the right thing. And I think tomorrow he should come to my office and look at more photos."

"From Northeast Munitions?"

"That's right. We need him to ID the redhead as soon as possible. But we have some ideas who it might be, based on Campbell's known associates."

"Are you going to tell me what the bigger story here is? Why was that man killed, and what does it have to do with a munitions factory?"

"I really can't say right now. I'm sorry."

"You seem to be saying that a lot lately."

A brief pause. "There are things happening that I can't tell you about yet. You have to keep trusting me."

She was tired of hearing this. "It looks like I don't have much choice."

"There's something else. Don't go to the parade today. The state rep, Cavanaugh, he's going to give a speech at the end, and I think it's going to be very unfriendly to people like you."

"Which is exactly why I need to be there. If a government official is going to stand before the public and spout Hitlerite nonsense, I plan on reporting it."

"Anne. I'm trying to help you here. I'm afraid that crowd could get ugly."

"I'm sure it will."

"You won't be safe. Jesus, I wish you weren't so goddamn stubborn."

"I don't need you to come to my rescue and be a hero, so don't get any ideas."

"Why do you really need to go? What does this have to do with your Rumor Clinic?"

She hadn't told him about the government censors who'd shown up at Larry's office and shut down the Rumor Clinic, or that she'd stormed out and told Larry she quit the *Star*. She partly regretted her decision, but at the same time, she had no desire to stay on staff just to write society pieces and whatever other lightweight jobs Larry deigned to give a "lady reporter."

"If something big happens at that rally," she told Devon, "I'll need to include it in the magazine piece I'm writing."

"I wish you'd let this be."

"Why, so it can all be swept under the carpet? If you really think something ugly is going to happen, then maybe the FBI should do something about it. Say, you don't happen to know any FBI agents, do you?"

"Anne, I'm trying to—"

"Or are you hoping to talk me into staying at your place for my safety, so you can fuck me again and hope I learn to be sweet and submissive?"

A pause, like he was shocked to hear a woman talk that way. "That's not fair."

"Well, sitting on your backside and telling a reporter to stay away from news isn't very fair either."

"I promise you, I am hardly sitting on my backside right now, but I can't tell you what—"

"Then if you can't tell me anything, maybe you should just stop calling. Goodbye, Devon."

She hung up before she could say anything else, and before he could hear her throat catch.

Harold had already left town for New York, having told Anne that one of them being at the Fourth of July rally would be enough. She couldn't help wondering if he was just chickening out, if after the windshield incident, he didn't want to put himself in danger again. Whereas this was Anne's neighborhood—she lived here, she had less choice.

The day was hot again, the open windows in the apartment helping only so much. It was impossible to get any breeze in the apartment, and the humidity made every surface and inch of skin sticky.

The bathroom door was open, and she saw Sammy standing in front of the mirror, combing his hair.

"I think you should stay in," she told him.

"Why?"

"I think it might get rough."

"If you're going, I'm going."

She realized she was having the same conversation she'd had with Devon, in reverse. Now she was the protective scold.

"I'm not the one who could be a star witness in a murder case," she explained.

"I'm tired of staying cooped up in this place all the time! It's bad enough we can't go out at night. C'mon, it's a parade, in broad daylight. Some of my friends want to meet up and get ice cream."

It seemed wrong to deprive him of anything right now. "All right, fine. But at the first sign of trouble, I want you to make a beeline for the apartment."

"And you'll do the same, right? No more being a martyr for the cause."

Devon had absorbed Anne's insults, realizing that he'd earned at least some of them. He wished he could have explained himself more, but she was a reporter, and he needed to belatedly erect some walls between them lest he risk ruining this operation.

He had not told her, for instance, that before sunrise that very morning—barely two hours ago—he and Lou had driven to the home of a federal judge and woken the old man up unconscionably early on a holiday to get him to sign a search warrant for the Christian Legion's offices.

Neither agent had slept all night. First they'd questioned Patty Campbell about the rifles and gotten the names of other Christian Legion members. Campbell fessed up because he seemed to believe Devon's offer that they'd go easy on him for the murder of Wolff, which he was still denying but that Devon was confident they'd book him for eventually. Campbell's assistance with the Legion wouldn't help him once they matched the print, but Devon saw no reason to tell him that.

Campbell wasn't terribly bright. He had given them the names of men whom he claimed to have heard talk about plotting to kill two Jewish city councilmen. These men—who did not include himself, Campbell claimed—believed that killing politically prominent Jews would cause "reds and Jews and such" to counterattack, leading to civil unrest and open warfare in the streets of Boston, which would then require the Army to subdue the revolt, which would then lead America to abandon the larger world war and focus on its problems here at home.

It all sounded absurd and paranoid and just crazy enough to be real, Devon felt.

Campbell also swore that he hadn't stolen any rifles himself, that he loved his job and wouldn't have done anything to jeopardize it. But he said he'd heard that some Legion men had bought M-1s secondhand, from some other worker who *had* stolen them. Wolff, Devon knew.

Whether Wolff had sold the guns to Italian gangsters who then sold them to the Legion, or whether Wolff himself had naïvely sold them to men who hated him for his religion and planned to use them against his own people, Devon didn't know, and maybe never would.

Very late that night—well into the morning, in fact—Devon and Lou had met with the SAC and gone over a game plan. Devon had been careful to tell them only what information he'd learned through legitimate means, or things he'd learned in the gray areas of the law and could lie convincingly about having discovered legitimately. The photographs of the counterfeiting machines with the crate of Northeast Munitions visible in the background? Those had come in the mail earlier that morning, he'd lied. They'd been mailed to him anonymously; he'd even saved the envelope (in truth, it was the envelope the blackmailers had used when sending him the compromising photos of himself and Anne, which he'd destroyed).

At not yet eight that morning, Devon, Lou, and two other agents announced themselves at the door of Nolan's office and, as no one answered on that holiday morn, broke the door down. They went about methodically removing paperwork and entire filing cabinets, moving them into a Bureau truck.

Devon did not let his colleagues know that he had been in this office before, had in fact broken in the previous night, removing several pieces of paper on which he'd seen his father's name. He knew it might well be inevitable that his father's role would come up in the many interviews the agents would soon be conducting with Legion members, but hopefully that would be only hearsay. He'd done his best to destroy any physical evidence of his father's involvement with the group.

If these actions of his were discovered, he would be in serious trouble—more trouble than his father.

At that same moment, other agents were visiting Nolan's house to search the premises for other files and, hopefully, the missing rifles.

Due to the continuing prohibition on fireworks, towns and neighborhoods that normally would have had festivities after dark had decided instead to put the focus on daytime parades and rallies. Anne could feel the energy in the air, Bostonians so pent up, everyone wanting to get outside and *do* something.

It wasn't clear what, though—the meaning of Independence Day felt both highly charged and in flux. We were at war, so flags were hanging outside more homes and businesses than ever. But people felt less free than usual, their lives proscribed in new ways: the gas and food rationing, the work shifts at odd hours. And of course the possibility—still remote, and still hard to believe, but an actual possibility, once unimaginable but now ever-present—that America might lose the war, and dictators and collaborators would reign, and true freedom would never ring here again.

The crowd was smaller than Anne had expected; even on our national holiday, many factories and warehouses were open, as the war industry could never shut down (her mother and Elias were among those at work).

The parade was silly, as parades always are. Rotary Clubs and Elks Clubs walked by in their goofy hats and ribbons, waving to the crowd. Firefighters slowly drove past in their big red engines, admired by young boys who pointed them out to their parents and yelled for the engines to blow their sirens (the firemen obliged, piercingly often). Dorchester High School's band marched in unison and played sped-up versions of "Over There" and "America the Beautiful" and other patriotic fare. The local Necco Wafers company sponsored a float decked out like a cloud, covered in cotton balls that could have been put to better use by the Red Cross, as pastel-hued executives tossed candy to ecstatic children.

And, not uncommon at events like this or St. Patrick's Day or Evacuation Day, Anne saw plenty of men and even teenagers carrying paper bags with thinly concealed bottles. It was barely noon, yet many were deep in their cups already.

She and Sammy met up with a few of his friends. Normally she would have let him wander off with them, but she felt protective today. She tried to give him a respectful distance, while not letting him out of her sight.

After the parade ended, the crowd gathered around a modest stage that had been erected in front of St. Joseph's, a tall white church atop a modest hill. The road was blocked on either side so pedestrians could wander. Anne guessed there were about two hundred people packed together, with more migrating this way from their earlier positions along the parade route.

"On this day, we remember how our forebears worked and sacrificed to throw off the yoke of oppression," Representative Cavanaugh intoned, sounding more funereal than celebratory. He was the second speaker so far, and he'd skipped over cheery icebreakers to go straight for the big themes. "How we told the tyrant King George: no more. How we told the British: we aren't yours. We aren't *you*. We are free."

There followed much venom about the British, how they had ruined the colonists' lives for generations, and how even after the war they didn't let up. A mention was made of the War of 1812, and then all those good American boys who lost their lives saving the Brits from their own mistakes in the Great War.

Anne also noticed something surprising: Charles Nolan, who was supposed to be one of the speakers today, wasn't on stage or anywhere in sight.

"And now we're back again, sending American boys overseas to fight for the British. Ladies and gentlemen, when does this end?"

The cheers and jeers made clear that he'd won the crowd, that he'd had them all along.

Anne had counted only three police officers along the periphery, including Officer Duffy, the man who'd impounded her car. They seemed to be here more to hear the speeches than to do any work.

Sammy stood beside Anne, his friends having wandered off at some point.

Cavanaugh detailed the many sins of the British and the evils they'd perpetuated against the good Irish people back in the homeland. "Just like the Yanks do it here," he went on. "How can they expect red-blooded Irish American men to give their lives to such a boondoggle?

"And we know who's really behind it, don't we?" he asked. "The Brits are bad enough, but we know it's Jews who are really yanking the Yanks' chains and putting *our* lives on the line."

Anne had been at a few awful speeches like this before Pearl Harbor. She'd felt unsafe before. But the tenor of this crowd felt different. Maybe it was because it was so large, and proudly out in the open instead of hiding in one meeting hall or another. That, plus the alcohol, gave it a more combustible air. Closer to violence.

She wanted to be taking notes, as it would help with her writing later, but she was afraid to be seen with a notebook. She would have to do her best to memorize Cavanaugh's worst lines.

"You heard about those Jewish businesses getting extra ration stamps, right? One of them is just down the road!"

She wasn't surprised, but still she had a sinking feeling in her stomach.

"Right there, stealing from our government and taking advantage of the rest of us, the ones who follow the rules and go without, the ones who sacrifice and do their part, the ones who send their sons into battle, all for a war that only helps *them*!"

Sammy turned and said to her, "I think we should go."

"I know this is hard, but we've made it this far, and I need to see what happens."

"No, Anne. I just saw the other man."

"Who?"

"The other one from the alley that night. The redhead. He's wearing a denim shirt. And he's staring at us."

Sammy had glanced to his left a few times, but Anne hadn't thought anything of it. He did so again, and she tried to follow his eyes. It took her only a moment; most people were facing the stage, but one man was turned toward them. She'd never seen him before, but she felt a shiver run down her spine. His eyes betrayed nothing but a terrifying focus.

"That's him," Sammy said. "We need to get out of here."

Campbell had given Devon and Lou the names of the men who led the Legion, in addition to Nolan. Other agents were knocking on their doors and raiding their offices today.

Devon had been deliberate in his decision to be one of the agents raiding Nolan's office and not his house. He was afraid that if Nolan saw him, he'd say something—elliptical or otherwise—about Devon's father. Or, if Nolan was involved in the blackmail photos, about Anne. It was best to stay away from the man for as long as he could.

It was past noon by the time he and Lou had driven to the office and unloaded the filing cabinets and other paperwork from Nolan's office. They'd heard from the other agents that Nolan, at his home, had stood there fuming as he watched the FBI remove evidence from his house, threatening them with lawsuits and calling them un-American.

No rifles had been found.

Given that they'd been up all night and this was the Fourth, Devon and Lou agreed to call it a day and get some sleep.

On the way home, though, Devon made one more stop.

His cousin Brian's wife, Patricia, answered the door. He didn't know her well, but she was friendly and social, and apparently forgiving enough to put up with her husband's surly personality.

"Hey, Devon. Looking for Brian?"

"I was, actually. He around?"

"No, he took the kids to the parade. I decided to stay home and get the place ready for later. Everything good? The phone's been ringing for him all morning."

"Really. Work calls?"

"I don't even know half the people who've called."

"I'm sure it's nothing." Other Legion members were no doubt spreading word about the raids. Thank goodness Brian had already left for the parade, or he'd know by now. Possibly he *did* know at this point, as word may have reached him. "I was just on my way home and thought I'd ask him something, but it can wait till another day."

She paused. "You okay? You have that just-got-off-the-night-shift look."

"I did indeed."

"Cop's wife's intuition."

"Remind me to never try getting anything past you." Then Devon snapped his fingers and pretended to remember something. "Oh, hey, while I'm here, could I possibly borrow some hedge clippers? I'm spending the day with my old man and promised him I'd do some yard work, but honestly his tools are older'n he is."

She told him sure, help himself to whatever was in the shed out back.

He followed her through the house, and she stopped in the kitchen while he let himself out the back door. Past the grill, the modest yard, the vegetable garden. The shed, however, was a large one, big enough for several bicycles and a lawn mower on one side, a workbench on the other. He ignored the garden tools and poked around the corners, lifting some tarps to see what was beneath them. Then he stood on a stepladder to see what was on the high shelving. He moved two small boxes out of the way, just to be sure.

Good thing, too.

"Goddamn," he said, flooded with relief and more than a bit of vindication.

Behind those boxes, way in the back, and hidden beneath a canvas tarp, lay something that did not belong: four brand-new military rifles.

Now that Anne had made eye contact with the redheaded man, he was navigating his way through the crowd, trying to reach them. He was a good twenty yards away, and moving through this mob would be challenging, so they had time to escape. But not much.

"Okay, let's go," she told Sammy. She turned and tried to excuse herself, but the bodies were tightly packed.

Cavanaugh continued with his rant: "And some of these so-called business owners have the gall to set up shop in our neighborhoods! They can sink their fangs into us and suck out everything they want, and supposedly there's nothing we can do about it!"

More jeering, more screaming.

Even as Anne and Sammy tried to move through the mass, the crowd itself was moving. She'd been distracted by what Sammy said and she had managed to tune out Cavanaugh for a moment, but people had begun moving toward Smith Street. She wanted to get out of the crowd, but it was like being caught in a riptide—every time she lifted her foot she was pushed sideways; it was the opposite of progress.

The crowd was moving toward Meyer's Meats, she realized. One of the businesses that had been "exposed" in the ration stamps story. The butcher's shop was only two blocks away.

She looked over her shoulder again and saw the redhead, now even closer. He didn't seem to be having as much trouble squeezing through this crowd as she and Sammy were.

She remembered what lifeguards had taught her as a girl: the trick wasn't to go toward the apartment but just to escape this current and figure out the next move once they were safe. If they ever *were* safe.

"Forget about walking home," she told Sammy. "Go this way."

Walking perpendicular to the current of the crowd was challenging. As she wedged her way through people, she heard comments about burning the place down, shattering windows. She couldn't believe her neighborhood had come to this. She hadn't seen a swastika anywhere in this mob yet, but she figured it was only a matter of time.

She turned her head again and couldn't see the redhead—a trio of taller men now stood in the way, blocking him from view. But he was out there still, surely, and not far behind.

Her first instinct had been right: she never should have let Sammy leave the house today. Not just because the crowd would get ugly, which was bad enough, but because, according to Devon, the second murderer was still on the loose. She was a fool not to have thought this through.

Sammy, the lone witness, was the killer's greatest threat.

As a girl she had always been taught that if a strange man tried to corner or chase her, she should call out for help. Neighbors and friends and family or even strangers would come to her aid—the trick was never to be alone. But now here she was, very much not alone, in a packed crowd, yet there was no one to call out to because she didn't trust her neighbors anymore. They had all been turned against her. If she cried out, more men in the crowd would have realized who she was, what she was—a troublemaker, a half-breed, a radical, a traitor—and the entire mob would pursue her, blot her out, erase her.

Sammy was in front of her and he'd reached back to grab her hand, to keep them together.

"Hey, watch it," a voice snapped as Anne stepped on someone's foot. She felt pressure at the back of her left knee until her leg gave way, and she would have fallen forward if there was anywhere to fall, but instead she leaned into the person beside her more heavily than she already had been, and someone else or maybe the first person shouted "Hey!" and she felt pressure all around her and though she'd always prided herself on staying cool under pressure suddenly her lungs felt empty, she realized she could be crushed by the crowd, she thought of stories about the Cocoanut Grove fire and all the bodies that were later discovered to have shattered rib cages because of the sustained force of all those bodies trying to escape through the same exit at the same time, oh my God she was going to suffocate out on the street only six blocks from her apartment, how had this happened, and her arms were bent into herself now and she'd lost contact with Sammy so she tried to extend her arms, to push out, to exhale, and then finally someone in front of her pivoted his shoulders and Anne fell out of the crowd.

Landed hard, skinning a knee and scraping her palms. She was in the middle of an intersection. A hand reached for her and she heard Sammy say, "Come on, come on!"

He pulled her up and she ran and only then realized she'd lost a shoe.

Thoughts popped into her head. Did their pursuer know their names? Where they lived? If not, running home might be a mistake, because he'd only learn how to find Sammy later. Maybe they should run somewhere else. But where?

Sammy was fast. She wasn't, and her lack of a shoe was a serious problem. She tried to call out to him, to tell him a smarter place to run, but she hadn't gotten her wind back since being barely able to breathe in the crowd and she felt the world fuzzing on her, dizziness nearly overwhelming her.

Behind her a car horn honked. She turned around even though it slowed her down.

She saw the redhead, holding his hands up in the middle of the road as if to apologize to the car he'd nearly run into.

She kept running. Sammy was nearly a block ahead of her now.

"Sammy, go to the Greens'!" she shouted. He stopped for a moment and turned, confused. "The Greens' backyard!"

"Not home?"

"No! Hurry!"

She hoped she was right. Aaron's first-floor apartment was only a block and a half away from where they were now. They'd be able to get in through the back door more quickly from this direction, plus Sammy had just been chatting with John, Aaron's younger brother, and had heard him say that his parents were home too, not being fans of parades.

She heard the redhead's footsteps getting closer. Now that they were out of the mob and away from traffic, he was gaining on them. He was taller and faster and maybe she'd made another stupid mistake. They should have run into a shop, she realized too late, if any were actually open.

They turned into a narrow alley that ran between two streets. The alley had some sparse grass but was mostly dirt, and on either side of them were old wooden fences leading to the backyards of three-deckers. When Sammy had been younger, Anne knew, he and John would walk home from school together, going to one house or the other. There was usually a key hidden somewhere on their back steps—hopefully Sammy still knew where.

Sammy reached the fence before Anne, pulled at the metal handle to the door. "It's locked!"

"Climb over it!"

A dog was barking. Marley.

"Get back here!"

Anne turned at the voice. The redheaded man was less than ten yards away.

Sammy climbed atop a beaten-up crate that looked like it wouldn't support his weight. It did, for the two seconds he needed to launch himself over the fence.

Marley got a lot louder.

"Easy, Marley!" Sammy shouted. "Easy!"

The man was running toward Anne and now he had a knife in his hand. The fence door finally swung open. She stumbled into the backyard and Sammy slammed the door shut again, latching it.

A second later the handle was jiggling, the man trying to force his way in.

"You can't hide from me, you little brat!" he shouted.

Giant Marley was barking at Anne now and she froze, uncomfortable around him in the best of times, but right now she was covered in sweat and panting, afraid that her racing heart and sudden movements would scare the beast into attacking her. But Sammy, a regular guest of the Greens since Marley was a pup, had his hands on the dog's front shoulders, petting him and holding him back.

"Easy, boy, easy," he said.

They hurried through the small yard, toward the apartment's back door. The fence gate was rattling still, then the entire fence shook—the redhead was trying to kick the door in. It wouldn't take him much longer.

Sammy let go of Marley and the dog darted toward the fence, barking and growling at the coming invader.

The Greens' back door opened, gray-haired Mr. Green staring out at Anne and Sammy in alarm. "Sammy? What's going on?"

"Someone's chasing us," Sammy said, and before he could explain further, Anne turned at the sound of splintering wood. She saw the fence door break from its hinges as the man stumbled in.

He made it only a few steps before the dog set upon him.

"*Ah!* Jesus, get back!"

"Sic him, Marley!" Sammy shouted as if he'd so commanded the dog before. Anne had never seen anything like this, the dog leaping up at the man and snapping at his neck and face, the redhead swinging with the blade and trying to knock Marley back. Again and again the dog jumped and snapped at him, and then Anne saw the knife hit the ground.

"Get in, get in!" Mr. Green called to Anne and Sammy, who followed him into a small kitchenette. He threw the locks and the dead bolt, then he lifted a cast-iron pot from the stove.

"Who is that?" he asked them.

"He wants to hurt Sammy."

"He'd better not hurt my dog." Then, before Anne could stop him, Mr. Green unlocked the back door and stepped outside.

Marley was still lunging at their attacker, his front paws nearly clearing the man's shoulders, as Mr. Green quickly walked over to them. The attacker had rotated so that his back was now to the house. Without hesitating, Mr. Green stepped up close and swung the pot into the back of the man's head.

The barking continued as the man collapsed to the ground.

"Easy, boy, easy!" Mr. Green was stroking the dog now, calming him down almost immediately. Just like that the chaos and sound died away, except for Anne and Sammy gasping for breath.

After what might have been only a few seconds, Mr. Green guided his dog into the house. Anne was no canine expert, but Marley was walking slowly and seemed hurt. One of his ears seemed less erect than the other, and a shred of denim hung from his mouth, soaked with blood or drool.

"Are you all right?" Mr. Green asked them, and Anne only nodded. "What's going on?"

"We're not," and she could barely talk she was breathing so fast, "completely sure." She was afraid to tell him more, to let anyone know that Sammy had been witness to a murder.

"We should call the police, right?" Sammy asked her.

Devon trusted Detective Jimmy Moore, he'd told her. She wasn't sure if she trusted either of them, but Moore had given them his home number, and it was probably better than calling the main police line.

"You call the police," Mr. Green said. "I'm gonna tie that *paskudnyak* to my fence."

Chapter Fifty-seven

DUTY

Two days later, Devon was sitting at his desk when he was surprised by a call from Sammy Lemire.

"Can we talk outside? I'm by the donut place across the street."

He told Sammy to give him five minutes, then hung up and sighed. He had an idea why the kid was calling, though he had hoped to avoid this. But if Sammy had gone to the trouble of coming downtown, he deserved to be heard face-to-face.

It was a cloudy day and breezy, feeling more like late spring than July. Sammy stood at a street corner beside the phone booth, smoking. He'd had his hair cut recently, almost military-short.

"Can I buy you a chocolate frosted?" Devon offered.

"No, thanks. I'm good." Sammy took a last drag, then dropped the cigarette and stepped on it.

"So, I was wondering. If you'd found her."

"I did, Sammy." Devon had guessed right. "She's okay. She's starting over someplace new; she's got a job. But she asked me not to tell you where she is, and I respect her decision."

He had tracked down Elena Wolff only yesterday, to Lowell of all places. Working at another war plant, sewing parachutes. Because she'd used her real name it hadn't taken long to find her, and he'd been able to question her a second time, get the answers she'd refused to give before.

She insisted she'd known nothing about the theft of the rifles, though her husband had hinted about some "deal" he'd been working on, told her that they'd have money coming their way. She said she hadn't known what exactly Abraham had been up to or whom he'd been dealing with, and Devon believed her. She knew only that she and her husband had been desperately trying to raise money to buy relatives out of Europe; she even asked Devon if there was anything he could do to look into where some of her relatives were, and if they were even still alive, but he'd told her there wasn't.

When he asked her about the upcoming FEPC hearing, she didn't know many specifics but confirmed what he now knew. She had heard Abraham complain more than once about the hiring practices at the plant, saying that he and some others had actually lied on their applications to indicate they were Christian because they'd been warned they wouldn't be hired if they put down they were Jewish. And saying that the plant hired Negroes only as janitors.

Devon had also called the Fair Employment Practice Committee down in Washington and had learned that, yes, Wolff had been scheduled as a witness in the upcoming hearing against Northeast Munitions. Apparently, Wolff had overheard managers talk about how to get around the law and avoid hiring Negroes for better positions, so he had offered to testify against his employer. Maybe the sale of stolen rifles had been a hedge in case he got fired, but Elena didn't know. And if any money had ever come in for those rifles, she claimed never to have seen it.

She told Devon that she and her husband had fallen out of love a long time ago; war and life as a refugee could do that. She admired her husband's politics, sometimes, but other times she resented how he hadn't learned anything from their time in Europe—that it was best to keep your head down, not try to force change, not try to step in front of any political issues that would only drive over you and keep going, oblivious to what you thought or cared or felt.

Devon had wanted to tell her she was wrong to think that way, but all the evidence in her life argued that she was right.

She had asked him at the end of the interview if he could not tell Sammy where she was. She was embarrassed by the affair and didn't want to string the kid along.

"She said that?" Sammy asked.

"Yeah. I'm sorry, kid. But she's been through an awful lot. She's trying to start over, and I think hearing from you would only make it tougher on her."

For a moment Devon feared the kid was going to cry, but it passed. He had known this answer was coming, Devon saw.

The Wolff murder case was proceeding, according to Jimmy Moore. The man who'd chased Anne and Sammy on the Fourth, and who Jimmy had arrested that afternoon, claimed he'd been minding his own business when a beast of a dog had attacked him, but Jimmy hadn't bought it. His name was Paul Whiteside, Dorchester resident, Northeast Munitions employee, friend of Patty Campbell, and his prints matched the swastika-marked cocktail napkin left in Wolff's pocket.

Whiteside and Campbell were in jail, charged with homicide. The police had searched both their homes looking for evidence and had turned up quite a lot of hate sheets at Whiteside's place—the same ones, Devon knew, that had been printed in his own father's warehouse. It sickened Devon to realize that words his father had helped distribute were having a direct influence on men like Campbell and Whiteside and all the other people causing trouble in Dorchester.

Anne and Sammy hadn't been hurt, but clearly they'd come close. While they'd been running from Whiteside, Cavanaugh had incited people at the rally to march down to a Jewish deli and throw rocks at its windows. A few fights had broken out, more men sent to the hospital, but no one had been arrested. Maybe the Legion had been planning to shoot Jewish leaders on the holiday too, but had been spooked into delaying by the heat the FBI was bringing. Or maybe the killings had been planned for some later date. Regardless, the rifles were in custody, as were Nolan and several other members of the Legion.

Including Devon's cousin Brian.

Immediately upon finding the rifles, Devon had called Lou and the SAC—from Brian's own house. Brian had been arrested a couple hours later, when he returned home from the rally. That scene—relatives everywhere, kids crying, Brian's wife, Patricia, screaming at Devon and insisting he do something—was not something Devon enjoyed thinking about.

I'll do what I can, he'd told Patricia. Just something to say. Not meaning it, but letting her think it.

He'd also grabbed Brian's son Johnny by the forearm, this kid who was watching his father being dragged off to jail, this budding tough guy who'd apparently been starting fights all over the neighborhood but now had tears in his eyes, and had spoken softly into his ear. *Stay out of trouble and stay off the streets. He doesn't need that from you right now.*

Devon's relationship with Boston's beat cops had deteriorated a great deal in the last two days.

Though the FBI had now charged several members of the Legion for conspiracy to commit murder as well as theft, counterfeiting, and working as undeclared agents of a hostile power, Devon knew there must be even more of them on the loose. He figured that the photos of him and Anne would be anonymously mailed to the SAC's desk any day now. Hadn't happened yet, but he felt that blade hanging over his head.

"So, listen," Devon told Sammy. "I need to get back to work. Tell your sister I said hi."

Devon had called Anne to ask if she was all right when he'd heard what happened, but she wasn't returning any of his calls.

He was about to step away when Sammy said, "I need you to do me a favor."

"Yes?" He'd thought finding Elena was the favor.

"I want to enlist. Today."

He hadn't expected this, though maybe it explained the hair. "Aren't you seventeen?"

"I'll be eighteen in five months. But I'm tired of waiting."

"Seventeen-year-olds can enlist with their parents' consent."

"My ma won't give it. That's why I need your help. Can you get the folks at the enlistment board to let me in? Maybe fudge my birthday a little?"

"Your sister would kill me."

"I won't tell her you helped. I promise."

Sammy seemed so young, ridiculously so. As were thousands of boys who were now shipping off to the bases, to the ports, and to the fronts.

"Look. I know getting dumped is no fun, but that's no reason to blow your life up. Take a few days to—"

"It's not about Elena. If anything, it's easier if she doesn't want to see me anymore. I just . . . had to make sure first."

"Sammy, you're a witness in a murder case. If they keep fighting the charges, you'll be needed to testify at the trial."

"But you said his fingerprints matched, right? You've got all the proof you should need. I'd be in basic training for weeks anyway—if you need me to testify, I can come back on leave or something."

Devon opened his mouth to reply, but he realized Sammy was mostly right.

"I'm tired of being here," Sammy said. "Being a target. Being a victim. I want to get to hold a gun and fight back. If I stay in Dorchester, I'm gonna wind up dead or in jail. So send me to the front and let me do some good."

Devon felt a weight he didn't want on his shoulders, even as he knew it was Sammy who would ultimately carry it.

The nearest enlistment office was just down the street, a block off the Common. It had been an old stationery store whose owner passed away just before the war; the walls were all filled with patriotic posters, most of the front window blocked by a giant flag. In earlier days, whenever Devon had walked past he'd seen a long line out the door, though that had become less common now that so many men had already signed up.

He opened the door for Sammy, and they saw that another enlistee was in front of them in line, so they waited as he was processed. Devon felt odd and out of place, his suit and very presence not right here, like he was a chaperone for something every other young man did solo.

It was also his first time inside one of these offices. This was now a rite of passage for damn near every American male of his generation, yet he'd never seen such a space before.

The young man in front of them walked out, gripping some papers, and the sergeant at the front desk silently beckoned them forward.

"Wait here a minute," Devon said to Sammy under his breath.

He stepped up to the desk and flashed his badge. "Agent Mulvey, FBI."

He lowered his voice and explained, "This fellow here, Sammy Lemire, is very excited to enlist. You're going to see that his birthday is in November, but you're accidentally going to record it as January. Just an honest mistake, writing one 'one' when you should have written two."

The sergeant wrinkled his brow. "That's not normally how we do things here."

"I understand. But you'd be taking a problem off the Bureau's hands and gaining one very enthusiastic soldier."

The sergeant considered this for a moment. "I don't like it. But I have bigger problems." He looked over Devon's shoulder and beckoned Sammy forward again.

"You know what you're doing, young man?" the sergeant asked Sammy as Devon stepped back.

"I do, sir."

"And are you here"—his eyes darted to Devon and lingered there—"of your own accord?"

"Absolutely, sir. I want to enlist, very much."

Devon knew Anne would never forgive him if she found out. But she already seemed to not be forgiving him. For being related to his father. For not doing more to magically dispel the sin of bigotry from all his fellow Irishmen. For not being a hero, or maybe, worse, for trying to be one and failing.

And Sammy was right: this decision solved many problems. The Lemire family still felt that they were in someone's crosshairs, even though Campbell and Whiteside were behind bars and Campbell was even cooperating. Whiteside surely had other friends on the loose. Hopefully they weren't stupid enough to try to come after Sammy again—now that so many other people had witnessed Whiteside trying to attack Sammy and Anne, there wasn't much point in eliminating the one witness to his earlier crime—but maybe they *were* that stupid. If Sammy removed himself from the household, he would divert the target from his loved ones.

Sammy was right about his neighborhood, too. Things weren't improving, at least not yet. The FBI had cracked down on the Legion, yes, but that only seemed to be outraging hundreds of households in Dorchester and beyond.

Devon lingered by the door while Sammy completed his paperwork, granting the kid some privacy. He thought of his brothers-in-law who were serving, his childhood and college friends, his neighbors. He felt useless and unworthy, but more so than before, to see this mere kid so enthusiastically signing on for certain danger.

The sergeant handed Sammy some forms and told him to report to a different office tomorrow morning for his physical. And with that, events were set in motion that no one would be able to undo.

He and Sammy stepped out onto the sidewalk. A few drops fell.

Devon told himself Sammy had made his own decision, that he himself wasn't condemning the kid to death. That the kid would make it, would be a true hero, would do some good in the world.

He extended his hand, and Sammy shook it rather limply.

"Good luck. I'm proud of you. Your family will be too, though they might not say it at first."

Sammy thanked him, and Devon turned and walked back to his office, cutting through the Common where the full tree branches might protect him if it started to pour.

EPILOGUE

A few days later, on July 10, Anne woke up to find that the Allies had invaded Sicily. Americans were fighting in Europe again. The isolationists' last-gasp attempt to stop it had failed.

A month and a half later, Harold's story—about the violence in Dorchester, the local police department's lack of interest (and even participation), and the FBI's just-in-time raid of the Christian Legion—finally went to press; magazines could operate agonizingly slowly. Anne felt she'd done the lion's share of the work, but she received no byline, as the editorial policy was not to run the names of mere "contributors" (she'd expected this, yet still it stung). Other than that, she was proud of the story, which was thoroughly reported and pulled no punches.

It made immediate waves. Within twenty-four hours Boston's mayor had given a speech excoriating the magazine and its clearly biased "anti-Boston" writer, who certainly didn't know a thing about this city "from his perch in snooty Manhattan." Anne feared that Harold's prediction was coming true, that the story wouldn't change anything.

But local politicians started asking questions, and a number of rabbis began speaking publicly about the violence.

The neighborhood watch continued, men like Elias breaking up a few fights and no doubt preventing many more from even starting. The American Jewish Congress wrangled meetings with a few Boston city councilmen, as well as one of the state's congressmen who was home on break from Washington. Eventually enough pressure was put on the police chief that certain officers were moved to different beats, replaced by some who actually seemed to care about the quality of life in Dorchester.

Life improved, gradually.

Anne was able to scrounge up just enough donations to print her first issue of the Boston Center for Democracy's newsletter since right after Pearl Harbor. She wrote a long piece on everything Harold's story had left out, such as the counterfeiters' attempt to entrap Jewish shopkeepers and get a few corrupt small-business owners to unwittingly play along with anti-Semitic tropes, all so that rotten politicians like Cavanaugh could manufacture a scandal and rally Bostonians against the war before American soldiers landed in Europe.

On that score, at least, the homegrown Fascists failed. As battles raged in Sicily and across the Pacific, America still had its pockets of antiwar sentiment here and there, and perhaps Anne's little corner of Boston was one of the worst, but at least lunatic Hitlerites were greatly outnumbered by patriots who were willing to make all necessary sacrifices to defeat the Axis.

In Anne's story, she also mentioned John Mulvey by name, tying his property to the printing press, the counterfeiting, and the hate sheets. She'd even called the man at home, seeking comment, but he'd cursed at her and hung up.

Weeks passed and Anne still hadn't spoken with Devon. He called a few times and she hung up on him, or her mother would answer and invite Anne to talk to him (she could be *such* a softie where handsome men were concerned) but Anne would refuse to take the call and her mother would apologize to Devon as if Anne was the one in the wrong, before wishing him a nice day.

He finally stopped calling. Anne suspected, but couldn't be sure, that he'd helped Sammy lie on his enlistment form, but she had plenty of other reasons to be angry at him.

She remembered one of the jokes he'd made the day they'd bumped into each other: *Whether or not you have dinner with me will have zero effect on geopolitical events.* She wondered if that prediction had been wrong.

She checked out of the library a book on Jewish history, wanting to fill the holes in her knowledge. And she made more time to attend synagogue with her mother and Elias, still unsure whether this culture was hers but wanting to be there for her mother, and wanting to be a part of something.

Meanwhile the Allies took Sicily, driving the Fascists back to the Italian mainland. Where more was in store.

She often woke in the middle of the night, thinking of her brothers. Of all the brothers out there. And of her friends, like Aaron Green, who'd just enlisted. Maybe the homegrown Fascists had failed, but the fight against millions of their worldwide brethren had barely begun. Staring at the ceiling when nothing would help her sleep, Anne felt helpless again, and small, and she knew she was only at the start of a long string of bad nights.

Sometimes she and her mother would share in that insomnia. They would talk about their fears, or try to cheer the other up, or just stare at the ceiling together, in silence, nothing to say, just glad that the other was there.

She was walking home from the train on an unseasonably cool day in mid-August, autumn impatient to begin. The setting sun cast a long shadow before her, and then the top of her shadow crossed over a pair of perfectly shined black shoes.

"Hello, Anne," Devon said. He'd been waiting at her street corner. He dropped his cigarette and crushed it under his right sole.

"Devon." She stopped, waited for him to walk through her long shadow until he was close enough for her to hit, or kiss, neither of which she was planning on doing.

"I know you've been avoiding me, so I thought I'd finally swing by."

"I'm not avoiding you," she clarified, "I'm just very busy, Devon. And I'm not sure I need to be making time for you, frankly."

Just yesterday she had accepted a job offer at a small publisher in Cambridge, copyediting painfully dull medical manuscripts. It would pay the bills while she looked for something more challenging, which was hard to do when she also spent most of her evenings on her poorly paid journalistic projects. She felt exhausted, and right now she wasn't in the right mood for seeing him. If she ever would be again.

"Well, it's nice to see you too," he said with an equal lack of warmth.

"What do you want, Devon?"

He looked around, as if checking that they weren't being watched.

"I told you someone was trying to blackmail me with photos of the two of us. Turns out my own cousin was part of that. Brian Dennigan, the one who got arrested. After I called his bluff, he or someone he was palling around with went ahead and shared those pictures with my boss after all."

"Oh?" She told herself she didn't care.

"I'm on temporary suspension. Possibly worse. They're double-checking everything I've been up to lately. My own partner even said a few things to my boss that aren't exactly helping my cause. I just wanted you to know. Other agents are picking up the case against the Legion, and prosecutors have all the evidence they need, so don't worry about that. I'm just not sure where this leaves me."

"I'm sorry to hear that. But I'm sure you'll land on your feet. Getting out of trouble seems to be a specialty of yours, for yourself and your family."

"What's that supposed to mean?"

"I've read every story I can find about the Christian Legion arrests. I haven't seen your father's name come up once."

"Except for the story *you* wrote."

"Ah, but he seems to be evading any legal troubles, doesn't he? I imagine he has his son to thank for that."

He looked down. It was hard to tell whether he felt unjustly scolded or if he knew he deserved it. He said, "I shouldn't even be talking to you right now. But I—"

"Then don't."

He ignored her interruption. "I wanted you to know what I've told my boss. And what's in your own record now. I figured you deserved that much."

"How gallant of you."

"I told him I'd been looking into that Center for Democracy group of yours because of an old tip that it was a Communist front—which we did receive a while back. But I told him there was no reason to think anything untoward was going on. That there was no reason for the Bureau to track you. And yeah, I said I kissed you in a moment of weakness. But I didn't say you'd ever spent the night at my place or anything like that."

"How kind of you to protect a lady's reputation."

He sighed. "Are you finished?"

"Are *you* finished, Devon? Because we certainly are."

"Yeah, you've made that pretty clear. And why—because I wouldn't throw my own father in jail? Look, he was kinder than he should have been to some crackpots, to let them use his old warehouse for something he didn't fully understand. He's an old man and he got talked into going along with some things and he should have known better. But he's learned his lesson."

"And how much evidence did you bury along the way, Agent Mulvey? You expect me to feel bad that you got suspended? They may have gotten you for the wrong thing, but you certainly deserve it."

An older neighbor, Mrs. Strolowicz, walked by, turning her head to Anne after she'd passed Devon, raising her eyebrows and smiling, silently seeming to say, *Nice catch, Anne! Hang on to that one.*

After she'd passed, Devon said, "I arrested my own cousin, for God's sake. Half my family isn't speaking to me. And most of the cops in town would run me over if I crossed the street near them. Look, we shut down a Fascist group that was turning into an all-out militia, hoarding weapons; we stopped them before they could do real harm. You helped with that, and I appreciate it."

"You don't need to give me your résumé, Devon. I'm not taking notes. We're not on the record."

"You can be awfully cold when you need to be."

"As can you. Once you brought your partner around, you acted like I was a stranger. Barely looked me in the eye."

"I was trying to protect you. Belatedly."

"You were trying to protect *yourself* and you know it. Your job and your family. That's what really matters to you. Not me."

She wasn't sure what he'd hoped to accomplish by coming here. Talk her into forgiving him? Sweep her off her feet somehow?

"My father does matter to me, yeah. But so do you. I wish you'd see that."

"And I wish you had a different way of showing it."

"Once I'm reinstated, *if* I'm reinstated, I'm going to make sure those bastards go to prison for a very long time."

"While making sure they never implicate your father, right? Good luck with that, Devon. And good luck with everything."

With that, she walked past him, ignoring the way he reached out to her halfheartedly with his hand, as if he thought he could stop her, and then pulled his hand back, apparently thinking better of it.

After a few steps, though, she turned around again. She wanted the last word, but it was so hard when you couldn't settle on which one was best.

"Remember at the restaurant, when you apologized to me? You said you'd done the wrong thing way back then, and you were ashamed. You do realize you've done the wrong thing again, don't you? Only this time it's so much worse, because you're an *adult,* and you have the ability to do so much good?"

"I'm still doing good, Anne. Maybe differently than you would."

"That's like a riddle. How 'different' can good be, before it stops being good?"

She saw him puzzling over that as she turned around again and left him behind. It was late, and she was tired, and there was so much more work to do.

Two days later Devon returned to the office where, as expected, he was stopped at the door by the young receptionist.

"I'm sorry, Agent Mulvey, but I'm not allowed to let you in."

He'd expected that, as he was still under suspension. He'd come to be less worried that he would be fired and had been braced for some lesser but still embarrassing form of discipline, and it felt insulting indeed to be rebuked by this twenty-three-year-old.

"That's all right, Cindy. I just need you to hand this to the SAC." He gave her a sealed envelope. He'd already turned in his gun and badge when his suspension began. "As soon as you can."

He took a last glance at the closed door behind her, then gave her a brief nod and left the building. He felt lighter already.

Again the short walk, again passing the Common, again the beleaguered-looking sergeant at the cheap desk. This time there was no line, so Devon stepped right up.

He could hear his father yelling at him in his mind, insisting he was making a mistake. *I helped you get that Bureau job so you'd never have to do this,* Pop would say. And that was one of the many reasons Devon stood here.

Maybe he was only running toward one fight to run away from another—the fight for his father's reputation, his legacy. But he didn't want to fight the old man's battles anymore.

It took a moment for the sergeant to recognize him. "You're that FBI guy."

Devon took off his hat. "Not anymore, actually. I'm here to enlist. I don't suppose Uncle Sam has any openings in intelligence?"

Over the next few days, Anne's anger at Devon cooled, and she wondered if she'd been too harsh. Maybe she was blaming him for things beyond his control. And as much as she was reluctant to admit it, she missed him. Missed what they'd had, whatever it was. The way he made her feel, like it was okay to be happy, okay to sometimes laugh at the things that usually made her want to scream.

She told herself she should call him, but she kept putting it off.

Then on the morning of September 3, she walked groggily into the kitchen and saw her mother and Elias sitting by the radio, rapt.

"We've invaded Italy," Elias said.

She pulled up a chair and the three of them listened to the report, which didn't have much information other than the fact that the invasion of the mainland had begun that morning at dawn. Only seven or eight hours ago, if Anne's knowledge of time zones was accurate.

They hadn't received a letter from Joe in more than three weeks and weren't entirely sure where he was these days. They wondered if his silence meant his ship had been sent to the theater, if he too was storming those Italian ports. Sammy was still training down at a base in Georgia—safe for now, but soon the very opposite.

As they listened to the radio announcer they wondered what role, if any, Joe might be playing, and when Sammy might join him. They hoped that one day they'd get to hear the boys tell their story.

AUTHOR'S NOTE

This is a work of fiction. Like my past novels, I've worked to ground the story in a historically accurate setting, though I have taken certain liberties with geography and timing in the service of story. Though I've settled in Atlanta, I was born and raised in Rhode Island and have deep family roots in Boston, so it was a joy to write something set in the city of my grandparents and great-grandparents, the Mullens and Mulveys and Lennons, the Comeaus and LeBlancs and Lemires.

The fictional Christian Legion is loosely based on several pro-Nazi, anti-Semitic organizations that still existed in the United States after the country entered World War II. In some ways the Legion is an amalgam of the Christian Front's pre- and post–Pearl Harbor iterations in New York and Boston. Many members of the Christian Front's New York chapter were arrested in 1940 by the FBI for, among other things, hoarding weapons (some of which had been stolen from a National Guard Armory) and plotting to assassinate Jewish politicians. They believed they could incite armed conflict between Fascist and Communist groups, which would lead to the imposition of martial law and eventually a Fascist government. Though they were arrested and charged with several crimes, they were later acquitted in court, partly because the accusations seemed so fantastical to jurors, and partly because much of the FBI's evidence was ruled inadmissible because it had been illegally gathered by the G-men.

After the arrest of the New York Fronters, leaders of the Boston faction insisted that they were different from the New York group; they claimed they were not violent and were merely expressing their constitutionally protected opinions. The Boston wing of the Christian Front continued to operate long after the New York trial, distributing anti-Semitic hate sheets and contributing to a hostile and violent environment throughout Boston (and other cities in the Northeast). The attacks on Jewish residents that my book dramatizes were not widely reported at first and were generally ignored by Boston papers; that changed in October 1943 when Arnold Beichman published a story, "Christian Front Hoodlums Terrorize Boston Jews," in New York's *PM Magazine* (the inspiration for Harold and Anne's project). As in my book, Boston authorities were initially dismissive of the story. Jewish organizations such as the American Jewish Congress and several rabbis, who initially had been reluctant to speak out publicly, stepped forward, substantiated the story's claims, organized protective associations, and worked with government leaders to address the violence, which nonetheless continued in some form throughout the war years.

Federal authorities seemed reluctant to crack down on the Front in Boston, possibly due to their earlier judicial failure against the Front's New York chapter.

One of the first places where I learned of this was in Stephen Norwood's article "Marauding Youth and the Christian Front: Antisemitic Violence in Boston and New York During World War II," published in *American Jewish History* 91, no. 2 (2003). The July Fourth rally in my book is modeled after a violent rally that occurred in Boston on Evacuation Day (March 17) in 1944, according to Norwood's account.

Some aspects of Anne's character are inspired by the journalist Frances Sweeney, an Irish American writer who dedicated her life to exposing Fascists both before and during the war, and who wrote a short-lived column debunking war rumors for the *Boston Herald*—until it was shut down via pressure from the Office of War Information, which claimed the column did more harm than good. A Catholic who was outraged by the Church's treatment of Jews, Sweeney was threatened with excommunication by her cardinal for writing unflattering stories about the Church, according to Nat Hentoff's *Boston Boy*. In the interest of story-telling, I ensured that Anne's character differed from Sweeney in many ways, not least her age, her degree of experience, her family, her ethnic background, and her health. Sweeney had been living with rheumatic heart disease for years, and she died of heart failure in 1944 at the age of thirty-six.

In addition to Norwood's and Hentoff's work, the following were all helpful in conjuring this world: *Nazis of Copley Square: The Forgotten Story of the Christian Front* by Charles R. Gallagher, *Undercover: My Four Years in the Nazi Underworld of America* by John Roy Carlson (pen name of Arthur Derounian), *The FBI and the Catholic Church, 1935–1962* by Steve Rosswurm, *Saboteurs: The Nazi Raid on America* by Michael Dobbs, *The Good War* by Studs Terkel, *Mafia Allies: The True Story of America's Secret Alliance with the Mob in World War II* by Tim Newark, *Radio Priest: Charles Coughlin, The Father of Hate Radio* by Donald Warren, *American Swastika* by Charles Higham, *Don't You Know There's a War On?* by Richard Lingeman, *The Fitzgeralds and the Kennedys: An American Saga* by Doris Kearns Goodwin, *Dorchester Streets: The Story of the Sheehan Family in Dorchester 1921–1943* by Robert Louis Sheehan, *Gellhorn: A Twentieth Century Life* by Caroline Moorehead, *The Rascal King: The Life and Times of James Michael Curley* by Jack Beatty, *African-Americans in Boston: More Than 350 Years* by Robert C. Hayden, *Fire in the Grove: The Cocoanut Grove Tragedy and Its Aftermath* by John C. Esposito, *Common Ground: A Turbulent Decade in the Lives of Three American Families* by J. Anthony Lukas, *An Army at Dawn: The War in North Africa, 1942–43* by Rick Atkinson, and the unpublished memoir of my maternal grandfather, Ernest Comeau.

My author's note at the end of *Midnight Atlanta* also lists many books about the first half of the twentieth century that came in handy when writing this book as well.

As always, thank you to my agent, Susan Golomb; my editor, Kelley Ragland; the fine team at Minotaur; my loving and supportive family; the many booksellers who put my work in readers' hands; and readers like you.